ALEX & ELIZA

ALEX & ELIZA

The Alex & Eliza Trilogy

BOOK ONE

MELISSA DE LA CRUZ

PENGUIN BOOKS

For Mattie,

who wanted to know more about them

PENGUIN BOOKS
An imprint of Penguin Random House LLC, New York

First published in the United States of America by G. P. Putnam's Sons, 2017
Published by Penguin Books, an imprint of Penguin Random House LLC, 2020

"From Alexander Hamilton to Elizabeth Schuyler, [August 1780],"
Founders Online, National Archives, last modified December 28, 2016,
http://founders.archives.gov/documents/Hamilton/01-02-02-0834.
[Original source: *The Papers of Alexander Hamilton*, vol. 2, *1779–1781*, ed. Harold C. Syrett.
New York: Columbia University Press, 1961, pp. 397–400.]

Visit us online at penguinrandomhouse.com

THE LIBRARY OF CONGRESS HAS CATALOGED THE G. P. PUTNAM'S SONS EDITION AS FOLLOWS:
Names: De la Cruz, Melissa, 1971– author.
Title: Alex and Eliza : a love story / Melissa de la Cruz.
Description: First edition. | New York, NY : G. P. Putnam's Sons, [2017]
Summary: "Before the world knew them as Alexander Hamilton and Elizabeth Schuyler, young Alex and Eliza fell in love amidst the turmoil of the American Revolution"—Provided by publisher.
Identifiers: LCCN 2016058743 | ISBN 9781524739621 (hardcover)
Subjects: LCSH: Hamilton, Alexander, 1757–1804—Juvenile fiction. | Hamilton, Elizabeth Schuyler, 1757–1854—Juvenile fiction. | United States—History—Revolution, 1775–1783—Juvenile fiction. | CYAC: Hamilton, Alexander, 1757–1804—Fiction. | Hamilton, Elizabeth Schuyler, 1757–1854—Fiction. | United States—History—Revolution, 1775–1783—Fiction. | Love—Fiction.
Classification: LCC PZ7.D36967 Al 2017 | DDC [Fic]—dc23
LC record available at https://lccn.loc.gov/2016058743

Penguin Books ISBN 9781524739645

Printed in the United States of America

Design by Jaclyn Reyes
Text set in Electra LT Std, MrsEaves, and Andrade Pro

1 3 5 7 9 10 8 6 4 2

ALEX & ELIZA

Beloved by you, I can be happy in any situation, and can struggle with every embarrassment of fortune with patience and firmness. I cannot however forbear entreating you to realize our union on the dark side and satisfy, without deceiving yourself, how far your affection for me can make you happy in a privation of those elegancies to which you have been accustomed. If fortune should smile upon us, it will do us no harm to have been prepared for adversity; if she frowns upon us, by being prepared, we shall encounter it without the chagrin of disappointment. Your future rank in life is a perfect lottery; you may move in an exalted you may move in a very humble sphere; the last is most probable; examine well your heart.

—**Letter from Alexander Hamilton to Elizabeth Schuyler,** August 1780

PROLOGUE

Mansion on the Hill

Albany, New York

November 1777

Like a latter-day Greek temple, the Schuyler family mansion sat atop a softly rounded hill outside Albany. Just over a decade old, the magnificent estate, called the Pastures, was already known as one of the finest houses of the New York state capital by dint of its exquisite furnishings and trimmings. The pièce de résistance was The Ruins of Rome, *a set of hand-painted grisaille wallpapers decorating the home's second-floor ballroom, which Philip Schuyler had brought back from a year-long trip to England in 1762.*

The local gentry was impressed by the mansion's square footage and elegant appointments, but they were more taken with the general's and Mrs. Schuyler's impressive pedigrees: Philip was descended from the Schuylers and the Van Cortlandts, two of the oldest and most prestigious families in New York, while his wife, Catherine, was a Van Rensselaer, the single most prominent family in the northern half of the state, whose tenure stretched all the way back to the Dutch days of the early 1600s. Rensselaerswyck, as their estate was known, encompassed more than half a million acres, an unimaginably vast parcel, rivaled only by that of the Livingston family, who controlled what Catherine derisively referred to as "the bottom half" of the state. As a married woman, Catherine wasn't entitled to any claim on the Van Rensselaer properties (or, for that matter, her husband's), but rumor had it that her sizable dowry had paid for construction of their Albany mansion, as well as the Schuylers' country estate outside Saratoga.

Just shy of his forty-fourth birthday, General Philip Schuyler was a handsome man, tall and fit, with a military bearing and a full head of hair that, like George Washington, he wore powdered and softly curled, rarely resorting to the elegant (but rather itchy) affectation of a periwig. As a commander in Washington's Continental army, Schuyler had organized a brilliant campaign against the British forces at Québec in 1775, only to be forced to resign his commission in June of this year, after Fort Ticonderoga fell while under his command. The defeat had been a double tragedy for Philip. Not only had the British taken the fort, they'd also seized his aforementioned Saratoga estate. Though not as grand as the Albany property, the Schuylers' second home was still sumptuous enough that John Burgoyne, commander of the British forces, chose it for his personal residence. But the coup de grâce came when the Continental army retook Saratoga in October, and a spiteful Burgoyne set fire to the house and fields during his retreat. General Schuyler had all but depleted his wife's inheritance building the house and bringing the land under tillage, which was expected to provide much of the family's income. The loss put a serious dent in the family's finances and cast an ominous shadow over their future.

Not that an observer would know it. Unused to idleness, General Schuyler had spent the past four months striding about the Pastures, laying out new beds in the formal gardens, regimenting the orchard harvest with military precision, supervising the construction of gazebos and guest houses and servant cottages, and generally getting in everyone's way, servant and family member alike. In a magnanimous gesture that indicated just how chivalrous he was—and how bored—Schuyler had even offered to put up the captured John Burgoyne before the British general was shipped back to England. Thus, did Schuyler's one-time rival and his entourage, some twenty strong, "occupy" the Albany mansion for a full month, and even if they didn't burn it down when they left, they still managed to eat a good-size hole into the family's provisions, comestible and otherwise.

Catherine Schuyler, one year younger than her husband, had been known as a "handsome woman" in her youth, but thirteen pregnancies in twenty years had taken their toll on her waistline. Practical, strong-willed, and stoic, she had buried no fewer than six of her children, including a set of triplets who hadn't lived long enough to be baptized. If the pregnancies had stolen her figure, the deaths had taken her smile, and watching her husband fritter away her financial assets had done little to improve her spirits.

Mrs. Schuyler's love for the seven children who remained to her was evident in the care she took of them, from the wet nurses and nannies she handpicked to raise them, to the tutors she hired to educate them, to the cooks she employed to keep them well fed. And somehow in the midst of the numbing cycle of births and deaths, declarations and proclamations, sieges and seasons, the Schuylers' three eldest girls had all reached marrying age.

Angelica, the oldest, was a whip-smart, mischievous brunette, with glittering eyes, her pretty lips set in a perpetual smirk. Peggy, the youngest, was a waifish beauty, with a waist so tiny that she rarely bothered with a corset, and alabaster skin set off by a mass of lustrous dark hair that was simply too gorgeous to powder or bury under a wig (no matter what Marie Antoinette was covering her head with at Versailles).

Eliza, the middle daughter, was as clever as Angelica and as beautiful as Peggy. She was also the most sensible, more interested in books than fashion, and, much to her mother's consternation, more devoted to the revolutionary cause and the mantle of abolition than to marrying one of its well-off colonels.

Her mother really didn't know what she was going to do with her.

Three daughters, each a prize in her own way (though Eliza would need a strong man to match her spirit). Under normal circumstances, marrying them off would be a feat of sustained diplomacy in which the first families of New York bound their blood and fortunes together like European aristocracy. But New York's respectable families were few in number, and word traveled quickly. It would be only a matter of time before people found out just how much the Schuylers had lost at Saratoga, at which point the girls would become damaged goods. It was imperative, then—both to their futures and the family's—that they married well.

But it was even more important that they married fast.

And so, Mrs. Schuyler resorted to a strategy that had served her own mother well in times of need.

She was throwing a ball.

1

Middle Child

The Schuyler Mansion

Albany, New York

November 1777

The mansion on the hill shone like a lighthouse.

Twenty windows stretched across the riverfront of the Pastures, each one ablaze from dozens of oil lamps and candlesticks. Shadows flitted behind the curtains as the household prepared for the party—servants busily rearranging the furniture to make room for dancing as well as laying out trays of preserves, candied nuts and cured meats. Inside the second-floor ballroom, hired musicians set up their instruments, ears tuned to their strings. Upstairs in their private quarters, family members stood before their looking glasses putting the final touches on their evening costumes. Hoops and panniers harnessed onto the women, jabots and lace cuffs fastened onto the men.

At least Eliza hoped it was just the household getting

ready. Her mother would scold them mercilessly if she and her sisters were to walk into the house after the guests were already there.

"Has anyone arrived yet?" she asked her sisters as she caught her breath beneath the weight of her load. Each of them was holding heavy bolts of blue wool and white cotton that they had gathered from the well-heeled women of Albany to make uniforms for the Continental troops.

"I don't think so," Peggy, the youngest, said, panting from exertion. "It was just past four when we left the Van Broeks' house, so it can't be five yet. Mama's invitation was for five o'clock."

"And we know none of these Albany ladies likes to be the first to a party," added Angelica knowingly.

Eliza bit her lip, doubtful. "Even so, we should go in through the back entrance. With any luck, Mama won't see us come in." She could practically feel the weight of their mother's censorious gaze as the sisters labored up the hill-side's sixty-seven stone steps hauling four dozen reams of fabric. At the top of the hill, the threesome quickly skirted around the south side of the mansion and passed through one of the covered porticos that connected the main body of the mansion with its flanking wings. The wing on this side contained her father's military office, and Eliza was surprised to see that it was as lit up as the rest of the house. Mama would be furious to find Papa still working so near to the ball's starting time.

"Were Mama and Papa quarreling this morning?" she asked her sisters. "I'd hate to think that Papa won't be attending the party because of some disagreement."

"I hope not; things can be so dreary otherwise. What Mama allows the musicians to play are practically dirges. It's positively funereal," said Angelica with a sniff.

"Did Dot mention anything?" Eliza asked Peggy, who was close to their lady's maid.

Some might find it strange that a servant was expected to know more than they did about the state of their parents' union. But the Schuylers, as befit their station, were a formal family and a busy one, and although there were seven children in the house, it was normal for them not to see one another until they gathered for dinner. The servants, by contrast, were in constant congress, and maids and valets and field workers kept one another apprised of the goings-on in the house. Thus Dot was much more likely than the sisters to have the temperature of the current state of their parents' marriage. Though solid and, in its own way, caring, the Schuyler union was conducted with as much diplomacy as Ambassador Franklin was even now using in Paris to persuade Louis XVI to bring the French into the revolution on the American side.

Peggy frowned. "Dot did mention that Rodger"—their father's valet—"said that the general is looking forward to the party as much as the missus is."

"But Mama will be quite cross with him for hiding in his office instead of helping her prepare," said Angelica.

"Nonsense," said Eliza. "Mama is probably happy to have him out of the way."

Peggy continued, struggling to keep her head above the bulky cloth she carried. "At any rate, Rodger said that Papa was expecting a visit from an aide-de-camp to General Washington."

"What!" the older sisters chorused. Eliza stopped so suddenly that Angelica crashed into her. "Is Papa being recommissioned?"

Since being relieved of duty after the loss of Fort Ticonderoga, General Schuyler had written innumerous letters asking for another command. The family felt his frustration keenly, and Heaven knows they could use the salary, but even Eliza, as patriotic as she was, was happy to have her father off the field of battle.

"Dot said Rodger didn't say," Peggy said, which was tantamount to saying that Rodger didn't know—General Schuyler's valet was an uncontrollable gossip, a trait the general himself was strangely ignorant of, and the rest of the family tolerated because it was how they got their news. "But he did mention . . ." Peggy let her voice trail off. A little smile played over her face.

"Yes?" Eliza demanded. She could tell from her sister's expression that Peggy was savoring a juicy bit of gossip. "Tell us!"

"The aide coming to the party is Colonel Hamilton," Peggy half squealed.

Angelica raised an eyebrow and Eliza tried not to blush.

Like every other girl in every other prominent American

family, Eliza had heard stories of Colonel Alexander Hamilton, General Washington's youngest but most trusted aide-de-camp, who was, if rumors were to be trusted, heart-stoppingly handsome and dashing to boot. Colonel Hamilton had been recruited by the commander of the American forces when he was still a teenager, just a few years after arriving in the North American colonies from the sugar-rich West Indies. Some said he was the son of a Scottish lord and could have claimed a baronetcy as well as a vast fortune if he'd chosen the loyalist side, while others said he was in fact a bastard, the illegitimate child of the disgraced son of some British aristocrat or other (there were so many!) with neither a name nor a penny of his own.

What *was* known, however, was that twenty-year-old Colonel Alexander Hamilton was brilliant, having made a name as an essayist while still a student at King's College in New York City. He was also known as having a bit of a reputation with the ladies. Eliza's old friend Kitty Livingston, who had met the young colonel on several occasions, had written Eliza about him after each meeting. She had been necessarily discreet in her letters (Susannah Livingston, Kitty's mother, was as much of a gossip as Catherine Schuyler), but it was clear she and the young soldier had carried on quite a flirtation. Eliza had been amused by Kitty's letters and curious about this young man who had captured the interest of Continental society.

Eliza peered through the second-floor windows of her father's office, hoping for a glimpse of the famous young colonel, but could discern no figures within the room, only the occasional flickering shadow.

"Perhaps Church will introduce us; I'm certain they are acquainted," said Angelica, meaning her rich suitor who was practically tripping over himself to ask for her hand. The oldest Schuyler sister was close to giving it, too, as John Barker Church was in the process of building one of the greatest fortunes in the new country, enough to rival or even eclipse their own father's (or at least before the British had burned a large part of it up at Saratoga). But Angelica was enjoying being the belle of the ball too much to relinquish it just yet.

"It will be interesting to finally meet this Hamilton fellow," said Angelica. "Livens up the party for once."

Eliza shrugged, attempting to appear disinterested, but her sisters knew her better than that.

"Maybe if you wore something a little more fashionable tonight, you'd catch his eye," said Peggy cheekily.

"And why would I want to do that?" Eliza retorted.

"As Mama says, honey catches more flies than vinegar," said Peggy, echoing their mother's perennial advice about reeling in the right suitor—and quickly.

"Honestly, Peg," Eliza said, rolling her eyes. "I have no interest in Colonel Hamilton other than to satisfy my curiosity."

"If you say so," said Peggy, sounding totally unconvinced. There was no hiding her feelings from her sisters, Eliza realized. They knew her too well.

"Peg's right, you could make more of an effort tonight,"

Angelica chided. "Most girls would love to have your figure. You could at least show it to its best advantage every once in a while."

"I suppose," said Eliza. "But why should I when no one need look at me when both of you are in the room?" It was an honest question, and said without the remotest hint of jealousy. Eliza was proud of her beautiful sisters, and much preferred the shadows to the spotlight.

"Oh, Eliza, your lack of vanity is sweet, but one day you must let us help you shine," said Angelica.

Unlike the perfectly turned-out duo, Eliza was not one for the latest vogue of cinched waists and pannier skirts and powdered décolletage and pompadour wigs. Just a month past nineteen, she favored simpler dresses in solid rose (which did, in fact, flatter her complexion) or soft blue (which made her dark eyes that much more radiant), with square necklines modestly covered by lace shawls whose translucence didn't so much conceal her cleavage as compel one to look harder. Her chestnut hair, darker than Angelica's but lighter than Peggy's, was never covered with anything other than a bonnet, and usually styled in nothing more elaborate than a pair of braided coils that accentuated the oval of her face, making her look that much sweeter. All of which is to say that, though Eliza may have been as "sensible" as her mother feared, that didn't mean she wasn't every bit as aware of the way young men looked at her.

Eliza huffed: "I want a boy who is attracted to me, not to my wardrobe."

"Pretty clothes are like the colors of a flower's petals. They tell the bee where to land. After that, it's what's inside that holds his interest," said Peggy, still quoting their mother.

Eliza rolled her eyes. "So I've heard. At any rate, you two should head inside to get ready; it grows later by the minute. I'll go back to the Van Broeks' for the last of it."

"Hurry back," said Angelica. "You don't really have much time, and the Albany ladies will arrive before you know it."

Already running down the hill, Eliza called over her shoulder, "I promise!"

2

Troop Inspection

Eliza's bedroom & the hallway, the Schuyler Mansion

Albany, New York

November 1777

It was almost an hour later when Eliza returned home. She stashed the last bundle of fabric behind a wall with the others and slipped into the house without being seen by anyone other than a garden boy raking the gravel paths of the garden and a kitchen maid ferrying foodstuffs from the kitchen in the north wing. Inside, half a dozen servants scurried up and down the stairs, but she came upon no one from the family or worse, any guests.

As she scampered down the hallway, a towheaded boy peeked out of the nursery. "You're late."

"Does Mama know?" Eliza asked her brother. John Bradstreet Schuyler, twelve, nodded somberly. The heir-apparent was deemed too young for the ball. Annoyed to have been left out of the festivities and stuck in the nursery with the littles, he frowned at Eliza's carelessness.

Philip Jeremiah, nine, appeared next to his brother and tugged on Eliza's skirts to entice her to play. Rensselaer, four, followed with glee and honey-covered hands. Cornelia, the baby, cooed from her nurse's arms, eager to join in the revelry.

Eliza laughed, took her little sister, and kissed her on both cheeks. "You're all getting me sticky!" she told the boys, who were running circles around her. "All right. One quick loop around the room. Catch me if you can!"

She was a favorite of the nursery, being the only older sister who would play on the floor with them or chase them around. After obliging them for one run around the chimney, she dashed upstairs and ducked into her room, which was the only dark one in the house. Inside, Dot was lighting the lamps on the wall sconces and atop the bureau.

Eliza collapsed in the middle of her four-poster bed. "I made it!"

"Miss Eliza! For shame!" said Dot. A stout woman of indeterminate middle age, Dot had once been the sisters' wet nurse, and long years of intimacy had led to an easy—some would say too easy— familiarity of discourse between the maid and her charges. "Your sisters are ready and you look as if you had just come back from a run in the countryside." She opened the wardrobe and reached into the thicket of clothing inside. "We don't have much time!"

Only then did Eliza notice the gown hanging on a dress form in a corner of the room. She caught her breath. The gown was undeniably gorgeous, with a burgundy overskirt and pale green brocade petticoats. It sagged awkwardly in the middle however, without a pannier to hold up its ample skirts—which is what Dot held in her hands when she turned from the wardrobe.

Eliza did her best to focus on the tangle of straps and slats of the pannier, which looked as cumbersome as a carriage horse's harness, rather than the gorgeous gown.

"But I *told* Mama I didn't want a fancy gown," she wailed. "It's unseemly for civilians to be dressed in frippery when our soldiers are fighting for our freedom in rags!"

Dot shrugged. "It's here now. And you didn't ask her to have it made." She stifled a giggle. "And it's not like our boys can wear it to battle."

Eliza frowned, unwilling to give in. "It's not right. For the past year I have spent all my time canvassing the ladies of Albany to spend less on themselves and more on the war effort. If I appear in a gown as sumptuous as this, they'll think I'm a hypocrite."

"If you don't appear in it," Dot said, "your mother will jerk a knot in your neck." She grabbed the loose end of the bow cinching the bodice of Eliza's dress and gave it a sharp tug.

Eliza slid across the bed, out of her maid's reach.

"And that hue is much, much too red for my coloring! I'll look like a bruised peach."

"A little powder," Dot said practically, reaching again for the ribbons on Eliza's bodice.

Eliza was shaking with fury. "This is so manipulative of Mama! She must know it contravenes all my principles! And she shouldn't be wasting so much money on a dress when the family fortunes are so tight!"

Dot bit back a smile, which Eliza wouldn't have seen, because her eyes were still glued to the gown. "Don't put it on for your mother. Put it on for Colonel Hamilton," she teased. Dot had been spending too much time talking to Peggy it seemed.

Eliza almost snarled. She did not care a whit what the celebrated soldier would think nor what any man would think. She dressed for comfort, not for competition.

"But, Miss Eliza . . . ," pleaded Dot. "Your mother."

"Fine! Fine! I'll wear it!" she said, as if she were agreeing to spend the day with her spinster aunt Rensselaer, who was so pious that all she would allow her nieces to do was to read to her from the Bible for hours on end, and so deaf that they had to shout themselves hoarse to be heard. Besides, she knew full well Mrs. Schuyler's wrath would fall on Dot if she did not put on the dress. "I suppose we'd better get started. It will take at least an hour to put it on—"

But she was interrupted by a pair of peremptory claps from outside her door.

"Girls! Inspection time! The first guests will be arriving any minute!" Mrs. Schuyler may have been the wife of a general, but there were times when Eliza thought her mother sounded more like a Prussian instructor before a drill.

With glee, Eliza realized there was no time to put on the fancy dress now.

"Quickly, just help me look presentable," she told Dot.

She smoothed her hair and straightened her dress as Dot brushed a little powder on her face and dabbed a little color on her lips. Her maid looked back longingly at the dazzling new dress.

Angelica and Peggy were already standing in the hallway when Eliza sidled behind them, hoping to escape notice. Angelica was resplendent in an amber gown, heavily embroidered with trails of green-leaved purple irises. Wide panniers beneath her dress gave her a striking hourglass silhouette, accentuated by a ribbed corset that cinched her already tiny waist even smaller, and pushed her breasts up and out. The expanse of bare skin was heavily powdered, as was her neck, face, and forehead, so that her skin had a moon-white purity, broken only by the pink pout of her mouth and flashing eyes. A powdered pompadour wig added nearly half a foot to her height, densely curled on top of her head and trailing between her bare shoulder blades in a few simple rag curls.

Mrs. Schuyler, dressed in a heavy gown of purple so dark it was nearly black, looked her eldest daughter up and down, then nodded once. "Impeccable."

She motioned Angelica back and Peggy forward. Her gown was sea-foam green, complementing her emerald eyes. It was embroidered with blooming flowers rendered in brilliant amethyst, and connected by a delicate tracery of vines woven from thread of gold. Her panniers were smaller than her oldest sister's, which only brought out the natural advantages of her lithe figure, as supple as a willow's branch.

Though her skin was more lightly powdered, her cleavage was just as pronounced as Angelica's. As usual she had elected to wear her own hair. The waist-length tresses had been elaborately piled on top of her head in a pouf nearly as tall as Angelica's wig. Eliza couldn't imagine how Peggy and Dot had achieved such a sculptural effect in so short a time, but judging from the whiff of bacon she caught, they must have used enough lard pomade to fry up a full rasher.

Mrs. Schuyler pursed her lips and pinched the fabric of her youngest daughter's sleeve between her fingers. "I do not believe I recognize the flower, Margarita."

Peggy smiled bashfully. "It is called a lotus, ma'am. Apparently, it grows in the gardens of Cathay."

Mrs. Schuyler was silent a moment. Then she nodded her head—the equivalent, for the sober matron, of a bear hug.

"Flawless," she said. Then, sighing: "Elizabeth. Step forward, please."

Eliza bit back a sigh of her own. She should have known she wouldn't get away so easily.

Angelica and Peggy parted like theater curtains, and Eliza took a step forward. She was dressed in what she'd been wearing all day, a simple gown of solid mauve, its skirt pleated but unamplified by hoops or panniers, and delicately draped to reveal a darker purple panel beneath. The purple lacing in the bodice ran up the front rather than back, leaving almost no décolletage in view, though what skin was left uncovered was all but concealed beneath an intricately worked lace shawl, which Eliza had stitched herself.

Mrs. Schuyler's expression didn't change, but when she pinched Eliza's sleeve as she had Peggy's, she caught a little skin with her fingers. Eliza did her best not to wince.

"Is this . . . *cotton*?" Mrs. Schuyler said in a horrified voice.

Eliza nodded proudly. "American grown and woven, in the province of Georgia." She shook her head. "I mean, the *state* of Georgia."

Mrs. Schuyler turned away from her middle daughter even before she finished speaking, her dark eyes finding Dot's, who stood well back against the wall behind her mistress. "I thought I selected the burgundy gown for Miss Eliza to wear."

"It's not Dot's fault, Mama," Eliza interjected. "The burgundy gown is too dark for my skin tone."

Mrs. Schuyler didn't take her eyes from Dot's. "If she would spend less time in the sun as I ask," she said, not to her daughter but to her daughter's maid, "she wouldn't have this problem. She is as freckled as a farmhand, and what boy wants to see that? A little powder to bring the down the tone and it will look regal."

"Yes, ma'am," Dot said.

"Mama," Eliza tried again, "I think it incumbent upon patriotic ladies to lead by example. How can we deck ourselves out in exotic frippery and stuff ourselves with sweetmeats and pastries when so many of our soldiers are shivering in threadbare rags and subsiding on bones and beans?"

Mrs. Schuyler didn't answer immediately. Then:

"Any moment now this house will be filled with more

than a hundred representatives of the province, including more than a dozen suitable bachelors. Your sisters are suitably prepared to meet them, but, alas, you seem bound and determined to alienate them by downplaying the gifts with which our Creator has blessed you. In a more perfect world, you might be able to attract a husband with your mind, but as women we must play the hand that was dealt us. You will put on the burgundy dress that I procured for you—at no inconsiderable expense—and the wig and powder, and you will appear downstairs with a smile on your face, whether that smile is painted on or genuine. And you will do so within the hour."

Eliza felt her cheeks color and wished she had used more powder, so she wouldn't give away her anger. "New York isn't a province anymore," she said. "It has been a state since fourth of July, 1776."

Mrs. Schuyler bit her lip. She drew in a calming breath before speaking. "Young men don't like drab dresses," she said in a clipped voice, "let alone girls who know more words than they do." She turned back to Dot. "You will dress Miss Eliza in the gown I selected and not let her out of her room until her skin is powdered as white as the Catskill range."

"No," said Eliza, "she will not."

"Excuse me?"

"I said no, Mama. I won't wear that dress. I am perfectly presentable and I have no wish to change, nor is there time. If I'm not mistaken, the first guests have arrived."

Mrs. Schuyler looked as if she would boil over like a

kettle, but the sound of carriages in the driveway seemed to change her mind. "I suppose there is always one spinster in the family," she said coldly. "You two," she continued, addressing Angelica and Peggy. "Downstairs on hostess duty. I want your smiles so bright that no one even notices the wallpaper peeling in the entrance hall. As for you, Elizabeth, try to be as inconspicuous as possible. Perhaps I can convince the gathering I have only two daughters."

Angelica and Peggy flashed sympathetic looks at Eliza before following their mother downstairs.

"I don't understand you, Miss Eliza," Dot said, tying the bows in the back of the dress a little tighter to accentuate Eliza's waist. "You had already decided to wear the dress. Why kick up such a fuss? It just draws Mrs. Schuyler's wrath down on you."

"Oh, if it wasn't the dress, it would be something else," Eliza said as Dot pushed and tugged at her dress. "Mama needs no excuse to scold me."

Dot had to agree with that.

"I don't know why she cares so much," Eliza said now. "This is hardly the most prominent party of the year."

"Yes, but the Van Rensselaers are coming and the Livingstons and, of course, that famous young Colonel Hamilton. Husband season is open. The hounds are on the loose."

Eliza's face brightened. "A good thing, then, that I have no intention of being a fox!"

3

Messenger Boy

Outside the Schuyler Mansion

Albany, New York

November 1777

It wasn't supposed to have been this way.

It was supposed to have been his triumph. After barely a year as General Washington's aide-de-camp, he had persuaded his commander to send him to Albany on a matter of vital military importance. He was to confront General Horatio Gates, the man who had replaced General Schuyler as commander of the northern forces, and demand that he surrender three of his battalions to the Continental army under the direct command of General Washington. Following the success of the Québec campaign and the recapture of Saratoga, the war in the north was essentially a holding game, and troops were needed farther south to liberate the British-held New York City and stem the onslaught of British troops besieging the southern states, where they were burning the vast fields of cotton and tobacco.

Technically, all Alex was doing was delivering an order from the commander in chief of the American military forces. But the United States was an almost two-year-old country, and the toddler nation was reluctant to be bound by rules. General Gates, like General Washington and General Schuyler and indeed every other patrician patriot—Jefferson and Franklin and Adams and Madison—had one eye on the war, but the other was firmly focused on what would come after. The new country would need new leaders, and a heroic general could parlay victory on the battlefield to high political office: president perhaps, if that was the direction the new republic went.

There were some who said the American states needed to replace King George III with their own monarch, and there were those who said Horatio Gates's autocratic style lent itself to a throne. Alex's missive would be less of an order, then, and more a request: one that would have to be delivered diplomatically but also persuasively. Success would bring Alex greater prestige—possibly even his own battlefield command, which he had been agitating for since the beginning of the war—while failure could condemn countless patriots to death. Alex relished the opportunity of putting the imperious General Gates in his place without the older man even knowing what was happening.

But just before he'd left Morristown, New Jersey, where the Continental army was wintering, General Washington had called him into his office and charged him with a second duty. The Continental Congress wanted someone to blame for the debacle at Ticonderoga. If the fort hadn't fallen in July 1777, the Continental army might have pushed as far north as Québec and brought eastern Canada into the United States as the fourteenth state. Instead the army had been forced to spend the past year simply to get back to where they started. The congress wanted to make an example of someone. And General Schuyler had been the commander at the time of the defeat.

General Washington rubbed his eyes in fatigue. "It appears the good general has been caught in the crosshairs of his own command."

Alex protested, saying General Schuyler wasn't even at Ticonderoga when it fell: He had been farther north, preparing the invasion of Québec. And the troops defending the fort had been vastly outnumbered and taken by surprise as well. There was nothing shameful in their defeat. There was, rather, much to be praised in the way they had acquitted themselves against overwhelming odds.

"Indeed, sir, if I may," Alex pleaded. "How to put it? Punishing General Schuyler for the defeat is akin to punishing a mule for being a born a mule, when its parents were a horse and an ass: Some things were simply meant to be."

The comparison brought a slight but much-needed smile to General Washington's face.

"If this were purely a military matter," he said when Alex had finished, "you and I would be advocating the same position. But, alas, there are military matters and there are political matters, and when the latter taints the former, the waters grow muddy. I am afraid General Schuyler must fall on his sword, if not for the sake of the army, then for the sake of his country."

Alex had traveled north to Albany with a heavy heart. The entire time he was arguing General Gates into submission, the pending confrontation with General Schuyler loomed in his mind. He had not yet met the New York patrician, but had heard only sterling descriptions of his character and his family—both his ancestors, whose pedigree was impeccable, and his descendants, which is to say, his children. His daughters were reputed to be each more beautiful and charming than the last. Perhaps one of them would look past his lack of pedigree and bring him the name and connections that had been denied him at birth by his feckless father. But it seemed unlikely, to say the least, that he would be wooing any of the daughters of a man whose head he was about to serve up on a platter.

Look on the bright side, he kept telling himself. *Maybe this will be another hurricane* . . .

THE HURRICANE OF 1772 had no name, but if it had, it would have been one of the Furies, those Greek goddesses whose only desire was destruction.

Alex also didn't have a name.

He called himself Hamilton, but he could have just as easily called himself Faucette, his mother's maiden name, or Lavien, the name of her first husband, because she'd never married his father. She never married his father because she was already married to another man, whom she had left before Alex's birth and refused to talk about, just as she refused to speak about Alex's father after he abandoned the family when Alex was nine.

That man, James Hamilton, was the fourth son of a Scottish laird who claimed that he'd given up the family manse—Kerelaw Castle was its grand name—to make his fortune in the New World. No one knew if his story was true, but his attempts to make money were well known throughout the wealthy Caribbean islands of St. Kitts and Nevis and St. Croix, as were as his absolute failures to do so. Indeed, the only thing James Hamilton was good at was disappearing. Just as he'd deserted his family in Scotland, he similarly left his children and their mother on St. Croix. Though Alex wrote to his father regularly and occasionally heard back from him, he never saw him again, and after his mother died, when Alex was eleven, he found himself truly alone in the world. He and his older brother had no relatives to take them in. James was fostered to one family, and Alex was sent to another. It wasn't an adoption. It was servitude. Alex had to earn his keep by working in the family's shipping office, but even that was tenuous. When Alex's foster family decided to leave St. Croix, they left him behind to fend for himself. He was barely in his teens.

His intelligence had already made itself known in the small island community, however, and he continued to clerk at the docks. On the one hand, it was dull work: counting inventory and keeping track of changing commodities' prices and calculating net profits and losses. On the other hand, it was fascinating. The great wooden ships, each as big as a plantation house, docked in the harbor with crews from all over the globe. West Africa . . . Lisbon . . . the Canary Islands . . . London . . . New York . . . New Orleans . . . Savannah. The sailors told stories of the wide world that made Alex realize how tiny and isolated St. Croix was and gave him his first yearning to see beyond it.

The stories were captivating, but their cargo was rather less appealing, for the great majority of the ships that docked in St. Croix were loaded with a single cargo:

Slaves.

By law, the freighters were required to "off-load" that portion of their cargo that hadn't survived the long passage over the Atlantic before they docked in the harbor, which is to say, the shippers were supposed to throw the bodies of any kidnapped Africans who had died in the holds into the ocean before the ships sailed into St. Croix. But there were always one or two dead in the gaunt parade of people who were marched or, often, carried off the great, dark, foul-smelling ships. Those who had survived the harrowing three-month journey chained to a splintery, rat- and lice-infested berth had muscles so atrophied that they could barely stand, their flesh pocked with sores.

It was their eyes that haunted Alex most, because even though they didn't speak his language and he didn't speak theirs, he could still read the knowledge of their cruel and unjust fate written there. Each tick he checked in the category of "live cargo" filled him with shame, because each one represented the length and breadth of a human life. A few hundred pounds that would change hands in the slave market, a few years of life in the cane fields before their abused body finally gave out from exhaustion.

St. Croix was part of the enormously rich Antilles, an archipelago of islands, whose plantations shipped endless amounts of sugar to satisfy Europe's sweet tooth, and consumed endless amounts of enslaved workers to grow and process the cane. Such was the demand for sugar that the small handful of islands, whose total area was smaller than that of New York or Massachusetts or Virginia, generated a hundred times more wealth than all the northern colonies combined. But all that wealth was generated at the cost of untold thousands of lives, each of which had had its total worth recorded in a single black check cursorily made by a white hand.

So, five years ago, when a hurricane had loomed out of the Atlantic like a great dark wall, its storm-force winds pushing twenty- and thirty-foot waves before it like a child's hand splashing drops across a pond, there was a part of Alex that hoped the storm would sweep away the entire island and cleanse it of its terrible deeds. Buildings collapsed like playing-card houses, hundred-year-old trees were blown away like dandelion fluff, and the ten-foot-tall cane stalks disappeared beneath floods that swept in with the ferocity of a pouncing lion. When the winds and floods retreated, carnage as far as the eye could see was left behind.

As a child of the Caribbean, Alex had weathered dozens of hurricanes, but this was like nothing he had ever seen or heard of. Struggling to make sense of the destruction, of the puniness of man's desires against the fury of the natural world, he sketched out a description of the storm's fury in a letter to his father. Before he mailed it, however, he showed it to Hugh Knox, his pastor, who had served as an intellectual mentor to Alex since his father's desertion and his mother's death. Alex had only been looking for an adult eye to make sure that he hadn't misspelled any words, but, far from criticizing the letter or correcting any errors, Knox extolled its virtues and even asked Alex's permission to publish a copy in the *Royal Danish American Gazette*, which carried news of the Caribbean to the wider world. Alex was flattered, and consented. Even then he wasn't thinking of any benefit accruing to him from his missive. Yet, when Reverend Knox told him that a group of wealthy residents in the province of New York had been so impressed by his account that they'd taken up a collection to bring the young writer north so that he could further his education, Alex thought his pastor was toying with him. But the offer and, more to the point, the stipend and the first-class ticket were all real, and less than a month after the hurricane devastated St. Croix, Alex left the tropical islands of his youth for the cold northern lands. At the age of seventeen he saw snow for the very first time. It was as white as sugar and, to Alex, just as sweet.

The following years were a blur, as he enrolled in King's College to pursue a career in the law and then dropped out of college to fight for the cause of independence. The patrons who sponsored his journey came from some of the northern colonies' most respected families, above all, William Livingston, a scion of the great New York clan, who took Alex under his wing and, often, into his home. Livingston's daughter Kitty was a beautiful, vivacious girl, fully aware of her good looks and good fortune, and unashamed to flaunt both. Though unspoken, Alex understood that Livingston's patronage didn't extend to bringing a nameless Caribbean immigrant into his own family. Like Alex, Livingston could trace his lineage back to the lesser line of a noble family, but unlike Alex's father, Livingston had done his family proud and had no interest in diluting its blood with unknown stock. This was the New World, where men made their own names. Alex would have to make the name Hamilton carry its own weight, rather than ride on the coattails of the name Livingston.

It was from Kitty that Alex first heard the name Elizabeth Schuyler. The Livingston daughters and the Schuyler daughters were all acquainted (and even distantly related, as were most of the families of New York). Though Angelica and Peggy were temperamentally more similar to Kitty, she'd always been closer to Eliza—most likely because there is only room for one flirt in any group of girls, and Kitty occupied that spot with pride.

Kitty knew marrying poor, penniless Alex Hamilton was out of the question, but was more than happy to trade witty banter with him at table and dance quadrilles until four in the morning. But between dances Kitty sang the praises of her friend in distant Albany.

As he made his dreaded way to the grand Schuyler mansion, Alex remembered what Kitty had said, even as he had already forgotten Kitty herself.

"Eliza's bookish, like you. She cares about fresh ideas. Independence. Democracy. Abolition, they say. I think she'd even marry a man with no name and no fortune, if he cared about the same ideas she did."

Hmmm, thought Alex, *a girl with a prestigious family name who might be open to marrying a man with no name of his own . . .*

4

Small Pitchers and Big Ears

Stairs Behind the Landing

Albany, New York

November 1777

Eliza followed her sisters down the stairs to the ballroom, where the musicians were playing a popular Italian violin concerto. At this point, there were still more servants than guests in the upstairs ballroom, and those who had already arrived were too busy plying themselves with food and drink to notice her entrance. Nodding at a few familiar faces, Eliza wove through the room and made her way toward the staircase at the rear of the house. As she descended to the middle landing, the lamps fluttered in a sudden breeze and she felt a rush of cold air around her ankles: Someone was coming in the back door.

Assuming it was a servant from the kitchens, she paused. She didn't want her entry to be accompanied by a steaming mound of turnips or glistening side of beef. But instead of a servant appearing below, she saw dark coats—

uniforms—and the murmur of deep voices. Her father was with a soldier.

"General Schuyler," an unfamiliar voice said nervously, as a slender, square-shouldered young man came into view. His back was turned so Eliza could not see his face, but his voice was deep and sincere as it grew more concerned. "I must apologize again for being the bearer of such bad news. I want you to know that General Washington has nothing but the greatest respect for your military capabilities and even more for your character. But His Excellency must answer to all thirteen states now, and there are too many voices calling for a scapegoat for the loss of Ticonderoga."

Eliza leaned over the banister a little more and saw her father next to the young man. If General Schuyler was stouter and shorter than his younger companion, his shoulders were just as square.

"There is no need for you to continue speaking, Colonel Hamilton," her father said in a curt voice.

Colonel Hamilton! Eliza's heart fluttered beneath her corset. Could it really be? She strained for a glimpse of her father's companion but could see nothing beyond the powdered top of his head.

"I applaud you for having the courage to deliver news of my court-martial in person, rather than simply sending a letter. Nevertheless, I find your decision to visit on the night of my wife's ball a little convenient."

Court-martial! The phrase exploded in Eliza's head like a cannon striking a buttress. *Her father? It couldn't be!*

"Convenient, sir?" Colonel Hamilton said in a confused tone.

General Schuyler did not explain, although Eliza knew her father meant to cast aspersions toward the young soldier's social aspirations for arriving at the Pastures on the night of an exclusive ball.

Her father sighed. "Still, you are a guest and, so I am told, a gentleman, and if I can surrender my own bedroom to General Burgoyne and his retinue for a month, I can certainly entertain a lackey of the Continental Congress for an evening. I would advise you not to stay too late, however. With so many of our men away at the war, the roads at night are not entirely safe."

There was a hint of accusation in her father's voice in the way he said "so many of our men away at the war," but Eliza was still shocked by his use of the term court-martial. Could it be that her distinguished, honorable, irreproachable father was really going to be called before a military tribunal? It didn't seem possible.

The top of Colonel Hamilton's head bent forward in a respectful nod. "Of course, sir," he said in an apologetic tone. "But, that is . . ."

"Yes, Colonel?" Her father had turned from Colonel Hamilton to gaze at his guests in the grand first-floor hall. Clearly, he was done with this unwanted visitor.

"Yes, sir. It's just that, you see, the army didn't arrange for an inn for me, and I myself am unfamiliar with Albany. I was rather hoping I could spend the night—"

"Here?" A chuckle burbled in General Schuyler's voice. "Well, that is a pretty situation, isn't it? I'm sorry to say"—in fact, he didn't sound sorry at all—"we're sleeping two to a bedroom as it is, and there's no way we could accommodate you in the house." He shrugged. "I'll see if Rodger can find you something in the barn."

He turned then and strode toward the front hall. Eliza quickly stepped back to avoid being seen, but as she did, one of her slippers brushed against the banister spindle and an embroidered bead popped off, bouncing onto the floor below.

The powdered head turned and tilted upward. A lean face, impossibly young, looked up at hers. It was a sharp face, with a wolf's sly intelligence. Long, straight nose, bright blue eyes. The most uncanny feature, however, had to be the eyebrows. For some reason, Eliza had always thought Alexander Hamilton would be dark-haired, but he was in fact a ginger and one who seemed to have a perpetual look of mischief on his face, even now, after he had just had his own head served to him on a platter. The rumors were right: Alexander Hamilton was terribly handsome.

Having been seen, she drew herself erect, then made her way down the stairs as regally as she could. With each step, Colonel Hamilton's face grew as red as his eyebrows, as he realized that she was a Schuyler daughter and that she'd overheard his exchange with her father.

"Colonel Hamilton," she said, without looking him in the eye, and swept past him into the party.

5

Tomcat and Canary?

Schuyler Ballroom

Albany, New York

November 1777

After his rough treatment by General Schuyler at the back door of the mansion, and the dazzling apparition of the Schuyler daughter floating down the stairs, Alex skulked in the rear foyer for a few minutes so that it wouldn't appear as if he were following her. He wondered who she was—was it Angelica, whom Kitty had said was the boldest of the daughters? Or Peggy, the prettiest? Or could it be Eliza herself, of whom Kitty had so often spoken? Whoever it was, the look she had given him cut him deeper than anything the general had said.

That wasn't his only trouble at the moment. He didn't usually affect a wig, but he'd put one on this morning. Not for the meeting with General Schuyler, but in anticipation of the ball tonight, news of which had been all over Albany since he arrived three days earlier. He had fiddled with the pins for ten minutes before giving up, and had spent the entire day with the distinct impression that his hair was on crooked. Plus it itched. Unfortunately, it was impossible to get a finger beneath the thick layer of hair without sending the hairpiece even more askew. But if he didn't scratch his head soon he was going to end up ripping the thing off and pulling his own hair out of his head.

He looked around for a mirror but didn't see one, so he squinted into a pane of the back door. He'd managed to worm his fingers under the wig without dislodging it too much, but just as he started to scratch, the door swung open and a servant's face appeared where Alex's reflection had been. Alex recognized him as Rodger, the general's valet, who had attended him in his office.

"Oh, ah, excuse me," Alex said sheepishly, jerking his hands from his head and feeling the wig grow even more crooked.

Rodger was perhaps thirty years old, a slim, regal man whose confident bearing suggested he was well aware how dependent his master was on him and not afraid to exploit his power. He smirked now, either at the thought of a young man asking his pardon or, more likely, at the mess that was at the top of Alex's head. "Allow me, sir."

Alex was about to step out of Rodger's way, but instead the valet reached his hands to Alex's head and, before Alex quite knew what was happening, had deftly slipped his fingers beneath the wig and began to knead his itching scalp.

"Oh . . . my . . . stars," Alex said, when he could speak again. "That . . . feels . . . *wonderful*!"

"It is a task I have performed for the general on occasion," Rodger said, his fingers giving Alex's scalp one last squeeze, then slipping out from the wig and quickly, professionally, fastening it back in place. "There you are, sir. You look like you could conquer anything now, whether it's the British or"—he nodded his head at the room behind Alex—"a ballroom full of belles."

Without another word, he slipped past Alex and disappeared into the house.

A burst of laughter from the door beyond him shook Alex from his trance and he reminded himself: There was a ball to get to. Smoothing his jacket, he squared his shoulders and marched into the party.

The jovial roar of voices struck him as soon as he entered. There were at least thirty people in the grand hall and, judging from the sound, at least that many scattered in the pair of opulent parlors that opened off each end. About a third of their number were men, equally divided between gray-haired ancients too old to fight and young men like him in smart blue uniforms, who were on leave or perhaps stationed to the local garrison. But the bulk of the party guests were women—seated grandes dames who spread their billowing skirts around their chairs and ottomans like fountains spilling over their basins and forcing their conversation partners to stand well back. The eyes of these half-dozen *femmes d'un certain âge* scanned the room as if hawks in search of prey, looking for suitable mates for their daughters.

And then there were the young ladies themselves—

their waists cinched and their cleavage pushed up high and proud—who made up almost half the room's number. Elaborate skirts cocooned each one of them in a richly colored aura, all of which set off their ghostly powdered complexions and the mountainous silver wigs perched atop their heads. Yet no amount of powder and makeup could hide the desperation in their eyes. With so many of the local boys away at war, there was almost no prey for this pack of fierce and brightly colored predators to track down and capture. Alex felt at least a dozen pairs of eyes fasten on him as he walked into the room.

He stood up a little straighter, glad that his wig was on right. Perhaps the night wasn't going to be so bad after all.

A HALF HOUR found Alex seated in a parlor whose tall windows offered a spectacular view of the Hudson River and the lights of Albany on its far bank. Six girls stood in a fan around him, their colorful skirts arrayed like a mountain range decked out in fall foliage topped by the first dusting of winter snows. If only their names were as delicate as their faces and figures: Alas, they all seemed afflicted with strange Dutch and English names like Van der Schnitzel or Ten Broek (pronounced "break," which is what his fingers nearly did when the girl shook his hand with a grip like a milkmaid at her chores) or Beaverbroke, which Alex had made its owner repeat three times to see if she were having him on.

"Oh, Colonel Hamilton," said a Miss Tambling-Goggin, or Tamblin-Gogging, he wasn't sure which. "How utterly fascinating it is that you work with General Washington himself! It must be so exciting."

Alex shrugged. "I wouldn't say it's exciting as much as . . . dangerous," he said, his bright blue eyes flashing. He knew how to play to this crowd.

A collective gasp from the gaggle of girls.

"I can't imagine anything more frightening than a battlefield," cooed a Miss Van Leuwenwoort, whom Alex was calling Liverwurst in his head. "The roar of the cannon and the smell of smoke and the cries of men in mortal ecstasy!" (Alex didn't mean Liverwurst as an insult, by the way; it was one of his favorite foods, and he hadn't had any in *ages*.)

In fact, while Alex had been in battle, he mostly served away from the front lines. Though the general always risked life and limb with his men, he often left his less-experienced aides-de-camp behind, a fact that made Alex feel like he was shirking his duty. But that wasn't his fault, and the image of his taking notes while fellow soldiers dodged musket fire and cannon balls or rushed toward the enemy with drawn swords wasn't going to loosen any of these ladies' bodices.

"Ah yes, mortal ecstasy," he said, looking into the middle distance as if recalling unsayable scenes of carnage. "It can indeed overpower the senses."

"As does the rich odor of India ink filling the nostrils with its terrible intimations of sealing wax and postage stamps!"

Alex looked up just as a new wig appeared among the peaks, looming like an iceberg emerging from an ocean fog. It crowned a long, magnificently sculptured face that would have been almost too severe but for the exuberance of a set of full, richly rouged lips, which were set in a smirk of private amusement.

"It is indeed a rich, ah . . . what?" he asked.

"Oh, one can imagine the terrible pain of a hand cramping after measureless hours curled around the barbarous scimitar of a raptor's quill!"

Alex turned to see a second new face, her glorious emerald eyes set off by a sea-foam gown. This beauty was without a wig, though the dark locks had been piled nearly as high as any of the other girls' pompadours. Her face was softer than that of the India ink jokester, yet there was a familial resemblance. He began to get a bad feeling in the pit of his stomach, as sweat beaded beneath his own laughable wig.

He managed a weak chuckle. "Ladies, you have caught me. I do indeed spend many hours serving as General Washington's amanuensis, assisting him in his communications with—"

"Amanuensis!" a third feminine voice cut him off. He turned to see—

The girl from the stairs, dressed in a simple gown unamplified by hoops. As his eyes darted between the three girls, he realized he'd been ambushed by none other than the beautiful and clever Schuyler sisters.

An image of Fort Ticonderoga, besieged on all sides, sprang to his mind.

The ladies who made up his breathless entourage of powdered hair and high heels glanced at one another peevishly before petulantly making room for the three newcomers.

It wasn't just that this was the Schuylers' house, Alex thought. These three were clearly used to commanding any room they entered.

"*Amanuensis* is such an impressive-sounding word," said the one he'd bumped into by the stairs. She stood in the middle of her siblings, glowing with good health, a little shorter than the one, a little taller than the other, and yet more vibrant than either, despite the plainness of her gown. "It must refer to some tremendously important position, like a bombardier or a charioteer."

A blush crept over Alex's cheeks. "There are no charioteers in the Continental army, Miss, ah, Schuyler, I presume?"

"He is correct, Eliza, the position is not as lofty as one might assume," said the first sister, the one with the sculptural face. "It is, of course, outside of the domestic purview of provincial females such as ourselves, but I do think what the word *amanuensis* describes is a position more akin to a . . . scrivener?"

"What's that you say, Ange?" the other sister said. "Scribbler?"

"Scribbler is a good word, Peg," the second sister—Eliza—answered. "And yet scribbler is a name often applied to novelists, who, after all, are the authors of the words they scratch onto the page. Whereas, an amanuensis is more of a copyist, don't you think, Angelica?"

"Indeed," the tallest sister answered. "It is a position rather akin to a ventriloquist's mannequin, who simply mouths the words of his master."

"There's another word for mannequin, isn't there?" Peggy asked. "*Dolt* or *dummkopf* or . . ."

"*Dummy*," Eliza filled in, looking directly at Alex. "I think that's the word you're looking for."

It was a rout, and revenge against what she had heard at the back landing. They were angry and defending their father from this court-martial, and they were out to shoot the messenger.

Alex looked up at the three faces arranged determinedly before him: elegant Angelica on the left; pretty Peggy on the right; and in the middle, the most bewitching of the three, seeming to combine the best features of both sisters and yet not resembling either of them. Angelica and Peggy were both lovely girls, but their beauty emanated from their visages. Eliza was certainly lovely as well, yet her distinction, her captivating quality, came from within rather than without.

He had eyes only for Eliza as he pulled a handkerchief from his coat pocket and waved it in the air. "I surrender," he said weakly. "Do with me what you will."

Eliza stared back at him for a long moment, a triumphant smile flickering at the edge of her lips. Then she reached out and, as if she were plucking a flower, pulled the handkerchief from Alex's hand. Examining it as though she'd never before seen a man's lace-edged, pocket handkerchief, she tucked it into her cleavage.

"He's all yours, ladies," she said to the Misses Ten Broek, Van der Schnitzel, Beaverbroke, Tamblin-Gogging, and Van Leuwenwoort. She turned her back on him, her voice dripping with contempt, "Do with him what you will."

6

Lovers' Reel

Schuyler Ballroom

Albany, New York

November 1777

At length the victuals had been consumed, another round of cider and whiskey quaffed, the chitchat dispensed with. A small army of footmen and stable boys suddenly appeared from the door beneath the stairs and in a manner of minutes had cleared the great hall of all its furniture. As the last sideboard was carted out the musicians, who had been playing quietly in the Red Room, took their place at the foot of the ballroom—a trio consisting of violin, viola, and cello. While the players were taking their places, the guests lined up on either side of the long gallery, and then Mrs. Schuyler separated herself from the crowd and stepped out into the center of the room.

"Ladies and gentlemen," she said with the air of a born master of ceremony, "it is time to dance."

A smatter of applause. Mrs. Schuyler waited for it to die down.

"In this time of war," she said, "it is more important than ever that we not lose sight of the traditions that bind us together as a nation, and the pleasures that we fight for as people. Hence this small party, which my husband and I throw in honor of the many brave men who fight for our new nation, and the stalwart young women who assist them on the home front."

As Mrs. Schuyler spoke, Eliza was busy retrieving her dance card from the credenza in the southwest parlor. Normally a girl carried her card with her, but on this occasion her mother had revived an old tradition of the female guests leaving their cards on a table, so that any gentleman could pencil himself in without fear of rejection. Eliza knew Mrs. Schuyler did this less out of a love of tradition but rather to make it impossible for her three headstrong daughters to turn down someone their mother thought would make a fine catch.

"As a mother," Mrs. Schuyler continued, "I am quite honestly relieved that my sons John and Philip are too young to go to battle, but I am also equally proud of the remarkable contributions to the war effort made by my three eldest daughters."

"Hear, hear!" The murmur of her guests' approval interrupted her. But not for long.

"Angelica, Eliza, Peggy—would you please join me?"

Just as Mrs. Schuyler called her name, Eliza spotted her card and snatched it up without reading any of the names written on it. She hurried into the ballroom where the crowd was dutifully applauding the famed Schuyler girls, and skipped out into the open space near her two sisters. As she took her place between Angelica, resplendent in her amber gown, and Peggy, dazzling in sea-foam green, she felt a small pang of regret for not deigning to wear the burgundy gown. Between two such fierce beauties, she felt a little like a servant girl, and only her sisters' hands in hers kept her from cringing into the shadows.

When the applause died down, the sisters began to move back to the sidelines.

"Peggy," Mrs. Schuyler called, "would you wait a moment."

Peggy pretended to gasp and look surprised, but it was clear she knew what was happening.

"Angelica and Eliza have both made their official appearances before," Mrs. Schuyler said to the crowd, "but as this is Peggy's first ball as a young woman, I am forgoing my right to have the first dance to give it to my daughter. It is not quite a coming-out ball, for such a celebration would be untoward in times of war. Nevertheless we can at least let her have her turn in the lights. Peggy, pray tell us the name of the gentleman who has the honor of sharing your first dance."

Peggy eagerly pulled her card from her reticule, a beaming smile on her face. Her smile flickered as she looked at the name at the top of the page.

"Ste-Stephen," she stuttered, "Stephen Van Rensselaer."

A great roar of applause went up, even as Eliza found Angela's and Peggy's eyes and shared in their shock. Stephen

Van Rensselaer III was the eldest son of Stephen the second. The Van Rensselaers were distant cousins on Mrs. Schuyler's side and the wealthiest family in northern New York State. In every way, Stephen III was the most eligible bachelor north of Albany—every way but one, that is.

A tall, thin boy in an exquisitely cut suit of midnight-blue overcoat and dove-gray breeches detached himself from the crowd. Despite his height, however, and the color of his coat, he was no soldier, for one simple reason: He was barely into his teens.

The eighth patroon of the largest estate in all of New York was all of fourteen years old.

Eliza felt a hand on hers and turned to see Angelica.

"I sense Mama's handiwork here," her older sister said, even as the band struck the first notes and Peggy and Stephen took their places at the end of the room.

Stephen's face was fine enough and might one day be handsome, but at the moment he looked like a stick doll in a suit. And Stephen had always been quiet and fumbling for words. A curious sort of fellow with a fondness for birding, he had earned himself the reputation of a loner.

"Stephen is at least four years younger than Peggy!" Eliza said indignantly. Their families had sat across from each other at the Dutch Reformist Church for years as the children grew up.

"Four? I think it is more like five. Isn't he only a year older than Johnny?" sniffed Angelica.

Eliza nodded, thinking it was a bit strange indeed,

watching the gawky young man dance with the belle of the ball in front of a cheering—or was it jeering?—crowd.

"It doesn't matter, does it? He is the richest single male in our circle, and we are the three marriageable daughters of a family fallen on hard times," said Angelica. "Oh dear," she gasped, as Peggy and Stephen danced past them down the line, a strained grace on her sister's face, a look of dogged terror on Stephen's. "She is leading him. She. Is. Leading. *Him*," she hissed.

"Let's hope the engagement is a long one," Eliza said with a sad laugh. She pulled out her own card to see whom her mother had arranged for her to dance with first, and soon she was as aggrieved as her sister. A small gasp escaped her lips. "It can't be!"

"What?" Angelica asked. "Who is it?"

"Major André!"

"*John* André? That is insane, even by Mama's standards!"

Major John André was a British loyalist, born in London to wealthy French Huguenot parents, whose ancestors, like so many Americans, had fled religious persecution in France. Before the revolution began, he and General Schuyler had served in the British army together, and André had been a favorite of their father's. Indeed, he was said to charm everyone he met, with his easy conversation in English and French and his ability to dash off the most remarkable likenesses in pen and ink, and above all, with his guileless brown eyes and open, honest expression set in a broad, handsome face.

But when the Colonies declared independence he had chosen to fight for the country that had taken in his own family when they had fled France. Such was General Schuyler's honor and fond memories of serving with André that he said he could not condemn the major's decision, and even went so far as to declare that he would be "most aggrieved" if circumstances forced him to shoot the dashing young officer. But that still didn't explain what he was doing on Eliza's dance card.

"How is he even *here*? Why is Papa not arresting him? Or—or shooting him?" asked Eliza.

"Apparently Major André was commissioned on a diplomatic mission to General Gates, for which he was granted safe passage up and down river," said Angelica. "It had to do with the prisoner exchange for General Burgoyne, and his transport to New York so that he can be sent back to England. When Papa found out he was in Albany, he invited him to dine."

"I declare, Papa's chivalry will be the death of us all. But chivalry wasn't why my mama let him sign my dance card. She is punishing me."

"For the dress, no doubt. Who do you have after him?"

Eliza looked down and turned paler. "Colonel Hamilton!"

This time, Angelica exclaimed loudly enough that people turned and looked at them. In a quieter voice, she added, "How could Mama do that, especially after his meeting with Papa?"

Eliza shrugged. She knew full well how to incur her mother's wrath. "How did you fare?" she asked Angelica.

Her sister held out her card with a smile. Only one name was written on it, albeit eight times, for every single dance of the evening: Mr. John Barker Church.

"What?" Eliza exclaimed. "How did you pull that off?"

"Simple," Angelica answered. "I was not foolish enough to leave my card out for Mama to commandeer. Not my first time at the ball," she added mischievously, flashing a little smile to Mr. Church himself, who stood on the far side of the room, patiently awaiting his dance.

John Church was almost a decade older than Angelica. Like Major André, he was British born and had only arrived in North America a few years earlier. Unlike Major André, though, he espoused the Revolutionary cause. But he also refused to renounce his British citizenship, and this, coupled with the fact that when he first arrived in the Colonies he set up business under the alias "John Carter," made many suspicious of his character. General Schuyler had said straight out that he thought Church was a gambler and a spy, and scented something devious about his business methods. However, Mrs. Schuyler, knowing her daughter's fondness for Church, as well as hearing stories about Church's growing fortune, had insisted he be allowed to attend the ball. "Until we have proof against him, civility directs us to be for him," she said diplomatically, and as General Schuyler valued decorum above all things in human society, he had reluctantly assented.

Eliza looked over at her sister's paramour. He was not what she would call ugly, but he was far from handsome. He was shorter than Angelica, for one thing, and rather thick through the waist, and his face always had a rather silly-looking smile on it, especially when he looked at Eliza's older sister, as he'd been doing all evening.

"Tell me again what you see in him, Ange? Besides his fortune, I mean?" she asked her older sister.

"I refuse to be an ornament in a gilded cage," said Angelica, lifting her chin. "And while a pretty face is nice to wake up to, an adoring face is so much more rewarding. Church talks to me like an equal and is grateful for my affection. I need never worry about him stepping out on me. And yes, his fortune is a most welcome quality."

"Papa will never allow it, though," Eliza warned. "You know how he feels about the man."

"We shall see," said Angelica, and Eliza knew her sister was determined to change their father's mind about her unsuitable suitor.

Eliza sighed, even as the first song came to an end. Sometimes her sister's pragmatism was too similar to her mother's. While Eliza professed no outward interest in romance, at heart she yearned to experience a lush, sweeping love affair of her own.

She was about to ask Angelica if she'd seen Major André, when she was tapped on the shoulder. She turned to face a fine-looking gentleman whose thick brown hair was pulled back from a high brow, his rich chocolate-colored eyes staring into hers.

"Miss Schuyler," a suave British voice announced. "I believe I have the honor of this dance."

Eliza's heart turned a little somersault. She had heard stories of how good-looking Major André was, but she had not been prepared for this. He was the picture of debonair in his dashing suit, which, though not a uniform (wearing his redcoat here probably would have gotten him shot in a duel!), was still sharply cut in a rich burgundy and accented with polished gold buttons and lace at collar and cuffs. She felt as though she were staring into a painting by Sir Joshua Reynolds.

She curtsied politely. "A pleasure to make your acquaintance."

"The pleasure is all mine," Major André said, leading her into position directly behind Angelica and John Church. "May I compliment you on your appearance this evening? You are among the brightest flowers here."

Eliza couldn't quite stifle her laugh. "No need to flatter me, Major André. I am aware that my dress is a little drab this evening."

The major turned to look her at her directly. "Your dress?" he said smoothly. "I hadn't noticed it." His eyes never left hers. "I'm sure it is the loveliest in the room."

The music started, saving Eliza from having to answer. For the next fifteen minutes she danced the line with her partner, whose light touch deftly guided her in the turns and twists and bows without ever once overpowering her. Because it was a quadrille, they kept spinning away from each other and coming back, dancing side by side and then turning to face each other. It was a complicated set of maneuvers, one that Eliza had spent many hours learning, and though she went through her paces gracefully, she always felt a little nervous, lest she make a misstep and bring the coordinated roomful of dancers to a crashing log jam. Yet every time she felt a twinge of anxiety she found Major André's hand in hers, or his eyes on hers, and he deftly set her to rights.

If, at the end of the dance, he had asked her to run away with him, she might have exclaimed, "Long live the King!" and run all the way to the docks by his side. But before she knew it the music faded out, and Major André was bowing to her.

"It was like dancing with a dove," he said. "I felt as though you carried me up and down the room."

"Oh, Major André," Eliza said, blushing, "you are too kind." It was not the most original line, but it was all she could come up with, rattled by how charming she found him.

Eliza caught Angelica's gaze across the dance floor as she was bowing to the handsome British adjutant, and her sister shot her a wink and a little smile. Then Angelica threw back her shoulders in an exaggerated signal to encourage her sister to lift her chest in a more enticing pose. Eliza quickly followed suit because big sisters know a thing or two.

And then he was gone, and a white-powdered wig took his place, capping a pair of russet eyebrows and piercing, amused blue eyes. Alexander Hamilton looked as surprised as she was to be asking her to dance.

"Miss Schuyler? I hope my name on your dance card wasn't too alarming, but your mother said she would make me sleep in the barn if I didn't sign up."

Eliza refused to acknowledge him just long enough to make him squirm, then finally took his hand and allowed herself to be led back to the head of the room. "I hate to be the bearer of bad news," she said as they walked, "but she's going to have you sleep in the barn anyway."

"Ah—" Alex's voice was cut off by the first strains of a reel. Almost reluctantly, he offered her his hand, and Eliza put her gloved fingers into it as though reaching into a pail of sour milk for a ring that had fallen. Yet she couldn't help but note that his hand had a sure and confident touch: light and attentive, and if she was being honest, not completely repulsive.

It irritated her, this confidence, and so she sought to undermine it.

"Colonel Hamilton, if you please," she said, adjusting herself beneath his grip. "I am not an apple on the tree to be tested for ripeness. If you could perhaps squeeze a little less tightly. I have worn corsets that took less liberty."

Alex's eyes went wide, and his fingers, which barely rested on her shoulder and waist, relaxed still more. "I do apologize," he said in a voice so aggrieved that she felt a twinge of guilt.

They began to move to the music. Alex's step was as assured as Major André's had been, but Eliza deliberately dragged her feet a little, so that he was forced to hurry her along to keep them from bumping into the other couples on the dance floor. A smile remained on his face, but it was a little strained.

They whirled by Major André, who had his hand in Henrietta Beaverbroke's. Eliza tried to catch his eye, but the music called for a whirl and they swept away from each other. Again, Eliza found herself face-to-face with the colonel's handsome but increasingly strained face. Spots of sweat had appeared on his temples beneath his periwig.

"I wonder that your parents would allow you to dance with a British officer," he said, nodding at the major.

Eliza frowned and did not answer.

"Miss Schuyler, have I offended you in some way?" he asked suddenly. The dance took them away from each other for a moment, and when he was back he continued: "If so, I do apologize. I can assure you that my errand today is as odious to me as it is to General Schuyler, for whom I have only the utmost respect."

"You have a strange way of showing it, then," Eliza shot back, but again she felt a little badly for her partner. His voice was genuinely full of concern, and her own father had told her innumerable times that war forced men to make compromises that in any other circumstances would be intolerable. But she didn't care. He had insulted her father's honor, and she didn't care if he was the most handsome soldier at the ball (much more handsome than even the British major, she had to admit); he would have to do a lot more than offer a de rigueur apology to get back in her good graces.

The colonel seemed about to say something more, but the dance called for a particularly complicated set of turns, bows, and weavings, and they were both forced to concentrate to move through them smoothly. But as they came to the end of the maneuver, their path brought them close to Major André and Henrietta. Eliza's eyes caught those of the dashing British soldier, who flashed her a smile, and she fell behind a half step. As she ducked beneath Alex's arm, her heel came down squarely on the bridge of her partner's foot.

Alex gasped, but he managed to repress a yelp. When they were face-to-face again, she glanced at him with equal measures of guilt and glee.

"Normally when a gentleman's foot interposes itself between his partner's and the floor, he apologizes for being so clumsy," she said in the kind of imperious voice that would have made Angelica proud.

"Did you drive the sharp wooden heel of your shoe into the top of my foot, threatening to break my arch?" he asked in the lightest possible tone. "I didn't notice."

Eliza couldn't help it. She smiled. And when he unexpectedly threw in an unscripted bound instead of the expected coupé, she let out the tiniest of whoops, and would have fallen if his strong arm hadn't pressed firmly into the small of her back.

"I beg your pardon," he said when she was upright again. "I didn't mean to leave you hanging."

She had to hand it him. He was *good*, this Alexander Hamilton. Under other circumstances, she might actually like him. But right now she had about seven more minutes of his time, and she was determined to make them as difficult as possible.

7

Gauntlet (Or Handkerchief?) Thrown

Schuyler Ballroom

Albany, New York

November 1777

As the night wore on, the frenzied pace of the dancing picked up. The officers' uniforms flashed with medals and a few gold braids. More than a snippet of petticoats could be glimpsed as the turns grew wilder and the men's hands around the ladies' waists began to intentionally miss their marks to hold on to something more interesting. Soon the ballroom grew overly warm despite the mid-November chill.

After taking his leave and bowing to Eliza Schuyler, Alex went back to drinking mulled cider from the Schuyler orchards spiked with apple brandy from the Pastures' own trees and followed that, perhaps a bit unwisely, with French wine spiced with cinnamon and cloves. In between dancing reel after reel with the eligible young ladies of Albany, he went back to regaling perfumed clouds of girls who clustered around him like life-sized lollipops with stories of battlefield valor and carnage.

Taking advantage of the general's lavish hospitality, he then stepped into the smoking room to indulge in fine Virginia cigars and whiskey brewed beyond the Kentucky frontier before intrepidly accepting a slug of some home-brewed spirit that unfortunately tasted like serpents' urine. At last, he returned to the ballroom and found himself once again surrounded by a clique of girls.

Well, two girls.

From the eight who had fawned on him earlier in the evening, the Misses Van der Schnitzel, Ten Broek, and Beaverbroke were all standing in a corner, waiting for their chance to dance with the British adjutant, one Major André, who seemed to have won the hearts of all the ladies that evening.

But the loyal Misses Tambling-Goggin and Van Liverwurst eyed Alex flirtatiously above their fans. They were comely lasses to be sure, the kind he would have happily spent the time with back in Morristown or Elizabeth, yet his eyes rolled right over them and shifted back to the dance floor.

For there were the Schuyler sisters, the undisputed queens of the party: Angelica, regal and self-possessed, even next to her less-than-graceful partner, a short and portly but jolly-looking older gentleman; and Peggy, laughing vivaciously and looking as though she were dancing with a French count rather than an awkward lad, the young Van

Rensselaer heir. But above all there was Eliza, wearing a dress more suited to the schoolroom than the ballroom, who had insulted his name and rank at every turn, and had even stepped on his foot—and who made him want nothing more than for her to step on the other.

Why was it he couldn't take his eyes off the one girl who failed to notice his impressive gifts? What was it about the sharp-tongued lass wearing a homespun gown, a modest cotton dress that touched his heart in its bold demonstration of her alliance to the patriot cause?

And why on earth was she dancing for the third time with that blasted British officer, Major André?

"I say, Colonel Hamilton, if you would like to return to the dance floor, I would be happy to join you," Miss Tambling-Goggin said, sounding anything but pleased. After all, no girl likes to flirt with a boy whose eyes keep wandering away.

"I do apologize, but I am quite satisfied where I am. Please, do not take my fatigue as a sign of lack of interest in your considerable charms," he said, flashing her a winning, but rueful smile.

"Since the colonel is unwilling," said a male voice. "Perhaps you will allow me to shepherd you to the dance floor."

The speaker was another man whom Alex didn't recognize and who, despite being in his early twenties, wasn't wearing a uniform. He was a tall, well-built man, though his soft neck and softer stomach spoke of a fondness for food and alcohol that were clearly getting the better of him, judging from the way he swayed back and forth. In fact, Alex was wondering whether the man had been drunk when he got dressed, because he was wearing one white and one brown hose beneath his expensive velvet breeches.

"So what do you say, Letitia?" he slurred.

Miss Tambling-Goggin turned toward the new speaker. "Alas, but like the colonel, I am quite satisfied with where I am as well."

"Don't be that way, come now," said the rude stranger.

"The lady has made her preference known," said Alex mildly.

"Yet I shall make her preference for her, Mister . . ."

Alex held out his hand, hoping to defuse the suddenly tense situation. "It is Colonel Hamilton, actually. I do not believe I have had the pleasure of making your acquaintance—"

The man looked down at Alex's hand, but didn't shake it. Only then did Alex notice that he was leaning heavily on a cane—and then, looking farther down, he saw that the brown hose was not actually cloth. It was a wooden leg.

"I would shake your hand, Colonel, but as you can see my right hand is otherwise engaged," the man said with a dramatic sigh.

"I do beg your pardon, sir," Alex said as the music stopped; he noticed Eliza, Angelica, Peggy, and their dance partners heading their way. A half-dozen pairs of eyes were trained on him, and he felt like a complete cad. "A war injury?"

"Indeed. Some of us haven't spent the past year and a half writing letters in an office. We spent it on the battlefield."

He snorted. "It's quite ironic when you consider it. Normally you would expect the person of highborn rank—that's me, by the way," he added contemptuously. "Normally you would expect the son of gentry to shirk the battlefield. But in this case it is the nobody commoner who flees glory and hides behind a clerical duty or some other equally flimsy excuse while the nobleman defends his country's honor. But then, it isn't really your country now, is it? Where were you born again? An island off the coast of nowhere?" the man sneered, as the Schuyler girls and their companions clustered around their little group.

Alex felt his cheeks go red and had to resist the urge to throw down his glove for a challenge—or just punch the man outright. No matter how important his work as aide-de-camp and ambassador for General Washington, his spending the war doing various non-combat jobs was a source of great shame to him. He wanted to risk life and limb for this country, which, though he hadn't been born here and had only lived on its shores for a few years, had nevertheless embraced him and inspired him with its ideals and potential. Only the fact that the man speaking so rudely to him was an injured veteran stayed his hand.

"I-I do apologize," Alex said again, letting the slur against his birthplace go. "Your country owes you a debt of honor."

"Yes, it does. Whereas all it owes you is a paycheck."

"Oh, put a cork in it, Peterson," said a young male voice. He turned to see Stephen Van Rensselaer rolling his eyes. "Everybody knows you got 'injured' when you stabbed yourself in the ankle with your own bayonet while you were loading your gun, and then you fell down drunk in a latrine and got it infected so that it had to be amputated. The mules who pull cannons serve their country more usefully than you do."

Peterson looked distinctly outraged, but before he could speak, Angelica's partner chimed in.

"Indeed, Peterson," said John Church. "Colonel Hamilton's contribution to the war effort is known throughout the thirteen colo—the thirteen states," he corrected himself with a wry smile, "and across the pond in England, France, and Germany. While we must never make light of bravery under fire, the skill it takes to load and shoot a gun is not a rare one, whereas the ability to address generals and diplomats—and indeed kings—is a truly singular gift. Hence General Washington's unwillingness to surrender his most valuable asset to the battlefield."

"Thank you, good sir," said Alex.

"John Church. A pleasure to make your acquaintance," said Church as Angelica looked at him fondly.

But that was the straw that broke Peterson. He whirled drunkenly on John Church. "You! A lobsterback! You dare to insult me in my own house."

Eliza, who had been silent throughout the whole exchange, spoke up. "Actually, Mr. Peterson, Mr. Church is not a soldier and hence does not wear a redcoat, and pray I remind you, the Pastures is my father's house."

Peterson looked confused. "Well, in my own country,

then! The Petersons have been respected landowners in the Hudson Valley for more than a century."

"Actually, Peterson," young Van Rensselaer drawled, not so very awkward anymore. "Your land belongs to my father, ever since you gambled away your income at gaming houses in New York City. You own no more land than Colonel Hamilton. No offense, Colonel."

"None taken," said Alex, feeling gratified at the swelling of support from Angelica's and Peggy's companions.

Peterson sputtered so hard that Alex was afraid he was going to fall over. "Oh, who cares what you think, Rensselaer. You're merely a Dutchman. My family are British through and through."

"I thought you didn't like the British," Eliza's partner, Major André, said smoothly. "You are fighting a war against us, after all."

Peterson's jaw dropped. He lifted his cane as if to strike the major, but the movement caused him to lose his balance on his wooden leg, and Alex had to steady him. "Careful there, Peterson."

"Unhand me! Why I . . . to be insulted in this manner by people who are on the raw edge of respectable!" An ugly sneer covered his face as he turned his attention to Eliza. "And you, girl. If your mother thinks you will make a rich match, she's sorely mistaken. No one is interested in a girl afflicted with intellect and opinion and a small dowry! It's why you only have a redcoat and a clerk as your dance partners this evening!"

There was a shocked silence from the assembled, until Alex spoke, his words cold as the first frost: "You will apologize to the lady."

"Apologize? For telling the truth?" Peterson sputtered. "Why? Is she your paramour, is that it? Oh, Colonel Hamilton, do not protest—everyone has noticed your interest in the girl. You can barely take your eyes off her."

Alex's grip on the man's arm became a vise, as Eliza's cheeks flushed with embarrassment and anger.

"Nonsense, my interest is purely to redeem something the gentle lady has been holding for me. I assure you it is most business-like in nature," he said, lying through his teeth.

"A fine story," sneered Peterson, practically apoplectic and sweating all over the place.

"But a true one," said Eliza, her cheeks reddening uncontrollably. "However, Colonel, I apologize as I do not have your handkerchief on my person."

"Nevertheless," said Alex, turning to Peterson, "you will apologize to the lady."

"Fine! Fine! My apologies! There!"

"Oh dear, Mr. Peterson," John Church said. "You seem to have exerted yourself."

"Here," said Angelica, "speaking of handkerchiefs, I believe Mr. Peterson needs one," and she reached into the pockets of her dress and handed one over to him.

"Thank you, my dear," said Church. And he used the handkerchief to pat down Peterson's face as if he were a little baby.

Peterson grabbed the handkerchief and waved it in Church's face for a moment before his hand fell and he stuffed it in his pocket. Publicly humiliated, he shook Alex off and stormed away in a huff, the butt of his cane striking the floor hard above the music.

"Oh dear, that's going to do beastly things to Mama's floor," Peggy lamented.

Eliza turned to Alex. "Thank you," she said quietly.

"It is an honor to come to your defense," he said with deep sincerity, his heart hammering under his uniform.

"And I must commend you on your restraint. An ugly situation could have grown much uglier had you not shown such decorum."

Alex smiled. "Those are the kindest words I've heard all evening."

Eliza looked as if she was going to take them back, but she held his gaze and didn't look away from him. He wished he could tell her how he really felt, but somehow he understood it would not be welcome at this juncture. Alex stepped back with a gentlemanly bow, watching Eliza walk away on the arm of the British major.

HOURS LATER, THE party finally came to its end and Alex retreated from the ballroom only to run into Rodger, General Schuyler's valet, under the stairs. The servant offered to help him to his accommodations for the evening.

"If you'll follow me, sir . . ." Rodger turned to the back

door and headed outside. Alex realized with a start that he really was going to sleep in the barn tonight.

Rodger guided him across the slippery gravel paths by the light of a single flickering lantern whose glow was swallowed up by a heavy clinging fog coming from the river. The dim light made it that much harder to negotiate the gravel, which rolled like marbles beneath his shoes.

The interior of the lofty barn at the foot of the hill was no less cold than the November night outside and reeked of a pungent mixture of manures: horse and cow and pig and sheep and chicken. Rodger led him down the barn's center aisle to a ladder whose upper reaches were lost in the darkness of the rafters. He pointed upward, indicating that Alex's bed lay somewhere up there.

"With the house so full of guests, Mrs. Schuyler was unable to find a spare blanket, but there's plenty of hay," Rodger said without sarcasm. He'd seen worse. "The boys will be in to milk the cows at dawn. That's about three hours from now. Perhaps one of them will give you a ladle or two before you have to be on your way."

Alex nodded wearily.

"Oh, and before I forget, I was told to give this to you." Rodger handed him a note folded with cloth. Without another word, the valet turned and made his way back down the aisle.

With a start, Alex realized it was his handkerchief—the one that he had surrendered to Eliza Schuyler earlier that evening, the same one she had tucked into her bosom. It smelled like her perfume, and he inhaled its sweet scent, bringing it to his nose, just as a scrap of paper fluttered out of it.

In the dim light of Rodger's retreating lantern, he saw a few words in a flowery woman's handwriting:

Wait for me. The hayloft. After the ball.

Alex stared at the note. A *midnight assignation? In the hayloft? With Eliza Schuyler?* Was he reading this correctly?

He looked around, as if the note writer might be nearby, but just then Rodger opened the barn door and stepped outside. When the door closed behind him, the last of the lantern light disappeared and Alex couldn't see past his nose. And it wasn't just the rafters that were dark. The entire barn was pitch-black. Thankfully he'd put a hand on the ladder to hold himself steady, or he didn't think he'd have been able to find it, and would have had to sleep beside whatever animal occupied the nearest stall.

But after a couple of swings with his foot, he found the first rung and slowly started to climb, somehow managing not to fall. The whole time his heart was beating in his chest at the thought of that marvelous girl making her way up to join him. He wasn't aware that he'd reached the end of the ladder until he found himself tumbling forward into a surprisingly soft and deep pile of something he assumed—hoped—was hay.

While he was excited about the possibility of seeing Eliza again, he was also too tired to care about the indignity of a colonel and aide-de-camp to General Washington being forced to sleep under such circumstances, and burrowed deeper into the hay. The sweet smell of straw filled his nostrils, and his body heat began to warm his little cocoon.

She would be here soon. It was after the ball. What would he say to her? So she had succumbed to his charms after all! And that strange, withering look she had given him after the incident with Peterson had belied a hidden affection! She had understood what was in his heart all along.

And now she was on her way.

He fought sleep, waiting.

And waiting.

BEFORE LONG IT was morning. When he awoke, he found himself staring into the eyes of the most colorful bird he'd ever seen.

It was a rooster with brilliant plumage of blue and red and golden feathers, and it came at him with beating wings and talons extended. Alex barely made it out of the loft with his eyes intact.

More Than Two Years Later

8

Reconnaissance

Deserted Road

Rural New Jersey

February 1780

The deeply rutted road was frozen, aggravating the bumpy pace of Eliza's wooden-wheeled carriage. With every detour the coachman took, she bounced up and hit her head on the low roof, landing in her seat with her bonnet knocked askew. She tightened the ribbon strings for what felt like the twentieth time. After six hours of this she didn't even consider tucking in the loose wisps of her hair.

Instead she pulled aside the window's heavy curtain and looked out over the snow-covered fields glittering in the late-afternoon sun. Her seat faced backward, so she could only see where she'd been, not where she was going. Here and there a farmhouse sat in a cluster of smaller work sheds, but these were few and far between.

Morristown, New Jersey, her destination, was a city of

several thousand inhabitants, but so far there was no sign of any kind of life.

"Miss Schuyler, please!" Her chaperone, Mrs. Jantzen, cried, a nervous woman who always seemed to be huffing at something. "You are letting out all the heat!"

If only I could, Eliza thought. The temperature inside the carriage was akin to a hot stove. But worse than the heat was the smell.

Squared away behind Mrs. Jantzen was a supply of lamp oil and scrimshaw, gifts sent along to General Washington from her husband, an Albany merchant who specialized in whale products. The collection was rounded out by the good lady's personal bottle of whale oil perfume, a cloying scent she had grown overly fond of. She rubbed it on her skin the way other women used soap.

Eliza took a deep breath, then let the curtain fall. *If I don't get out of here soon, I'll be stinking of whale oil myself.* She turned to her chaperone with a sigh. "How much farther is it to Morristown?"

Mrs. Jantzen rolled her eyes and huffed once more. She reached into the folds of the fur spread over her lap and pulled out an imaginary map, unfolding it with theatrical fastidiousness.

"Let me see, let me see. Yes, here we are," she said, stabbing a gloved finger into thin air. "It is exactly seventeen miles and three feet."

Mrs. Jantzen pressed her lips together just so, tucking the imaginary map back into her blanket.

Eliza fell silent. Her mother was to have accompanied her on the trip south, but Mrs. Schuyler had fallen ill with a violent cough, serious enough to make it unwise for her to travel. Eliza was willing to make the trip on her own, but her mother wouldn't hear of the notion of a girl her age making a journey without a chaperone.

"The roads are overrun with soldiers too long denied women's taming influence," she said from her bed, propped up by pillows and swaddled in down.

"But, Mama," Eliza insisted, "I can take care of myself."

Mrs. Schuyler waved her handkerchief in the air, ending the discussion. "I'll not have my daughter be the first feminine face they see in who knows how long."

Eliza wasn't convinced the presence of Mrs. Jantzen would safeguard her, but if that's what it took to make this trip, then she was willing to bear it. Perhaps her mother had realized her chaperone's abominable perfume was weapon enough against a soldier's advance.

She stifled a laugh and smiled to herself.

The fragrant Mrs. Jantzen tightened the fur pelt around her knees. "I beg your pardon, Miss Schuyler. Did you just say something?"

"Oh. Why, yes. I-I was just wondering whether you had ever met my aunt Gertrude?" Eliza hid her smile behind her hand. "Yes, that's it."

"Her that married Dr. Cochran, General Washington's personal physician? She is sister to your father, is she not? I can't say that I've had the pleasure of making her acquaintance, but I have heard the kindest things about her character." Mrs. Jantzen, an accomplished gossip, mumbled to herself, "Imagine the stories she's privy to . . . surrounded by all those soldiers and what-not."

"Indeed, she is a remarkable woman and a great inspiration to me. Aunt Gertrude insisted her husband train her in the ways of a nurse so that she could remain at his side to assist in the recuperation of our brave patriots."

Mrs. Jantzen's pinched face took on a saintly look. "Just as I have spent many a day swabbing the sweat from the brow of a feverish soldier."

And suffocating those poor invalids with your ghastly perfume, Eliza supposed. Aloud, she said, "But my aunt Gertrude does so much more! She washes the blood from wounds, and runs the threaded needle through lacerated limbs as calmly as stitching together a torn overshirt. Why, she's even held the hand of a soldier while Dr. Cochran saws off the other—"

"Miss Schuyler, if you please!" Mrs. Jantzen held up a gloved hand. "I do not consider such subjects fit conversation for a lady!"

Eliza smiled a tepid apology. Of course the details were gruesome, yet she found them fascinating. It was bad enough that women weren't allowed to fight for their freedom. But to be denied the knowledge of what fighting cost its soldiers seemed too much to bear. How could one help the country's bravest young men if their needs were kept silent?

The carriage hit another pockmark in the road, sending Mrs. Jantzen's bottle of whale oil perfume sliding across the coach floor.

"Begging your pardon yet again, ladies," hollered Mr. Vincent from the coach box. The coachman was one of General Schuyler's retired old soldiers, now employed as the trusted family driver. "It's a bit of a rough go out here."

Eliza reached down and caught the bottle, which leaked onto her hands. But by the time Mrs. Jantzen could tighten the lid and settle the bottle more securely under her seat, a fresh wave of whale oil perfume had filled the coach.

Aching to be done with this journey, Eliza decided to look on the bright side. "Well, at least there'll be no fighting this winter while the army shelters in Morristown. Aunt Gertrude will be working alongside Dr. Cochran inoculating the local population against smallpox. I believe it is heroic work."

"Variolation!" Mrs. Jantzen said, sneering. "Tell me why anyone would think that infecting someone with pestilence ought cause but further disease."

"It's a milder form that's used for inoculation." Eliza slowed her words as if talking to a child. "The scratch method is much safer. Look at how many of our soldiers have stayed healthy."

Mrs. Jantzen huffed once again. "If God had wanted His subjects to resist the pox, He would have made us so."

Eliza thought about saying that if God had not wanted

His subjects to be so creative, perhaps He should have made them less ingenious. But she held her tongue. A little blasphemy would likely induce a faint in the good Mrs. Jantzen, and the thought of having to fan her awake—and send fresh clouds of perfume through the coach—was not to be borne.

Instead Eliza abandoned the conversation and peeked through a slit in the heavy curtain. Aunt Gertrude had written the family two months ago with news of Dr. Cochran's plans to continue the inoculations while General Washington's army wintered at Morristown. She had called it "work of the gravest importance" as military hospitals were overrun with soldiers confined in crowded wards that were breeding grounds for disease. "Inoculation," she wrote with palpable hope, "could save hundreds—if not thousands—of lives."

Eliza wanted desperately to be a part of the mission. She'd fired off a letter to her aunt to ask if she could help give the inoculations herself. If she could not fight, she could at least do everything in her power to make sure that those who did fight were as well equipped as possible. There were far fewer troops in the Albany area than there were farther south, of course, but they were vital to the capital's security. Thanks in part to Eliza's efforts, the battalions were all kitted out in smart new uniforms, stuffed with beef and porridge, and housed in some of the most comfortable mansions in the area, which had been seized from British loyalists. Inoculation seemed like the last noble service she could offer them.

She had begged her mother to let her make the journey south. Surely old Vincent was up to the task. Mrs. Schuyler had refused at first, saying it was far too dangerous, but Eliza had pleaded. She reminded her mother General Washington himself was spending the winter in Morristown, along with his senior staff and thousands of his troops. There was no safer place on the continent.

The mention of General Washington had not endeared Eliza's plan to Mrs. Schuyler. General Schuyler's court-martial was only recently completed, and even though he'd been exonerated of all wrongdoing in the Battle of Ticonderoga, she still felt that the military trial ought not to have taken place at all. Indeed, General Washington had gone so far as to write General Schuyler a letter of congratulations on his acquittal, but Mrs. Schuyler was unmoved. She was a steady woman, and slow to ire, but once one had earned her wrath, her forgiveness was hard to come by.

Almost as an afterthought Mrs. Schuyler had warned Eliza, "I suppose that foul Colonel Hamilton will be there as well."

Colonel Hamilton had served as clerk to the prosecution during the trial. He had been studying to be a lawyer before the war broke out, and though he had left school to serve the revolution, he was still competent enough in the ways of the law and the military that he had been called upon to liaise between the court and General Washington's office. It was yet another honor for one so young, but clerking for the prosecutor had supposedly caused him great pain, given his regard for the Schuyler family and his belief in General Schuyler's innocence. He had written as much in a letter to General Schuyler, but Eliza's father insisted on his presence. If General Washington was not going to preside over the farce of a trial, then he wanted someone close to the commander in chief to attend, so that Washington would be fully apprised of all that had gone on, and would feel that much more shame at capitulating to the political whims of the Congress.

Eliza thought to remind her mother of all this, then decided against it. Not that Eliza had given any thought to Colonel Hamilton's presence in Morristown, nor did she have any opinion as to the high level of his intelligence. Not at all. Besides, recalling the past would only cause Mrs. Schuyler to get her back up.

But to her surprise, her mother had relented rather quickly. She saw the silver lining in Eliza's plan. "There will be any number of unmarried officers in Morristown. Perhaps you will meet a suitable bachelor to replace the one who courted you so diligently and turned away."

Her mother was talking about Major John André, the British officer who had strived to win her hand. Eliza had been a bit infatuated with him for a while, but in the end had turned down his suit. Perhaps she was too much of a patriot to accept the man, unlike Angelica, who was holding steady with her Mr. Church, despite his having left her and the country without proposing. Almost three years after her illustrious ball, Mrs. Schuyler was irritated to find her three oldest daughters still unmarried and mentioned this unfortunate state of affairs often.

"Oh, Mama," Eliza said, running off to pack.

ELIZA PULLED BACK the curtain again and peered out. She felt Mrs. Jantzen's glare and ignored it. The snowy fields and barren trees looked no different from those of ten minutes earlier, and soon enough she let the curtain drop of her own accord.

"I wonder how much farther," she couldn't help but say aloud.

Mrs. Jantzen opened her mouth for a retort, but was caught up by a jarring thump, followed by an even louder crack.

"Whoa!" came the faint voice of the coachman. "Whoa there!"

The carriage lurched to a stop and then slowly, with a splintering sound as of a branch breaking off a tree, the right rear of the compartment sank slowly, heavily down, until it was some three feet lower than the left. Eliza had to grip both sides of the carriage to keep from falling upon Mrs. Jantzen, who was lying on her back, her legs sticking straight up in the air and protruding from the ruffled yardage of her petticoats and bloomers.

"What on earth!" Mrs. Jantzen exclaimed, desperately trying to right herself, but having little more success than a turtle flipped on its shell.

Eliza couldn't decide which was the more frightening

prospect: falling on Mrs. Jantzen, or being shrouded in that terrible perfume, but she wasn't about to find out. She toed the older lady's skirts aside as delicately as she could, spread her feet, and braced them against the opposite seat.

"Driver!" she called out. "Driver, there seems to have been some kind of . . . tilt."

The left-hand door of the carriage flew open, and the bearded face of Mr. Vincent appeared. "Begging your pardon, my ladies," he called out in his thick Irish brogue. "I'm afraid we've broken a wheel. Allow me—"

He reached a meaty hand into the carriage, wrapped it around Eliza's arm, and pulled her from the skewed compartment with no more effort than if she'd been a weaning puppy. The left side of the carriage was some five feet above the ground, and once free of the narrow door, Eliza had no choice but to jump down.

The road was frozen hard as stone, and sharp, hot pains pierced her feet as she landed. Convinced her daughter was likely to meet eligible bachelors along the trip, Mrs. Schuyler had insisted she wear fancy shoes of thin embroidered cotton—hardly proof against a New Jersey winter. The shoe heels were a full inch tall. Their thin soles gave way almost immediately to the chill of the frozen roadway.

She shook her feet to warm them, looking up just as the coachman lowered himself into the carriage to help Mrs. Jantzen. Eliza had once seen a pair of fighting squirrels chase each other into a pumpkin that had been hollowed out to hold a candle. The pumpkin had shook like a kettle on the boil as the animals tore at each other inside its orange shell, until suddenly the top burst off and one of the squirrels flew into the air and dashed off, leaving the other one poking from the cracked gourd. As the coachman attempted to free Mrs. Jantzen, the tilted carriage vibrated with nearly the same violence as that long-ago pumpkin.

The stranded lady's yelps and squeaks pierced the otherwise silent afternoon, interrupted by the coachman's half-desperate requests. "If you would just hold still, m'lady . . . Beg pardon, m'lady, but if you want to be liberated you will have to allow me to place my hand *just there* . . . Well, I'm sorry, dearie, but I thought that was just swaddling!"

Popping like a bubble, Mrs. Jantzen was fully ejected from the open door and rolled over and off the side of the carriage. Eliza rushed forward to help, only to be thrown aside by the bulk of the older woman's skirts as she sprawled onto the ground.

"My ankle!" the older lady screamed in pain. "It's broken!"

The coachman appeared and, despite his ample build, jumped nimbly to the ground. "Forgive me again, m'lady," he said, unceremoniously hefting her skirt and reaching for her ankle.

"Sir!" Mrs. Jantzen protested. "I must remind you that I am a married woman, and a lady!"

The coachman ignored her. His nimble fingers slipped inside her booted ankle and squeezed tenderly. Mrs. Jantzen winced and pulled away, but he held her in place. "It's not broken. Probably just a sprain. Best keep the boot on to hold in the swelling. We're only five miles from Morristown, but this does complicate things."

"Complicate things! I shall in all likelihood lose my leg!"

Eliza couldn't resist. "My uncle John is an excellent physician. And I shall be honored to hold your hand while he cuts."

"Now, now, ladies, let's not get carried away," Mr. Vincent said, though he grinned at Eliza out of view of Mrs. Jantzen.

He looked over at the ruined coach wheel. It was thoroughly shattered.

"No fixing that. I'm afraid we'll have to ride."

"But there are only two horses!" Mrs. Jantzen protested. "And no saddles! And we ladies in skirts!"

"Aye, there's that." He pondered a moment. "This will require some rope."

A half hour later, Mrs. Jantzen lay awkwardly across one of the horses, tied onto it like a saddlebag and covered in a voluminous fur, so that she looked like a bear carcass being brought in from a hunt.

"This is most indecorous," she said. "I assure you that you will not be receiving a tip at the end of this journey."

The coachman ignored her and turned to Eliza.

"Mrs. Jantzen's ankle is starting to swell up like a puff adder. I'm afraid of proving her right in her fear of amputation if we don't get to a doctor in short order. I was going to put you on the second horse and lead you, but I really do think we need to ride."

Although she had wrapped herself in the other fur from the carriage, Eliza had no protection from the winter other than her waistcoat. Her feet, however, were freezing and starting to go numb.

"Of course," Eliza said. "I would not wish further injury to Mrs. Jantzen. But with no saddle, sir, and me encompassed by all this fabric"—she indicated the expanse of her dress—"I do not think we shall both fit, or that I shall be able to remain astride."

"I shouldn't blame your dress, m'lady, as much as my own belly." He patted his large stomach. "The wife's shepherd's pie is too tasty for my own good, I'm afraid. Well. I am at a bit of a loss, I must admit."

"It is only five miles to Morristown, you say? Mr. Vincent, you've known me to walk that kind of distance on a daily basis back home in Albany. Why don't you ride with Mrs. Jantzen to aid, and I shall come on foot?"

"Your self-sacrifice is admirable, m'lady, but I can see how ill shod you are for such a journey."

"Nonsense. We Dutch girls rarely even bother with shoes on a day as warm as this."

"She's fine, coachman!" Mrs. Jantzen called. "Do please let's hurry! I'm DYING!"

The coachman shook his head anxiously.

"Night's coming on, too, and the moon's waning crescent. One step off the road and I fear it'll be you who meets her end on this day."

Eliza could see no other solution, and wished the

coachman would get going with things. The sooner she started walking, the sooner she would reach her destination.

Before she could speak again, however, she heard the *clip-clop* of horse hooves from farther down the road.

"Is it redcoats?" Mrs. Jantzen moaned. "We are killed!"

The British had been confined to the eastern shore of the Hudson River in New York City, but even so, Eliza was tense as she turned on her aching feet and stepped from behind the broken carriage to see who was approaching. A large bay horse was galloping toward them, mounted by a figure in tricorn and dark blue overcoat.

"Never fear," she said to Mrs. Jantzen. "It is one of ours."

The soldier's face was obscured by a scarf, Eliza saw as he approached, no doubt to protect it from the cold. She wouldn't have minded one herself. The rider was not tall, but certainly not short, with broad shoulders and a perfect, martial posture, wearing a long, slightly curved sword at his waist. The only part of his face that was visible, however, was a pair of piercing blue eyes staring at her—almost, she could have sworn, with amusement.

A voice came through the scarf with a fog of breath.

"Looks like we've had an accident." The mirth was audible in the words as well as visible in the eyes.

"Sorry to say we have," the coachman replied. "And our precious Mrs. Jantzen has injured her ankle. I wonder if perhaps you could give our Miss Schuyler the use of your horse."

"Oh, I'd be happy to give the daughter of General Schuyler a lift," the scarved figure answered. "That is, if Eliza does not object."

The soldier pulled back his scarf then, revealing a shadow of reddish stubble. Eliza's hand flew to her mouth.

It was Colonel Alexander Hamilton.

9

Knight in Shining Armor

Not-So-Deserted Road

Rural New Jersey

February 1780

"Slow there, Hector." Alex inched the big bay closer to the three stranded travelers, bringing him to a precise halt with his nose against his chest. Swinging both legs over his saddle, he landed before them in an elegant dismount.

"The sun will be down soon. We should make haste."

He dropped to one knee next to Eliza and laced the fingers of his gloved hands together to offer a lift up onto Hector's back. "A leg up, m'lady?"

An unmistakable quiver of embarrassment and annoyance ran through her but indeed the sun had already dropped behind the trees and darkness was fast setting in. In spite of the frozen cold ground under her delicate cloth shoes, it appeared her wounded pride was enough to make her lift her chin and press on.

As nimbly as she could, Eliza set her feet in the cradle of his sturdy hands in order to allow herself to be hoisted into place. She placed one hand on his shoulder and reached for the saddle pommel with the other as their bodies passed in close proximity. Calculating the full weight of her body, Alex inhaled the edge of her bonnet and found himself caught off guard by a vague whiff of what could only be whale oil.

Eliza settled herself with as much dignity as she could muster, both legs to one side of the cavalryman's saddle. Gathering up the reins, she clutched at some wisp of control. She looked down into the faces of the two men staring up at her and addressed them through a clenched jaw.

"Now, sirs, I must ask you to kindly turn your backs while I . . . I, I take a moment to, ah . . . arrange myself," said Eliza. "I'm afraid there's nothing else for it."

"It's a pity but I agree," said the young colonel, although he didn't sound at all disappointed.

The two men pivoted 180 degrees in perfect tandem.

The red-faced coachman pulled off his cap and stared straight down into it, a signal he planned to wait as long as this might take. Still strapped across the coachman's horse like a duffel bag, Mrs. Jantzen swiveled her head to survey the scene. To her right, two men stood staring off into the sunset with their backs to her ward. To her left, General Schuyler's devoted daughter Eliza was busy hiking her skirts up to her waist, all the while perched atop a sixteen-hand gelding.

"Lord have mercy upon us all!" wailed the incapacitated chaperone. "This must surely be the devil's doing."

Eliza thought she glimpsed a slight shaking of the much-too-obliging Colonel Hamilton's shoulders.

And yet . . . she had real work to do. She raised her skirts and opened her knees wide enough to swing her right leg across the saddle. There! Eliza had grown up riding the fields alongside her father and always felt most in charge on the back of a horse.

Sitting astride, Eliza leaned forward into the saddle's polished leather, which was disconcertingly warm. She certainly fit, but the problem was the dress. Between skirt, underskirt, petticoat, slip, and ankle-length, form-fitting pantaloons—which were new in style and considered a bit French and risqué—there was too much fabric for her to ride sidesaddle or otherwise. Her dress ballooned in front of her, spilling out around the horse's neck, spooking him in the early evening light, and making it impossible to grasp the reins as well. Behind her rose a mountain of petticoats and skirts, leaving no room for a second figure in the saddle.

"Well, then," said Eliza. "I'll need another moment, please, gentlemen." She slid down from the saddle, aware of the cold ground under her silly shoes and, taking her skirts in her hands, ripped them apart clear up to her knees. But she wasn't done. Grasping the paler petticoat and underskirt in her hands, she tore them until her legs were covered only by pantaloons and hose.

Apoplectic at the rending of the garments, the halfway-upside-down Mrs. Jantzen hollered out from the back of her horse. "Do speak up, Miss Schuyler. Is your honor in danger? Say the word and I shall set these ruffians to rights!"

"Never fear, madam, all is well," Alex called over his shoulder. "Miss Schuyler's dress has merely become a bit entangled, and she has freed it from its, ah, entanglements."

"Don't presume to speak to me as if I were a spinster ill versed in the ways of the world, young man. Next thing you know, she'll be wearing a sack cloth."

Eliza had heard the unforgiveable laughter in the young colonel's voice and her blood started to boil. "Mrs. Jantzen, let me assure you I am in full control of my well-being now, as well as in the foreseeable future."

Looking every bit the rag doll, Eliza pulled her waistcoat in close for warmth. As she stretched her spine to her full height, a twinkling of vanity flashed through her mind. In five miles she would arrive at the army's winter quarters as a victim of her mother's fashion sense. With her bonnet ribbons bouncing around her head, she stuck her left foot in the stirrup and hoisted herself back on Hector. Her legs dangled straight down alongside the leathers, heels down and toes up like the experienced rider she was.

"Sirs, you may now return me your gaze."

The two men turned her way slowly, neither wishing to be the first set of fresh eyes.

"Crikey!" gurgled the coachman. The stunned Irishman buried his face in his hands. "Oh, miss, please. Forgive me. I am, I am—quite amazed."

Alex couldn't resist a smile. Nor could he pretend that he wasn't above finding a certain amount of guilty pleasure at the sight of the general's daughter perched atop his wary steed in a much shorter dress than any girl has ever worn in public.

"Well, then, coachman! We must all be on our way before the frigid night air sets in. Miss Schuyler and I shall push on at a faster pace than you, due to Mrs. Jantzen's unfortunate condition. We will ride ahead and send back a flatbed wagon and blankets for a more comfortable and, shall we say, dignified arrival for such a . . . brave lady."

The coachman squinted at the brave lady's rump.

"Yes, sir," he said, yanking his cap down over his eyebrows. "It's sure to be slow going on this end."

"Yes, slow indeed." Alex turned to a shivering Eliza, who was staring resolutely in the opposite direction, pretending not to notice how little she was wearing. He spotted the extra fur blanket on the ground where Eliza had let it fall and handed it up to her.

"Now then, miss, if you will permit me to come aboard?"

Eliza gave him the slightest nod. "You may. If you must."

It took a single heartbeat for Alex to maneuver himself onto the horse, declaring the space behind the saddle his own. His legs slid beneath Eliza's ripped skirts, pressing against them. Reaching for the reins, his arms surrounded her but he felt her body stiffen as she shrugged him off.

"I am perfectly capable of directing Hector, Colonel Hamilton. If you will let me see to the reins, then you can offer the spurs in a proper way."

"Indeed, my lady," Alex said, handing over the reins. Then, with a firm kick to the horse's withers, he started Hector up with a force that jerked Eliza's head back against the young officer's chest. Again, he imagined he smelled the vaguest hint of whale oil. Whale oil? And could it be that for once he found it sweet smelling if only because she was wearing it?

THEY RODE ON for some minutes without speaking. *He doesn't know,* Eliza realized. *This conceited officer doesn't believe I know how to ride.* And yet, the partnership between Eliza and Hector had already begun as she held the reins like they were tiny birds, directing the bit gently inside Hector's mouth. She watched his ears fall forward into the way of a contented horse.

Meanwhile the young officer behind her was having some trouble maintaining his seat. Having neither stirrups nor reins to hold, he bounced on the horse's croup like a rowboat tossed by waves.

"Pardon me, Miss Schuyler," he said hesitantly, "but could you kindly keep Hector to a walk? Forgive me but I'm afraid I absolutely must . . ." Suddenly his hands came to rest on Eliza's waist.

Eliza started, but didn't speak. Instead, she slapped the reins against Hector's neck, sending him into a sudden trot. Alex's quick reflexes were all that kept him on Hector, that and his hands now gripping the saddle's edge for all they were worth.

"Easy, boy. That'll do." Eliza tightened the reins to bring the horse to an abrupt halt. She turned her chin toward Alex.

"Sir, you may place your hands around my waist, but only with my prior consent. Is that clear?"

"As clear as the night air, Miss Schuyler, and every bit as cold."

Eliza couldn't help but smile at that.

"Then may I assume I now have miss's permission to remain comfortably attached to the back of this saddle—even though it involves some slight contribution on her part?" he asked.

Eliza lifted her chin. It felt fine to be in control again.

"You may, sir, and I trust that to mean we will continue our journey with no further breach of decorum. Agreed?"

"You shall have no protest from me, miss."

They rode on in silence once more, with the colonel settled into position with his legs narrowly touching Eliza's and his hands surrounding her rib cage like a belt.

THE WINTER SUN was well below the tree line now. Hector stumbled on a root growth along the dark, rutted roadway. Alex instinctively tightened his grip on Eliza's waist and was surprised when she didn't seem to mind. The softness of her back revealed she wore no corset, no doubt because she was traveling, but until now her posture was as unyielding beneath his fingers as if she were all laced up. Her shallow breaths barely disturbed her rib cage, and he'd found himself inhaling deeply, breathing against the back of her neck as if to lend her the warm air from his own lungs.

Now he noticed how her shoulders had dropped some

of their previous tension. Something about her poise in the saddle reminded him of how she held herself on the dance floor.

"I must say, Miss Schuyler," he began, "I have nothing but fond memories of your family from the time of my last visit."

"A visit? Is that what you're calling it? It felt more like an ambush."

"Miss Schuyler, I want you to know that my official relationship with your father in no way mirrors my personal feelings toward him. Indeed, I have only the greatest level of respect for him. I do apologize for having been the bearer of bad news that evening and for my strong words about Ticonderoga. And I hope you will accept a belated apology for my repeated offenses against your father's good name the night we last met."

"Do go on, sir."

"I take you into my utmost confidence when I tell you that none other than General Washington himself believed your father to have been a patriot during the fall of Fort Ticonderoga. Indeed, he praised the way the troops defended themselves, greatly outnumbered as they were. It is to your father's everlasting credit that he refused to let the blame rest on any shoulders but his own."

"For all the praise you heap on my father, you had a fine way of showing it then. Prosecuting him in a court-martial for dereliction of duty!" she retorted.

"I assure you that if there had been any way to avoid the embarrassment of the trial I would have."

"If you feel that way, then why did you pursue the matter? Let me guess: You were only 'following orders.'"

"But I was," Alex replied. "Your father's."

"If you expect me to believe that my father insisted on his own trial, you take me for a fool."

"But it's true," Alex insisted. "I thought you knew. Your father did not want the slightest shadow of doubt hanging over his actions concerning the Ticonderoga battle. He refused to accept the resolution of censure offered by the Continental Congress and insisted on a full trial instead, where he was convinced he would be exonerated—as indeed he was."

"But, but why would Papa not tell his own family this?"

"I cannot say. Perhaps he thought to spare you the ugly details of politics, or did not want his own family to think ill of the government to which he has dedicated his life."

"So you did not want to prosecute him? You thought him blameless in the fall of Ticonderoga?" she asked.

"Not just blameless, but exceptionally farsighted. If your father had not instituted the measures he put in place, not only Ticonderoga would have fallen, but all of New England."

"You know we lost our house and farm at Saratoga," Eliza said with injured pride. "General Burgoyne burned it all to the ground."

"I am aware of that. Aware, too, that your father, out of a font of gentlemanly generosity, allowed that same General Burgoyne to shelter at your house after he was defeated."

A heavy sigh from Eliza gave Alex a little hope that she might be warming up finally.

"Yes, he surrendered his own marriage bed to th
for well over a month. And I must say Mama found that
a bit *too* generous." Eliza sniffed at the memory of it all. "She and Papa were forced to sleep in one of the guest rooms."

Alex murmured absentmindedly, "I am sure it was more comfortable than the hayloft."

"I beg your pardon?" Eliza's posture went suddenly rigid.

Alex didn't answer, and once again they rode in silence. When it seemed clear that she wasn't going to speak to him again, he attempted a new way in.

"So," he began, "may I assume it is your mindfulness of the rift between your father and me that forces you to hold back any semblance of a smile?"

Eliza puffed her way through a laugh, leaning as far forward as she could to distance herself from him.

But he pressed on. "You see, I have been waiting for more than two years to tell you it pleased me wholeheartedly to receive your note after the ball, and I was sorely disappointed when you failed in your promise," he said, in a rush of sudden emotion that took both of them by surprise.

"Pardon me? What note? What promise? If I'd written a note to every gentleman I met, my days would be wasted complimenting clumsy men on their knack for walking the line or turning a reel. Must I remind you there is a war going on? I have more pressing things to do with my time."

"Turning a reel—is that what they're calling it these days?" Alex clucked his tongue against his cheek. "Forgive me if I seem old-fashioned, but I'd imagined I was the only one to whom you had written!"

"My word, Colonel Hamilton, you are besotted with yourself. Do you truly think you are such a fine dancer as all that? Would you be surprised if I said that I have but the dimmest recollection of that evening? Frankly, sir, of your time in my parents' house, I remember your affront to my father better than anything that passed between us."

"Ah, miss. You cut me to the core."

"I find it hard to believe that a woman's free speech could so unnerve you. For a man of war, you are easily shocked."

"It is not your speech that shocks me. It is the actions to which it refers, and the apparently trifling regard with which you consider them."

"Your dance maneuvers?" Eliza laughed.

"You cannot seriously think we were to dance in the hayloft?"

"I beg your pardon, Colonel Hamilton! I must confess myself unimpressed by any other aspect of your character other than your grace on the dance floor."

Alex shook his head, flabbergasted. He yanked off a glove and reached into his inner pocket to pull out one of his most prized possessions. "Do you profess ignorance of this?"

Eliza turned and regarded the square of wrinkled cloth in Alex's hand. "A somewhat soiled pocket handkerchief?"

"I have not washed it for more than two years!" he said, affronted.

"That would explain the dirt."

"Miss Schuyler, are you asking me to believe you have no memory of my giving this very handkerchief to you?"

Alex could see only the profile of Eliza's face, but it seemed clear she was mystified.

Suddenly a fresh detail from that night popped into her mind. "Oh yes! 'I surrender,'" she parroted. "As I recall, Angelica and Peggy and I routed you in the parlor where you were trying to impress Miss Tambling-Goggin and Miss Van Leuwenwoort with your military prowess. I had completely forgotten about it until just now."

"So you are saying, then, that you have no memory of returning this handkerchief to me later that evening with a note?"

"Did I?" Eliza shrugged. "Well, that was awfully kind of me, wasn't it? Although, given its rather sorry state, I can see why I was so eager to be rid of it."

Alex was doubly confused. Could it be that Eliza Schuyler—the most sensible of the Schuyler sisters, the one who was said to care more about the revolutionary cause than dresses or even books—was so featherheaded that she had no memory of a romantic missive she had sent? It was inconceivable!

"You must forgive me, Miss Schuyler," Alex said, his breath escaping in puffs in the frigid air. "Although I knew you were no shrinking violet, I still thought your sensibility was less jaded than this."

"Oh, good heavens, Colonel Hamilton. It's just a handkerchief."

"Indeed it is not 'just a handkerchief.' It is the very foundation of the male-female connection."

"Once again, Colonel Hamilton, I must beseech you not to take our present physical proximity as an excuse for licentiousness. Do not assume that it is anything other than necessity alone that has caused me to compromise my physical boundaries in this manner."

"Oh?" Alex said drily. "And I suppose you did not send me a note with the handkerchief that said you would meet me in the hayloft?"

Hector stopped in his tracks to snort, blowing hard enough to make Eliza lift her chin and laugh.

"*Meet you in the hayloft?* I beg your pardon, Colonel, but even your loyal horse finds this a bit ridiculous!"

"Miss Schuyler, do not play the innocent with me. Though society may think you a girl consumed with nothing more than patriotic fervor, not even you could convince anyone that you are quite as brainless as you pretend."

"My dear colonel, I do not know what is causing these wild insinuations, but I assure you they are as unwelcome as they are preposterous. If anything in my actions misled you to believe otherwise, I am both mortified and unapologetic."

"Misled!" Alex couldn't help himself. "Far from it! It was you who never showed up, after promising to meet me for a midnight assignation!"

Eliza gasped. She turned around in the saddle, mere inches separating her from her accuser. "As God is my witness, sir, there was never a note from my hand to yours."

Alex could see the truth as plain as the soft moonlight on her face.

Eliza turned her back to him and slumped over the saddle.

In that moment, Alex felt two years of expectation slip away onto the cold road to Morristown. In the past two years he had started to write but then discarded a number of letters addressed to this very maiden. He had stayed his hand for fear of sending the wrong message. What to write, after all, to a lady who sent midnight missives? He worried about being too presumptuous a lover, and instead had waited patiently for the right time to make her acquaintance once more, and had been champing at the bit when he'd heard she was to join her relatives in Morristown.

But alas and alack, of course it hadn't been Eliza who had sent him the note! She was made of sturdier stuff than that. Someone else had sent his handkerchief back to him. Someone had been playing a trick on him—a trick that happened to be at her expense.

But who could have done it?

A memory came to him: of John Church swabbing Peterson's pink face with Alex's handkerchief, and Peterson snatching it up and pocketing it.

Eliza seemed to have come to the same conclusion that he had been pranked, and badly. "Peterson!" she said. "It must have been Peterson who sent the note. You see, Colonel, I'd lent your handkerchief to Angelica to wipe a stain off her dress, and when you were arguing, she handed it to Mr. Church, who—"

"Gave it to Peterson! And the man decided to return it to its owner." Alex shook his head. "Ill-minded mischief, and one I was a fool to fall for. I do apologize, Miss Schuyler."

"It was Peterson, for certain," said Eliza.

"I have half a mind to go straight back to Albany and confront the man," said Alex grimly.

Eliza spoke in a dull whisper. "I do not know which is more offensive to me—that you think me capable of such an action . . . or that you find this an attractive feature."

"Miss Schuyler, please," Alex stammered. "I am undone. I genuinely thought the note was from your hand . . . that is to say, I would never think you, of all girls, capable of such—"

"And yet you did," Eliza said. "And not only that, you used it as an excuse to extend your flirtation with me. I am appalled."

"I assure you the appallation is all mine." Alex banged a fist against his forehead, nearly knocking himself off the back of the horse. *Appallation?* On top of everything else, he suddenly seemed to have forgotten how the English language worked.

"If you please, Colonel, I would prefer if you did not speak for the rest of our journey." Eliza sat tall in the saddle, her back stiff as a board. "Were circumstances less unwelcoming, I would run for safety. But given that I am for all intents and purposes your prisoner, I am forced to remain in such repulsive proximity to you until we reach our destination. But for God's sake, please, cease speaking, or I really will throw you from this horse."

Alex opened his mouth, thought better of it, and closed it. There was nothing to say to make the situation any better. He could only make it worse. Alexander Hamilton, widely reputed to be the most eloquent man in the United States of America, had, for the first time in his life, been rendered speechless.

10

Lean in to Me

Near the Cochran Residence

Morristown, New Jersey

February 1780

The moon slipped under a blanket of clouds as the first snowflakes landed on Hector's shoulders. It had taken the big bay a mile or so to get used to the current arrangement on his back. While a warhorse is able to withstand the roar of cannon fire without flinching, tolerating the tickle and swish of petticoats behind any horse's head is something altogether different. This brave gelding could neither see them nor shake off their bothersome lacy itch. But he quickly came to trust that the lightweight human perched on his back had the sort of skilled hands he could put up with.

Eliza reached out and patted the bay's strong neck. "Walk on, Hector."

A mile or so back, the young colonel had pointed out final directions to the encampment before lapsing once more into an abashed silence. Thankfully it wouldn't be long before this nightmare was behind her.

The soft *clip-clop* of Hector's hooves beat quarter time to the racing march of her thoughts. It riled her to think about how Alex had accused her of the basest harlotry. The absolute cheek of the man—to think she of all people would have acted in such a way. To think he had believed her the type of girl who would send a boy notes outside of an approved courtship, with a tryst in a hayloft of all places!

And yet the memory of taking his handkerchief was clearer now . . . the saucy way she, Angelica, and Peggy had cut the legs out from under the young aide-de-camp—that is, secretary—who was busy putting on airs in front of a posse of second-rate society girls, who were only flirting with him because they had neither fortune nor beauty enough to attract a more prestigious suitor. It was easy to see how her words could be misconstrued as flirting—pretending to cut down a boy to test his mettle. She had even felt the same thrill she got when she flirted with other boys. So maybe she had been flirting with him. Still, that gave him no right to make such gross presumptions about her.

But he said there had been a note that he believed was from her hand. So they weren't really presumptions, were they?

He seemed quite disappointed that she had not met this assignation. *Until he realized his mistake.*

It was bewildering. Eliza knew that she should think less of Alex for this and assume him to be the sham of a gentleman that her mother claimed he was.

But Eliza had met true roués before—men who pretended to be respectable in public and then indulged in the most repulsive behaviors in private. Alex hadn't behaved like a man who was removing a mask or like he was trying to entice Eliza into something illicit or nefarious. No, his behavior seemed natural. Grateful even, as if she had given him a rare but not unusual gift—an exquisitely wrought charcoal sketch, say, or the first crocus of spring.

Still, Eliza couldn't let it go. The fury she felt was not near enough protection from the horrid cold, although the realization that for two years he'd kept the handkerchief she'd once stuffed into her bodice had a peculiarly warming effect of its own.

But this was still February in New Jersey. An uncontrollable shiver raced down her spine, shaking her from her reverie. The nice thing about anger was that it distracted you from the cold. But it didn't actually make you any warmer, and now Eliza's teeth began to chatter. She grabbed a hunk of Hector's thick black mane, hoping to find some warmth there, and didn't let go. Her body ached with fatigue from the cold and she wasn't sure how long she could hold her seat.

"You're shaking," he whispered. "Lean in to me and let me take the reins from here."

Eliza had no willfulness left in her. The cold had stripped it away. She closed her eyes and let go of the reins, melting into the warmth of his chest and shoulders as they closed in around her.

In a feverish dream-like state, she was suddenly at home again in the warmth of her family's parlor. The young colonel was there, twirling her in his arms as he turned a reel with a graceful step. His hand on the small of her back and his breath against her neck made her feel as if she were floating in time and space. She had once found a young lady's delight in his arms. Now the closeness of the man hemmed in behind her brought solid comfort.

The steady *clip-clop* of horse hooves and the mournful hoot of an owl lulled her toward a deeper calm. And somehow, she slept.

Later, in the arms of the man she had told never to speak to her again, Eliza opened her eyes and looked into his face.

"But how could it be that you were on the road today, just as we approached?"

"*Shhh,*" Alex whispered. "*Shhhh*. It won't be long before we'll have you sitting in front of a fire with a hot bowl of broth. For the moment, just lean back, close your eyes, and let Hector do his job."

"Yes, yes. That sounds fine. So lovely and warm."

Eliza looked up into the clouded night sky, no longer sure of her whereabouts. As she nodded off in Alex's arms, she mumbled one last thought, "But where on earth did you come from?"

THROUGH A FAR-OFF stand of pine trees, the first traces of campfire light appeared. Shadows played over the soldiers' tents in the slant of the moonlight. As they crossed a crusted field of stubble, the gelding picked up the scent of familiar horses in a nearby pasture and began to dance in place with excitement. Alex tightened the reins to keep the horse from sprinting back to his field mates. Lifting his head with nostrils flared, Hector roared his magnificent neigh, announcing his return to the encampment.

It was only a short ride away from the center of the town, where the Cochrans' white two-story house stood, not too far from army headquarters.

"Ease up there, fella. This is the place."

Alex nudged Eliza's cheek. "Miss Schuyler? Are you yet awake? We have reached our destination."

Sensing that she was strong enough to sit up in the saddle, he leapt off Hector's rear and came around to his left side. "Here we are, once again, m'lady. May I offer some assistance?"

He laced together his fingers to aid in Eliza's dismount, aware of how dainty her foot felt in the cradle of his hands.

But when she slid from the saddle she nearly collapsed in the snow, possibly because her feet were frozen numb. Indeed, she did fall, but Alex caught her in his arms. Caught her and, when it was clear that she couldn't walk, carried her up the walk to her aunt and uncle Cochran's house.

A butler opened the door with Mrs. Cochran close on his heels, elbowing him out of the way to get to her niece. She guided Alex to a sofa inside the parlor where he laid Eliza down with care.

"Oh dear! Eliza! Is she quite all right?" she fussed worriedly. "Mrs. Jantzen returned to us hours ago!"

Piling her niece high with blankets, Mrs. Cochran directed the servants to fetch hot broth and bank the fire higher in the grate, while she herself undertook the task of rubbing Eliza's poor feet.

In the confusion, Alex quietly slipped out, even as he wished he could stay.

11

Absent Without Leave?

The Cochran Residence

Morristown, New Jersey

February 1780

"Was that Colonel Hamilton who carried you into the house like a bride?" Aunt Gertrude was more teasing than proud. Since both her husband and the colonel worked closely with General Washington, of course she knew him well, and it was clear she was really asking about how such a strange circumstance came to be. Eliza, however, colored deeply at the mention of the word *bride*, and Aunt Gertrude, being as attuned to afflictions of the psyche as she was to the body, let the subject drop. "You must be exhausted!"

Eliza thought she would never be warm again and had only a dim recollection of how it was that she was finally inside, and in the comfort of her aunt's home, not freezing on the road to Morristown still.

When Eliza's feet were finally as pink as a newborn's,

Aunt Gertrude rang the bell for a maid to take Eliza up to her room with a brazier to warm the sheets. The maid plucked several coals from the fire and laid them in the brazier, which sizzled all the way up the stairs. She ran the brazier under the bedclothes for a full five minutes until the sheets were fairly smoking, then helped Eliza off with her dress and into one of Aunt Gertrude's nightgowns because Eliza's trunks were still lashed to the top of the broken carriage seven miles away.

The blanket was flannel and smelled lightly of Aunt Gertrude's scent, a pleasant mixture of rose oil and witch hazel, and the warmed sheets were almost *too* hot, yet from the moment Eliza slipped into bed she was shivering. She wrapped her arms around herself and, almost against her will, recalled the heat from Alex's body.

She told herself her chill was the result of three hours outside in silly shoes and without a coat, but she knew this wasn't the whole truth. What plagued her was more unsettling—the memory of the light touch of his hands on her as they rode and how naturally his fingers had curled around her waist.

And how soft his voice was in her ear, all tenderness and concern, when the man was a rogue and a rake as far as she was concerned.

WHEN ELIZA WOKE in the morning, the bedclothes were damp with perspiration. Her joints ached and her face was flushed with fever. Uncle John checked in on her before heading out and pronounced her symptoms "probably not life-threatening," but nevertheless prescribed bed rest until the fever broke. The idea of spending the day in a strange (and rather small) bedroom with neither books nor fire nor company made the prospect of a cold that much more disheartening, and Eliza was able to commute the sentence to the parlor sofa, where, though she did feel somewhat weak and light-headed, she was nevertheless able to visit with her aunt.

The parlor was a grand room with four tall windows set against rose-flocked wallpaper. In keeping with the latest French style, the plaster on its high ceilings had been worked in a rococo pattern. Servants kept the fire high and water in the coffeepot piping hot, and there were cellar pears and cheese to snack on, and strained broth to sip. It was, all things considered, the least unpleasant way to be sick that Eliza could imagine.

"This is a beautiful room, Aunt Gertrude, and the bedroom I slept in was also lovely. I am sorry I'm not well enough for a complete tour—you and Uncle John have an exquisite home."

"Oh, pshaw," Aunt Gertrude said. Where another woman would have busied herself with embroidering a pillow sham or handkerchief, Aunt Gertrude was sewing buttons onto military uniforms. Eliza wanted to assist her, but had been forbidden to strain herself.

"Your uncle and I found this house as it is, furniture and all. I shall say that, for loyalists, the Kitcheners—the former owners—did have rather good taste. Those are they," she added, indicating a pair of portraits that hung in the bays to either side of the fireplace.

Eliza studied the pictures. Mrs. Kitchener looked to be in her early forties. She was dressed in high fashion with an ornate gown and elaborate wig, yet her soft chin and round, pink cheeks suggested an equal fondness for the conviviality of jokes and sweets.

Mr. Kitchener was perhaps two decades older than his wife, a somewhat distant-looking man. Eliza thought he seemed a little lost inside his elaborate suit, as if, without it, he would be like any other sixty-year-old man, weathering his twilight years with less poise than patience.

Not knowing the subjects, she couldn't judge the likenesses. However, the paints themselves testified to professional rather than amateur ability, which made her think they must have presented a fairly accurate representation. "They seem a most respectable pair," Eliza said. "It must have grieved them dear to have to sell a home to which they obviously devoted much labor and love."

"Sell?" Aunt Gertrude scoffed. "I hope you do not think your uncle and I would give our money to a pair of loyalists."

Eliza was confused. "I don't understand. How came you to have their house, then?"

"In the same way that General Burgoyne once helped himself to your father's house at Saratoga: It was claimed as a military prize."

"Ah, so!" Eliza said. "Of course."

"I've been meaning to take down their pictures and just haven't gotten around to it. And I don't have anything to hang in their stead, so . . ."

Eliza nodded. Yet she couldn't help looking up at the couple and feeling sorry for the Kitcheners. She had been devastated when she learned that the Saratoga house had been seized, and even more heartbroken when she learned it had been burned. Though her father rebuilt it quickly, the house that held so many childhood memories no longer existed for her. Those happy times could never be re-created with a cover of wood and stone.

"Had they children?" she asked quietly.

"I would assume so." Having had none herself, Aunt Gertrude was unsentimental when it came to the subject of children. "There was a crib in the bedroom upstairs where you're sleeping, and another was bedecked with a young girl's furnishings. I think perhaps they lost a son in battle, as well, for a sword tied with a black ribbon hung in another room."

"And they left it behind!"

"Indeed they did! When General Washington's forces took northern New Jersey, the Kitcheners, like all the other loyalists, left in such haste that they took naught with them, save their clothes and jewels, and not all of those." Aunt Gertrude tapped a cameo on her dress. "I found this precious bauble upstairs, fallen behind a bureau."

The butler, Ulysses, entered. Once his presence had been acknowledged, he said, "A Colonel Hamilton is here to inquire after Miss Schuyler's well-being."

A bright smile flashed on Aunt Gertrude's face, but it disappeared as soon as she saw Eliza's. The blush had come back, and she was shaking her head rapidly. She wasn't ready to see him, not at all, not when her mind was still a confused jumble of emotion, from irritation to embarrassment to something too much like excitement at the prospect of seeing him again.

It was clear that Aunt Gertrude wanted to ask the reason for Eliza's objection, but declined to do so in front of Ulysses.

"Tell Colonel Hamilton that Miss Schuyler is well. Well, but tired, and resting after yesterday's ordeal. Please convey Dr. Cochran's and my immense gratitude for his assistance and inform him that we look forward to thanking him properly for his chivalry when Miss Schuyler is fully recovered."

Ulysses nodded, closing the door behind him to keep the heat in the room. Eliza listened intently to the voices in the hall, but the walls were too thick to admit more than a faint murmur. The conversation did go on for longer than she expected, though; she thought she heard the colonel insisting that he wanted to check on her with his own eyes before finally being persuaded to leave. At length there was the sound of the front door's opening and closing.

Eliza turned to the window, half expecting the colonel to appear, but nothing came in save the light of a late winter's morning. She was strangely disappointed even if she was the one who had sent him away.

When she turned from the window, she saw her aunt regarding her quizzically.

"So tell me, dear. Did Colonel Hamilton happen to say how came he to be on the post road yesterday?" she asked lightly—too lightly, Eliza thought—as though she were not seeking information, but was already in possession of all the facts. Apparently, even the saintly Aunt Gertrude wasn't above enjoying a little innocent gossip.

"He said that he was making the rounds of the outposts along the Hudson River."

"Really? I would have thought it was the outpost's job to report to him, and not the other way around."

Eliza hadn't considered this, though now that it was said out loud, it did make sense to her.

"Perhaps he felt that their diligence needed the extra prod of supervision. Papa has remarked on more than one occasion that nothing maintains both discipline and morale like the occasional unexpected visit from authority."

"Perhaps," her aunt said. She snapped the thread on the button she had just sewn on, set the jacket aside, and retrieved another from the pile beside her.

"You sound unconvinced."

"It is just that your uncle John remarked on Colonel Hamilton's absence yesterday. Or, more accurately, he said that General Washington had noticed the colonel's absence. So if this were a surprise visit, it would seem that his superiors were as surprised by the errand as his subordinates."

Eliza felt a flush coming on. "I am not sure I understand, Aunt."

"Your father wrote to General Washington to tell him of your trip, did he not?"

"Of course, but Papa would never let me take the trip without our family coachman, Mr. Vincent. For my sake, the dear old soldier pretended that he was carrying military information, but given my father's two-year absence from a command post, this seemed merely a ruse to keep me from being alarmed."

Aunt Gertrude nodded. "I wouldn't want to speak out of turn, but I always felt you were your father's favorite—even more than John or Philip Junior or the other boys. Of all his children, you are most like him in spirit. So, it makes sense that he would go to the extent of informing the commander in chief of the Continental army that his daughter was coming to visit his aunt. Although, let me see, *hmmmm* . . . a letter to General Washington would not be first read by him. It is initially vetted by— "

Eliza interjected before she could help herself. "Are you telling me Colonel Hamilton knew I was coming?"

Aunt Gertrude gave Eliza an impish shrug.

"Dr. Cochran remarked last week that he asked after your trip. At first I thought nothing of it—your uncle and the colonel are in regular communication, and I thought it was simply a pleasantry between colleagues. But when I saw you in his arms yesterday, well, you can forgive an old woman for wondering whether romance was in the air."

Now Eliza was blushing wildly, and her heart was

beating too fast to be healthy. "While I admire the romantic spirit that leads you to such a conjecture, Aunt, I have to doubt its veracity. If Colonel Hamilton had, in fact, read my father's letter to General Washington, he would have known I was due to arrive not yesterday but the day before. So it seems likely that he was on the road yesterday on official business."

It seemed to Eliza that her aunt's expression was almost pitying, as if her niece were too guileless to be believed. "Perhaps. But Dr. Cochran did say that Colonel Hamilton was missing for several hours the day before yesterday, much to the consternation of General Washington."

Absent without leave because of me? That note that Peterson wrote must have been a doozy, that had to be all it was. Eliza could not meet her aunt's gaze. She reached for her cup, but it was drained dry. She was about to ring the bell for more when her aunt's hand settled over hers.

"Eliza, I must ask. Have you and Colonel Hamilton met before?"

Eliza wasn't sure how to answer that question. An affirmation seemed so inadequate to the spirit of the inquiry. But to say anything more risked a conversation that she knew not how to broach, let alone conduct.

"He was a guest at an assembly my mother threw more than two years ago. Our encounter was . . . trifling," she said, even as her mind flitted to the knowledge that he had kept a handkerchief with her scent on his person for over two years.

Aunt Gertrude laughed. "Your uncle and I met one week

before our wedding. Your grandparents were, I think, more despondent about the possibility of marrying me off than I was myself; they'd promised Dr. Cochran a handsome dowry if he would have me. It was not a romantic match, is what I am trying to say."

Aunt Gertrude took a moment to rearrange the cameo on her blouse. "Ah. But it was an apt union, my dear, and one that has only deepened in respect and regard as the years have passed. Nevertheless, I know love—not least from the example of my brother and your mother, whose passion—"

Eliza sputtered. "Passion! My mother? Are we discussing the same Mrs. Schuyler?"

"Be gentle, dear. Please do not think that the forty-seven-year-old matron busily raising eight children is the full representation of your mother's life. She was young once and lovely, too—just like you."

Eliza pursed her lips together and shook her head in doubt.

"But that is not my point," said Aunt Gertrude, speaking before Eliza could throw her off her game. "My point is, I know a swain when I see one. Colonel Hamilton is clearly smitten with you. And though he is handsome and intelligent—indeed, brilliant—perhaps even bound up in the very future of our young nation . . ." Here Aunt Gertrude's shoulders slumped. "But I sense you find his suit unwelcome somehow?"

Eliza's esteem for a woman who had forged such a singular role for herself—despite the expectations and constrictions of her gender was such that she could not lie to her. Nor could she bring herself to speak the truth, not least because she was not sure what the truth was. With facts, she was comfortable. Give Eliza Schuyler yards of fabric or pounds of mutton, and she could tell you exactly the yield of breeches or stew. But emotions were not the stuff of stitchery or recipes. She believed it was impossible to know what they would make until all the elements were right before her eyes.

"Unwelcome and quite impossible," said Eliza stiffly. "And I doubt the veracity of his interest. I am sorry, Aunt. Colonel Hamilton is quite the catch, but he is not the fish for me."

Her aunt regarded her in silence for a moment before turning back to her sewing. For a long moment there was nothing in the room besides the crackling of the fire and the rasp of thick thread pulled through coarse, sturdy cloth.

Then, almost under her breath, her aunt said, "Do not sell yourself short, Niece. You are the quarry and Colonel Hamilton the hunter, and I daresay if he cannot catch you, then he doesn't deserve to claim you as his prize."

12

Bold Moves

Ford Mansion: Continental Army Headquarters

Morristown, New Jersey

February 1780

Alex stared uncomprehendingly at the sheet of paper before him. Though he recognized his own hand, he had to remind himself to whom he'd just written. As the only member of General Washington's staff who was fluent in French, Alex frequently wrote as many as twenty letters a day to French military commanders and the noblemen who paid for them.

The boulder Alex had to get around was General Washington's famously terse directions. *His Excellency*, as Alex referred to the commander in chief with equal parts admiration and filial mockery, might say, "*Tell La Bochambreaux to move his troops to Charlotte*" or "*Ask the Duke of Normandy for another 5,000 francs for the Georgia campaign.*" Then leave it up to Alex to transform a half-dozen words into full pages of *discours diplomatique*, complete with flattery, appeals to one's better nature, compliments to one's children, wives, and mistresses, and cleverly veiled threats. No small task.

Though Benjamin Franklin was the official ambassador to France, credited with bringing the French into the war on the American side, it was Alex's attentive and delicate correspondence that kept them in it. Despite the snail's pace of the conflict and the absence of any immediate benefit to the French, the humiliation of the British was a goal the French needed little encouragement to embrace.

Alex looked down at the letter again to remind himself who would receive it. *Ah!* John Laurens—a lieutenant colonel in the Continental army currently serving in his home state of South Carolina. He was also Alex's best friend.

"My dear Laurens," he read, looking up guiltily to see if anyone could read over his shoulder.

The missive had begun formally enough with the latest military news, but halfway through his letter he veered off into personal matters. He had told Laurens about the handkerchief incident the years prior. Alex wanted to pursue the matter immediately, but John persuaded him to wait until General Schuyler's trial was over, as Eliza would undoubtedly refuse any advances made by the man who was persecuting her father.

Alex noted the wisdom of his friend's argument, although it took all of his self-control not to inundate Eliza with one love letter after another. But when he giddily told John that Eliza was coming to Morristown for the winter, John knew his dearest friend was smitten.

"The way I see it, Hamilton, is that it's time to make a bold move."

It was John who came up with the idea that Alex haunt the post road to intercept Eliza's carriage, although not even he could have foreseen the broken wheel. It should have been a complete triumph. Instead Alex had ruined everything by revealing himself to be a rake and mortifying poor Eliza.

For over two years he'd pined for the spunky girl who'd put him in his place so deftly at her mother's ball. Every moment from that evening stung as if it had happened last night—and he could not stop thinking about those laughing eyes, the biting wit. And as for the hours they spent on the ride to Morristown together, he could still feel her small waist in his hands, and her soft hair against his cheek, as well as recall the easy way she had bantered and parried with him. A chaste and sensible girl, with a good shape and a generous nature—qualities he had enumerated to Laurens years ago that he desired in a mate—and here now, he saw in Eliza. He found he liked her even more, knowing that she had never sent that note.

But was he a fool to think she might ever return his ardor?

After all, she had made her repulsion clear during their ride together, and had made it more clear when he visited the Cochrans' residence and she didn't want to see him. But Alex knew enough about the game of love to know that there was no surer way to make a fellow interested than to show no interest in him.

Was Eliza Schuyler rebuffing him to egg him on, or because she actually had no interest in him?

If he could see her again he could attempt to sound her out, if only she would allow him to call. Or perhaps he was chasing after an illusory El Dorado and should set his sights on a more realistic goal.

But that was the thing about Alex, a nameless orphan from the Caribbean, who had written his way up to General Washington's side, he was nothing if not determined.

IT WAS SNOWING lightly when Alex turned up in front of the two-story white house on Chapel Street, a quarter mile down the road from His Excellency's headquarters. The only light in the Cochran residence radiated from the good doctor's study. Alex pulled up Hector outside the house to stare at the darkened second-floor bedroom. This was his self-imposed mission tonight—to keep guard duty in the shadows of the Cochran house, to watch for redcoats, of course, but in truth, to hopefully get a glimpse of Eliza's figure if she happened to pass by the window, God willing.

He sat in his cavalry saddle, hidden from the road by a tree, keeping watch. He rubbed his gloved hands together for warmth, then leaned forward to give his loyal pal's neck a good long scratching.

Hector was happy to be out for an easygoing moonlit stroll with his human and was feeling a bit spunky himself.

The snow stopped, and the blanket of clouds pulled away from the moon. From far off in a field behind the house came a whinny Hector recognized as decidedly feminine. The horse stamped his feet and tossed his head, half cantering in place with a lusty kick from his hindquarters. Alex's hands were strong enough to steady him but he knew old Hector had a mind of his own.

"Easy, boy. Quiet down. Suppose somebody saw me out here. They'd think I was a ruffian—or worse, a lovesick lunatic."

Every bit the good warhorse, Hector needed all of his willpower to hold himself together for his master. He gnashed his bit and stomped the snow under his hooves. Still, nature has a way of its own.

When a second sensuous whinny came floating through the air, Hector's eyes flew open and he let out a bellowing neigh that would've woken the dead. Or certainly everyone in the Cochran household.

Light flooded the downstairs parlor as Dr. Cochran stepped out onto the front porch with a lantern. "Who's there? Speak up, man! What business have you here?"

Alex froze. He'd been spotted. He eased his horse forward into the closest reach of the lamplight. Alex noticed a shadowy female form pass by the second-story window frame.

"Why, it's Colonel Hamilton, is it not? What brings you out on such a bitter night?"

"Evening, Dr. Cochran. Not to worry you, sir, but there's word of a ne'er-do-well highwayman out along the post road tonight; I thought it worth a trip to make sure you and the missus are safely protected. Is all well indeed in the Cochran household?"

Dr. Cochran looked around the empty yard. Quiet as ever. "We are safe, sir, and your concern is much obliged."

Alex struggled to give off a serious air about tracking down this supposed ne'er-do-well, but his eyes had zeroed in on the second-floor bedroom where a candle flickered behind the lace curtain. The shadowy figure paused near the window and captured his complete attention.

"Well, it's getting on a bit past my bedtime, young man. Will there be anything else you're in need of tonight, Colonel?" the good doctor asked heartily, and Alex had a feeling Dr. Cochran could easily diagnose a case of lovesickness in a young soldier. "Ahem. Colonel?"

"What's that? Oh yes. I mean, oh no—no, sir. That is, if you're sure my services are not needed here, Doctor, I suppose I'll be on my way." Alex tipped his cap to the doctor and dug his spurs into Hector's flanks.

"Good night, sir!"

"Good night to you, Colonel, and I'll be sure and tell Elizabeth you stopped by to see her."

The candle in the second-floor window went suddenly dark.

13

There Is No Inoculation Against Love

Continental Army Headquarters

Morristown, New Jersey

February 1780

"Well, Eliza, my dear," Dr. Cochran noted the next morning, "you seem *remarkably* rejuvenated."

Her symptoms did not indicate the onset of a cold, and after a second day in bed, Eliza was pronounced fit to resume her daily activities.

An elated Eliza asked if she could assist her aunt in administering smallpox inoculations to the soldiers in camp.

"That would be a fine thing, indeed," agreed the doctor. Aunt Gertrude would appreciate her lovely niece's enthusiasm. She had four hundred soldiers waiting to be inoculated and she could certainly use a second pair of hands.

"You know, dear, most of the troops are quite suspicious of this newfangled hoop-de-doodle and since you've already been inoculated and lived to tell the tale, you're living proof that the treatment works!"

It was true. Eliza had been inoculated three years ago when General Washington ordered that all American troops should receive the treatment. Eliza recalled that when General Schuyler found out his troops were nervous about the procedure, he had taken it first, stepping up to demonstrate its safety. When doubts still prevailed among the men, he made a great show of instructing Dr. Cochran to administer it to the entire Schuyler clan.

Eliza had never seen such a battle of wills between her parents. Tough-minded Catherine Schuyler had squabbled with her husband over using their children as guinea pigs because of doubts of her own. After all, they had lost so many friends and family to the scourge of pox. But when the general convinced her that the treatment made it all but impossible that their beloved children would fall ill, not only had Catherine Schuyler consented, she volunteered to sit for the procedure, surrounded by all of her children. Eliza and her siblings were nervous, but they were more frightened of crossing their mother than contracting a disease. There was no choice but to grin and bear it for the sake of the troops.

Eliza was surprised to find the treatment was simple enough: The family received a scratch on the wrist and then the administration of the poultice. A rash and a light fever followed. Within a week the rash had flaked away and General Schuyler declared them all immune. Although it seemed to Eliza a remarkable scheme, she took her father's words on faith.

Eliza actually found it to be a fascinating business, shrouded in a magical aura. The treatment materials were stored in a heavy wooden box fastened with an iron lock. Aunt Gertrude kept the key in a tiny velvet drawstring purse pinned at her side. The wooden box held a dozen tightly sealed glass bottles, each one filled with an innocuous off-white powder, coarser than flour but less granular than cornmeal. There were odd tools: a mortar and pestle fashioned from locust wood that had been cured into a rich brown finish; a spatula that looked a little like a fish knife; and the most fascinating of all, a good-sized silver fork, whose tines were bent at ninety degrees to the handle, so that it looked like a miniature rake.

Eliza took note of every step of the process. She watched Aunt Gertrude remove one bottle at a time, then immediately lock the box. She mixed a dram of powder with an equal amount of water and whirled it into a paste in the mortar, which was then scraped onto a bandage with the spatula.

Next came the application. Aunt Gertrude looked up at Eliza. "Now, here's where you will come in most handy, so pay close attention. We begin first thing tomorrow, dear, so be sure to wear your layers. The enlisted men's medical tent can get awfully drafty!"

"WHO'S NEXT?"

Aunt Gertrude nodded toward the long line snaking out of the tent. The men stood by with their shoulders slumped, smoking and telling jokes to ward off the creeping doubt they had about the mysterious goings-on.

"Bring along the next fellow, Eliza."

Eliza treated all of the soldiers with the exact same can-do spirit. It amused her to see each soldier's face switch from suspicion to surprise upon being greeted by a warm smile in the cold setting. As her aunt had predicted, Eliza's presence made the procedure go much more smoothly.

"Take a seat, if you will, sir. Remove your jacket," Eliza said over and over, "and roll up your sleeve."

"Happy to, miss." "Whatever you say, miss." "Anything else, miss?" Each one of them seemed eager to oblige. Then it was time for Aunt Gertrude to go to work.

Once the soldier had his sleeve up, Aunt Gertrude took firm hold of his arm with one hand and drew the rake across his wrist with the other. She dragged it heavily, scoring sharp red welts in the skin, sometimes drawing blood before finally announcing, "This one's ready for you now, Eliza. You may apply the poultice."

At first, this was the only task Aunt Gertrude allowed her niece to handle. Somehow Eliza managed it with a gentleness that moved each one of the soldiers in her care. She folded the poultice over the wound and wrapped it in place, finishing it off with a soft squeeze before the soldier was sent on his way. Every man left the tent with a smile on his face instead of the worried look he'd stepped in with, believing that gentle squeeze was only for him.

But Eliza was a quick study and by the second day was every bit as capable of handling the entire procedure as Aunt Gertrude. Working in studied tandem, they performed the repetitive task twice as fast.

Each administration took no more than five minutes, but there were upward of four hundred men to treat. It took four full days, and a good part of the fifth, to get through them all.

Early in the afternoon of the fifth day, just as they were finishing up, a ginger-haired soldier poked his head inside the tent.

"Is it too late for one last soldier?"

Busy as they were, the women didn't bother to look up. "Come in, come in," Eliza said, sighing. *Four hundred and one*, she thought, but she would treat this soldier exactly like the hundreds of others she'd assisted over the last five days. "Take a seat if you will, sir. Remove your jacket and roll up your . . ." Eliza caught her breath as she turned.

"Happy to oblige, miss." Colonel Hamilton shucked off his jacket and was making quite a show of busily rolling up his sleeve, showing off a well-muscled forearm. "And I must apologize for the lateness of my arrival."

Aunt Gertrude didn't hide her amusement. "Colonel, it is never too late to be at your service. We are all quite aware of your extraordinary *vigilance* as to our family's protection. As such, we are certainly bound to do all we possibly can for your well-being in return. Isn't that right, Eliza dear?"

Eliza's hand flew to her bonnet to tuck in a few stray tendrils of hair. "Yes, Auntie, of course. Quite right."

She could barely maintain her composure. Without his military jacket on, Colonel Hamilton was so much more real to her than in her daydreams. She had forgotten how square and strong his shoulders were. And wasn't that a fresh shaving cut on the swale of his jaw? Surely, the timing of this mission must've been carefully planned.

She avoided his gaze and it appeared he was doing the same, looking resolutely at the wall in front of him as Aunt Gertrude prepared the treatment. And the wily matron seemed to be taking her sweet time. When she'd mixed the paste and readied the spatula, she handed the application to Eliza and smiled. "Here we are, Eliza, will you do the honors?"

"I would be glad to, Auntie."

"B-but . . . ," Alex stammered, "I had assumed the good doctor's wife would be doing this." He showed his teeth in a nervous smile. "Are we quite sure Miss Schuyler, ah, well, that she knows what she's doing?"

"Quite certain indeed, sir," said Aunt Gertrude. "And I'm confident the two hundred troops who have already sat in this same chair for her would attest to it as well."

"Well, if it's good enough for my men, then I suppose it's good enough for me, too." Alex swallowed hard, his Adam's apple playing along with his doubt.

"Ah, Colonel. Shall we say, *ahem*, this is not my first time in the . . . *saddle*. Now, if you'll just give me your forearm and relax, it will all be done in no time at all."

Unconvinced but steeling himself like the dutiful soldier he was, Alex extended his arm with a face full of misgiving.

"Are you ready for me, sir?"

"I am that," said Alex, with a raise of his eyebrow.

Eliza blushed, and when she hesitated, he took the opportunity to address her again. "Will it hurt?"

"Only if you let it," she said sternly.

"You wound me, mademoiselle," he said.

"Colonel, really. It is a mere scratch in comparison to the dangers of the battlefield."

"Ah, but I am exposed mostly to the dangers of the inkwell, if you remember." He was teasing, and the twinkle in his eye was hard to ignore.

"I do," she said, now blushing even more furiously. "It was unkind of me and my sisters. Especially as I have heard you have survived several battles since then."

"I was lucky," said the colonel, his face suddenly grave. "The others, not so much."

She looked up at him then, met his eyes, and tried to stop her hands from shaking. It was truly frustrating how his presence affected her. She was right to keep him from visiting her. Her uncle kept teasing her that there was no safer place than their home with Colonel Hamilton guarding the post road.

"Please," he said, and she looked down once more at his tensely corded arm.

She felt his gaze upon her, but quickly set her face straight to get to the work at hand. She took firm hold of his arm and drew the rake across his wrist, scoring sharp red welts in the skin, drawing blood. Then she folded the poultice over the little wound and wrapped it expertly in place, finishing it off with a soft squeeze. Only this time, she held the squeeze a fraction longer than she had for the hundreds of other soldiers who'd come before him.

Alex must have felt it, too, because the doubt dropped from his face and a tenderness crept into his eyes. He put his free hand over hers and left it there.

"I am glad to see you well, Miss Schuyler. I was worried about you," he said.

Eliza gave a brisk nod. "Thank you for your concern, I am fully recovered."

"I see, and yet you have not graced us with your presence at the town's social delights."

"Are you keeping track of my whereabouts, Colonel?"

It was Alex's turn to blush. "I admit I was disappointed not to see you at Marquis de Chastellux's ball the other day. Or the dinner hosted by Baron von Steuben."

"I have been here, Colonel," she said simply.

"Every day? At headquarters?" asked the handsome soldier.

"Every day."

"If only I'd known," he murmured to himself. "You are more interested in service than sleigh rides, then?"

"I go where I am needed."

"A pity, for Hector pulls a great sleigh," he said with a sigh.

At the mention of the horse, Eliza's interest piqued. "How is Hector? Is he all right?"

"Right as rain, miss," said Alex. "Although I have to admit I never expected to feel this way."

"What way?" Eliza asked, intrigued.

"Jealous of my horse."

Aunt Gertrude cleared her throat, and the two of them jumped aside, as if caught in something naughty. She looked at Alex and Eliza in amusement. "Are we all done, then? Yes? I suppose that does it, Colonel. *Ahem.* You may put your jacket back on now, sir."

"Indeed, indeed, Mrs. Cochran." Alex reached for his jacket and was halfway out of the tent before he could button it back up. "I'll say thank you for your time, ladies, and be on my way. Good afternoon, Mrs. Cochran." He shot Eliza a parting look. "Miss Schuyler."

He pushed aside the tent flap and made to leave.

"Wait!" said Eliza.

He turned back, his eagerness all too apparent in his eyes. "Yes?"

"I like . . . I mean . . . I like sleigh rides, too," she said finally. "I mean, it would be nice to see Hector again."

Alex almost laughed. "Of course. Hector would like it very much. Perhaps in a day or two?"

She nodded.

He gave her a small bow and was gone.

Eliza began quickly gathering up the last of the bottles

of white powder, the mortar and pestle, the spatula, and the rake. Her hands felt clumsy as she arranged them in the wooden box they arrived in and stepped back. Thankfully Aunt Gertrude did not notice as she pulled out her key and locked the box.

"Well done, Eliza. You make a fine second pair of hands indeed." Aunt Gertrude dropped the key into her velvet purse and drew in the strings with a flourish. "Now, what say you, my dear? Shall the new medical team of Mrs. Gertrude Cochran and Miss Eliza Schuyler retire to the parlor for a well-deserved cup of hot chocolate?"

14

A Disease, an Affliction

The Cochran Living Room

Morristown, New Jersey

February 1780

Mrs. Cochran's cook was famous for her scones. She filled them with dried cranberries and glazed them with orange syrup, making them sweet, tart, and delicious despite the strict rationing of flour and sugar.

Fatigued but satisfied from the long day's work, Eliza sat back in her aunt's fine parlor chair. Seeing Colonel Hamilton again had produced the oddest thrill, and one she couldn't help but ruminate on. But she was determined to push all thoughts of him from her mind, even as she could still picture his strained forearm and the muscle underneath, as well as his bright blue eyes staring into hers. So she stretched her legs, resting her heels on the little footstool in front of the fire, and addressed her aunt.

"I must confess, it is a little hard to believe that the activity we engaged in for the past four and a half days was a medical procedure. It is so simple that it seems more like a child's game, or a spell."

In truth, Eliza did not feel this way at all. When her father had informed the family that they were to be inoculated, she read all about the procedure and knew as much about it as anyone outside of the scientific community. But Aunt Gertrude, for all her singular feminine independence, had a view of the female intellect that was in some ways dimmer than the most chauvinist male's, and loved nothing more than dispelling what she saw as typical girlish naïveté.

"Medicine is a bit like love," she began. Eliza recognized the opening of another of her favorite aunt's lengthy if genial lectures. "There are the theatrical outer forms gone through by the players—the bandages and injections and extractions, the flowers and love notes and dances—but the real work is always happening out of sight. In here," she added, tapping herself on the heart.

Eliza couldn't help but laugh. She had not been expecting quite this response.

"I am not sure if you make medicine sound more exciting than it is, or love more dull," Eliza said, smiling. "But I should think that the biological processes by which immunity is stimulated and the more ephemeral alchemy of love are much related."

"Have you ever seen a germ?" Aunt Gertrude asked without waiting for Eliza's reply. "Neither have I, yet I have no doubt they exist, because I have seen their effects on the body. Likewise I have never 'seen' love, yet I have witnessed again and again its transformative effect on human beings."

"But a germ is a real thing," Eliza, who had, in fact, seen drawings of them, protested. "A physical thing, I mean. Whereas, love—love is a feeling. It can no more be caught than it can be inoculated against, because it cannot be contained in powder or paste."

"I myself have seen many a young woman catch love from being exposed to the amours of her social circle. And, as well, I have seen many a young man harden himself to love by overexposure to its coarser varieties."

"I do not follow your meaning, Aunt Gertrude."

"It is like the poultice we have been administering to our brave soldiers. By only scratching the surface of the skin rather than drawing blood, a less potent infection arises. There are many young men who dally with love or even engage in activities that would be improper for me to describe, and by so doing, harden their hearts to the gentleness that love requires."

Now Eliza understood what her aunt was referring to. As the daughter of a general, Eliza had absorbed more of the cruder details of a soldier's life than even her father would have suspected. She had seen the soldiers staggering in and out of the unpainted house on Whitelawn Street in Morristown, whose occupants numbered five single women. Aunt Gertrude explained that the women were war widows, but Eliza noted nothing mournful in their countenances.

"At any rate," Aunt Gertrude continued, "I hate to retreat behind the privilege of age, but permit me to say that one day after you have been married for a few years you will understand what I mean. Suffice to say, love is not a business to be attended to haphazardly, no more than medicine. You must research the matter as you would a disease and make a plan of attack and follow through with all possible rigor."

"A disease! An attack!" Eliza exclaimed. "Aunt Gertrude, you run the risk of confirming every assumption about scheming women that the most belligerent bachelor has ever concocted. Oughtn't love appear of its own accord and on its own terms? Isn't anything else not love, but mere manipulation of certain social conventions?"

"Men are already manipulating them, Eliza. We women must formulate our own strategies or risk our entire future happiness on a man's emotional intelligence. And that, my dear, would be akin to letting one's horse choose one's hotel based on the quality of the straw in the stables!"

Aunt Gertrude ended her diatribe with a little snort.

Eliza was not entirely sure she followed her aunt's comparison, but the older woman's next words put it completely out of her mind.

"There are still a few more inoculations to perform. We have not yet administered to the officers in General Washington's headquarters, Colonel Hamilton being the exception. Therefore, first thing in the morning that will be your duty. Dr. Cochran has requested my presence for his rounds tomorrow, so would you be so kind as to attend to the officers yourself? You are certainly capable of it."

Eliza was determined to keep her aunt's respect. "It will be an honor, Auntie. Thank you for your confidence in my work."

"You have earned it, my dear."

Eliza discovered her aunt's motivation as they discussed the preparation of a small basket of supplies containing the necessary bottles of inoculum and the tools Eliza would need to administer it.

"Pay attention, Eliza. No doubt several of the officers will try to tell you they've already received the treatment, but if a name doesn't appear in my record books, it is not so. They may need some encouragement. So hold up Colonel Hamilton's voluntary inoculation this afternoon as a brave and shining example for the rest of them. Tell the officers it is Dr. Cochran's orders, which is akin to an order from General Washington himself." Aunt Gertrude waved her hand toward her niece. "You're a clever girl. You'll know what to say . . ."

But before Eliza could protest, the butler announced that they had unexpected guests.

And standing in the doorway were none other than Angelica and Peggy themselves.

"Eliza!"

"Angelica!"

"And Peggy, too!" said Eliza, jumping up from her chair to give each of her sisters a warm hug. "What are you doing here?"

The sisters exchanged a look with Aunt Gertrude, who did not seem a bit surprised to see them. Angelica batted her eyes with forced innocence. "We wanted to help the cause."

"No, really," Eliza said drolly. "What are you doing here?"

Angelica was only able to keep a straight face for a moment. "Albany is so boring!" she exclaimed. "Mama is always fretting about money, and Papa orders the servants about as though they were troops, and the same four families throw the same four parties."

"It's true!" Peggy assented. "If I have to dance with Cornelius Van der Toothless one more time!"

Eliza laughed. Cornelius Van der Shoot was a notorious bachelor in his mid-fifties whose fortune was only matched by his inability to get anyone to marry him for it, not least because of the dental issues Peggy's nickname alluded to.

"Have you heard the latest?" Angelica chimed in. "He got a new set of false teeth—made out of real teeth! He is chewing with someone else's teeth in his mouth!"

"No!" Eliza gasped. "That is too foul!" The sisters fell into each other's arms in a fit of giggles that went on for several moments. At length Peggy pulled free. "There is also this," she said in a more serious tone. She handed Eliza an envelope addressed in her mother's familiar handwriting. "You might want to sit back down, Eliza."

Eliza tore open the envelope and caught her breath at her mother's tortured first words.

Dearest Elizabeth,

How it pains me to bring you this news. The burning of our Saratoga estate by that vile General Burgoyne seems to have no end to its cruel spiral into our lives. As much as your father endeavored to revive our precious second home, it has become clear that due to the total devastation of the house and most buildings on the property, the Schuyler finances have been dealt a crippling blow. Indeed we have had a glimpse of what it must feel like to be poor and struggling. Papa says it is only temporary but with so many mouths to feed, a real depression has descended on us all. To that end, my Darling Girl, your loving parents have decided you three sisters would be more satisfactorily engaged this dreary winter in the generous arms of Uncle John and Aunt Gertrude. My heart swells with pride at what a team you'll make, lifting the soldiers' morale with your fresh countenances and unblemished hopes. Oh, that I were only young and spry enough to work alongside you—

Eliza stopped reading, her eyes trembling with tears. But then something strange and wonderful happened. She looked into her sisters' faces expecting them to fall apart, but instead was surprised to see something she'd never seen in them before: total resolve. They had come to Morristown not in surrender, but to continue the good fight by supporting the brave patriots the only way they knew how. They would stand with Eliza and do the work—sew the torn overshirts, mop the fevered brows, provide inoculations—whatever must be done to help set to rights their broken world.

"All right, ladies. We've all had an exhausting day. We'll get started on the officers' inoculations first thing in the morning. But for now? Let's take the chill off your bones. Come, step out of your furs and settle down next to the fire. Cook has the most extraordinary gift with glazed scones."

Aunt Gertrude rang the tiny silver bell, and a shy servant girl appeared with more cranberry scones.

"Thank you, Louisa," said Aunt Gertrude with a twinkle in her eye. "I'll handle it from here."

It was 1780 after all, and the vibrant and spirited Schuyler sisters were joining the fight for independence—their proud and unruly young nation's as well as their own. Plus, each one of them had her own dream to follow, and it was high time to get started.

15

Ministering Angels

Continental Army Headquarters

Morristown, New Jersey

February 1780

The next morning, an arctic chill blew in as Eliza led her sisters up the front walk of the old Ford mansion, appropriated for General Washington's headquarters. The stately white house sat on an estate owned by a local judge who had died. While the general had use of the master's quarters, Colonel Hamilton and the other officers slept in the smaller upstairs bedrooms, sometimes two to a bed, and worked in a log office annex by day.

Would he be there this morning? *Remain cool headed*, Eliza reminded herself. The thought of seeing Colonel Hamilton again confused and excited her, but she hadn't had time to think it all through before her aunt bundled her and her sisters out the door, their heads swimming with directions for the treatment.

As the sisters stepped inside the mansion, a cloud of

warm air rolled out with the heady scent of tobacco smoke. Down the hallway they overheard the boisterous voices of men unrestrained by the presence of women. Eliza walked to the doorway, which opened into what had once been the judge's study, and knocked on the doorjamb.

"Good morning," she said. "Dr. John Cochran sent us—"

Her voice faded as she made out the room's occupants, a pair of young men hovering awkwardly over a disheveled desk. Loose papers and an inkwell had been pushed in a jumble to one side. The men sprang up guiltily, and it was only as they were straightening their vests and jackets that Eliza realized they had been arm wrestling.

"That's funny, Larpent," the fellow beside the desk said. He was a pale blond youth of no more than nineteen. "Usually it is the man who saves the damsel from distress, but in this case it is you who have been rescued by the arrival of this fair young lady."

The other fellow behind the desk was as fresh faced as his companion but thin and soft. A redness of his cheeks revealed that he had been on the losing side of their struggle.

"Good morning, miss!" The one called Larpent ignored his friend's jibe. "How may we help you today?"

Eliza smiled officiously as she walked in the room. "My name is Eliza Schuyler, and these are my sisters, Angelica and Peggy. Dr. John Cochran requested that we administer the smallpox inoculation to the men working in this office today, in compliance with General Washington's orders."

Larpent frowned. "The Schuyler sisters? I had been told

that Mrs. Cochran assisted Dr. Cochran in administering the inoculation, Misses, ah . . ."

"Schuyler," Eliza said. "As in General Philip Schuyler?"

The name did the trick for the heavier fellow.

"Of course, Miss Schuyler, Miss Schuyler, and Miss Schuyler. I'm Corporal Weston. Please give me a moment to collect the men. Where would you ladies like to perform the procedure?"

"Over there by the fireplace," Eliza said with immediate confidence. "The room is sufficiently warm that the men won't be chilled when they remove their jackets, and there are extra chairs, which I shall need."

Peggy held the supplies basket while Angelica looked around with an unimpressed air.

"May I?" Angelica sat herself down on the nearest chair. Peggy followed suit and moved to unload the supplies in the basket.

"Stop, Sister! Germs! Germs!" Eliza blanched. "First clear the table for our equipment. Nothing must touch the floor."

Angelica was taken aback by her middle sister's bold new confidence in this strange arena. Clearly in the brief time she had been away from Albany, she had taken on some impressive new strength, but then Eliza had always been the quickest study of the three of them. Angelica turned to Peggy, who was staring openmouthed at Eliza.

"Well, what are you waiting for, Peggy? You heard Sister. Put the basket on a chair and help me clear this table for her. She's got important work to do!"

Corporal Weston glanced nervously at the basket and gave it a wide berth as he headed for the door. Eliza thought him a bit dim. His companion looked equally skittish and made to follow his friend, but Eliza stopped him.

"Larpent, isn't it?" Eliza spoke briskly. "The building is not so large that it will take two of you to gather everyone, Mr. Larpent, so why don't we start with you? Peggy, fetch me a pitcher of water from the kitchen."

Larpent glanced desperately at Weston, but his friend was making a grand show out of leading Peggy to the kitchen, despite the fact that she had just walked through it.

"Of course, Miss Schuyler," Larpent said in a resigned voice. "What should I do?"

"You need do nothing but remove your jacket, roll up your left sleeve, and have a seat here."

Larpent took off his jacket, unbuttoned the lace flounce from his cuff, and began to roll up the sleeve.

"Is there any reason why it's the left arm?"

"The procedure will cause a slight rash that can make writing a bit uncomfortable."

"And suppose I am left-handed? Oh, well, it's a pity. Perhaps I'll come back another day." Larpent jumped up in relief.

Eliza grabbed his sleeve. "Please relax, Mr. Larpent. The treatment is just as effective on the right arm as the left."

Larpent sat down. "It doesn't matter," he said dejectedly. "I'm not actually left-handed."

"Mr. Larpent!" Eliza said with a laugh. "Are you nervous

about the procedure? I assure you, there's nothing to worry about. I have had it myself, along with my entire family, including my seven-year-old brother, and both of my sisters."

"A remarkably courageous act for such a young boy," said Angelica. "Of course, he was holding on to Mama's petticoats at the time." She delivered Larpent a tight smile packed full of derision.

Peggy returned from the kitchen, sloshing water from a full pitcher.

Eliza began to prepare the paste, measuring conservatively. Though there were only a dozen or so treatments to administer and more than enough medicine, she didn't' want to waste any of it. She could feel the young soldier's nervous eyes on her as she mixed the powder and water. At length he cleared his throat. "I-I've heard that the treatment doesn't work for everyone."

"If it doesn't work, we'll administer it again."

"But how do you know if it doesn't work?"

"As I said before, if it takes, there will be a rash, as if you had been exposed to itch ivy."

"Will it itch like itch ivy? I had that once when I was a boy and my mother had to sew socks on my hands to keep me from scratching myself to bloody pieces."

"I assure you, Mr. Larpent, the pox itches far, far worse."

"It's Lieutenant Larpent, actually."

"Of course," Eliza said. "I apologize. So young to be an officer!"

Larpent shrugged. "It doesn't mean much in a new

army. They hand out ranks like apples in October around here. There are even colonels my age—Colonel Hamilton for one—but he earned it the hard way, didn't he, fighting at Brandywine Creek one year, and the next alongside Washington himself at the Battle of Monmouth."

Thrilled to hear Colonel Hamilton's name come up so naturally in the conversation, Eliza wished he would say more. But Larpent had moved on from the subject and was complaining about the lack of rations.

"Buck up, Lieutenant Larpent," said Eliza. "Surely the blockade will be over soon. I'm just happy to be able to do my small part for the cause. Now, if you will extend your arm, please."

Larpent gave her his left arm as though she were going to chop off the hand. Eliza grasped it firmly by the forearm and reached for the rake. "This may sting a bit," she said, and before he could react she dragged the rake across his wrist. Larpent groaned.

"Lieutenant!" Eliza chided. "It is just a scratch!"

"It's not the cut that bothers me," Larpent said. "It's just—I've heard some people get sick from the treatment."

"There will be a rash, as I said, and a light fever—"

"I've heard some people die," Larpent cut her off.

"Lieutenant, would it put your mind at ease to know I have just this week given an inoculation to your colonel Hamilton? And not for a moment did he doubt its worth or question its aftereffects. He merely said that if the inoculation was good enough for his general, and good enough for his general's men, then it was certainly good enough for him. General Washington would be proud of the example of this brave man. Do you not agree, sir, that we are all fighting the same battle?"

Larpent dropped his chin to his chest. "If you say so, miss, but Colonel Hamilton is awful brave. If there was ever anyone among the officers I admire more than the colonel, it could only be the general."

"Brave, is he?" said Angelica, exchanging a look with Peggy. "Pray, tell us more about this brave young colonel."

"I heard all about it from the boys, ma'am. Yes, indeed! It was at Monmouth—the day Colonel Hamilton had his horse shot out from under him. With redcoats swarming over the hill, he was charged head-on by a pistol-wielding cavalryman. So what did he do? He stood his ground. He cut the man down with his sword, swung himself into the empty saddle, and galloped away. At least that's the way it was handed down to me . . ."

Angelica rolled her eyes. "Ah, so the legend begins!"

But Eliza was thrilled to hear it, even as she noticed Peggy looked a little green around the gills.

"Please, Sister, take a seat before you faint. Lieutenant Larpent, I'm afraid our Peggy is not used to such fantastic stories. Why don't we get on with the less disturbing task of the inoculation treatment, shall we?"

Eliza was aware of the mortality statistics surrounding the smallpox inoculation and knew there was some truth to what the frightened young fellow was saying. For every hundred inoculations, one or two people did in fact develop full-blown smallpox, sometimes fatally. But given that the fatality rate among uninoculated individuals was thirty times higher, she understood that it was a more than acceptable risk. Still, she was too honorable to lie to the worried young man.

"Be of good cheer, soldier. You are far, far more likely to die of the pox *without* this treatment than with it. For that matter, you are more likely to die on the battlefield than from this treatment. Now then—" She laid the poultice over the scratches and wrapped it in place. "It's in God's hands now."

Larpent blanched.

"I'm teasing you, Lieutenant," she said as she knotted the wrapping in place. "Everything will be fine. You'll be arm wrestling again in no time."

16

Officers and Gentlemen

Continental Army Headquarters

Morristown, New Jersey

February 1780

Just as Eliza finished, Corporal Weston returned to the room with eight men. Most were younger than twenty-five, though a couple were older. Eliza scanned the faces eagerly, telling herself she wasn't looking for one face in particular.

The officers were surprisingly much more nervous than the enlisted men, and to the degree that Eliza and her sisters could bring themselves to converse with any of them, they gathered that it was because the men had been told just enough about the procedure to fear it and not enough to understand it. A little education, Eliza reckoned, could sometimes be more dangerous than no education at all.

But Eliza had no time for idle talk. The men were mostly young, and all of them extended chivalry to the point of flirtation. They were besotted with Peggy and intimidated by Angelica. It was clear that they didn't get to spend much time in the company of females other than dowagers and servants, and all were eager to make them laugh or secure some promise of a future dinner or perhaps even a dance at some point.

Eliza tried to answer them in kind, but her words were listless. She had to admit it; she was disappointed that Colonel Hamilton wasn't there. She told herself that she wanted the opportunity to chastise him yet again for his gross assumptions of her imputed behavior two years ago, and to call him out in front of an audience. But that argument was losing steam. More than anything now, she wanted to know what it was about her in the first place that would make a young man think she was capable of such wanton actions and whether those assumptions stood for a more complex affection on Alex's part, or if it was only a baser emotion at the heart of it.

She felt a flush spread over her cheeks as, for the hundredth time that week, an image of Alex waiting for her in her father's hayloft appeared in her mind.

Just yesterday, she had agreed to let him take her on a sleigh ride, if only to see his horse, Hector, once more. Although as much as she wanted to admit it, she was feeling a welling of affection toward Hector's master lately as much, if not more, than for Hector himself.

Her current patient, a Colonel Martins, tried to escape.

"You look flushed, Miss Schuyler. Please, allow me to fetch you a glass of cold water!"

Eliza held on to his arm and kept him in his chair.

"I am quite comfortable, Colonel. Please remain seated until I've finished the procedure."

She was just administering a final dose to the genially named Lieutenant Colonel Friendly when she heard the door open in the hallway behind her, and a jovial male voice exclaimed:

"Where is he—that scoundrel, Hamilton! Tell him to come downstairs with his saber drawn! His fate has caught up with him at last!"

At the sound of Colonel Hamilton's name, Eliza's heart tumbled over in her chest in delight.

"Nope, not here, sir!" said Corporal Weston, getting out of the loud officer's way.

Eliza did her best to hide her disappointment once more. She glanced up at the three men still in the room who had come up with excuses for not going to work (or whose rank was high enough that no one could order them to stop flirting with the doctor's pretty aides). But none of them seemed particularly bothered when a pair of flamboyant figures appeared in the door.

Both were about Eliza's age, or a year or two older, and both wore particularly smart uniforms cut from the finest wool. One's sleeve declared him a lieutenant colonel, while the other was a major general, and it was hard to say which of the men was the more dashing specimen. The general had dark wavy hair combed forward over pale cheeks tinted rosy from the cold. His nose was long and thin and aristocratic, but he smiled in real pleasure when he saw Eliza, who was alone in the room, having sent Angelica and Peggy to search the house to make sure there were no more officers hiding in a cupboard or wardrobe.

"Well, I have certainly come to the right place today! I just passed two stunning beauties in the hall and now find myself face-to-face with a third! A good day, indeed!"

The colonel's features were less refined, the complexion ruddier, but his uniform was, if anything, even more turned out than his companion's, the blue jacket as crisp as if it had just been ironed, the boots still in high polish, though the officers must have been riding for some time to get here from wherever they were coming from. A few wisps of brown hair showed in his whiskers, but the rest of his hair was freshly powdered. This was a man who cared about how he looked—how others saw him. When he saw Eliza looking at him, he put a hand to his chest and bowed low.

"I beg your pardon, miss!" he said in a comically loud southern accent. "Had I known there were female presences in this house of fallen men, I would have tied up my companion with the horses outside!"

"Had you known there were women inside, Laurens," the general scoffed, "you probably would have slunk around to the back door, to save yourself the embarrassment of being passed over for a man of both higher breeding and higher rank."

Laurens! Eliza recognized the name instantly and the southern accent reinforced her thinking. Henry Laurens from South Carolina was the president of the Continental Congress. This must be one of his sons.

The dark-haired officer's accent was also intriguing. It was definitely European, but it had a certain aristocratic universality, which made it hard to tell if it was French or Spanish or Italian. Eliza had just decided it was French when the general said, "Allow me to introduce myself, mademoiselle. I am Marie-Joseph Paul Yves Roch Gilbert du Motier, Marquis de Lafayette, but you may call me Gil—"

"Or you can just call him Marie, which is what everyone else calls him." Colonel Laurens cut in, extending his hand with American frankness. "John Laurens," he said. "A mere three syllables next to my friend's five and twenty, but what I lack in letters I make up for in charm."

Eliza watched this display with increasingly widened eyes. At length she said, "I would shake your hand, but I have smallpox on my fingers."

Colonel Laurens couldn't have jumped back any faster had a cobra come out of her mouth. In half a second he was on the other side of the room, the marquis well on his heels. Eliza burst out laughing.

The marquis was the first to recover. "I beg your pardon, mademoiselle, but I thought you said smallpox."

"I did say smallpox, General."

Angelica and Peggy swooped back into the room, empty-handed.

"It appears word has gotten out"—Angelica sent a scowl in Corporal Weston's direction—"there's suddenly not a soul left to be found out there."

"You see, General," said Eliza with a wave of her hand,

"my sisters and I are here on an errand of medicine, inoculating the good soldiers of our army against an enemy more fearsome than all the British and Hessian troops."

"You girls?" The southern gentleman seemed surprised. "Inoculating our troops?"

"Every one of them!" replied Eliza. "Why, the man you were calling out for, Colonel Hamilton, just received his yesterday. Would you like to follow in his footsteps?" Eliza smiled her first real smile of the day. There was something immediately likeable about this fellow Laurens.

Laurens scratched at his arm. "The marquis"—he pronounced it "mar-kwiss" in a mocking tone—"and I had that procedure done some years ago. I commend you for your bravery, but I found the whole affair unnatural and unnerving."

"What? You have been inoculated? Then you have nothing to fear." As she spoke she stood up, motioning to Peggy to begin packing up the supplies. Laurens retreated farther behind a chair.

"I must take my American friend's side in this matter. If God had not wanted us to catch smallpox, he would not have made it in the first place," said Lafayette.

Angelica had finished packing and made to leave the room, but could no longer hold her tongue. "That is the most absurd statement I have ever heard! The Lord presents us with trials so that we may use our God-given gifts to overcome them, not to give in to them. By your logic we would all be naked and living in caves—a condition that I am sure Colonel Laurens would find not at all appealing."

"Touché, mademoiselle! You are quite correct." The marquis snickered more at her than with her. He gave her a frank, appraising look that started at the top of her head and landed at her toes. Angelica smiled to herself as she scooped up the last of the supplies and laid them in the basket.

"Peggy, it is high time we left here. Eliza can join us back at Aunt Gertrude's after she finishes her *duties* with these gentlemen."

Eliza didn't understand why Angelica was rushing Peggy off—neither did Peggy, apparently, judging by the confused expression on her face. Then her older sister caught Eliza's eye with a wink and a nod in the direction of the charming Colonel Laurens, and Eliza realized: Angelica was playing matchmaker!

"Forgive my friend's lack of faith in your brave efforts," the marquis called to Angelica and Peggy as they headed out of the room. "Our Laurens is full of hubris. Indeed, I have discovered vanity to be endemic among southern men."

"Said the man who goes on campaign with three servants, two jewelry boxes, and wears knickers lined with mink," Laurens teased.

Angelica smirked. "Good day, gentlemen," she said, as she pivoted on her shoe and left the room, Peggy right behind her.

The marquis's legs squeezed tightly together. "*Mon Dieu!* I see your northern winters are as blasted cold as your women!"

"They are not *my* northern winters," Laurens said, laughing. "I would give anything to be home in Carolina right now.

But at least there is something here to relieve the cold. And, since the mar-*kwiss* has, despite his many names and titles, failed to ask, may I inquire as to your name, mademoiselle?"

"Unlike you, Colonel Laurens, I value my name highly, and don't just hand it out to any lieutenant colonel or major general who asks, even if one of them is a mar-*kwiss*. So, what will you give me if I tell you my name?"

Laurens smiled. "I would offer you my heart, miss, but I fear it is not worth a tenth of what you offer in exchange."

"Indeed, Colonel," Eliza said. "Especially since you seem to deal it out like playing cards."

"I, on the other hand," the marquis said, reaching a hand into his greatcoat and pulling out a bottle of amber liquid, "have a bottle of ten-year-old cognac shipped from my estate on the far side of the Atlantic. Perhaps you would do me the honor of sharing it with me, Miss—"

Eliza put down her basket of supplies and extended her hand to the marquis. "Schuyler. Elizabeth Schuyler, but you may call me Eliza. Thank you kindly, but I have quite a bit more work this evening and will have to decline your good hospitality."

"Eliza Schuyler?" said Colonel Laurens, with a piercing gaze.

"Yes, the one and the same," she said, and wondered at the look he gave her.

17

Guess Who's Coming to Dinner

The Cochran Residence

Morristown, New Jersey

February 1780

Eliza awoke the next morning to someone knocking insistently at her bedroom door. "Yes?" she called.

"Eliza, darling, it's Aunt Gertrude. Your uncle John and I were asleep last night when you three returned home. I just want to make sure all is well. May I come in? I have coffee."

"Of course, Auntie, I'm so sorry to have overslept. It was a long day."

Aunt Gertrude entered, bearing a small tray with a covered pot and cup and saucer. There was concern on her face, as well as amusement as she set the tray on the bedside table. "Exhausted, no doubt! I'm afraid your mother would be quite displeased with me, working you girls so hard."

Eliza smiled back ruefully.

"By the by, Colonel Hamilton was nice enough this morning to bring over the inoculation supplies you left in

General Washington's office. I think he hoped to return them personally."

Eliza felt a blush spread itself on her cheeks as she reached for the coffee cup on the bedside table and sipped at it.

"Well," her aunt said, "I hope yesterday didn't take too much out of you, because there are festivities tonight."

"Really? Is one of the officers' wives throwing a party? Or the baron?"

"No, we are!" Aunt Gertrude said mischievously.

"You! Mama always said you had the festive sensibility of a . . ." Eliza didn't finish the sentence. "I meant, she said that you and Dr. Cochran were both too busy with your important work to entertain much."

What Mrs. Schuyler had actually said was that her sister-in-law was about as much fun as a Puritan on All Hallows' Eve, dressed in black wool, clinging to a cross and seeing devils and witches in every shadow, but Eliza thought it better to rephrase her mother's barb.

"Well, it's not a party, per se, just a dinner gathering. Stephen Van Rensselaer is in town. I wager he couldn't keep away from Peggy and followed her here, so we're holding a small dinner for him. And when we heard that such prestigious figures as Colonel Laurens and General Lafayette were here as well, of course we had to invite them along . . . with Colonel Hamilton."

Hearing that Colonel Hamilton would be at the party quickened Eliza's pulse. Try as she might to pretend it wasn't so, that rascal had gotten under her skin somehow. Suddenly the confident girl with the practical clothes was wondering what sort of fancy dress she might find for the dinner. *Maybe borrow something from Peggy?*

And that was surprising about Stephen Van Rensselaer. She had to give him credit for following Peggy to Morristown. He certainly couldn't be faulted for lack of interest. She turned her attention back to her aunt.

"The marquis has already agreed to bring a barrel of wine with him. He seems, despite the British blockade, to have an endless supply. The French are of different priorities, I suppose," said Aunt Gertrude, adjusting her cameo broach. "Well, perhaps you should rest this afternoon, dear, so that you have energy for the dinner." A twinkle appeared in her aunt's eye. "Colonel Hamilton accepted our invitation 'most eagerly,' and said that he was 'especially excited' to have the chance to continue his acquaintance with you."

"Did he!" Eliza exclaimed before she could stop herself.

"He did indeed." Her aunt smiled at her slyly. "Shall I have the maid bring up some toast in a bit?"

"Yes, thank you!" Eliza said. She barely heard her aunt as the older woman slipped out of the room.

SIX HOURS LATER found Eliza ready for the party, dressed in a violet gown lightly embroidered with gold threads and pearls. Her aunt had sent Louisa, the servant girl, up with it and Eliza decided not to pursue the same old argument about how it was unbecoming for a woman of her stature to dress in finery while the soldiers went about in rags.

They were in the headquarters of the Continental army, for

one thing, where the soldiers were as well appointed as it was possible for soldiers to be. And the truth is she wanted to look especially nice on this occasion. Angelica's and Peggy's arrival had made her acutely aware that she was the only one of the grown Schuyler sisters without a beau. And after all, she had not picked the dress out herself. Her mother had packed it for her. To let it wrinkle in a trunk would be wasteful. *Not practical at all!*

She even consented to wear a wig. Once it was on, she wondered that she did not wear one more often. It kept drafts off the head, for one thing, and for another, one did not have to sit still for half an hour or an hour while a maid teased and styled and powdered and sprayed every strand of hair in place. One need only pin one's own hair up and sit as the great silver confection was lowered onto the head—et voilà—an ordinary girl was transformed into a ravishing mademoiselle.

When she came down the stairs, nearly twenty people were sitting down to dinner already, tables had been lined up in the hall downstairs and covered with several sheets of embroidered ivory linen. The plates were embossed with a gold-and-green Chinese pattern, and edged with a gold rim, the silver heavy and ornate. The stemware was pewter, but polished to such a high sheen that it shone like silver in the light of the three eight-stemmed candelabras gracing the table.

"The Kitcheners did set a fine table," Aunt Gertrude noted, as Eliza appeared downstairs. "But you'll be its jewel tonight. Come," she added, "your sisters have already taken their places in the front parlor."

Peggy and Angelica were chatting among a half-dozen other early guests, including Stephen Van Rensselaer. In the two years since that first dance with Peggy, he had grown by nearly eight inches and now stood a full head taller than Eliza's sister. She was glad to see he had turned out to be a fine-looking, if rather serious, young man.

"Rensselaerswyck, my father's manor, amounts to some 768,000 square acres, or 1,200 square miles, which is roughly the same size as Long Island. We rent to more than three thousand tenant farmers and their families, who together manage thousands of cattle, sheep, pigs—yes—and turkeys, ducks, rabbits, and—"

Angelica came up and whispered into Eliza's ear. "And titmice and seventeen-year locusts and seventy-two different varieties of flea!"

The sisters laughed softly. Angelica added, "Mrs. Witherspoon made the mistake of asking him what he wanted to be when he grew up. He said he would be 'patroon of the manor' and has been detailing exactly what his holdings will be for nearly fifteen minutes. I can't tell if people are too afraid of his wealth to interrupt, or if they've simply been stunned into silence."

"—wheat is the primary grain crop, but also oats and rye and corn and alfalfa and milo and—" droned young Stephen.

Eliza laughed into her gloved hand. Perhaps the young man still had a few social graces to master.

"We shouldn't be so hard on him, Ange. He is so young, after all, and his responsibilities will be vast indeed." She glanced at Peggy, who was managing to regard her pontificating suitor with an expression that attempted to pass for genuine interest. "Do you think that Peggy will really marry him? I would hate to see her trapped with a bore for the rest of her life just because he was rich."

"Rich?" Angelica said. "He's so far beyond rich there isn't a word for him. There are some who say that his father is the wealthiest man in all the colonies—wealthier even than John Hancock or Benjamin Franklin—which means he will be, too."

Eliza nodded, but corrected her sister. "You mean, the United States."

"Oh, can we not talk about the war tonight?" Angelica moaned. "It's all Papa ever talks about, and my Mr. Church, too. Can we not be happy mademoiselles for once, and talk about dresses and dinner courses and Samuel Richardson's novels and secret rendezvous?"

Stephen's voice carried on. "—made it a personal goal to travel each and every foot of the 4,649 miles of roads and paths that crisscross the manor. By my calculation, I have traveled approximately 949 and one-half miles, which means I have three thousand—"

"Who says 949 and a half is an 'approximate' number?" Angelica moaned. She was about to go on when Eliza stopped her.

"Did you mention Mr. Church? Are you still seeing him?"

Angelica coyly looked away. "Not exactly."

"What do you mean, not exactly? Have you broken things off?"

"Not exactly," Angelica said again, clearly enjoying being mysterious.

"Angelica Schuyler, don't make me pinch you in a parlor full of people!"

Angelica turned to Eliza and grabbed her hand. "Church is on his way here!"

"*WHAT?!*" Eliza spoke so heartily that everyone in the room—except Stephen—looked over at her.

"—sometimes I use a whip when I travel, other times I ride horseback, and still other times I go on foot," Stephen continued, oblivious. "When on foot I find it expedient to employ a walking stick. After much trial and error, I have found that an ash limb has the appropriate combination of strength, lightness, and springiness for—oh, hello, Miss Schuyler," he interrupted himself, nodding at Eliza, but, mercifully, not crossing to her and trapping her within his conversational prison. "I did not see you come in. I was telling Mrs. Witherspoon how I prefer to employ an ash limb as a walking stick when I—"

Eliza nodded and turned back to Angelica. "When?"

"I am meeting him tonight! I think he means to propose!"

"And you will accept him?"

Angelica only smiled.

"But how will you get Papa to consent? He thinks Mr. Church to be a scoundrel and a knave."

"*Scoundrel* and *knave* are redundant, but thank you for the vote of confidence," Angelica said drolly.

"And Mama has made it clear she believes the continuing

source of his wealth to be suspicious, if not altogether ill-gotten!"

"That hurdle, at least, has been cleared. John's business is stable and doing rather well," said Angelica.

"—the revenue for the farms amounts to some ten thousand shillings, which comes to approximately one hundred thousand Continentals—" droned Stephen.

"And what *is* John's business?" Eliza asked. "He has always been rather mysterious about his affairs."

"It is rather exciting," Angelica said. "He 'runs guns.'"

"Runs them? Like an infantryman?"

"No. It is a euphemism for arms dealing. He procures weapons from French and German munitions manufacturers and sells them to—"

"The redcoats? But that's horrible! He is helping our enemy!"

"Eliza! Do you think I could align myself with a redcoat or a sympathizer? He sells weapons to the Continental army. That's why he has to be so quiet about it. He is still a British citizen, after all. If he were to get caught, he would be stripped of his citizenship at the very least, and more likely executed as a traitor," said Angelica, quite indignant.

"Oh!" Eliza exclaimed. "That is romantic. And patriotic. Well, not patriotic for him, I suppose, if he remains British. Why doesn't he become an American?"

Angelica shrugged. "He says he admires America greatly, but that he cannot help being British to the core. He would like to introduce our reforms to England—to reduce the power of the crown and see Parliament become more democratic. He says the Old World can learn much from the New, and must learn, or it will be left behind."

Eliza absorbed all this with some surprise. So that was why John Church was always so vague in conversation. But now she understood—he was protecting himself and his interests. It explained Angelica's interest in him, too. She had assumed that her headstrong older sister was attracted to John simply because he was everything their parents despised—which was fine for an adolescent crush, but didn't explain the endurance of the attraction over several years. But now she realized that her sister had fallen in love with a man of principle. She wished he was a handsomer fellow, to match Angelica's beauty, but looks fade, after all, and intelligence and character are what sustain a relationship.

"Oh, Angelica, this is so exciting! Church is on his way! How romantic! If Mama approves, I'm sure she'll be able to wear Papa down."

Angelica shrugged, as if the blessing of their parents were of little concern to her. "Papa will do what he wants to do. And so will I."

"You wicked girl!" Eliza said, scandalized and titillated at the same time.

At that moment a heavy round of footsteps landed on the front porch. Ulysses opened the front door to a jocular crowd of men streaming in, pulling off their coats and hats and dumping them into the servant girl's thin brown arms.

"Girls—our guests!" Aunt Gertrude said to the Schuyler sisters. "The officers have arrived!"

18

Goose Is Cooked?

Cochran Dinner Table

Morristown, New Jersey

February 1780

Dr. Cochran sharpened the carving knife and fork high in the air over a crispy brown duck while the rest of the table looked on. "My word, Dr. Bones," the marquis said in a teasing voice, "from the way you are sharpening that knife, one would think you are preparing to operate on General Washington himself. By all means, proceed!"

Alex sat back, downright jolly. It had been a long week, and at last, after haunting her window and missing opportunities to see her at headquarters, where she had been near but so far, he was finally in the same place as Eliza Schuyler. His generous hostess had even seen to it that he was seated next to her lovely niece. Alex hoped dinner would go on until the wee hours as was custom lately; there was nowhere else he would rather be than at the Cochran dinner table. He smiled as the servants set a variety of savory dishes before the guests. There were three large courses with duck and venison roasts to be carved, with jellies, dried fruits and nuts served alongside. An endless pile of fresh oysters from the Hudson River was set in front of each officer.

Laughter ricocheted from every table, as Louisa raced around the room, filling and refilling the wine glasses. Across from him, Laurens and Lafayette spoke animatedly in bawdy, good-humored French. Alex looked fondly at his fellow aides-de-camp. It was good to see them so relaxed.

He turned to his right, stealing a glimpse of Eliza, ravishing in the candlelight. He watched as she leaned in to catch wisps of what French she could figure out. Fluent in the language from his childhood in the West Indies, Alex was charmed by her struggle to understand the officers' racier phrases as she strove to translate them. *A good student*, he smiled, as he absentmindedly scratched the last of the rash on his wrist left over from the inoculation she'd given him.

"What is so amusing?" Eliza asked, turning to him. "Are they being very naughty?"

Alex shook his head. "No, I am just enjoying the view," he said. "It is not every day that we are graced with such pleasing company."

She blushed, and he liked seeing the rosy flush on her cheeks; it gave him a wellspring of hope.

"You look very beautiful tonight, Miss Schuyler," he said bravely. "I hope you will allow me to compliment you."

Eliza lowered her lashes. "I'm afraid I did not pack many party dresses but thankfully, my sisters did."

"I do not think it is the dress," he murmured, finding her dark, almost-black eyes—and the gentleness in them—her most appealing feature.

Halfway through the second course, Alex pinged his fork against his wineglass to signify he was making an announcement and stood up.

Conversation ceased and the entire party gave him their attention.

"Ladies and gentlemen, if I may intrude on your serious conversations for a moment, I'd like to propose a toast of thanks to our host and hostess tonight for giving us the pleasure of eating and drinking . . . *at someone else's expense.* It puts to shame the many nights we poor soldiers have shared a pint or two of ale at Jacob Arnold's tavern and pretended it was a meal."

"Hear! Hear!" came the agreeable shouts from the other officers.

"And what more can be said of the lovely company you have chosen to surround us with tonight, Mrs. Cochran? The work these ladies are doing is quite sure to save battalions of lives. I salute you for your attention to our country's most basic of needs."

Alex raised his glass toward Eliza, whose dark eyes sparkled with good cheer in recognition of his kind words. He sat back down and leaned over to whisper into her ear. "Your aunt was overly generous to include me in tonight's dinner party," he confided. "I owed her a few words of praise."

"I think it's fair to say Aunt Gertrude is already quite taken with you, sir, and her seating you next to me at the table is more than just a coincidence. Indeed, she's made it a point to repeat how contentedly she sleeps through these long cold nights lately, knowing that you are out there . . . *guarding* the house."

Alex bit his lip, trying to suppress a smile at the thought of Aunt Gertrude blissfully snoring away in her night bonnet.

As if she had read his mind, Eliza smiled as well.

"It is nice to see you smiling at me. I take it my presence is not as objectionable to you as in the past?" he said.

"I wouldn't go that far," said Eliza, still smiling.

"The weather has been atrocious, and I am sorry for it."

Eliza took a delicate bite from her fork. "Why? Does Mother Nature usually attend to your wishes?"

"Not in the least, but there was to be a dancing assembly on the morrow, but it has been canceled due to the snowstorm. I wished to take you in the sleigh . . . only for Hector's sake, of course."

"Of course," said Eliza, turning pink once more.

AS THE MEAL was winding down, Eliza noticed that Stephen and Peggy had pulled their chairs closer together in a sort of silent pact. She thought perhaps the plethora of words from the shy young man's earlier monologue had squeezed all the air out of him.

Angelica started in on him innocently enough. "And what brings you to Morristown in the bleak midwinter, Stephen? Surely it must be a business matter of the utmost importance." She gave Eliza a little wink.

Stephen put down his fork and looked Angelica in the eye. "I came to see Miss Peggy."

"And . . . ?" Angelica pursed her lips and tilted her head in a way that begged for more information.

"That is all." Stephen picked up his fork again and continued with his dinner.

Angelica dabbed her lips with her napkin. "My goodness, Stephen. You are quite the conversation stopper—isn't he, though, Peg!"

Peggy glared at her sister as a cool hush descended over the dinner guests.

Aunt Gertrude stepped in to break up the awkward moment. "Perhaps now would be a good time for something sweet?" She held the tiny silver bell in the air to ring for Louisa. "And who will be wanting coffee as well?"

Once the dinner plates had been removed, Peggy turned to her aunt with a simple request. "Aunt Gertrude, supper was perfectly splendid and we know your cook is famous for her lovely desserts. But will you forgive me?" Peggy rose from her seat, squaring her eyes at Angelica. "I-I feel a bit of a chill in the air."

Stephen stood up clumsily and pulled back her chair. "Thank you, Stephen. Shall we take our coffee in the parlor by the fireplace, then?"

"Of course, Miss Peggy, as you wish."

Stephen turned to Aunt Gertrude and bowed low. Eliza noticed the crown of his head where his hair was starting to thin and something inside her softened toward him. Sometimes Angelica pushed too hard.

"Mrs. Cochran," he said stiffly, "I am most obliged for the respectable food tonight." He pushed the two empty chairs back against the table and followed Peggy out of the room.

Perplexed, Aunt Gertrude looked around at Eliza and Angelica. "He's not much of one for light conversation, is he?"

Eliza, ever the hopeful pragmatist, said, "Perhaps Peggy sees something in him that we do not."

"Indeed," said Angelica drily. "He comes from one of the wealthiest families in the state of New York."

AT ANGELICA'S SMART jibe, Alex felt his ears burning. Could he himself be justly accused of similar selfish calculations in regards to his feelings for Eliza, the second Schuyler daughter?

"Nevertheless, Angelica dear," Aunt Gertrude wisely intervened, "is that reason enough to tie oneself down to a lifetime of masculine silence?"

Alex watched Angelica flinch. He thought her reply seemed touched with an unflattering tinge of bitterness.

"Well," said Angelica, "I for one think they are perfectly suited to each other—he's as passive as a sheep and Peg is a pretty shepherdess."

Nervous laughter streamed around the table at Peggy and Stephen's expense before the topic quickly moved on to some of Morristown's more scandalous gossip.

Alex noticed Eliza had remained silent and did not seem eager to go along with the unkind joke.

Aha, thought Alex. *Here beats a softer heart than Angelica's unsentimental one.*

The room was suddenly too hot for his taste, and he excused himself from the table, saying he needed a bit of fresh air.

He went out and took a few deep breaths, his cheeks hurt from smiling at Eliza Schuyler all night. But he was worried, too, that she was too far above him in station for him to even think about courting her.

Lost in his own thoughts, he didn't notice Stephen Van Rensselear stride past, red in the face, and disappear around the corner.

Peggy followed him, looking upset. She stopped when she saw Alex. "Oh! Colonel Hamilton."

"Everything all right, Miss Schuyler?"

She nodded, then changed her mind and shook her head. "No, Stephen doesn't like Angelica's teasing," she confided. "My sister can be a little too sharp-tongued than is good for her."

"She is only being protective," he said soothingly. "Older sisters tend to be."

Peggy drew herself up to her full height. "Perhaps," she said. "But you will see one day, when the lash falls on you."

He raised his eyebrows, not quite knowing what to say.

"I spoke out of turn, I apologize," said Peggy.

"There is no need," he assured her. After a short silence, he said, "You know, maybe if you told your sisters how you felt about the young man, they would be a little more gentle with him and your feelings."

Peggy appraised him, as if taking his stock for the first time. "Thank you, Colonel. I might just take your advice."

WHEN ALEX RETURNED to the table, Eliza's aunt was standing at the head of it. "Ah, lovely," she announced. "Dessert is ready."

Laurens walked around the table and clamped a hand on Alex's shoulder. "So, Ham, what do you think of my plan to free southern slaves who are willing to join the fight for independence? Let's take these men out of the fields and let them live like human beings. Free them and train them to fire a musket! Pay them to maintain their loyalty like any enlisted man! Think how it would swell our ranks against the British overnight!"

Growing up in the West Indies had given Alex a hatred for slavery and the vile practices he had witnessed firsthand. He admired his wealthy southern friend for feeling the same way when Laurens came from a long line of slaveholders himself and had much to benefit from the practice.

"I support it duly, John, not as your closest friend, but as someone who has seen the depravity of slavery during my childhood. No man could ever find satisfaction in being owned by another. We are all the same in God's eyes, are we not? And General Washington agrees with me. If only I could persuade him to act on it . . ."

"Yes, there's the rub. Too much talk when immediate action is needed. Tell me true, Alex, is the plan anything more than futile?"

Alex turned his palms up to the ceiling. "Ah, friend. I am doing all that I can and yet—"

Eliza cut in on the conversation. "Though you will continue to press the idea upon him, yes, Colonel? It is the right thing to do. Surely, His Excellency understands that?"

Alex and Eliza shared a moment of mutual surprise.

"You support the abolitionist cause?" he asked.

"Fervently," she said. "We Schuylers have always, always espoused a belief in the equality of black and white souls."

It moved him to hear the same perspective coming from this young maiden. Here was something concrete that spoke volumes to the natures of their respective souls.

"I am glad to hear it," he told her. Without thinking, he reached over the table and grasped her hand, giving it a meaningful squeeze.

Laurens coughed and turned away with a smile, and for a moment, Alex enjoyed the feeling of Eliza's small hand in his.

Though Mrs. Cochran was seated too far away to have heard their conversation, it was clear that she noticed something had changed between the soldier and her niece. In a moment, she all but confirmed his supposition with one arched eyebrow. "Cook has discovered a recipe that should put a smile on everyone's face. Tonight we're having a little *tart*."

19

Girl Talk

Eliza's Bedroom

Morristown, New Jersey

February 1780

The dinner over and the guests gone home, the Schuyler sisters retired for the evening. Eliza readied for bed, thinking dreamily of the passionate way Colonel Hamilton had spoken to her at the table that evening. His brilliance, his enlightened mind, and his mischievous good humor were hard to dismiss, and in fact, she kept dwelling on the small, precious moments they had found together all evening. The way his eyes shone when hers caught his across the room upon his arrival. The feel of his hand on her back when he led her out of the room to the ladies' parlor before retiring to her uncle's study for whiskey and cigars. The way he had sought her out afterward, to say a particularly sweet good-bye.

She closed her book and plumped up her pillow, knowing she wouldn't be able to sleep for a while; she was too excited, thinking of him. But she licked her fingers and snuffed out the candle like a good girl nonetheless, just as a knock came at the door.

"Can I come in for a moment?" It was Peggy, shivering in her cotton nightgown and bare feet.

Eliza pulled back the covers and patted the bedding beside her. "Of course!"

Peggy hopped up on the bed and snuggled in beside her older sister. The both of them let out a contented sigh, reveling in the warmth of each other's bodies.

Peggy spoke first. "Remember when we were children and how we shared a bed and all our secrets, too?"

"Yes, Peg. Happy memories, those." Eliza closed her eyes, thinking back to the lively Schuyler home with each of the sisters playing a musical instrument. The brothers would chase them all through the fields with their dogs. As often as not, Eliza would lead the way in the footraces.

"Well, I have another secret for you, Sister." Peggy sat up in bed and turned toward Eliza. In the darkness, Eliza could barely see Peggy's perfect nose.

"I have found the only man I shall ever love. And I intend to marry him."

"But, dear Peg! You are younger than I. How can you know such a thing at such a tender age?"

"Because of his . . . kindness. He is the only suitor I've ever had who doesn't pretend to know all there is about me, or tells me how beautiful I am, then proceeds to step all over my toes in the most careless ballroom manner. In fact, I can see it in his eyes that he is most comfortable when I am at his side. Of course, Stephen says relatively little but—"

"Stephen? We're talking about Stephen?" Eliza said, trying not to sound too shocked for her sister's sake.

"Yes, of course. I know you and Angelica find him tedious."

"We do not!"

"But he is just young; he doesn't know yet not to ramble."

"He is very earnest, that."

"Earnest and sweet. And you see, Eliza—do not think me a silly goose—but I have always been the one people took care of. First Mama babied me, then you and Angelica. Now I find men want to baby me, bolster me up with fine words and fine promises, and wear me on their arms like a gaudy bauble. Stephen does none of that. Rather, he looks to me—to me!—for strength, as if he can scarce believe that I should care for him. For the first time, I have found someone whose life I want to make better. It's like coming upon a bird with a broken wing and nurturing it back to full strength. Yes, that's it! Here's a fellow who needs *me* to take care of *him*."

"Dear sweet Peg." Eliza wanted to believe it, too. "I suppose when you have the opportunity to do something of value for someone you love, you have the responsibility to do it. If that is the case, then I am truly happy for you."

"But surely Papa will not approve," Peggy moaned into the pillow. "He thinks Stephen is much too young and untested, and he would prefer a bold soldier like your colonel Hamilton who marches around with medals clanging against his breast."

"What do you mean, *my* colonel Hamilton?"

"Oh, dearest Sister. For all of your intelligent ways, are you too pious to recognize a lovesick man when he stands before you wearing his heart on his sleeve? Everyone seems to see it but you. He was mooning over you all evening."

The bedroom door flew open and moonlight streamed in behind a tall figure.

"Brrr . . . what have I missed?" Angelica lifted the covers and slipped in bed between them.

"Where have you been?"

Angelica smiled mysteriously. "You know where."

Eliza did not press. "Peg is telling me what she really feels about Stephen."

"Is that so? And what do you feel?"

"I love him, Ange. And you will do well to keep your claws away from him. He is young and has a soft heart."

"Truly? You love him?"

"With all my heart!"

Angelica cackled. "A marvelous twist! The quietest man at the table wins the family beauty by coming up with nothing at all to say."

Peggy bopped her oldest sister over the head with her pillow. Goose feathers floated in the air. "He's a quiet man, not a fool."

"I'm teasing, Peg. To tell the truth, he has rather grown on me. And no one can deny he is turning into a handsome young man, which is more than I can say for my suitor.

"Speaking of which: Did you see Church? What happened tonight?" asked Peggy.

"Oh my goodness," Eliza said, laughing. "This bed may be too fragile to withstand any more surprises!"

"How surprising could it possibly be that I have found a suitor with wits to match my own," announced Angelica, "and a fortune that will sustain me in high society for as long as I may live?"

"Church has proposed at last, has he?" said Eliza.

Peggy turned toward her sister and said softly, "But do you love him?"

"Let's not overegg the pudding, dear Peg." Angelica tugged at a ribbon on her younger sister's nightcap. "Perhaps for me to love and be loved is an impossible quest. I simply know that in John Church I have met my match. And in one way or another, whether by elopement or a fine wedding, he will be my husband."

Angelica pulled up the covers and stared up at the dark ceiling. "I trust that Papa will be but temporarily dismayed."

The deal was as good as done. Her sisters knew it, too.

"That's all fine and well for you, Angelica," said Peggy. "You have always gotten whatever it is you wanted by sheer force of will. But what of me and my Stephen?" Peggy sounded as though she might burst into tears at any moment. "Surely Papa will be swayed by the Van Rensselaer wealth and the long-held trust between our two families. But do you think he can be persuaded to allow the marriage?"

"My dear little Peg," said Angelica, "you have always dragged along behind me, imitating me at every turn since you were a child. Be aware that I now have a plan and fully intend to carry it out. So here is my advice to you: Perhaps this is just one more time you dare not hesitate to follow your big sister's lead."

"And what about Colonel Hamilton?" said Peggy.

"What about him?" said Angelica.

"He means to take our Eliza away," said Peggy.

"Does he now?" said Angelica impishly. "And what say you, dear sister? Shall you allow yourself to be swept off your feet?"

Eliza hid underneath the covers. "I have no idea what you both are going on about. You are both the ones with secret romances, not me. He has not even announced his courtship yet."

"Maybe he is shy," said Peggy.

Angelica snorted. "Of all the things he is—I don't think *shy* is quite the word."

"Perhaps," said Eliza, muffled from under the blankets, "we are just friends and he does not fancy me at all."

"Oh, Eliza," said Angelica. "You really are dense sometimes."

"He was very kind to me this evening," said Peggy loyally. "Said I should tell you both how I feel about Stephen so you can stop your taunting. I think you should accept him, Eliza, if he asks. You can do worse than to marry a kind man. I think kindness, out of all the virtues, is the best quality to have."

"He does have a good heart," said Eliza, popping up from the pillows. "The men love him."

"But he lacks a great fortune and has no name and no family," reminded Angelica.

"Well," said Peggy. "We have name and family, if not fortune, enough for him, don't you think, Eliza?"

For once, Eliza had to agree with her sweet younger sister rather than her smart older one.

20

First Comes Friendship

Continental Army Barracks
Morristown, New Jersey
February 1780

Laurens and Lafayette remained in town for three more days, but the snows were still so bad that there was no possibility of sleigh rides to dancing assemblies or dinner parties. Work was busy, and Alex's time was split between taking meetings with General Washington and the rest of the top brass, and carousing with his comrades till all hours of the night. Several times Alex attempted to pull rank as the aide-de-camp to the commander in chief of the Continental army in order to be alone with his friend before he left, but General Washington was almost as fond of the son of Henry Laurens, Washington's southern counterpart in the Continental Congress, as Alex was, and always invited him along to meetings and inspections.

On the afternoon of the third day of Laurens's visit, a messenger arrived from Charleston. Reports had come in that General Clinton, the commander in chief of the British forces, was shifting the focus of the war to the South. After being driven from Philadelphia a year and a half ago, General Clinton had holed up in New York City, but since Ambassador Franklin and the Marquis de Lafayette had persuaded the French to enter the war on the side of the Americans, Clinton had come to the conclusion that the northern states, with their close proximity to French Canada, were increasingly vulnerable to a combined French-American attack, and he should shift their efforts south.

The South was the engine of the American economy: Much of its food came from below the newly surveyed Mason-Dixon Line, as well as two of its most valuable exports, tobacco and cotton. If Clinton could cut off the South from the North, the cash-strapped nation would soon run completely out of money.

Even before the messenger had finished delivering his news, John Laurens was shifting about in his seat. As soon as General Washington dismissed them, he raced out of the building. It was all Alex could do to keep up with him.

"Laurens!" he called after his friend, fleeing out of headquarters without even bothering to put on his coat amid the winter chill. "Laurens, wait!"

At the sound of Alex's voice, Laurens halted, panting wildly. He waited until his friend caught up to him.

"I have to go," he said. "Charleston is my home. My family is there. My mother and brothers and sisters, and Mepkin."

"Your beloved estate. You talk about it as though it were your child."

"More like my parent. I would not be the man I am were it not for what I learned at Mepkin. One day when you establish an estate of your own you will feel the same way about it. I must return home to protect her."

"Of course," Alex said, even though he had no real experience with what having a home meant. "I wouldn't dream of trying to persuade you otherwise."

"Then give us a good hug farewell, Alex."

The two men embraced there on the path to the Ford mansion. When Alex stepped back, though, Laurens held on to one of his hands.

"And take the advice of your fondest friend—the Schuyler girl is yours for the asking. It's time to rally, soldier. Do not wait to speak your heart."

Alex was surprised to see tears in his friend's eyes, and he felt an upswell of emotion in his own chest. He knew Laurens was right, and that he was perilously close to losing his chance.

"Be safe, my friend, and send me a lock of hair from General Clinton's head when you drive him from Carolina," said Alex at last.

Laurens bowed with mock formality, then turned and strode off toward his quarters. His shoulders were square, his back straight and proud, yet Alex couldn't shake the idea that his dear friend was marching off to his doom.

THE NEXT MORNING was taken up with routine administrative duties, although routine was hardly the right word. The weather of winter of 1779–80 could hardly be compared with that of 1777–78, which the Continental army had spent freezing at Valley Forge. During that terrible season, one in four American soldiers died. Diseases and injuries, which would normally have been no more than inconveniences, were made rapacious by poor shelter and few provisions. The current season was milder, but the war had been going on for two additional years, and supplies were meager. Storeroom ledgers were alarming; reports from the infirmaries were dispiriting. Among Alex's most dreaded tasks was writing the letter to the family of a fallen soldier, informing them that their son had died, not in battle like an Asgardian warrior, but in a cot, of a fever, because he could not get warm enough or fill his belly with enough sustenance to fight off the ravages of injury and infection.

"My dear Mr. and Mrs. Willey, it is with great sadness for your loss, but also great respect for your son's commitment to the cause of freedom, that I write to inform you of the passing of Josiah, on the 19th day of February in the year of our Lord 17 hundred and 80 . . ."

Alex had penned no fewer than sixteen such letters that morning, and on no fewer than seven different occasions he had to abandon his draft and begin again, because he'd mistakenly used the name *John* for whatever fallen soldier he was meant to be commemorating. When the letters were complete, he told Corporal Weston that he was off to run an errand; he grabbed his coat and hurried from headquarters.

He had no fixed plans when he left. He only knew he needed to get away from his dismal task and worries about his friend, who was riding south toward the fiercest troops the British had mustered. But his feet knew where to take him. Within ten minutes of leaving the Ford mansion, he found himself back again at his post on Chapel Street, standing before the two-story white house.

It was one o'clock in the afternoon when Alex banged the knocker on the Cochrans' front door. He had no idea whether anyone would be home or not, especially since Eliza's sisters had arrived in Morristown. No doubt she was off somewhere *doing the Lord's work* with them. But he thought about what Laurens had said. *I'm a soldier. It's time to rally!* But maybe he should just go and get back to his—

The door pulled open and Ulysses greeted him. "Colonel Hamilton," he nodded, motioning that he should enter.

Alex thanked the old butler and walked into the hall, which in truth was not much warmer than it was outside. Ulysses beckoned him to follow him into a parlor, which was considerably warmer. A fire blazed in the hearth and the scent of spiced cider oozed from a brass kettle hanging over it. Alex's soldier-trained eyes peered into the shadowed room—its windows faced northeast—but did not spy an occupant.

"Miss Schuyler, Colonel Hamilton is calling."

A shadow detached itself from the recesses of a high-backed wing chair, and Eliza's face, turning toward the door, greeted his.

"Colonel Hamilton!" Eliza jumped to her feet, sending an embroidering ring and several spools of thread and a pair of long needles flying. "No, no, not to worry," she said as Ulysses stooped forward to pick up the fallen objects. "I'll get it. Please bring Mr. Hamilton a cup. I'm sure he would enjoy a glass of hot cider. It is particularly frosty today."

She knelt down as the butler retreated from the room, her nimble fingers retrieving the scattered articles. "Indigo, indigo, I am sure I was working with—oh!"

She started as she looked up and found Alex kneeling beside her, his gloved hands proffering the spool of blue thread. He pressed it into her hand more firmly than he needed to.

"Here you are, Miss Schuyler."

"I—thank you, Colonel."

He helped her stand, taking her hand once more. He didn't seem to want to release it.

"Somehow I take it you are not here to invite me to a sleigh ride," she said with a hint of smile.

Alex shook his head as the door opened behind them, and a maid entered with a pewter cup. He crossed to a chair and waited till Eliza had taken a seat before he, too, sat down. Louisa brought them each a tall drink of cider, poked the fire, then asked if there was anything else needed.

"No, thank you, Louisa. You may go." She waited until the maid was gone before speaking again. "I am sorry to say that my aunt and uncle are not at home. Dr. Cochran is attending to the troops, and my aunt is, as always, acting as nurse and assistant, and my sisters are out at the moment."

Alex spoke frankly. "I did not come to see them." Then, fearing he was insinuating too much, he said, "Colonel Laurens left yesterevening. I thought you would like to know."

"Oh! That is too bad. I know you are dear friends. Did he take the marquis with him?"

"No, General Lafayette remains among us, though he will be off soon. There are rumors of British activity in coastal Connecticut, and he is going to investigate."

"Ah. So you will be left quite friendless and bereft!"

"Not entirely bereft, I hope," Alex said, staring directly into Eliza's eyes. But his gaze must have been too intense, for she turned away suddenly and reached for her embroidery. He saw now that it wasn't a ring for a pillow sham but rather the sleeve of a uniform she was working on—she was sewing on an insignia of rank.

"You give so much to our troops," Alex said now. "If there were decorations for noncombatants, you would be the first to receive one."

"I fear I do not do nearly enough," Eliza said. "Especially since coming here, to a strange town where I have not the network of friends and acquaintances to tap for resources for our boys."

Alex knew that he should tell her that what she did was more than adequate, but something held his tongue. At length he spoke.

"You will forgive me, Miss Schuyler. I am afraid I do not know why I came here this afternoon, but I could not help but want to see you. I think I wanted . . . consolation?"

"Colonel Hamilton? Have you lost someone dear to you?"

Alex thought of Laurens walking away, and the number of times he had written his name in the place of one or another fallen soldier. "I hope not," he said.

"Colonel Hamilton?" Eliza said again, concern etched all over her gentle face. It was a face he could imagine waking up to every morning, and in his dreams, she was always there.

"I beg your pardon, Miss Schuyler," Alex said. "I—" He broke off. Then a thought came to him, unbidden: "Have you ever been to the infirmaries?"

Eliza knew what he meant. "You mean the wards? Where the soldiers recuperate? I am afraid I have only been to the examining rooms when I helped my aunt administer the inoculation for the pox."

"It is a difficult thing to recover in the coldness and anonymity of a hospital as opposed to the comfort and familiarity of one's home. There are no books, no mother or servants, no little brothers and sisters to distract one from the boredom or the pain. I think that our soldiers would appreciate it very much if they had a visitor every now and then."

Eliza looked taken aback at first, and then chagrined. "Of course! And here I am sewing on silly little epaulets that turn an ensign into a lieutenant and a lieutenant into a . . . major? Did I get that right?" As the daughter of a general Eliza knew the insignia well, but she felt the need to be a little self-deprecating. She continued: "I shall make arrangements with my uncle to visit them as soon as possible."

"Yes," Alex said. "That is, I was thinking—perhaps I could take you there now?"

"Oh!" Eliza said, then "Oh!" again. "Of course. Just let me put on something warm."

She stood up and only then did Alex notice that she was wearing a simple woolen dress: warm, if one were inside, near a fire, but hardly suited to the freezing weather.

He stood up, too.

"I'm sorry, I'm being stupid," he said. "I should have written and given you advance notice. We can do this another day. Tomorrow or—no, tomorrow I have to drill. Friday, then—"

"Nonsense," Eliza said. "If the truth be known, I am half crazy with boredom. Peggy has been spending all her time with Stephen, and Angelica is off who knows where. While Aunt Gertrude and Uncle John are off saving lives, I am left here for six or eight or ten hours at a time sewing epaulets on sleeves. Please, I beg of you: Put me to real use."

Alex waited while she slipped from the room. She was back some fifteen minutes later. It was unclear to him whether she'd changed her dress or not, but now she was bundled beneath several layers of coat and shawl and hat and gloves. He did see that she had replaced her silk slippers for a pair of sturdy leather boots with a pointed toe and tiny heel.

"I am ready for the fiercest storm," she said. "Please, lead on."

It was only when they were outside that Alex realized he should have commandeered a buggy for this trip. The nearest infirmary was half a mile away, and though Eliza was dressed for the weather, he had only his greatcoat and tricorne. From chest to knees he was snug, but his exposed neck and poorly shod feet immediately felt the nip of the cold. Yet when Eliza crooked her elbow to accept his, all thoughts of the cold vanished from his mind, and he set off toward the infirmary at a leisurely pace, half hoping the journey would never end.

As they strolled, he told Eliza of his gloom at Laurens's departure, and the strange vision he kept having of his friend's death as he wrote out letters of consolation to the families of fallen soldiers. He kept telling himself to change the subject—talk of death and war were not the things to win a girl's heart—but the words came of their own accord. Though Eliza said very little as he spoke, her step never faltered and her arm in his never shook. More than once, he felt her reach across with her free hand to pat his.

Was he mad? Wooing a girl by taking her to the infirmary? What was he thinking? But Eliza Schuyler did not seem to mind.

Romance during wartime, he thought. *In exceptional times, none of the usual rules apply.*

Then again, perhaps it's not the times that are exceptional, he thought. *Perhaps it's the girl.*

21

Soldiers and Suitors

C Infirmary

Morristown, New Jersey

February 1780

The C Infirmary was housed in a long stone barn. The structure had been crudely winterized during its conversion, and the roof had been lowered to keep the heat from disappearing into the rafters, but even so, the barn had not been designed for human habitation, and the four cast-iron stoves deployed along its length barely raised the temperature above freezing. Ten cots stretched up each side of the long space, twenty in all, and puffs of breath could be seen floating in front of pale faces.

Eliza shook her head at the sight and pulled a small notebook and pencil from her reticule and scrawled a note.

"What are you writing?" the colonel asked, intrigued.

For a moment she was consciously aware of his presence and felt the quickening beat of her heart, but she took hold of herself and her emotions in order to concentrate on the task at hand.

"Lists! We need more stoves," she told him. "More stoves and blankets." She waved a hand at the vast space. "This simply will not do."

"If anyone can find them, I have no doubt it's you."

An orderly dozing near one of the stoves snapped to attention as they approached.

"Good afternoon, Colonel Hamilton!" he barked, saluting. His face was flushed from the heat so close to the stove, his collar undone, revealing a slightly moist neck.

"Corporal Weston!" exclaimed Eliza, delighted to recognize a familiar face.

"You know this man?" Colonel Hamilton demanded, sounding just a bit jealous.

Eliza turned to him, smiling. "Of course. I inoculated him from the pox. What on earth are you doing here, Corporal?"

Weston looked sheepish. "I got a bit ill from the inoculation."

"I am sorry to hear that, it should pass sooner rather than later. But I have to ask, Corporal Weston, why *is* your chair pushed so close to the stove? It seems to be rather uncomfortable for you, if the floridity of your cheeks is any measure."

Weston's eyes widened in surprise. "Why, it's the warmest spot in the room, miss! In case you haven't noticed, it's winter!"

"Indeed, I have noticed. As have, I suspect, the twenty men who lie on these cots, much farther from the stove than you are."

"Nineteen, miss," Corporal Weston said defensively. "One of the beds emptied earlier this morning."

"Emptied?" Eliza repeated. "You mean, its occupant died?" Her voice was all but an accusation.

"Y-yes, miss," Corporal Weston answered weakly. "There are three more stoves, miss."

"And nineteen more patients. Might I suggest that you move one or two of the cots closer to this stove, and find a place to sit that will be less uncomfortably hot? I do so hate to see one our brave soldiers suffering."

"It takes at least two men to move a bed, miss. I'm the only attendant on duty."

"I'm sure Colonel Hamilton would be happy to assist?"

She turned to him for the first time since they'd entered the infirmary, brave enough to meet his piercing gaze, which never seemed to leave her face. Why on earth was he looking at her like that? Was that what Peggy and Angelica meant when they said he mooned over her all during dinner? And if so, did he notice that she looked at him that way as well?

"Colonel?"

As if roused from a reverie, he snapped to attention. "Corporal, grab the foot end and be quick about it," he said, trotting toward the nearest bed. Its young occupant appeared unconscious; a downy peach fuzz sprouted along the edge of his jaw. Eliza watched as Alex tucked the soldier's blanket around his shoulders and tenderly patted his hand.

"Get some rest, boy. You will need it for the long journey ahead."

Eliza pulled gently away from Alex's side and approached the fellow in the next bed. Another pale young face peered at her curiously, having obviously heard the commotion when she came in. Eliza introduced herself, and the soldier said his name was Private Wallace. He was perhaps twenty, but his hand in hers was as weak as a boy half his age.

"How are you today, Private Wallace? Is there anything I can get you?"

"Just the sight of a female face is enough to brighten up the day," Private Wallace answered.

"Have you no other visitors?"

"None besides the doctors, and they're so busy they only come once a day, usually."

"No family? That's terrible."

Private Wallace just shrugged. "We hail from all across the north, and some even as far south as Virginia. The mails being what they are these days, most of our families don't hear that we've been injured until we've been discharged or, you know, *discharged*."

His eyes floated up toward the heavens, but Eliza's fell to the bed, where she couldn't help but notice the flat spot beneath the blanket below Private Wallace's left knee where his ankle and foot should have been.

"I'm one of the lucky ones," Wallace said, seeing where she was looking. "Bullet hit below the knee, so I still have the joint left. And the doc says I'm past the risk of infection. I just have to get my strength up, and then I'll be making my way home to Massachusetts. I've been practicing my letters," he said, indicating a small volume that sat, in lieu of a table, on the floor beside his cot. "I thought I might apprentice myself to a printer when I go home. If it was good enough work for Ambassador Franklin, I figure it's probably good enough for me, too."

Eliza passed a few more words with him before moving on to the next bed. The stories were much the same, at least where the patients were awake. The room was cold and the food was poor, but what they claimed really bothered them was the boredom.

Out of the fourteen to sixteen hours they were awake each day, they had human companionship for perhaps twenty or thirty minutes. Eliza decided that she should visit the ward every day; she would commission Peggy and Angelica to visit some of the other infirmaries in the camp. If she couldn't gather supplies or money as she had done in Albany, and if she had not the medical skills her aunt possessed, she could at least read a story to a convalescing soldier, or listen to his stories about his home hundreds or thousands of miles away.

DARKNESS HAD FALLEN by the time she and the colonel had finished the rounds. Eliza turned to him. "I must thank you for bringing me here, Colonel Hamilton. I believe I can procure some more blankets for this ward, and even one or two more stoves. My aunt tells me that there are many empty houses in town."

"It's I who should thank you," Alex answered. "I really had no intention of bringing you here today. Any other girl would have run away."

"I'd like to think I'm not like any other girl," Eliza answered. She hadn't meant her answer to sound flirtatious—two hours in an infirmary can take that right out of you—but the words came before she could stop them.

"I like to think that as well," Alex answered and, to her surprise, he laughed. "I swear, if ever there was a more ungainly swain than myself, I have not heard of him."

"A swain, are you? Are you courting me, Colonel Hamilton?" she asked with a shy smile.

"If you can call courting taking a girl to an infirmary as an afternoon's outing. And this after only recently getting her to talk to him!"

"That seems like ages ago now. I can't even remember what I found so objectionable about you," she said bluntly.

He grinned. "Well, I shall not remind you, then. Although I find it to be a fine twist that you ended up joining me in a barn after all!"

She almost gasped, but her smile betrayed her amusement, and they were back at her aunt's house sooner than she would have liked.

She turned to him at the door. "I do not know that I should describe this afternoon as pleasant," she said. "Nevertheless, I must admit that I did enjoy my time with you, Colonel Hamilton."

"May I take that as permission to call again?"

"Somehow I don't think you would stay away even if I asked you to," she said, feeling quite as bold as Angelica all of a sudden.

"Oh, but I would. I would stay away, and ache for want of seeing you."

Eliza had to laugh. She knew she should scold him for pressing his suit so insistently, but the visit to the ward had reminded her that these were not normal circumstances under which to entertain suitors. It was a war, and war laid bare the urgency of things. What might have taken months under different circumstances was now unfolding over the course of days.

"I expect to be busy during the afternoons seeing to the ward, but my evenings are likely to be free. If you wish to come by, I know my aunt and uncle always welcome your visits."

"But will you?" The laugh lines at the corners of his eyes tightened into a fine squint. "Welcome my visits?"

"Please, Colonel. A girl must hold on to some mystery." And, tapping on the tip of his reddened nose with a gloved finger, she went inside, but her heart was pounding all the while.

"WAS THAT COLONEL Hamilton?" Peggy's voice greeted her. She rushed into the hall and pulled Eliza into the heated parlor after Eliza had removed her frozen, wet boots. "Louisa says you've been gone for hours! Tell all!"

Eliza opened her mouth, but didn't know where to start. She shrugged.

"Colonel Hamilton and I paid a visit to Infirmary C."

"You— " Now it was Peggy's turn to be speechless. "I do not know what to say to that."

"Neither do I," Eliza said. "But I think I like him," she said in a small voice.

It took Peggy a moment to process this. Then she squealed. "You like him!"

"I do! I like him!" Eliza exclaimed, admitting what she had felt for a while now.

"I can't believe it! At last, a suitor the Schuyler parents will approve of. Washington's most-trusted aide! And neither too British nor too young nor—"

"Nor too rich. Mama will not like that, I fear."

"Pshaw," Peggy scoffed. "Stephen's fortune will more than make up for any deficiencies in Colonel Hamilton's accounts. And Church is not doing so badly, either," she added as Angelica joined them.

"Is there more news?" asked Eliza, turning to her older sister, whose beau had left town for a few days.

"Yes, He arrives on the morrow. He writes that he comes with 'a question in his heart.'"

"A question? But he has already asked you to marry him, and you have already accepted. What other question could he have for you?" asked Peggy.

"He has been pressing me to get Papa to bless our union. I have mentioned it to him several times, but Papa always shuts down the subject. He says that it's bad enough that John is British, but his past is simply too shady. He has heard rumors that John left gambling debts behind him in England, and he couldn't bear to see him do the same with my dowry."

"But Papa knows what you told me the other night, does he not? That John is—how did you phrase it—running guns? For our troops? An activity that is both lucrative and honorable," said Eliza.

Angelica shrugged. "You know Papa. Once he's made up his mind about someone, it never changes."

"So then what do you think Mr. Church's question will be?" Peggy persisted.

Angelica looked at her sisters nervously. "I think he is going to ask me to elope."

"What?" Eliza gasped as Peggy literally clutched her pearls. "You cannot be serious! Surely you did not lead him to think that you would accept—oh, Angelica!" Eliza stopped herself when she saw her sister's face. "You're not going to run off with him!"

"I think—" Angelica broke off and was silent for a long time. "I think I am."

Peggy grabbed her sister's hand. "But does this mean you love him?"

More silence from Angelica, who smiled whimsically and stared off into space. "I think I see us as Mama and Papa are. Not enthralled with each other, but respectful and supportive. Two people joined together in a partnership to create something enduring. A family. A legacy."

"But do you love him?" Eliza pressed. "You are too young and too beautiful to give up on love yet. There are more young men out there!"

"Are there?" Angelica said, getting up and heading to the door. "Or are they all ending up in the infirmary, or the kirkyard?" She paused at the door. "Mama and Papa raised us to expect a certain lifestyle. You were always less enamored of material comforts than other girls, but Peggy and I, well, we like our things, don't we? And John will provide me with all the things I want, and adventures as well." She smiled at her younger sister. "Dearest Eliza, you'll have to have the romance for us."

And she slipped into the hall, letting a shiver of cold air into the room.

22

Sweet Nothings

South Street
Morristown, New Jersey
February 1780

Being that Alexander Hamilton was a man of many words, he decided to put them to use to win over his Eliza. He began with a series of letters to her sister Peggy, where he poured out his feelings, knowing the sentiments would be transferred to Eliza forthwith. Since confiding in him at the dinner party, he and Peggy had a sibling-like friendship, and it was to her that he entreated his courtship of Eliza.

When he wrote, he appealed both to Eliza's vanity and her practicality. "*She is unquestionably lovely, yet she lacks the petty affectations of women who believe themselves very beautiful.*" He admired her love of nature and the outdoors. "*Eliza's face glows with the expectation of morning sunshine and I happily imagine her as a rollicking, good-natured tomboy as a child.*" No woman, he wrote, could match her sister's unlimited passion for reading. He even begged Peggy to encourage her sister to continue studying French so one day they might share secrets in their own private language.

These, Alex wrote in reams and reams of pages, were all things he would choose to champion in the perfect woman.

Peggy wrote him back with a much simpler plan. "My dear Colonel Hamilton, if you want to win over my sister, why not simply tell her so yourself?"

THE COOL BLUE evening under the pine trees smelled sweet, and the air called for a thick coat, even standing in front of a roaring bonfire. Alex had taken Peggy's hint and invited Eliza to step out with him along the Morristown green where a seasonal lighting of the bonfire on South Street was set to begin at dusk.

Alex and Eliza squeezed toward the front of the crowd where a tall boy with long fingers and thin beige bangs played his mandolin. People began to cough and clear their throats after two songs. In due course, somebody tossed a turpentine-soaked rag into the bonfire's brushwood and lit a match. There was a wind-sucking *VA-roomph* and the faces of fifty awed souls flashed orange in the firelight. The bracing, sweet smell of the burning pinewood surrounded them.

When he sensed she was feeling cold, he wrapped an arm around her shoulder and rode his fingertips up and down her elbow to create warmth. He lowered his mouth to her ear and whispered, "You are so special to me, my dearest Betsey. And I want you to know it this very moment. Do you think you could ever be persuaded to feel the same toward this poor soldier?"

He had taken to calling her Betsey when they were alone, a name only he called her, and no one else.

"Perhaps one day," she said. "You have yet to take me on that long-promised sleigh ride, Colonel."

"Only say the word, my sweet nut-brown maid," he said, "and I shall make sure Hector will be at your door with bells on. And Alex, please, call me Alex."

"Alexander," she said with a smile. "You take too many liberties, just like our congress against the British."

"My darling, you are the declaration of my heart," he said, enjoying this game.

"Alex," she said at last. "It is nice to be with you here, tonight."

He thrilled to hear the sound of his given name on her lips.

"At the very least, my sister will finally stop pestering me about you," she said.

"They may pester away, for it is to Peggy I thank that we are here together."

They stood in front of the bonfire, enjoying its warmth and each other's.

At the end of the next song, a fellow stepped into the slant of firelight in front of Alex. At first he didn't recognize the tall elegant figure wearing civilian clothes, backlit by the blaze. In the low light beyond the edge of the bonfire, it was unlikely that Major John André would have been recognized by anyone but Alex.

"Good evening, sir!" said Alex. "And what brings you here?"

Alex took a step forward in the firelight. He noticed the major's face was flushed and beads of sweat tracked along the swale of his high cheekbones. He seemed to be in a hurry.

"Ah, Colonel Hamilton. And Miss Schuyler as well—what a . . . pleasant surprise! But please, you mustn't get too close to me. I was merely passing through Morristown only to have been waylaid by a nasty bout of a cold, which I now fear is racing toward pneumonia. I'm out of my sick bed to get to the apothecary for a remedy. Yes, yes, that's it. And now I really must be on my way. Good evening to you both."

The major tucked his chin under the scarf around his neck and cut through the crowd enjoying the bonfire. John André stepped out into the street and took a turn in the direction of Whitehead Street.

"Strange," Alex pondered out loud. "The apothecary is in the other direction. I've always admired the fellow for his fortitude of mind. But this time it is as if he's hiding something."

He looked down at Eliza, who was pensive. "What is it, my darling?"

"He asked me to marry him once," she confessed.

Alex stiffened. "Your dance partner. You danced with him three—no, five—times, I remember. I counted."

She saw the look on his face. "I didn't say yes."

"But you were . . . fond of him?"

"A schoolgirl's crush, that is all."

He breathed in sharply. A British officer—asking the hand of American aristocracy! But of course André would feel confident enough to ask for Eliza's hand. He was wealthy and, enemy or no, had family and fortune that Alex lacked. He was ashamed, all of a sudden.

Now it was Eliza's turn to ask him what was the matter.

"It is nothing," he said weakly.

"I didn't want him," she said.

"But why not?" he asked, unable to help himself. If Eliza would turn down someone as worthy as André, what hope did he, Alex, have of success in his suit?

Eliza contemplated her answer. Walking through the infirmary ward with Colonel Hamilton these past days had shown her a softer side of what an officer must be. The one who cares for his men above all else and is willing to see them honored for their service to the new country he believed in so fervently.

Yes, she had seen Alex's temper flare over his disappointment with a lack of his own regiment to command, but she saw that as merely the fighting spirit of an ambitious and confident leader. Yet, wasn't that what appealed most to her about him? A spirit and impetuousness that could match her own and challenge her to better herself in this new democracy? A man who could honor her own values?

Yes, it was true: Once she had been quite enamored of the elegant Major John André. But here and now, for Eliza, all of Major André's former appeal seemed to vanish in the night air, snuffed out like the pine needles curling orange in the blazing bonfire before her.

In its place, she would enjoy the light dancing in Alex's eyes and the fire ignited in her heart forever, and told him so.

"I didn't accept him," she said. "I fear I am too patriotic to marry against the cause."

He seemed satisfied with the answer.

I didn't accept him, Eliza thought but didn't say, *because he wasn't you.*

23

Full Hearts, Empty Pockets

Continental Army Headquarters & Cochran Dinner Table, Part Deux

Morristown, New Jersey

February 1780

Walking on a cloud after another evening with Eliza, Alex had lost all track of time. He arrived back at headquarters well after the evening guard had been posted, a young corporal huddled in the small shelter in front of the Ford mansion. Swathed in a half-dozen blankets topped by an enormous bearskin, the sleepy fellow made some motion beneath the pile of rugs as Alex approached. It might have been a salute aimed at the familiar figure of Colonel Hamilton, but there were so many layers of fabric over the man's body that Alex wasn't sure.

"Password, Colonel?"

Alex opened his mouth, only to draw a total blank. *The password?*

He had forgotten the password—which was rather awkward since he was in charge of coming up with them.

"Er . . . Eliza?" he said after a moment.

"Colonel?" For the past month the passwords had all been names of birds.

"Elizabeth?" Alex said. "Beth? Betty? Betsey? Bits? Lisa? Liza? Eliza?"

"You tried that one already," the guard said.

"And I shall keep trying it"—Alex saluted the guard as he sauntered past him toward the mansion—"for it is the only name on my mind. Feel free to shoot me, Corporal," he added. "I am so in love that bullets will only bounce off."

The lieutenant in command appeared suddenly and motioned to the young guard. He had heard the colonel's frank revelation of love and felt pity for him. "Laurens is right, you are a gone man. It's *nightjar*, Colonel Hamilton. The password is *nightjar*," said Lieutenant Larpent.

"Nay! It's Elizabeth Schuyler!" Alex called back over his shoulder. "That is the key that opens all locks, or at least the one to my heart!"

As he spoke, he grasped the door handle to the mansion and pulled hard, smacking his nose on its oak panels because it was locked. He tapped at his pockets, but he already knew they were empty: He had left his keys behind when he snuck off to see Eliza.

"I've got it, sir," said Larpent, amused, as he got up to unlock the door.

"Yes, yes, thank you, Lieutenant," he said sheepishly. "Long day, don't you know. Running the army and, uh, that sort of thing."

THE NEXT MORNING he received a note from Gertrude Cochran asking him if he would like to dine *en famille* with them that evening.

> *I know you graced us with your presence just a few days ago, but Angelica's beau, Mr. Church, is in Morristown, as is Peggy's Mr. Van Rensselaer, whom you met the other night. It seems a shame that Eliza should not have her own young man to dote on her, lest she feel left out. I am afraid we are only offering the usual venison stew, but the portions will be plentiful, and there is as much perry to quaff as you can hold.*

Alex immediately dashed off a short note—"It would be my pleasure to be a guest at your table"—and spent the rest of the day contemplating the significance of Mrs. Cochran's missive. Eliza's aunt had attempted to play matchmaker before and could simply be doing so again. But there was something leading in her use of the words *her own young man*. Had Eliza spoken to her aunt? Had she told her that there was something between them? If so, this was the best news he had had all winter. Certainly their time together so far had been encouraging, but he didn't want to assume too much. But he didn't want to play it too cool either, lest she think he was careless of her feelings.

Fortunately General Washington was away and the workload was relatively light: the usual appeals to wealthy American businessmen and plantation owners asking for money or munitions or wool or food; the various summaries of troop movements and intelligence; the flood of letters of condolence for soldiers who had succumbed to their wounds or illness. There were only three today, a blessing.

By five, he was out of the office and back to his quarters, where he bade the manservant he shared with four other officers to press and brush his uniform into crisp neatness and polish his boots. There wasn't time to heat a proper bath, so he stripped down to his tunic and hose and washed his armpits and nethers with frigid water from the basin, then splashed himself with rosewater and dressed in his freshened uniform. He would have liked to have brought flowers but it was the middle of the winter in northern New Jersey: Flowers were but a distant memory. But as he headed out he spied a small bowl of oranges on a side table. They glowed like little suns in the dim room, and he couldn't imagine how they'd survived from whatever tropical clime they'd originated in. He shared this house with seven other officers and he knew the oranges were intended for all of them, but he knew that fresh fruit in February would be more welcome than three dozen red roses. He grabbed a sack and tipped the oranges into it and quickly headed out into the evening.

Lights were blazing in the main parlor of the Cochrans' appropriated house, and multiple shadows could be seen moving around beyond the heavy curtains, drawn against the cold. Alex rang the bell and Ulysses let him in. He took Alex's coat and hat in the hall, and showed him into the parlor.

The room radiated with heat. The three Schuyler sisters were present, Angelica and Eliza seated on a sofa and Peggy on a chair nearby, while Stephen Van Rensselaer and a short, portly man in his early thirties occupied a pair of cane chairs on the other side of the room. Van Rensselaer was out of earshot, yet the drone of his voice could be discerned from the expression on his face. Church stared at him blankly, clutching a goblet as though it were the only thing that kept him from bolting from the room.

Alex tried to catch Eliza's eye, but Aunt Gertrude rose from the same wing-backed chair Eliza had occupied days before and interposed herself between him and his object.

"Colonel Hamilton! It is so good of you to grace us with your presence on such short notice, and so soon after your last visit." She glanced at the sack in his hand. "And you brought your laundry!"

Alex laughed at her joke. "Actually," he said, opening the top of the sack. "They're—"

"Oranges!" Aunt Gertrude almost shrieked. "Oh, what a blessed sight. We ate the last soft apples from the cellar just after Candlemas and haven't seen a rind of fruit since. Oh, I feel healthier just looking at these. Eight of them! My stars, these must have cost as much as a good mule!" She leaned in close, and as she did, Alex got a good whiff of perry on her breath: Aunt Gertrude, it seemed, was tipsy. "Dr. Cochran is away until Monday. I'll split his with you, and it'll be our little secret."

"It's a deal," Alex said. He handed the sack over and turned toward Eliza, only to have Mrs. Cochran grab him with her free hand and turn him toward Van Rensselaer and Church.

"We're too small a party to segregate into separate parlors," she said as she led him to the pair of men, "and wood is so dear to heat a second room as well, so just pretend that you gentlemen are in your own chamber and we ladies are in ours. Mr. Van Rensselaer, I believe you know Colonel Hamilton. Colonel Hamilton, this is Mr. John Barker Church, an Englishman, I'm afraid," she added mischievously, "but one who aids our side at no inconsiderable risk to his own person. Dinner should be ready in a half hour or so," she said, retreating to the far side of the parlor.

Alex shook the men's hands and took a seat on his own cane chair. The chair had its back to the women and he didn't want to appear rude by turning it, so he sat at somewhat of an angle so he could at least glance at Eliza out of the corner of his eye. At least her sofa faced his side of the room, and he could make occasional, if brief, eye contact.

"Colonel Hamilton," John Church said now. "You honor us with your presence. It is well that we should have at least one soldier among us."

"I'll join up next year as soon as I'm seventeen. I wanted to join this year," said Stephen, "but Papa wouldn't let me."

"I'm sure you'll make a fine soldier," Alex agreed. "And it's not too late for you to join our side, Mr. Church."

John Church sat up straighter in his chair. "I think you will agree that I have done much for the Americans, Colonel Hamilton. One out of every four bullets fired by an American rifle was procured through me. Yet I remain an Englishman and will not commit treason against my country."

"But the bullets we fire are against British soldiers," Alex replied. "Does that not distress you?"

"Of course it does," Church replied. "As it should distress you, and all people with an open heart. To see so many of my fellow countrymen cut down in defense of an unjust policy grieves me, yet neither will my conscience allow me to support continued colonial domination. War is a degrading business all around. Thank God, it's profitable or it would have no use whatsoever."

Alex chuckled along with Church and Stephen, though he was not sure if he should be offended. Angelica's beau was either a shrewd man or a buffoon, he wasn't sure which.

"I make light of a foul situation," Church parried, "but I cannot wait for this war to be over, and to return to England. It is my hope that we can bring a bit of American-style democracy to our side of the pond."

"And Angelica?" Alex responded. "Does she want to bring some American-style democracy to your side of the pond?"

"It is my fondest wish," he said, glancing over Alex's shoulder. Alex turned, but it was Eliza who caught his eye. For the first time that evening she was able to smile directly at him. Alex felt the sudden need to loosen the buttons of his waistcoat; his heart was full to bursting.

The door opened, Ulysses entered with Loewes, the young footman, and after conferring briefly with Mrs. Cochran, pulled a table out from a wall and set it in the center of the room. Louisa and a chambermaid appeared with china, plate, and linens and set it quickly, as the men stood and allowed their chairs to be pressed into service, while chairs were brought for the women's side as well. Mrs. Cochran's wing chair was pushed to the head of the table, and soon enough, everyone was seated in front of steaming bowls of stew.

To Alex's dismay, though, he was seated directly across from Peggy, with Angelica in the middle and Eliza at the far end. Church was seated next to him, and Stephen across from Eliza.

"Colonel Hamilton," Angelica said, almost before they had begun eating, "we have been seeing a great deal of you lately. Or should I say, my sister Eliza has been seeing a great deal of you."

Alex felt his cheeks warm. "Not nearly as much as I would like," he said quietly, and dipped his spoon into his stew.

"Is that so? Then are we to conclude that you have proper intentions toward our sister?"

Alex struggled to keep his spoon steady as he brought it to his mouth. He chewed and swallowed slowly, hoping that someone would speak, but the table remained silent save for the occasional clink of metal and china.

"I would not like to characterize my feelings toward Miss Schuyler in public, if that is all right with you?"

"Dear me, Eliza," Angelica continued, turning to her sister, "I hope he has more gumption on the battlefield than he does with females, or the war is doomed."

Eliza didn't meet her sister's eye or Alex's.

"Like I said, I hope Colonel Hamilton has more gumption on the battlefield than in courtship if he is hesitant to publicly announce his affection. Why, I told Mr. Church he was too old and too short for me the first time we met, and he still told everyone that he was going to marry me!"

"I believe you said I was too fat, too," Church said, laughing and rubbing his belly."I have grown very fond of your *softnesses*," Angelica said coyly, "though take care that they remain firm *softnesses*, as it were, and do not begin to sag. I should not like it if I were seen on the arm of a man who . . . drooped."

"Oh, Angelica, you are too saucy!" Aunt Gertrude said, though it was unclear whether she was amused or outraged. "You would not speak so if Dr. Cochran were here."

"What did she say that was so saucy?" Stephen asked. "She just said she didn't want a man who—" He clapped a hand over his mouth, less than quick on the uptake in social settings.

"I don't know," Alex said now. "I don't think a man should presume too much. A proposal isn't a battlefield charge, after all. It's much more a game of diplomacy."

Eliza smiled at him when he said this, but Alex's gaze was caught by Angelica's. She had the strangest look on her face. Of determination, mixed with chagrin. It was as if she were determined to put him on the spot, yet she also felt guilty about it.

She is under some external pressure, Alex said to himself. *I can only hope she manages to resist it a little more effectively than she has been.*

Alas, after another moment of hesitancy, Angelica drew a deep breath, as if preparing a second salvo.

"The more significant absence tonight is that of our parents, who, though they have some knowledge of Colonel Hamilton—you remember he tried to have Papa thrown in jail last year—do not know nearly enough about him to judge whether he is a suitable candidate for one of their daughters."

"Angelica, please," Eliza said now. "You are being too bold."

Another pause on Angelica's part, another flash of pain on the tightly drawn features of her face. "Sometimes boldness is necessary," Angelica said. "You have never had any sense when it comes to men, and if someone else doesn't look out for you, you will end up penniless and cooking your own food."

It is the parents, Alex said to himself. *It must be.*

"I assure you that I would cook for Miss Schuyler, if it came to that," he said, attempting levity.

"I have no doubt you would," Angelica said, "by which I mean that I have no doubt that you probably *do* know how to cook, as you were raised without benefit of servants or, if I understand correctly, without benefit of family."

Alex's eyes widened. He did not know that he had ever been spoken to so bluntly in his life—or at least since he had arrived in the north—and certainly not by a lady.

"My father . . . *traveled,*" he said, choosing a word that was not, at the most literal level, a lie, "and my mother was taken home when I was quite young. I was raised by friends of the family. My family were but recent immigrants to the West Indies, and alone there, and it was impractical to send me back to Scotland."

"Well, one certainly can't fault your resourcefulness," Angelica admitted. "You have certainly made a name for yourself, and done great service to your country, despite the fact that you come from, well, nothing."

Alex startled and coughed. "I must say, Miss Schuyler, I have never had a compliment feel quite so much like a knife in the bowels."

Angelica colored beneath her powder. "Oh, damn it all!"

Peggy tittered. Eliza gasped. Aunt Gertrude reached for glass and downed it in a single quaff.

"Good God, Miss Schuyler!" Stephen said, the urgency of his words undone by a squeak in his voice. "Have you quite lost your senses?"

Angelica put her left hand on Eliza's right and squeezed visibly, but her eyes were trained on Alex.

"You must know, Colonel Hamilton, how inordinately fond we all are of you. Even my father, whom you tried to imprison, has nothing but praise for the alacrity with which you performed your duties. But I am honor bound to remind you that the Schuylers are one of the oldest families in New York, with connections to the Van Rensselaers, the Van Cortlandts, and the Livingstons on our mother's and father's sides. Your own people do not have the same depth as do ours, neither of blood, nor, more pointedly, of pocket. To see my sister wedded to a man whom she loves and admires would give me nothing but joy, but you can't possibly expect to claim her with a bag of oranges, can you?"

Alex glanced at Eliza to see how she reacted to her sister's words. She was clearly aghast, and Alex took this as a sign that Angelica's words, if ostensibly on Eliza's behalf, were not also at her behest. Peggy and Stephen looked embarrassed, whereas Aunt Gertrude's eyes, when they met his, were positively heartbroken. But the most unhappy person at the table (save perhaps him) was clearly Angelica, and Alex was once again convinced that she spoke on behalf of someone else. It could only be General and Mrs. Schuyler.

"Miss Schuyler," he said then, turning back to the eldest sister, "at the risk of public hubris, may I remind you that I am the chief aide-de-camp to His Excellency, General George Washington, the commander in chief of the Continental army. On his behalf and on behalf of our country, I have corresponded with the representatives of no fewer than four kings, thirteen princes, twenty-one dukes, forty-seven earls, and more marquesses and counts and knights-errant than you could fit on the island of Manhattan. Further, in my defense, my name—*my name*, I tell you, and not my father's or my grandfather's or some other moldering ancestor—*my own* name is known to every American of any distinction whatsoever, from Ambassador Franklin to Thomas Jefferson and James Madison to John Adams, and John Hancock to John Jay. Why, even Patrick Henry and Robert Morris know me by name, and it is by their high standards, and not by a list of names in a kirkyard, that I judge myself, and expect others to judge me."

Angelica listened to Alex rattle off his list with a growing smile on her face.

That put her in her place, he thought. But he had underestimated the eldest Schuyler sister.

"That's quite an impressive roster of names, sir," she said when he had finished. "It sounds like my mother's Christmas card list."

It took Alex a moment to realize she was toying with him—Christmas cards?—but it was not until Peggy tittered and Eliza covered her eyes with her hands that he realized her joke had undone all the work of his list of accomplishments and contacts. The reaction from the others came gradually with Church spitting out an uneasy chuckle while Stephen searched everyone's facial expressions for clues as to how to respond. When Aunt Gertrude joined in with an almost masculine guffaw, Alex realized Angelica's trick had hit its mark again.

But someone came to his rescue. "Oh, come now, Angelica, you know Mama has only ever corresponded with two kings, and one of those was an exile from some Italian isle that is hardly larger than the Pastures," said Eliza, setting the joke squarely back on her sister.

Alex smiled, relieved, and the merriment gradually ran its course and the rest of the evening passed in a noisy swirl of cigars and hard cider. He made the effort to be the bon vivant but Angelica had unintentionally struck his Achilles' heel. It was true; he belonged to no one.

IT WAS NEARING midnight when Alex headed toward the coat closet, steeling himself for the cold outside air. Angelica rounded the corner like a nighthawk and caught his arm, fixing him with a smile that was both challenging and a little sad.

"In truth, Colonel Hamilton," she said, "you haven't got a penny to your name, do you? A pity, for it appears you are quite taken with my sister, and it bereaves me to say that the feeling is mutual. Alas."

And for the second time in his life Alex found himself struck speechless by a Schuyler girl.

24

Mother's News

Eliza's Bedroom

Morristown, New Jersey

February 1780

With Aunt Gertrude tucked away all cozy in bed, Eliza pulled both sisters into her second-floor room. She shook her head and punched a pillow, bouncing on the bed. "Angelica Schuyler!" Eliza began. "What were you thinking?"

Angelica sighed and didn't say anything for a long moment, then pulled a letter from her purse and handed it to her sister in silence.

"You need to hear this, too," she said to Peggy. "It concerns all of us."

It was chilly in the room, and Peggy joined Eliza beneath blankets that had been warmed by a brazier. Angelica slipped behind a screen and began changing into her nightclothes as Eliza read their mother's letter aloud:

"My dear Angelica,

"I write to you as the eldest of my daughters, not because I think that the information I am going to share with you is the sort of thing that a girl of your age should concern herself with, but because there are times when a girl of any age must concern herself with things that seem masculine, or foreign, or otherwise unpleasant. I speak frankly when I say that you are not as intelligent or educated as your sister Elizabeth, but you possess a capacity for captaincy that she, who is independent rather than a true leader, does not. I therefore confide this information to you with the trust that you will see that it is put to its proper use.

"I am informed by General Schuyler that, though the house at Saratoga has been rebuilt and the fields and orchards replanted, the harvests have not yet reached fruition, and as a result the farm is consuming far more money than it is bringing in. General Schuyler has considered selling it, but there is no one in these conditions of uncertainty who is willing to pay even a tenth of its worth, and parting with it would only be cutting off one's nose to spite one's face. Additionally, General Schuyler has not received his stipend from the Continental Congress for nearly two years, and though there is every reason to believe that he will be rewarded amply with land and other in-kind goods when the war is concluded, it is impossible to say when that day will come, or even if it will be decided in our favor.

"What I am trying to say, my dearest daughter, is that we are on the verge of ruin.

"It is therefore imperative that you and your sisters marry immediately, and marry well. In this regard, only Margarita is fulfilling her duty, but Master Van Rensselaer is still some years away from attaining his majority. Though the connections between his family and ours go back several generations, I worry that the Patroon will discover to what circumstances we have been reduced and will call off the engagement. So great is my fear that I urge you not to share this information with Peggy, who has not the discretion the Almighty gave to a screech owl and is likely to unnecessarily share this information with young Stephen, who would then be well within his rights to communicate it to his father."

"Mama!" Peggy exclaimed when Eliza reached this point. "You libel me!"

"Oh, hush," Eliza said. "You know you're an unrepentant gossip."

Peggy hushed. It was true.

"As for you, Angelica, I am going to advise you to do something that directly contravenes General Schuyler's wishes for you and, as such, causes me no amount of consternation. Though Mr. Church's family connections remain hazy to us, as do his business dealings and debts from his time in England, his

successes here in America are plain enough to assess. Even General Schuyler has admitted that, though he dislikes Mr. Church personally, the man is remarkably adept at providing munitions to the Continental army at reasonable prices while simultaneously retaining a handsome profit for himself. I am told by both General Schuyler and other sources that those profits number in the thousands, and as such they outweigh any marks against him. Therefore it is with a heavy heart I am advising you—nay, directing you—to accept his offer of marriage and to finalize the union posthaste. If necessary, you should elope with him, for, though the news will wound your father, the general will take comfort in the fact that you are paired with a man whom you respect, and who can provide for you and ease the lot of his relations."

"Angelica!" Eliza called to her sister behind the privacy screen. "Are you really going to do it? Are you going to elope?"

"Keep reading," Angelica grunted as she writhed free from her dress. "We will discuss everything when you have finished."

"Which brings us to Elizabeth. We sent her to Morristown with the expectation that she would meet some suitable young gentleman among the many officers in General Washington's entourage. But it has come to my attention via Gertrude that Eliza has allowed her time to be monopolized by that nameless and penniless scoundrel

Hamilton, who only last year oversaw the prosecution of dear Papa for crimes against his country, even though he was exonerated on all charges. I do not wish to go into that again.

"Undoubtedly, it is a testament to your father's goodness of character and breeding that he speaks in the highest terms of Colonel Hamilton's intelligence and potential despite that fellow's transgressions against him. Nevertheless, Colonel Hamilton is an unacceptable candidate.

"Suffice it to say, as a woman I judge him with my heart and my purse. My heart does not forgive him for what he did to your father, and my purse hangs empty at my side—he will not fill it.

"In short, he will not do, and since Eliza is making no attempt to find a more suitable beau, I have decided to take matters into my own hands. I have been in correspondence with Susanna Livingston, the wife of Governor William Livingston and mother to your friends Kitty and Sarah. Their brother Henry is the same age as Eliza and has served as aide-de-camp to both General Schuyler and Major General Benedict Arnold, who led our boys to victory at Saratoga and regained for us our once and future beloved estate. Though his efforts on behalf of his country are nothing less than commendable, Mrs. Livingston tells me

that she has seen certain signs of restlessness in Colonel Livingston, and indeed indications of incipient waywardness that suggest he is in want of a wife to cut short these libertine tendencies before they can become true vices. To that end, Mrs. Livingston and I mutually agree that is in both families' best interest if he and Eliza marry immediately—"

"No—!" Eliza cried out, pressing the letter into Peggy's hands.

There were two or three more paragraphs, but Eliza couldn't bear to read further.

"Angelica?" she called in a forlorn voice. "Is it . . . oh, can it be . . . true? Am I to marry Henry Livingston?"

It was Peggy who answered her.

"Mama's letter says he arrives on the twenty-fourth. That is tomorrow. He will only be in Morristown for one week. She wants the business concluded before he leaves."

The business, Eliza thought grimly, *as though I were so many bushels of corn to be sold at market.*

"I have not seen Henry in some years," Peggy said, squeezing her hands, "but Kitty wrote me last winter to say that he had turned out a fine young man."

"He pulled my pigtails," Eliza said dazedly. "When we visited the Livingstons in Elizabethtown when I was eleven. Henry would sneak up on me and pull my pigtails from beneath my bonnet." She looked at her sister forlornly. "That is all I know about my future husband."

"You know he's rich," Angelica said, stepping out from behind the screen. "What more do you need to know?"

Eliza looked up in surprise to see that her older sister had not changed into her nightgown, but into a simple traveling dress in dark wool, without corset or bustle.

"Sister? What are you doing?"

Angelica shrugged. The look on her face was one of defiant resolution. "I am doing what Mama directed me to do: I am eloping."

"What—tonight?! That cannot be."

"John sends the carriage for me at midnight. We will travel to Elizabethtown, and Governor Livingston himself will perform the ceremony. Not even Papa can object, if his daughter is married by a governor. We travel thence to Philadelphia, where John is establishing a base for his business so that it can better cater to both north and south."

"But, Angelica! You cannot marry like . . . like a milkmaid in trouble, in front of a judge in a plain wool dress! You must have a trousseau and a dowry and a wedding at home like Mama and Papa's, in bright silks, with family gathered around you."

Angelica smiled benignly. "That will be your wedding, dear Eliza."

"I will not marry Henry Livingston! I do not even know him."

"That may be so, but you won't marry Colonel Hamilton either. Mama and Papa will not allow it. They cannot afford it."

Eliza was aghast.

"And you can't elope either." This last from Peggy forlornly.

"What do you mean?" Eliza said, turning to her younger sister.

"Mama writes that she worried that you might attempt to run off with Colonel Hamilton, but Papa assures her that Colonel Hamilton's own sense of decorum will prevent such an outcome. She says he feels too much loyalty to Papa as a fellow soldier in the cause of revolution to betray his trust in such a manner. His guilt at being forced to prosecute Papa last year will only reinforce his desire not to further harm a man whom he esteems so greatly."

Even as Eliza turned her back to Peggy's words, she knew they were true. Alex was too honorable to steal a man's daughter, especially the daughter of a man he had been forced against his will to do harm. She was trapped. Besides, as Angelica pointed out at the dinner table, Alex had yet to declare his courtship or define his intentions concerning their relationship, whatever they were.

So now she was going to have to marry Henry Livingston, a boy she had last seen nearly a decade ago, when he had pulled her pigtails until her head was so wobbly she thought it would fall from her neck.

"If he so much as touches my hair now," she said out loud, "I swear I'll cut his hands off."

25

No Guts, No Glory

Continental Army Headquarters
Morristown, New Jersey
March 1780

The news of Angelica Schuyler's elopement with John Barker Church made the rounds of the Morristown encampment with the magical haste of gossip. Upon hearing the news, General Washington remarked to Alex that if he could learn of British troop movements with the same speed as he learned of love affairs, he would have won the war two years ago.

In the long run, few were surprised that the marriage had finally come to pass after Mr. Church's extended courtship. To the degree that people were familiar with the character of Miss Schuyler-that-was, she was understood to be a brilliant young woman who would only accept a husband who could gain her access to the very highest levels of society. And John Barker Church, despite the questions that remained about his past, was obviously the kind of man who could provide it.

If his bearing was not quite as martial or athletic as some other young men's, he had the wooer's gift of giving a girl his undivided attention—of flattery, yes, and the sorts of gifts and romance that the modern girl expects from a suitor—but also of genuine interest in the things that held a girl's fancy. Where another man would be content to charge a lady's maid with procuring a bolt of cloth from which a dress could be made, Mr. Church would not only pick out the fabric himself, but commission a seamstress to craft the most flattering cut for his belle. If a girl expressed an interest in Daniel Defoe's *Robinson Crusoe*, he would gift on her a complete set of the Englishman's work—including even the scandalous *Moll Flanders*!

"They are well met," Lafayette said to Alex when he heard the news. "He will keep her on her toes, but she will keep him honest as well. It will be a tempestuous marriage, but if they can handle each other's tempers, I predict a successful union."

Alex had found the news out from Eliza herself. She had written him a brief note apologizing for Angelica's outburst at the dinner table, saying that her elder sister was feeling the pressure of the coming elopement, which had occurred that very evening. The words were obviously meant to mollify him, yet the note's being addressed to "Colonel Hamilton" rather than to "Alex," and signed "Yours very sincerely, Miss E. Schuyler" instead of "Yours, Eliza" left him on pins and needles. More devastating, she pointedly did not encourage him to visit her or make any mention of coming to see him. Perhaps Angelica's words had had their effect on her?

Regardless of Angelica's motivations for speaking so bluntly to him, Alex knew that she was right. The Schuylers would expect Eliza to marry someone rich. Indeed she, and they, deserved it. The family had worked hard for three generations to establish and increase their status as one of the first families of the northern states, and they would not grant access to their inner circle to just anyone. To be sure, the New World was a place where a man could come from nothing and become a person of great power and wealth. Look at Benjamin Franklin, who had started out a humble printer's apprentice yet became one of the wealthiest men in America.

But Alex had not Mr. Franklin's scientific mind. He would not invent a kind of spectacles or a type of stove, let alone discover something as momentous as electricity itself! He had only his wits—his ability to see through to the heart of a situation quickly and to render that truth persuasively in words. Such a talent boded well for a career in law or in public service, perhaps even newspapering or literature. But none of those paths was a route to quick wealth, and he could not propose to Eliza—let alone to her parents!—on the basis of some hypothetical future success.

However, Alex did have a head for numbers as well. After his mother died, he had been apprenticed as a clerk in the mercantile house of Beekman and Cruger. There he discovered a flair for keeping books and anticipating the movements of the market and knowing when to sell and buy to maximize profit. Alex had been all of fourteen at the time. To him, it was a game, but many men made careers of this kind of trading—and fortunes. It was base work, to be sure, devoid of glory, and full of questionable morality as well. What man wants to make his living peddling the vices of tobacco or alcohol to the besotted, or manipulating the price of vital goods such as grain or mutton so that he would profit greatly while his thousands of customers might lose? But if he didn't do it, someone else would.

And yet . . . could he give up everything just for Eliza? Could he be miserable in business for the sake of a happy wife? And would she be happy, if he were miserable? It seemed to Alex that Eliza did not care for money the way her parents did, or her sisters. It might be that, as a rich girl, she had never had to worry about it, but that was selling her short. She was simply not a material individual, and if she saw Alex throw away his beliefs for the sake of buying her from her family like a piece of livestock, she would lose all respect for him.

There was one other way, but it was uncertain and dangerous to boot. In all the world, for all of history, there has always been—for men, at least—one aspect of their character worth more than money, and that was glory. The kind of glory that only valor on the battlefield can gain. Horses churning beneath a soldier's body as swords flash and rifles sound and bullets cut the air. To risk one's life for a worthy cause—and what cause was more worthy than democracy?—was the kind of endeavor that made a man beloved of his fellow countrymen, and granted him influence in the highest circles, whether it be government or industry or society. Glory brought fortune more surely than an investment in gold bullion or Barbados rum. And unlike those other endeavors, it brought respect, too. The kind of respect that even the Schuylers must surely acknowledge.

And though Laurens and Lafayette liked to tease him for clerking away the war while other men his age risked their lives, Alex had been on the battlefield. As General Washington's chief aide-de-camp, he was never more than a few feet away from the center of command. But a modern general did not ride into the fray like a medieval king. He stood apart, usually on a hill or other prominence, observing the action and directing its course, and his secretaries were likewise sidelined. Alex had been present at battles on a half-dozen occasions, but in every instance save one he had never drawn his sword or fired his weapon. He had instead taken notes—of General Washington's orders, of the enemy's troop movements and the Americans' response, of request for aid or supplies. The rules of engagement prohibited firing on commanding officers (although that didn't prevent the occasional "mis-aimed" cannon from coming dangerously close), but Alex's only real taste of combat had come at the Battle of Monmouth in 1778. When it seemed like Cornwallis's forces would overcome the Americans, General Washington had ridden into battle and Alex had thrown aside his pen and paper and ridden after him. Together they had rallied the American troops and saved the day, and if the battle ultimately ended in a draw, the result was far better than the rout it could have been. Indeed, it was the first time that American troops had met the British counterparts on an equal basis and held their own, and reports of their bravery had inspired other battalions up and down the line.

Alex remembered little about the day save that it had been unbearably hot. Later it was discovered that more than half the men who lay dead on the battlefield were not wounded—they had died not of bullets or bayonets but of the heat itself. General Washington's own horse, a magnificent white charger given to him by the governor of New Jersey, William Livingston, had died of heat stroke, and Alex's own horse had fallen beneath him, from a bullet that could have just as easily killed Alex. The fall knocked him unconscious. His leg and arm had both been badly sprained, though by some miracle neither was broken. When he awakened, he found he had been dragged from the field. His clothes had been soaked in blood, though whether it came from his horse or the enemy he couldn't have told you. His sword was also bloodstained, but he had no memory of running anyone through. He had been brave, yes, but no stories would be told about a man whose own horse had been the one to remove him from battle.

He needed to prove himself once and for all. For himself. For his country.

But above all, for Eliza.

It was just after two o'clock in the afternoon when Alex knocked on the door of the first-floor rear parlor that

General Washington had taken as his private office, and let himself in.

"Your Excellency."

Even seated, the blue-coated figure at the square, paper-covered desk cut an imposing figure, with his erect posture and broad shoulders and thick hair heavily dusted with powder. He did not look up immediately but continued with his writing for some minutes while Alex waited patiently.

At last the commander in chief of the Continental army placed his quill back in its holder. He sifted a little ash over the sheet of parchment in front of him to soak up any excess ink, then blew the ash to the floor and folded the parchment into thirds. On the outside of the letter he wrote a simple large *M*, and then, finally, he looked up at Alex with the letter in his outstretched hand.

"For Mrs. Washington," he said.

Alex had already known to whom the letter was intended. The only correspondent to whom General Washington himself wrote was his wife.

General Washington turned back to his desk and reached for a passel of letters when he noticed that Alex had not left the room.

"Yes, Colonel? Have I overlooked something?"

"No, Your Excellency," Alex said. "That is, I was hoping that I might have a word with you."

General Washington paused a moment, considering Alex's question as seriously as if he had been asked for a loan of a thousand shillings, or his decision on whether or not to execute an enemy soldier. At length, he said, "Tell me what is on your mind, Colonel."

Alex would have liked to sit down, but General Washington was the kind of man who grew only more formal with those whom he spent the most time. There was a joke—a very private joke—that the *M* he wrote on the outside of letters to his wife was not for Martha but for Mrs., which was the only name by which anyone had ever heard him refer to her. Alex took a calming breath before addressing his general.

"It is about a matter we discussed last fall. You said that I should bring it up with you this spring.

"Ah," Washington said, turning to the window. He gazed out over the snow-spotted boughs of an ash tree, and from thence to the fire in the hearth behind him that barely kept the outside chill at bay. "It does not look like spring to me."

"It is the second of March, Your Excellency. The ice is cracking in the Passaic and Hudson Rivers. The war will resume sooner rather than later."

"Indeed," General Washington assented. "I wonder that you are so eager for the resumption of fighting. Most men would avoid it as long as possible."

"I am eager to fight only in as much as the sooner we fight, the sooner we win, and free ourselves from having to fight again."

"Indeed," General Washington repeated. He looked at Alex. "May I assume that you are resuming your petition for a command of your own?"

"I am, Your Excellency."

"You have never commanded a battalion before. Why do you think you are up to the responsibility?"

"As a youthful country, many of our battlefield commanders have assumed their duties with little or no previous experience. I have learned what I know about war from the best of them all."

Something close to a smile flickered over General Washington's lips. "I would disagree with you, but that would mean admitting that I am not the best of our men, which would smack of false modesty."

The story went that the general was a mirthless man, but this was not entirely true. The general's teeth were notoriously rotten, and he was afraid his dentures would fall from his mouth if he smiled too widely, let alone laughed aloud. Certainly no one had ever seen the general laugh aloud. But Alex suspected the general had just made a joke, though whether at Alex's or his own expense, he couldn't be sure.

"I have been present at some of our most contested battles," Alex said now. "I know the enemy's tactics and again, if I may make bold, I know yours as well, not the least of which is your ability to inspire troops with your words and your bravery."

"I could not disagree with the first part of that statement," General Washington said, "since many of my most inspiring words were written by you. But I will say that there is a fine line between bravery and recklessness. A commander of an army cannot be so fearless that he unnecessarily jeopardizes his own life."

"You are referring to Monmouth, Your Excellency?"

"It is not I who refer to Monmouth, but other soldiers and officers who saw you on the field. None would dispute your bravery, but many would question your ardor."

Alex was about to defend himself when General Washington spoke over him. "Many would, but I do not. Monmouth was a messy affair, and at the end of the day, only one thing saved us from defeat, and that was the fighting spirit of our men. I was very proud of you that day."

"Thank you, sir," Alex said humbly.

"But it is difficult for me to conceive of my own role—of this office—without you by my side. Quite simply, you are too good at your job. You make me a better commander, and that is good for our army and our country."

"You flatter me, Your Excellency."

"I think you know that I have never flattered anyone in my life, nor, as I have already indicated, am I much impressed by false modesty."

"Then allow me to speak immodestly, Your Excellency. For as valuable as my services are to you as a clerk, a hundred times more valuable will they be to you on the battlefield, where I can fire off not letters but bullets, and finish off our enemy the only way he will ever truly be vanquished, which is not with ink but with blood. Other men can craft pretty sentences that persuade men to surrender their money or their supplies, but only a few men can persuade men to give up their lives. I believe I am one of those men, and for the sake of my country I would like the chance to prove it."

"Your eloquence *is* persuasive, Colonel Hamilton, yet it also works against you, for true eloquence is far more rare than bravery. I am not convinced that I could replace you and, more to the point, I do not want to."

Alex felt his heart sink, but he pressed on. "Your Excellency," he said urgently, "would you call yourself a soldier if you had never set foot on the field of battle, but only directed men from a protected promontory? Would you feel that you had served a country as great as this one if you had only written letters like a tradesman, ordering troops about like so many bales of cotton or hay? I know you, sir. I have seen you wade into the thick of the action like an enlisted man, and I know that this experience has made you a better general, because you know what is at stake when you give an order.

"Your Excellency," he continued, "this nation has the potential to be something that no other country has been, a beacon of freedom and opportunity. But it is as yet very far from realizing those goals, and it never *will* realize those goals if its men cower behind desks and windows. The war is being fought out there," Alex wound up, "and out there is where I need to be."

General Washington absorbed all of this without giving away a clue as to how it was affecting him. *He must be a formidable opponent at the card tables*, Alex thought.

At length the general turned back to his letters. "I make no promises," he said. "But I will consider it."

"Your Excellency," Alex said, bowing low, then retreating from the room. He knew he would get no more that day.

26

Timing Is Everything

Down the Street from the Cochran Residence

Morristown, New Jersey

March 1780

"That white house in the ash trees is the Ford mansion, where General Washington maintains his office," Eliza pointed, "and that brown house is Jacob Arnold's tavern where many of the officers take their mess, though for the life of me, I cannot fathom why anyone would refer to food by such an unappetizing name."

"If you saw what passed for food in most army camps, Miss Schuyler, you would understand immediately."

Henry Livingston had changed dramatically in the decade since Eliza had seen him last. He had grown into a tall, well-formed young man, with lamb chop whiskers and a thick head of chestnut hair he kept heavily powdered, in the manner of General Washington himself. His eyes were dark and mercurial, rarely resting on one object for long, be it a house or a painting or even the face of a young woman. On meeting Eliza at Aunt Gertrude's house, he had said only, "Well, I guess I won't be pulling your pigtails anymore," and then walked right past her to the pair of portraits on the far wall.

"I say, are these the Brits who used to live here? What a sad lot they look, huh?"

"The Kitcheners," Eliza said.

"I wonder that Dr. Cochran keeps their portraits still." He lifted the portrait of Mrs. Kitchener and peered behind it. "Aha, I knew it. Wallpaper's all faded. Have to keep these here to cover it." He regarded Mrs. Kitchener's face rather longer than he had Eliza's. "Probably wasn't a bad-looking woman in her day. Can only imagine what she thought when she was married off to that old buzzard." He jerked a thumb at Mr. Kitchener. "At least you can say your parents didn't sell you off to an old man, or an ugly one, if I do say so myself."

Eliza stared at him blankly. She had never heard a man speak quite so crudely about the marriage contract—least of all about his own.

"I'm sure our parents were thinking of our welfare as well as our families' when they chose us for . . . for each other." Eliza found it hard to say the words aloud.

"It's a nice thought, but I'm pretty sure ol' Mrs. Schuyler would've made you marry me even if I'd been an ugly cuss twice your age. And I know my mother wouldn't have winked if you'd weighed fifteen stone and drooled when you drank your coffee. 'She's a Schuyler,' she would have said," he mocked, putting on an accent that was even more posh than the one he already affected, "'her bloodline is impeccable.' Well, I'm just glad you're not a hag."

"I . . . thank you?" Eliza had no idea what to say.

"The dress, though," he said, waving a hand at her blue wool jumper. "I'll get Kitty and Sarah to go fabric shopping with you, or maybe just send you fabric. Something more feminine. As a Livingston, you'll be doing a lot of meeting and greeting, and I'd rather no one mistook you for the housekeeper."

Eliza did her best not to gasp.

"Yes, well, my jumper *is* appropriate to the weather. It is not so cold today, and I thought perhaps you might enjoy a turn about the town after your long carriage journey."

"Absolutely." Henry shrugged. "I mean, if you've seen one town on the Eastern Seaboard, you've seen them all. House, house, steeple, steeple, village green, cow patty. But I'm sure you want to show me off." He grinned crookedly, as if he were making fun of himself, but Eliza decided he was just showing off his grin.

An hour later, and Henry's demeanor had not changed. Everything was too familiar, too old-fashioned, and too quaint. The only time he perked up was when they passed the house on the corner of Whitelawn and Farrier Streets, where even at this early hour a soldier could be seen making his way down the alley to the rear entrance, his hat pulled low over his face.

"Well, I know a house of ill repute when I see one," Henry said bluntly. "If you come looking for me in the middle of the night and I'm not in my bed, you might consider asking for me around there."

"Mr. Livingston!" Eliza struggled to regain control of her voice. "I most certainly will not come looking for you in the middle of the night!"

"Oh, I'm supposed to come to you, then?" Henry said, and actually dug his elbow into her ribs. "You'll 'play hard to get' and I'll 'pretend' to ravish you, is that it?"

"Mr. Livingston!" Eliza said again. "I find this line of conversation most inappropriate!"

"Oh, come on, Eliza, I'm only trying to break the ice. We're going to be married in a week."

"Well, we are not married now, and indeed we have only known each other for a few hours. I would appreciate a little delicacy before the secrets of the marriage chamber are thrust upon us."

"*Thrust* being the operative word," Henry said, sotto voce.

Eliza made to pull away but Henry had locked his arm in hers.

"Oh, come on, Miss Schuyler. I'm just teasing. I promise to be good for the rest of our walk."

They continued on for ten more minutes, and if Henry refrained from any more off-color comments, he had not said much of anything else. Indeed, Eliza heard him yawn once.

At length they came to the Ford mansion. Eliza peered up at the stately residence, thinking, *Was it really only a few weeks ago when I was inoculating soldiers against the pox and bantering with Colonel Laurens and the Marquis de Lafayette and dining with . . .*

But she couldn't bring herself to say his name. It seemed impossible that her life could have been upended so quickly.

Oh, Alex, she thought, staring at the front door and willing it to open. *Where are you? What happened to us? Did Angelica scare you away? I have no care for name or fortune; you are more than enough for me.*

To her shock, the door opened and Alex flew out in a whirlwind. He ran down the path, but it was only when he was near the end that he seemed to notice her.

"Miss—Miss Schuyler! I was just coming to see you!"

Eliza's heart was beating so fast that she couldn't actually speak.

"How do, Colonel," Henry said in a mocking rendition of a southern accent.

"Henry Livingston!" Alex said, his eyes going wide with shock. "Is that really you?"

Eliza remembered then: When Alex had first come to the United States, he had stayed with the Livingstons. It was Kitty, Henry's sister, who had first described the young Alex to her.

Eliza couldn't help but notice that the two men did not embrace each other—a brief handshake sufficed. Kitty had described Alex as almost joining their family, but this greeting was not exactly brotherly.

"What brings you to Morristown?" Alex said now. "I thought you were stationed in Connecticut. Are you on leave? Visiting family?"

"After a fashion," Henry drawled. "The powers that be—by which I mean our mothers—have arranged for Miss Schuyler here and me to tie the knot."

Alex's face went blank. "Tie the knot?" he said, as if he didn't speak English.

"You know, get hitched, jump the sword, and become one, as they say in more refined circles." His hand slipped dangerously low on Eliza's hip and he patted her like he was inspecting a horse at the fair. "You are looking at the dam of the next generation of the Livingston brood. Enjoy this waist now, because after eight or ten babies it will be naught but a memory."

"I . . . I . . ." Alex shook his head, looking downright miserable. "I don't know what to say."

"How about commiserations? I mean congratulations, ha-ha."

"I, um, con—" He clearly couldn't bring himself to say it. "Miss Schuyler?"

"The news was quite as much of a shock to me as it was to you," Eliza said, doing her best to keep her voice level. I learned of it only two days ago myself." She forced herself to smile, but it felt like her cheeks were cracking. "You were coming to see me, you said. Had you some news you wished to share?"

"Oh, am I sensing a bit of history here," Henry said now. "Am I spoiling the party, as it were? Never fear, Hamilton, there are plenty more in the sea—for you at least. I'm stuck with this one forever."

Alex's head whipped back and forth between Henry's and Eliza's, as if he still couldn't believe what he was hearing.

Eliza had a sudden urge to strike Henry Livingston, that oaf.

"Your news, Colonel Hamilton?" she prompted, hoping for some kind of a miracle.

Alex turned back to her. He looked at her for what seemed like an eternity, his blue eyes brimming with disbelief.

"I was coming to tell you that I've received a posting," he said finally. "A command."

"A command," Eliza repeated. "You are going into battle?"

Alex nodded. "It is a great honor for me." His eyes bored into hers and it seemed as if he wanted to say more, but that was all he said.

If Eliza went by what her father told her, or what she saw in certain paintings and prints, she would have thought battle was a man on horseback with a sword raised in the air and a standard flying behind him. But, though she had been sheltered from the realities of war, she knew it was a much bloodier business than that—why, think of poor Private Wallace and his missing leg. The idea that Alex was facing similar peril—or even worse—made her knees tremble inside her skirt, and she silently pleaded for Alex to tell her that he would never be in harm's way. But of course he wouldn't do that. He was too honest to lie to her.

Finally, because it was getting awkward, Eliza spoke. "Yes, it is a great honor. Congratulations, Colonel. Your first command, how exciting." She stared back at him, feeling herself tremble all over at the thought of him going to war. *If I cannot marry him, at least let me know that he is safe!* But aloud all she said was, "When do you leave?"

"In two days," Alex said, looking so distraught that she worried he would keel over.

"Two days," Eliza echoed.

"What unfortunate timing!" Henry's braying voice cut in, making both Alex and Eliza jump. "You're going to miss the wedding!"

27

Command Performance

3rd New Jersey Regiment

Amboy, New Jersey

March 1780

S*pringtime!* All across New Jersey, tender shoots of new grass reached for the sun. Amid the delicate green of new leaves, the purplish-pink flash of the first redbud blooms hinted at a change in the air. Birds gathering in the yellow forsythia appeared tethered to a cloud as they heralded in a glorious new season with their songs.

Along the post road, iced-over puddles cracked like broken glass beneath the wheels of wagons delivering morning goods, but by midafternoon the ice had melted into the muddy earth. The last few pockets of snow lingered in the northern shadows of barns where the cows were full of milk, and the farm wives were busy making butter and cheese. The farmers sharpened their plows and oiled their harnesses. It wasn't time to plant yet, but soon, soon.

It wasn't time to fight yet, either. That would come soon enough.

AFTER THREE DAYS of consideration, General Washington had announced that Alex was to be given command of the 3rd New Jersey Regiment. Its previous commander, Colonel Elias Dayton, had been wounded in a skirmish on Bedloe's Island, when his raiding party ran afoul of a group of British soldiers making their way up the Kill Van Kull, north of Staten Island, to sabotage activities in Newark Bay. During the melee Colonel Dayton took a musket ball in his thigh. The wound festered, and gangrene set in before the leg could be taken. Lingering close to death for more than a week, Dayton finally succumbed.

But the 3rd New Jersey would prevail. It was the youngest of the three regiments of the New Jersey Line, having been commissioned on the first day of 1776, three months after the first two Jersey regiments had been formed. Nevertheless, it was quite experienced, fighting in more than half a dozen campaigns, including the Battle of Monmouth, where Alex himself had been injured. It was a typical Continental regiment consisting of eight companies, each with ninety soldiers and a captain.

The plan was to go south.

Reliable intelligence had it that General Henry Clinton, the commander in chief of British forces in North America, had sailed south in December at the head of a massive army of over 8,500 men. General Clinton was believed to have been in Savannah since early in the year, where he had been joined by Generals Cornwallis and Rawdon, who had swelled the British forces to 14,000 men. It appeared the British general had his sights set on taking the crucial city of Charleston, which, in addition to its trading importance, was also garrison to some 5,000 Continental troops.

Colonel Hamilton and the men of the 3rd New Jersey, in conjunction with seven other regiments, would sail to South Carolina and establish a second American position on Sullivan's Island, where in 1776 Colonel Moultrie had successfully defended Charleston against a far smaller British force.

The second garrison would make it impossible for Clinton to lay siege to the forces inside Charleston proper without exposing his rear flank to constant ambushes by the American forces at Fort Moultrie.

SHE WAS GOING to marry someone else. Someone with a name, a family, and a fortune. Of course she was. He had to forget about her. He had 728 men under his command. At first they were no more than a list of names on sheets of paper, but as he perused the litany of Alcotts and Kilkelleys and Williamsons, the Josiahs and Ezekiels and Franklins, Alex had a sense of the awesome responsibility that had been placed in his hands. Each of these men was someone's son, someone's brother, someone's husband—someone's future. And all of them would be risking their lives at his sole discretion. Alex's wisdom would be their salvation. His folly would be their death.

When he got the word from General Washington, Alex poured his heart out to his friend Laurens.

May I say, the news of an imminent reunion with my Dearest Friend is the only thing that consoles me during these dreary days, when I am separated from my adored Eliza not just by a distance of some hundreds of miles, but by the dispiriting prospect of her marriage to that bounder Henry Livingston! Dispiriting, I write, as if I were talking about a loss at cards or a poor yield from an orchard. The truth is, John, I am crushed. So dismal am I that I have bethought myself to decline General Washington's commission on the grounds that I am not fit to assume responsibility for the lives of Seven Hundreds of our boys when I care not a whit for my own. If I had my druthers right now, I would not lead these brave lads but fight amongst them as one of them. I would charge the enemy line with my bayonet outstretched and gorge myself on British blood till they were all strewn about me like a covey of partridge happened upon by a rabid dog, or until I myself was gored and fallen. Indeed, I sometimes think it better that I die in the upcoming battle so that Eliza may be free of me and not have the regret of not marrying me to compound the woes of what I cannot help but conceive of as a difficult marriage. And yet it is a marriage that I have no right to contest, for I have not the fortune nor the name to claim her as my own. Laurens, the fighting cannot come soon enough . . .

And yet, he would still have to wait a little longer.

DURING THE COURSE of the long winter, one of Alex's many tasks was negotiating with Wilhelm von Knyphausen, a general in the army of England's Hessian allies, and the erstwhile commander of British-held New York City in General Clinton's absence, over a plan for an exchange of prisoners of war. After Clinton's departure to South Carolina, Alex began corresponding with the German general. Both sides claimed to long for the prisoner exchange, yet during the four and half years of fighting, no steps forward had been made.

By this point, each side held thousands of prisoners, which was onerous for the captors, but excruciating—and often fatal—for the captives. King George, in violation of the rules of war, had gone so far as to declare that American soldiers should be treated not as enemy combatants but as traitors, and thus were denied many of the protections that were afforded to prisoners of war by international custom. Wallabout Bay off the coast of Brooklyn was filled with the hulks of more than a dozen so-called prison ships—ancient vessels too decrepit to go to sea. Conditions on board were unspeakable, with reports that thousands of Americans had died of starvation, disease, and exposure. Captured Britons were treated more humanely by the Americans, but only to the degree that supplies permitted. This was wartime, after all. It was hard enough feeding one's own army, let alone some seven thousand enemy troops. It would be a tremendous relief to be rid of them, but of course that wouldn't happen if the British did not consent to release a compensatory number of captured Americans.

The negotiations had progressed well, with General von Knyphausen proving more amenable than General Clinton to divesting himself of the responsibility for thousands of captured Americans. No doubt as a mercenary and someone with no national loyalty to England, he took the rebellion less personally than did General Clinton, who seemed not to care how many American boys died on his watch. With spring approaching and with both sides in need of more troops for the resumption of hostilities, von Knyphausen requested a personal meeting to move the negotiations forward. General Washington refused to meet with him, on the grounds that von Knyphausen was not his equal in rank and it would be beneath him to parlay with an inferior.

His Excellency directed Alex to go in his stead.

Alex was torn about the mission. It was, in its own way, an even greater responsibility than command of a regiment, with perhaps twenty thousand lives hanging in the balance. Yet Alex was tired of telling powerful men how powerful they were. It would be tedious work, more a matter for an accountant than a statesman, with dozens of egos to play off and assuage.

He longed for the straightforward heroism of combat. And he also wanted to be away from Morristown, with its constant reminders of Eliza and her upcoming nuptials to Henry Livingston.

But General Washington's directive was not a request—it was an order. Alex had no choice but to delay his journey to Carolina.

So on a chilly morning in early April, accompanied by

Lieutenant Larpent acting as his secretary, Alex set out on horseback for the town of Amboy, New Jersey, a bucolic hamlet at the confluence of the Raritan River and Arthur Kill, across from the southern tip of Staten Island. It was a ride of less than thirty miles, which would take no more than three or four hours on horseback, depending on the condition of the roads.

Along their journey, the crisp air was laced with chimney smoke and the smell of the morning's bread. Housewives and maids tossed seed to chickens, gathering the eggs into their aprons; farmers set off armed with muskets for hunting or axes for felling trees. From a distance, the men and women might have been mistaken for married couples, but on closer inspection, the males were either very young or very old. Every man of fighting age was off at war.

AS THEY TROTTED past yet another frame farmhouse set back from the road, Lieutenant Larpent eyed a shapely milkmaid dragging a stool toward the cow shed. Larpent slowed his horse to a walk.

"It's hard to believe there's a war going on. If you ignore the fact that we're in uniform, I mean."

Alex spoke sharply to the listless soldier. "Were you speaking to me, Lieutenant Larpent?"

From the corner of his eye, he saw Larpent sit up straighter in his saddle.

"Sir! I said, Colonel Hamilton, sir, that it's hard to believe there's a war going on. Everything seems so . . . *peaceful*, sir."

Alex smiled out of sight of the lieutenant's eyes. He had learned from General Washington to ignore the temptation to fraternize with those beneath his rank. It only made it that much harder for them to accept one's orders when the time came. Though Washington often referred to Alex as "my boy," he had never referred to him by his Christian name or offered Alex permission to call him anything other than "Your Excellency."

Alex had adopted the policy for himself. If anything, he found it even more necessary than did General Washington, for he had not the latter's family connections and long history to fall back on to command respect.

"Aye, Lieutenant. It's a beautiful morning. Let's hope the day ends on a high note as well."

"Do you think Knyphausen is serious about exchanging prisoners, sir? It's hard to believe, given General Clinton's refusal to do so, that he would allow one of his subordinates to act in his absence."

"General von Knyphausen tells me that he has full authority in this matter, and that General Clinton is eager to be rid of the headache." He shrugged. "I'd say the chances are one in two that he'll bother to show up, and one in ten that he'll agree to an exchange of any consequence. But it is worth the effort, given the thousands of lives that hang in the balance."

They mulled over the subject until it was exhausted, then lapsed into a companionable silence. Alex's thoughts flitted back and forth between the praise he would elicit from General Washington should he succeed in negotiating the prisoner exchange, and images of Eliza's face framed by an ivory wedding bonnet, saying "I do"—but not to him.

A half hour passed before Lieutenant Larpent cleared his throat and said, "Pardon me? Colonel Hamilton?"

Alex roused himself from his thoughts.

"Yes, Lieutenant?"

"I was just wondering, sir, whether you knew when we would be getting back to Morristown? That is, will it be by tomorrow night, sir?"

"I cannot say with certainty, Lieutenant. If, as I suspect, this is just another overture, our business may well be concluded by the evening, and we can return first thing tomorrow. But General von Knyphausen placed no constraints on our discussion, and if the conversation goes well, it could take several days or more to work out a large-scale exchange."

Lieutenant Larpent sucked in a breath. Alex resisted the desire to scold him.

"Have you pressing business back in Morristown, Lieutenant?"

"Well, not exactly, sir."

"For some reason your 'not exactly' sounds unerringly like 'exactly.'"

"I—sir?" Lieutenant Larpent had clearly not understood Alex's wit.

"What is it that you need to get back to Morristown for?"

Lieutenant Larpent opened his mouth, then snapped it shut. After a long moment, he said in a guilty voice, "Oh, it's nothing, sir."

"Lieutenant, don't make me order you."

"It's just a, well—it's a party, sir?"

Alex's eyebrows raised. He had not heard of any upcoming party for the officers, junior or senior.

"Is there a birthday among the ranks?"

"Eh, not exactly, sir."

"*Lieutenant.*"

Lieutenant Larpent sighed heavily. "It's more of a, well, a send-off, sir."

"I was not aware that any regiment beside the Third had been given marching orders. I would hate to think that a party is being thrown for my own men, and I was not invited."

"It's not that kind of send-off, sir."

"My God, Lieutenant, I think you should take my place in the upcoming negotiations with General von Knyphausen. You can withhold better than anyone this side of an Algonquin brave."

Another squirming sigh from Lieutenant Larpent. "It's more of a, um, a party, sir."

"A party? What on earth could the men be celebrating?"

Suddenly Alex understood. It was a party for Henry Livingston to celebrate his upcoming marriage to Eliza Schuyler.

"I'm sorry, Colonel Hamilton. I shouldn't have brought it up."

Alex wasn't in the mood to be charitable.

"Indeed, you should not have, Lieutenant Larpent. We are on a mission of state. There are thousands of American soldiers festering on British prison ships whose freedom depends on what we do in the next several days. And you can think only of getting drunk on cider and sherry!"

"With all due respect, sir, that's not why I'm sorry I brought it up. I'm sorry because I know how much you love Miss Schuyler, sir."

Alex whirled on Larpent, ready to lash out at him. But the face he saw staring at him sympathetically wasn't that of an underling but that of a boy a few years younger than him, who felt keenly the heartsickness of an admired comrade. Alex's rage melted on his tongue. He brought his horse up beside Larpent's.

"At ease, Lieutenant. I confess I have been rather on edge this last week." He managed a laugh. "So, you feel my pain, do you—but not so much as to decline the invitation of my rival?"

Lieutenant Larpent risked a chuckle. "As you said, Colonel, there'll be all the cider and sherry you can drink. It's been a long winter with nothing stronger than the corn mash Sixth Massachusetts brews behind the Langleys' barn. A man has to treat himself once in a while."

Alex nodded. "Well, then, let's get a move on, and I'll do my best to get you back in time to the celebration."

He spurred his horse, and Lieutenant Larpent kicked his up beside him. "If it makes you feel any better, Colonel," he said as they galloped toward the river, "the troops all think Colonel Livingston's nothing but an empty purse, and you can be sure I'll be drinking his liquor all the while—and having him on in your stead!"

28

Hen Party

The Cochran Residence

Morristown, New Jersey

April 1780

"Oh, Eliza, isn't it thrilling! We're going to be sisters! It is a prospect almost too delicious to contemplate."

Kitty Livingston, Henry's older sister and Eliza's friend since the earliest days of their childhood, had been tasked with throwing Eliza a little celebration of her own. And here it was, coming off as something of a failure

Due to such short notice and Kitty's lack of acquaintance with the local mademoiselles, she had been unable to round up any guests besides herself and Peggy and Aunt Gertrude, who was now sleeping soundly over in the wing chair next to the fire.

To make up for the lack of guests, however, Kitty had dressed herself in enough fashion for ten women. Her wig was so tall it would have made Madame de Pompadour jealous, and her heavy makeup was done in exquisite grisaille.

Her face and décolletage had a silvery sheen, so that she looked like Pygmalion's statue of Galatea come to life in all her perfect beauty, polished yet nubile.

Her dress was a separate work of art. Acres and acres of laurel-green silk moiré embroidered with the most ornate arabesques of saffron and oxblood, the tones muted yet exquisitely deep, like sugar candies tinted with mint and lemon and cherry. The bustle was three feet wide and the skirts twice that, so the only spot she could find to sit was in the middle of Aunt Gertrude's longest sofa, which was so crowded with Kitty's dress that no one else could join her. Eliza thought perhaps Kitty had done that on purpose.

"Can you imagine, Eliza?" trilled Kitty. "One day soon we'll be able to send out invitations that proclaim 'Catherine and Elizabeth Livingston and their husbands wish to invite you to Liberty Hall to officially open the season at Elizabethtown' and 'Catherine and Elizabeth Livingston and their husbands invite you to—'"

"But, Kitty," Eliza interrupted her. "If it's 'Catherine and Elizabeth Livingston and their husbands,' won't your surname be necessarily different after you marry?"

"Oh, I've already thought of that. I've always said that I'd refuse to marry anyone less distinguished than a Van Rensselaer or a Livingston—or maybe a Schuyler, though Philip is a little too young for me to wait around for," she added with a wink at Eliza. "And since Peggy seems to have snatched up *the* Van Rensselaer to have, I've set my eye on a couple of cousins on Papa's side."

"Oh, Kitty," Peggy said with a laugh. "You speak of a husband as though he were a long-term investment, like a parcel of land to be cleared and sowed with some slow-growing orchard crop."

"And isn't he? How old was Stephen when you began to reel him in? Eleven? Twelve? You have been playing that boy as expertly as a courtesan."

"Kitty!" Eliza clapped her hand over her mouth. "You go too far."

"You think I'm speaking ill of dear Peggy, but I'm complimenting her. Your sister will be the richest woman in the United States. If," she added slyly, "she can ever get him to propose."

"And what makes you think he hasn't?" Peggy said coyly.

Like Kitty, she had gone full stop for tonight's party. Even though the ever-thrifty Catherine Schuyler had slashed her daughters' dress budgets, Stephen was constantly sending his beloved bolts of the most exquisite silks from Europe. Her dress tonight was made of a shocking orange damask, a color that Eliza would have thought no living girl could pull off. Yet Peggy had gone the extra mile, having her maid dye her hair with ancient Egyptian henna, giving it dramatic umber tones. Piled up high, it sat atop her head like the crest of some exotic bird from the jungles of South America, perhaps, or one of those elegant long-legged cranes that wade through the shallow waters of southern wetlands. The summery palette highlighted the rosy hue of Peggy's skin, which was sprinkled with enough flecks of mica to rival Kitty's silvery sheen.

"Has he proposed?—oh, do tell!" Kitty urged, jumping ahead of herself. "I know he is not yet of age to access his fortune, but you could always elope like Angelica did and wait until he is twenty-one. That is, assuming his parents don't disinherit him."

"Disinherit him?!" Peggy said.

Eliza was unclear if her sister was outraged or merely pretending to it.

"For marrying a Schuyler!" Peggy laughed out loud. "The Van Rensselaers should be so lucky as to join their family to ours!"

"Aren't you already related to the Van Rensselaers? On Mrs. Schuyler's side? Or perhaps Mr. Schuyler's? Or both?" asked Kitty.

"Mama was a Miss Van Rensselaer, and of course a Livingston on her mama's side. Papa's mother was a Van Cortlandt, not a Van Rensselaer."

Eliza couldn't help but laugh. "Oh dear, we are so related, it is a wonder that we do not turn into those poor Habsburgs, marrying cousin after cousin until we start giving birth to misshapen idiots."

Eliza had meant her words to come out in jest, but there was enough truth to them to cause Kitty and Peggy to stare at her in incredulity.

"Oh, Eliza, you are too morbid, even for yourself!" Kitty said at last. "Come let us have a bit of fun, as I know my brother certainly is!"

KITTY WAS REFERRING to Henry's festivities, which were going on in full force near the officers' barracks several blocks away. Henry had invited every officer from the rank of lieutenant on up—some one hundred men, most of them under the age of twenty-five, and all eager for one last party before the war went hot again with the return of warm weather.

Earlier in the day when she was out for a stroll, Eliza had seen dozens of casks of beer, cider, and sherry being rolled into the long stone barn that housed the C infirmary.

Curious enough, she had peeked in, only to find that all the beds had been cleared out. The four cast-iron stoves had doubled to eight, and large stacks of firewood were piled beside each of them—enough to heat the large space moderately for a week, or to keep a single party raging all night long.

"Pardon me, Corporal," she'd said, pulling aside one of the enlisted men setting up the party. "But—where have all the patients gone?"

The corporal had blushed deeply. "You will forgive me, miss, if I decline to answer that question on the grounds of decency."

"And you will forgive me, Corporal, if I tell my fiancé, Colonel Livingston, that you declined to assist a lady."

"Ah, Miss Schuyler, I didn't know it was you. I do apologize." He blushed. "Colonel Livingston had us take the sick to the house on Whitelawn."

"The house on—" Eliza's jaw dropped. "You mean, the one on the corner of Farrier Street?"

"Aye, Miss Schuyler. Now if you'll excuse me, Colonel Livingston said that if we get the party set up by sundown he'll let us have a cask of cider for ourselves."

"ELIZA?" KITTY'S VOICE cut through her reverie. "Are you all right? Or is it just the thought of the momentous cusp you stand upon that has you so preoccupied?"

Dazed, Eliza looked up at her friend—her cousin, her dreadful fiancé's sister.

"Cusp?" she repeated. "A cusp is the top of a hill whereupon one can see clearly in every direction. This is not a cusp. It is a . . . it is a cliff, a drop into some unfathomably deep and foggy abyss. And, and—and below it all, I hear the thunderous roar of waves crashing upon rocks, like those that dashed Prospero and Miranda upon Caliban's island!"

"Eliza!" Kitty said sharply, placing her hand on her friend's knee. "You are overwrought! I tell you, you must calm down, dear. It is a marriage, for God's sake, not a shipwreck!"

"Isn't it, though?" Eliza said glumly.

"Sister!" Peggy spoke up. "You insult our cousin!"

"It's . . . *acceptable*," Kitty said, though the color had come into her cheeks, visible even beneath her makeup. "I-I understand that you haven't known Henry long enough to love him. I even know that Henry can be . . . difficult, but I promise you, I know all his secrets and his weaknesses, and once I've shared them with you, you'll have him under your thumb in no time. And Papa is grooming him for a career in politics, which means that he'll spend most of his time in Philadelphia or New York or wherever they decide to place the capital, so you'll hardly have to deal with him at all!"

"But is that what a marriage *is*?" Eliza said. "Learning how to 'manage' your husband so that he doesn't oppress you? Praying for his departure rather than yearning for his return?"

"My word, Eliza, everyone always said you were the sensible Schuyler sister!" Kitty laughed. "And here you are, mooning about romance like some latter-day Juliet. Listen to me, Cousin. We live in a new country—a country that will be larger than any in Europe by three times, and with unlimited possibility for expansion. And we are our country's gentry—its kings and queens, princes and princesses, dukes and duchesses, its barons and earls and—"

"I am quite familiar with the order of ranks," Eliza snapped. She did not appreciate the turn this conversation had suddenly taken.

"Then you are also familiar with our responsibilities." Kitty fluffed up her enormous flounces. "Yes, we command great prestige and power and wealth compared with the rank and file. But we also owe a duty to our position in society. The common man and woman are free to marry whom they choose based on nothing more than base physical attraction, but we are bound to make unions that preserve our fortunes and estates, which provide the structure and indeed the occupation on which plebeian lives depend."

Peggy tittered.

"Indeed," Eliza said, turning to her sister. "And no offense intended, Peggy, but I've heard Stephen wax on about his holdings and tenants more than once."

"No offense taken. He does tend to go on and on about the patroonship."

"But," Eliza continued, turning back to face Kitty, "isn't that what we're revolting *against*? The unfair advantages of aristocracy? The tyranny of a distant king deciding one's fate based on what suits his interest, rather than one's own?"

"You talk of politics, Eliza. That is men's business." Kitty took a long pull from her glass and banged it down on the side table. "We are women. We tend to the home front."

"And why should that be?" Eliza demanded. "This is a new country, as you say. Why shouldn't it have new laws, new customs? And why should not those customs extend to the home itself. To—to love!"

For the first time this evening, Kitty's expression cracked, though her makeup almost managed to conceal it.

"I sense your heartache, Eliza," she said finally. "The news of your flirtation reached us, too. You mourn the loss of a great love that you think could have surmounted the difficulties of rank and fortune. And I agree, he is quite a charming bastard—in every sense of the word. However, I must point out that Colonel Hamilton never proposed to you. You may have thought love conquers all, Eliza Schuyler, but he knew the rules of the game."

Eliza steeled herself for Kitty's next words.

"And the truth is, dear sister-in-law, even Alexander Hamilton realized he wasn't good enough for you."

29

Tortoise and Hare

Continental Army Headquarters
Morristown, New Jersey
April 1780

The meeting with General von Knyphausen had been a wash. Alex was unsure whether the acting commander even bothered to come to Amboy, but when it was conveyed to the British contingent that Colonel Hamilton would be negotiating in General Washington's stead, a terse note arrived from the British warship docked so boldly offshore: General von Knyphausen would not meet with anyone other than General Washington. To parlay with an underling was beneath him. It was, Alex reflected, the same language General Washington had used when he refused to meet with General von Knyphausen.

These aristocrats! Alex thought with some annoyance. *Their infatuation with rank and face make their own lives ridiculously difficult! And even worse, they don't recognize how it inconveniences the lives of the rest of us.*

Although in the case of thousands of prisoners of war, *inconvenience* seemed like a deeply inadequate term. While generals and colonels jockeyed about whose sleeves were decorated with the most epaulets and tassels and stripes—as if rank were measured in gold thread!—their privates and ensigns and corporals huddled in rags in prison cells and work camps.

All in all, not a great day for diplomacy.

But what made everything worse was that now he had no excuse to stay away from Morristown, which meant that he would be in town when Eliza married that Livingston bounder—not in the actual church, perhaps, but it was right across the square—and he would hear the bells ringing and see the throngs of well-wishers cheering on the new bride and groom from his windows. He tried to delay the journey back to headquarters, but Lieutenant Larpent was in such high spirits about making the night's entertainments that he wouldn't be held back, and Alex, though miserable, was not so mean-spirited that he could spoil his assistant's fun just because he himself was not going to partake.

It rained the whole way, adding insult to injury. The roads were a soup of mud, and even though their mounts were as eager to be out of the chilly drizzle as their riders, they refused to move beyond a canter, lest their hooves slip out from under them in the mire. The journey to Amboy had taken but three and a half hours. The slog back to Morristown took more than six. By the time the men arrived, they were sodden and iced to the bone. Alex charged the grooms at the stables with brushing out their weary mounts until they were thoroughly dry and serving them a double ration of oats, and then he and Lieutenant Larpent hurried as fast as their chilled bones would carry them to the Ford mansion. Despite the exhaustion of the journey, Larpent was still excited for the party, but all Alex could think about was grabbing a few bites to eat and crawling beneath the covers.

Alas, when Alex and Larpent entered the Ford mansion, they found it deserted and frigid, the fires gone cold in their grates. The larders had been stripped bare of comestibles and beverages. Even the bottle of cognac Lafayette had given him before he went off had been pilfered from its hiding place beneath a loose floorboard in his bedroom.

When Alex was absolutely certain that there was not one thing to eat or drink in the house, nor even a single coal to start up a fire, he turned to Lieutenant Larpent with a rueful smile on his face.

"Permission to speak freely, Lieutenant."

Larpent looked at him with confusion. Alex was his superior officer. He need ask for nothing from him.

"Uh, permission granted . . . sir?"

"God damn his soul to hell!" Alex said, and collapsed atop his bed.

"Oh, sir!" Larpent cried out. "Buck up, sir, it's not so bad. Here, look, just let me get some tinder and I'll have a fire going in no time." He raced from the room and down the stairs, returning shortly with a tinder and twigs.

Alex hardly noticed him. He had shucked off his wet coat

and rolled himself in his blanket like a caterpillar wrapping itself in silk, his head buried beneath his pillow. With one half-open eye he watched as Larpent knelt before the grate, expertly arranging wood shavings and splinter into a neat cone, and then striking the flint against steel in steady streams of sparks.

The men had lit a lamp when they came in, yet Larpent seemed content to start the fire from scratch, and on just his fifth spark a little glow appeared in front of him. He blew on it gently. The glow grew and sprouted a little tongue of flame. Larpent fed splinters of wood to it, with the delicacy of a farmer feeding an abandoned weanling, then twigs, then small branches. Within minutes a small fire was crackling in the grate, and a pile of larger logs suggested that the blaze would grow to a conflagration quickly.

"I must say, Lieutenant, you light a fire with admirable alacrity."

"We didn't have servants to light fires for us when I was a boy on the farm, sir. As the younger, I was charged with lighting the stove in the mornings while my father and older brother tended to the cows."

"No mother to attend to the task?"

"Alas, sir, my mother died giving birth to me. My father never found a suitable replacement."

Alex could feel the fire warming the tip of his nose, which was all that poked from the covers. He pushed the pillow back, feeling the warmth on his cheeks, his forehead.

"I, too, lost my mother when I was very young, though I was blessed to have her in my life for its first decade."

Larpent nodded. "I sometimes think that's worse. Having a mother, then losing her. My older brother and father miss her to this day, whereas I only wonder what she would have been like. Excuse me, sir," he said then, and walked quickly from the room. He was back a moment later with a pair of towels.

"If we don't get out of these wet clothes and dried off, we'll catch our death of cold."

Alex knew he was right, but part of him didn't care. He had failed at today's mission, had failed at securing a command, had failed at winning the hand of the girl he loved. When he came here as a fourteen-year-old, he had been told by everyone he met that he was going to be a great man. But all he had managed to become was the secretary of a great man.

Larpent went to look for dry clothes and came back several minutes later dressed in a mismatched and somewhat ill-fitting uniform.

"Cadged from Weston's, Tilghman's, and McHenry's tack, I'm afraid," Lieutenant Larpent explained. "Not even General Washington himself could command me back into my own uniform. Now, let me see if I can find us some provisions," he said and left the room.

Alex changed out of his wet garments and into the dry ones. He was a miserable human being still, but at least one who didn't feel like a drowned rat.

Larpent returned with a frown. "Not much here but salt beef and crackers," he reported.

Alex didn't respond. A moment later, Lieutenant Larpent cleared his throat.

"I say, sir, why don't you come along to the party? There'll be food there and wine and good cheer, and you look as though you could use all three."

Alex couldn't help but laugh. "Go to my rival's pre-wedding celebration. Yes, that does sound like a fine time."

"You won't have to see him, Colonel. The party's in the barn by Gareth's Field. It's a huge building. You can keep as far from him as you like."

Alex just laughed again. But then something came to him. "Wait. You said the barn by Gareth's Field. The stone barn?"

"Yes, sir," Lieutenant Larpent answered.

"But that's the barn being used as the C Infirmary, is it not?"

"Yes, sir. It's my understanding Colonel Livingston had the wards moved to Miss Jane Dawdry's establishment for the evening."

"To . . . a . . . brothel?!" Alex roared. "Are you joking with me, Lieutenant?"

"Ah, no? Sir? Colonel Livingston said that even the sick and injured need to have some fun."

"This is outrageous!" Alex said, jumping up and dropping his blanket and rushing to his wardrobe. I'll have him court-martialed! I'll have him flogged! I—" He stopped in front of the open doors. "I'll call him out."

"Sir?" The shocked word dropped Lieutenant Larpent's lips like a dribble of chaw.

"I'll call him out!" Alex hurriedly pulled on his pistol. "I'll challenge him to a duel. Don't you see, if he's dead he can't marry Eliza!"

"Sir, please," Lieutenant Larpent said. "Calm down! I don't know that a breach of protocol, if that is indeed what you are calling him out for, necessitates a duel, sir. Isn't it simply something for a military tribunal?"

"Then I'll make him call me out," Alex declared. "I'll go to his own party and insult his honor and integrity in front of his own guests. He'll have no choice but to challenge me to a duel. You know these milquetoast aristocrats! They cannot bear to lose face in front of their peers, but even less so in front of their inferiors."

"Sir, please," Lieutenant Larpent pleaded as Alex stuffed his feet into his boots. "I don't think this is a good idea. It will look like—"

Alex turned sharply on the lieutenant. "Like what, Lieutenant?" he demanded.

Larpent's chin trembled as he answered. "Like you are manufacturing a reason to duel him. Like—" Larpent bit back a gulp. "Like murder."

"It's not murder if *he* calls *me* out," Alex said, striding from the room. "It's proof of how unsuitable a mate he is for any gentlewoman. Arrogant, quick-tempered, foolish . . ."

"Forgive me, sir." Larpent panted as he hurried along after Alex. "But do you not see how all those words could describe you in this moment, sir? She chose *him*, sir. For whatever reason, she accepted *his* proposal, and not *yours*."

Under ordinary circumstances Alex would have wheeled on the man and dressed him down until he was a quivering ball of jelly. But Larpent was right; Eliza had accepted

Livingston's proposal, while he, Alex, had never even proposed. It suddenly dawned on him. *That was it!* He had never told her what he felt about her. He had never formally presented his suit, never courted her properly.

He had let her sister cut him to the quick, and Angelica was right. He was penniless. Without a name or family. Who was he to think he could be worthy of such a girl as Eliza Schuyler? An American princess.

But the thought of that bright, wonderful girl marrying that slug filled him with an intoxicating brew of anger and hope that he picked up his pace, grabbing his damp hat from the tree in the hall and dashing out the front door.

Maybe it wasn't too late. Maybe he could still do something about it. Call the man out, duel him for her honor.

It was his last chance to save Eliza. To save himself.

BUT THE DAY wasn't done with him yet. After a brisk, rain-soaked trot of some twenty minutes, Alex and Larpent reached the stone barn, his assistant pleading with him all the while to see reason. Alex burst through the doors into a throng of men in various states of disarray and undress. The cavernous space blazed with heat from Colonel Livingston's appropriated stoves, and a spicy fog of alcohol and sweat laced the air. The revelers were clustered in three distinct throngs.

Alex scanned the leering faces, looking for Colonel Livingston's, but saw no trace of him. He made his way to the second group of men, then the third, but though he saw two scantily clad lasses dancing for tips and kisses, he found no trace of Henry Livingston.

Suddenly Corporal Weston's face appeared before his. His cheeks were rosy with heat and his speech was addled by alcohol. "Colonel Hatilmon!" he exclaimed. "I mean, Curling Hallinom! You ma'e it to the par'y!"

He grabbed Alex by the shoulders and would have bestowed a slobbery kiss on him if Alex hadn't pushed him back.

"Corporal Weston!" he demanded. "Have you seen Colonel Livingston!"

"Corna Who?"

"Livingston!" Alex shouted, trying to make himself heard through the noise of the fog and Corporal Weston's drunken stupor.

"Corna Livy-ston?" Corporal Weston laughed. "Never met him!" He held up his glass. "But I'll drink a toas' to him. Here's to Corna Livy-ston, whoever he is!" He swilled a gulp of some frothy lager.

"But this is his party!" Alex persisted.

"Livyston's party? Oh, right-right-right!" Weston said, nodding his head enthusiastically.

"Where is he, then?"

"Not a clue. He's gone. Definitely gone!"

"Gone! But isn't he to be married to Miss Schuyler tomorrow?" Alex demanded, his frustration rising.

"Miss Schuy'er!" Corporal Weston, his eyes lighting. "She's a beauty, in't she!" And then, unbidden: "She eloped!"

"What?" Alex gasped. "It was Miss Angelica Schuyler who eloped. I refer to Miss Elizabeth Schuyler."

"Don't tell *me* no," Corporal Weston said with great outrage. "I know Miss Angelabeth, Miss Elizica, Miss"—he took a deep breath to steady himself—"Miss Elizabeth Schuy'er, and I know she eloped. Gone since yes'erday mor'ing."

Alex could only stare at the corporal in shock.

"Miss Elizabeth Schuyler," he said at last. "Eliza. She—she's already married? You are certain?"

Corporal Weston nodded cheerfully, as if he were delivering the most felicitous news in the world.

"Miss Schuy'er," he said dreamily, even as his eyes flitted to one of the dancing girls, who had wrapped her shawl around the waist of a shirtless soldier and was using it to pull him behind her toward a ladder that led to the hayloft. "Wouldn't've minded a trip to the haylof' with the general's daughter myself."

Alex's jaw dropped open, but his fist was faster. A moment later, Corporal Weston was sprawled unconscious on the stained planks of the barn floor, a drunken smile still plastered across his rapidly swelling lips.

Alex stared down at the man in surprise. He had not thought that punching a man in the face would make him feel better, but in fact it had.

Pivoting on his heel, he stalked out of the barn into the rain.

30

Taking Liberties

The Cochran Parlor

Morristown, New Jersey

April 1780

The "party," such as it was, was over. Kitty Livingston's coachman, who had spent six hours asleep in a shroud of blankets, had been awakened and clambered sleepily up into his box, to save Kitty the trouble of having to walk a quarter mile to the house she was staying in with her brother and mother, who had come west for the wedding. She had taken Peggy with her, saying Eliza needed a bed to herself on last maiden night, while Aunt Gertrude, who had had perhaps one glass of Madeira too many, had taken herself rather unsteadily up to bed, while Eliza remained downstairs to supervise the lone housemaid still awake in the cleanup of the party.

There was little to do. Dinner had been eaten and cleared more than four hours earlier. The furniture was pushed back into its usual arrangement, the coals banked in the fire, and then Eliza had urged Louisa to get a few hours' sleep before the madness of the wedding day should dawn.

She, however, remained in the parlor, which was still quite warm, and, taking the lamp near a bookshelf, rummaged through until she came across an edition of Richardson's *Clarissa*, which she and Angelica and Peggy had taken turns reading aloud to one another some years ago, when they felt the first stirrings of romance in their hearts. She pulled the first volume from the shelf and flipped through idly for some minutes, until at length a passage leapt out at her, bold on the page despite the dim light cast by a single wick.

> *I declare to you, that I know not my own heart if it not be absolutely free. And pray let me ask, my dearest mamma, in what has my conduct been faulty, that, like a giddy creature, I must be forced to marry, to save me from—From what? Let me beseech you, Madam, to be the guardian of my reputation! Let not your Clarissa be precipitated into a state she wishes not to enter.*

Eliza sighed. She remembered the passage well, of course. She and Angelica and Peggy had each taken turns declaiming it, competing to see which of the three could be the most dramatic, the most forsaken, the most imploring. Now she wondered whether the passage had appeared as some kind of sign, telling her to follow the truth of her heart and flee this marriage, or whether it was simply the idle workings of her mind, looking for an author's eloquence to express feelings she was too despondent to put into words.

She could run, she told herself. It would be like Angelica's elopement, except instead of an escape *to* marriage, she would escape *from* marriage. The Schuylers had not the ready access to cash they had had before the war, but there was still enough money to get her to Philadelphia, where she could find Angelica and John Church and persuade them to let her reside there until such time as Henry had abandoned his suit. She would take a job, as a governess perhaps, or a schoolteacher, or even as a lady's maid. She would depend upon neither father nor husband to determine the course of her life. She would be free to pursue those great inalienable rights that Mr. Jefferson had enshrined in the Declaration of Independence: her own life, her own liberty, her own happiness.

But even as a brand-new sort of life flashed before her eyes like a series of paintings in a gallery, she knew the images were no more real than pigmented oils applied to canvas. She was Eliza Schuyler, after all. The middle sister. The sensible one, whose intelligence was steady where Angelica's was cunning, whose beauty was human where Peggy's was statuesque. She was the daughter of whom Papa had remarked when she was but seven years old, "A part of me does not mind if I never have a son because I have Eliza. She has a boy's fortitude and ingenuity without the terrible vanity that afflicts our sex." Even after Philip was born and had lived past the childhood illnesses that took almost half of the Schuyler children, Papa always said to his namesake and heir, "Take care that you follow your sister Eliza's example, and you will never bring shame on the family name."

Because when all was said and done, she was a Schuyler, and she was proud of it. Her family had been present at the birth of this country under the Dutch and had seen it through its first great political upheaval when the English took over, and now were seeing it through to independence. She didn't want to run from that legacy. She wanted to add to it, to build on it, to help make the United States be what it wanted to be, a place where all souls—black as well as white, and female, too—could realize their full potential, regardless of the circumstances of their birth.

So she would not run. She would stay. She would do her duty. She would hold her head up high, and no one would ever reproach her.

And would it be so bad? Eliza understood that Angelica had chosen John Church not for his jawline or waistline, but because he was attentive to her, and would give her access to the society she craved. They would build a good life together—the life that Angelica wanted. And Peggy had been corralled into allowing Stephen Van Rensselaer to court her for two and half years now, though he was too young and too earnest. Yet he did dote on her, and he was kind, and when they finally married, Peggy said, it wouldn't be a case of two strangers awkwardly maneuvering around each other, but of two friends progressing in a relationship that had developed for years—although in this case one of the friends had carefully shaped the other into exactly what she wanted in a mate, certain that he would treat her as the drone treats the queen bee, attending to her every need. Eliza was twice as resourceful as Angelica and Peggy. If they could mold their men, then why couldn't she?

But the heart of the matter was simple. She didn't want to marry Henry Livingston when she was desperately, helplessly, in love with someone else. Someone who, while he had wooed and whispered sweet nothings into her ear and had hinted at the depth of his feeling and affection, had never declared himself. Had never asked her aunt and uncle for permission to court her, and as Kitty had pointed out, he had never proposed or made his intentions clear.

His reputation preceded him. Alexander Hamilton was a tomcat and a flirt, and she had fallen for him anyway, but it didn't make a difference, as he was nowhere near. He was gone, to the 3rd New Jersey Regiment, to battle and to glory, had left town without looking back once.

SUCH THOUGHTS AS these were flitting about her head when she heard a sound in the rear of the house, near the kitchen. One of the servants, she thought, sneaking in for a bite to eat now that the mistress is asleep. Or who knows, maybe it was Kitty and Peggy. But a moment later she heard a heavy clatter of crockery and, even through two closed doors, a pained curse followed by a self-mocking laughter.

Eliza placed her book down and took her lamp to the hall. Cool air swirled about her and she pulled her shawl over her bare shoulders and chest.

"Hello?" she called in a low voice, not wanting to wake anyone upstairs—if indeed they had not been awakened already.

The kitchen door swung open, and a man's face appeared. It staggered unsteadily toward her, but only when it was a few feet away did the light reveal who the visitor was.

"Why, Colonel Livingston! What on earth are you doing here?" *Besides being intoxicated,* she added to herself.

Henry placed a sweaty hand on the wallpaper to steady himself.

"What? Eliza? Have I wandered into the wrong house in error? All these colonials look the same." But even as he said that, a smile flickered across the edges of his mouth, and she knew he was pretending.

"I think you should not be here, Colonel. It is bad luck to see the bride before the wedding, for one thing, and for another we have a long day tomorrow, and both of us could use some sleep to restore us from the excesses of our celebrations."

"Celebrations, eh?" Henry slurred.

"We had some hot chocolate," said Eliza.

"Chocolate! Of course. Eliza the sensible Schuyler. Plain dresses, no wigs, not even a bit of décolletage to give us something to look at." And as he spoke, his free hand darted forward and swatted at Eliza's shawl, dragging it roughly from her shoulders.

"What! I spoke too soon! Look at those, I had not realized you were so . . . blessed!"

Eliza knew she should be shocked, yet she felt an eerie calmness descend upon her. Henry's actions were so far beyond the pale that condemning them was almost beside the point. What she needed to do was disarm him.

"It is quite chilly here in the hall. Let's go into the parlor, where the fire still burns. I can make you some chocolate."

Without waiting for answer, she turned and headed back into the parlor, fixing her shawl as she went.

"Chocolate? No, thanks," Henry groused, falling onto the sofa where Kitty had held court less than an hour before.

"Miss Livingston was nice enough to bring several tins from her latest trip."

"Kitty?" Henry's head whipped back and forth, as if his sister might still be in the room. "She is overfond of European luxuries, that one. I tell you, Liza, if there's one thing I'm looking forward to at the end of this war, it's kicking out all the foreigners. All the Brits and Germans and especially the French, with their dandy men and frosted women. Give me good, solid, earthy American men and women, unpowdered, unwigged, and, hell, unwashed."

Eliza winced inwardly at Henry's profanity, but kept her face calm. She handed him his cup. Caught unawares, he started coughing, his cheeks reddened and his forehead sprouted drops of sweat.

"What is that?" he said when he could speak again.

"Chocolate, as I said," Eliza said demurely, reaching out with the pot, which she had brought with her, to refill Henry's cup. "It's a little bitter, but warming."

"This is terrible," Henry panted, tossing back a second shot, which went down smoother than the first. "You women were drinking this?"

"Yes."

"My God! I underestimated you. You must have the constitution of a goat."

"I think it's lovely," Eliza said, even as she leaned forward with the pot once more. "More?"

"No!" he said, spilling half its contents on the chintz fabric of the sofa.

"Whoa, what happened?" His head lolled around his shoulders. "I feel as though we are in a dollhouse, and a little girl is shaking it in a tantrum."

"The room feels quite still to me," Eliza said. "Perhaps you ought to lie back and close your eyes."

She took his cup and saucer from him and set it on a small table placed before the sofa; even as Henry allowed himself to fall against the back of the sofa so heavily that his hat, which he had not removed, fell off his head and disappeared behind the sofa. His eyes drooped and so did his jaw, while the fingers of his right hand pawed weakly at his cravat, yet could not seem to remember how to untie a knot.

Eliza sat very quietly, waiting for what she assumed would be the inevitable sound of snoring, at which point she would make her escape. And indeed one loud snort tore from Henry's throat, but the sound seemed to startle him awake and he lurched from the sofa unsteadily, kicking the table before it and smashing it to splinters. The porcelain cup went flying, crashing loudly against the floorboards.

"Worse!" Henry moaned. "Oh, lying back makes it so

much worse." He fell forward, catching himself on the side of Aunt Gertrude's wing-backed chair. "Poison!" he moaned. "You have poisoned me!"

Eliza thought to say that she and Kitty and Peggy had all drunk the chocolate without any ill effects, but when Henry looked up at her, suddenly she saw a strange leer in his eye, and her words died in her throat.

"It was all your plan, wasn't it? To lure me here and take advantage of me?"

"Take advantage of you how?" Eliza said drily. "Braid your hair like a little girl's, and paint your lips like a courtesan's?"

Henry giggled uncontrollably at this image, so much so that Eliza thought he was going to fall backward into the fire.

"You are funny! And saucy! I think marrying you won't be so dreadful after all. If I promise to always stay drunk, do you promise to always inflame me with that naughty tongue of yours?"

"Inflame you? Is your ego so damaged that you take insults as entreaties?"

Henry giggled, but a little less certainly, as he tried to make sense of her words. Then, quite before she knew what was happening, he had lurched across the parlor and half leapt, half fallen upon her.

"Don't pretend you don't know what you're doing. We men like to think that you girls are all innocents who know nothing about the world, but I know better. You little minxes are always trying to control us to satisfy your own craven pleasures. And you know what I say? I say satisfy them!"

His hands pawed at her shoulders and his glistening lips made for hers. She turned her face away in disgust and felt a wet smear across the side of her chin and neck.

"Colonel Livingston, have you quite forgotten yourself? You are a gentleman, and my fiancé as well. You degrade us both with this behavior!"

"You're right," Henry slurred, pulling her close when she attempted to slide free. "I am your husband. By this time tomorrow we will be married, and then the law itself will compel you to submit to me. So why not submit to me now. Start your marriage right: by giving your husband what he wants."

He grabbed at her, and Eliza heard fabric rip as she pushed him away. For the first time she began to be afraid. With another strong push, she was able to get out from under him, and she stood up quickly. Her fingers closed around something of their own accord. She looked down and saw it was the pot of hot chocolate.

Eliza thought of calling out, but to whom? Kitty and Peggy were gone and the servants had retired to their quarters. Only Aunt Gertrude remained in the house, and assuming she even heard Eliza through her alcohol-laced slumber, the prospect of such a reputable woman being confronted with Henry's scandalous behavior was even more shaming than having to suffer it herself.

She sat up straight and summoned a breath.

"It is time for you to go, Colonel Livingston. If you wish to salvage this marriage, and indeed your reputation, you need to leave now."

"Or what?" Henry said in an ugly, amused voice. "You'll hit me with a porcelain pot?"

He took a step toward her, and she took a step back.

"I'll do it!" she cried, raising it. "Don't think I won't!"

"Oh, I think you will," he said, taking another step toward her. "That's what I like about you—you've got spirit." He laughed at his weak pun. "This is going to be fun, breaking you in. Now come, give your fiancé a kiss."

31

Heroes and Villains

Outside Infirmary C

Morristown, New Jersey

April 1780

The rain had stopped while Alex was at the party, but it didn't matter. His change of clothes was as wet as the uniform he'd worn during the ride from Amboy. Only his feet were dry, protected in the sturdiest pair of boots that man could make, and his face, shielded by a tricorne that could have withstood an Atlantic crossing. No rain got past that formidable hat, but he had worked up a sweat in the barn, though whether it was from heat or agitation was anyone's guess.

Married, he thought. *Eloped, just like her sister*. It didn't seem possible.

He let his boots choose his path. Morristown was gently hilled, and his tired legs skirted the bases and avoided the hills, taking him by more farms than houses, which had been built on higher ground to enjoy the advantage of light, breeze, and view. The great trees that had been left behind when the land was cleared were still leafless but somehow heavier of limb, as their thick sap began to run in anticipation of spring. Their branches cast shadows as heavy as down blankets on the fields and pastures, which lay bare in the moonlight, awaiting the kiss of the plow. The houses were on the small side, but finely made, and sparingly but elegantly appointed with handsome cornices, their chimneys as dormant as the fields at this late hour, though a faint tang of wood smoke still hung in the air. All in all, it was a picture of American handiness and probity, one that filled Alex with pride that he had chosen this side in the war, when he could have just as easily defended the land and traditions of his parents. This continent had put its stamp on him, whether it was the Indies or the northern colonies, making him a person from the New World and an American through and through. If in the future the buildings grew larger and more numerous, Alex hoped that the American cities would never lose this sense of modesty and hardiness.

As for his own hopes about the newly married Eliza? *Gone. All my plans—all my love—undone at a stroke. Married already, and to that cretin.*

A figure emerged from beneath the shadow of one of the great maples. Alex thought to duck away to avoid human congress, but a thin male voice, not yet done with the slide whistle of adolescent tunes, halloed:

"Colonel Hamilton?"

He didn't recognize the speaker until he was closer,

however, and the sight filled him with a strange mixture of jealousy and tenderness.

"Mr. Van Rensselaer," he called. "You are up late."

Stephen was young enough that Alex would have been well within his rights to call him Master Van Rensselaer rather than Mr. Van Rensselaer, to say "up past your bedtime" rather than "up late," but he wasn't feeling much like teasing anyone at this moment.

"As are you, sir. Are you coming from Colonel Livingston's party?"

Alex turned on him sharply, but there was no trace of enmity in the boy's voice. He was too young to realize that his words might sting. Might make their hearer want to pull his sword from its scabbard and slice off the head of the speaker.

"Aye," he said, "Colonel Livingston seems to have commandeered every bottle and every plate of food in camp. Lieutenant Larpent and I went there upon our return from Amboy to get something to eat. Were you there? I didn't see you."

Stephen nodded. "A strange party. The host was never seen by anyone."

That's because he's off being married somewhere. Although the marriage would have taken place hours ago by now. By now, he was—

No, Alex told himself. *Do not think of it. It is uncharitable of you and will just torment you more.*

"Indeed," was all he said to Stephen. "Though his guests seemed to have had a good-enough time. I suppose they need it. It has been a long, hard winter, but I fear a harder spring."

"So I understand. The war seems to be shifting to the south. You yourself are to lead the Third New Jersey to Charleston, I hear."

Alex laughed. "I should be shocked that you know that, given that you are not a soldier, let alone an officer."

"I would enlist!" Stephen said defensively. "Papa forbade it, but I went anyway. But when I got to camp the sergeants refused to accept me. They said my father's money was more valuable to them than his son. Apparently he pays a lot for the privilege of keeping me alive through this war."

"You are young, Master Van Rensselaer," Alex said in a teasing but tender tone. "There will be plenty of other wars. You may yet die in one of them."

Stephen laughed, his adolescent voice cracking again, and Alex continued: "I must ask, though, how did you learn of my assignment? Although it is not exactly top secret, still, it is surprising that it should have circulated so quickly outside of officers' ranks."

"My fiancée is a general's daughter and rather gifted at wheedling secrets from even the most reticent men. Not as good at keeping them, however," he added, laughing.

"What, your fiancée! Is it official, then?"

Stephen slapped his cheek. "Look at me! Teasing Peggy for gossiping even as I fall guilty of it myself. It must be the beer," he added, though Alex smelled no alcohol on his breath. "Well, yes, since the cat is out of the bag: I asked her some months ago, and she accepted me. We are keeping it a secret, though, because I am not yet of age. My father has approved the marriage, but General Schuyler is rather strict about his daughters' prospects. I think he doesn't approve that I am not in uniform since I am already seventeen, even though my own father has made it impossible for me to enlist."

"General Schuyler is a man of such great honor and wherewithal that he sometimes fails to realize not all men can act with his independence. He will come around." Alex cuffed the boy on the shoulder in a brotherly way. "Congratulations."

"Thank you, sir," Stephen added. "And may I add . . ." His voice caught nervously.

Alex thought he knew what he was going to say. "It is not necessary, Mr. Van Rensselaer."

"Perhaps not. But I would still like to say that I would very much have enjoyed having you as a brother-in-law. We would have made a fine trio, you, me, and Mr. Church. They would have called us the Schuyler husbands, I think."

It was a moment before Alex trusted himself to speak.

"They are a unique set of girls, it is true. Formidable as individuals, but terrifying together. A set of modern-day Furies. But not as vengeful I hope."

"And without the snakes for hair, thank heavens," Stephen said, laughing. "And look, they have called us to them without our even knowing."

Alex looked up, and there indeed was the Cochrans' handsome home. All its windows were dark save for those in the downstairs parlor.

"Someone is up late there as well."

"They had their own party for—" Stephen's voice broke off nervously. "Peggy told me it was just her and Kitty Livingston."

"Kitty Livingston," Alex mused. "You know, she was the first American girl I met."

"What an introduction!" Stephen said. "I'm surprised you didn't run back to the Indies."

"Indeed. I wasn't sure if I loved her or wanted to run in terror. She is like the three Schuyler sisters rolled into one, yet she hasn't the . . . restraint that they have. It will be a strong man who marries her, or else—I say, it seems rather agitated in there."

Shadows thrashed about behind the drawn curtains, as if some sort of melee were taking place within.

"Could it be the maids, cleaning up the party? Modern girls, you know," Stephen said. "Anything we can do, they have to do better, just to prove they can—"

He was cut off by the sound of a crash from within.

"That is no party!" Alex said, rushing forward. He vaulted the picket fence and ran to the front door, Stephen hard on his heels. His fingers clutched at the front doorknob, but it was locked.

"Stop!" a familiar female voice called out from within, clearly in distress.

"Eliza!" Alex yelled. He shook the door, but it refused to open.

"Let's try the back," Stephen said. "Peggy said the servants—"

But Alex was already running around to the rear of the house. He stumbled through some bush and nearly fell, but soon enough made it around, where he found the rear entrance hanging open. He dashed through, Stephen right behind him. In the kitchen beyond the floor was a treacherous field of broken crockery.

"My God!" he said to Stephen. "It looks as if a raiding party has broken in!"

They ran into the hall, where the sounds of feminine agitation could be heard more clearly, and from there into the parlor, where he was shocked to see Eliza thrown back on the sofa, while over her stood—

"Colonel Livingston?" she said. "Someone is here."

Henry turned around with a snarl on his face. "Get out of here, Hamilton. She's not your concern anymore."

Alex was upon him in an instant. Henry tried to gather himself, but Alex hit the taller man with a hard jab to the jaw before Henry could he even raise his fist. He spun wildly and crashed to the floor.

Alex leapt on him. "You miserable cur," he yelled, rolling him over and pummeling the splotched face with blow after blow.

"Alex, stop!" Eliza called behind him. "You'll kill him!"

He felt hands on his shoulders. It was Stephen, pulling him back. It was all he could do not to throw the boy off him. Henry made no move to get up now, but merely curled himself into a ball, hiding his face and moaning like a piglet separated from its mother.

"He deserves to be killed," Alex said now. "In fact—" He gathered a breath. "Henry Livingston, I challenge you to a duel in defense of the honor of your wife!"

"My wife?" Livingston barked a laugh. "Not quite yet!"

Alex turned to Eliza, his heart in his throat. "Is it true?" he asked hoarsely.

"Is what true?" she asked, mystified and shaken.

He wanted nothing more than to take her in his arms and comfort her, but he had to know for sure before his agitation got the best of him. "What he just said. You are not yet married. You are still Miss Schuyler, then?"

"Pardon?" Eliza said. "Of course I am. Why would you . . . ?"

"That damn Weston," Alex said. "He was so drunk that he told me you had eloped."

"No, that was Angelica."

"I thought so, but he repeated it, so—"

"I always thought Corporal Weston a bit dim," said Eliza.

Alex shook his head angrily. "Never mind. You will never have to marry him now. I will kill him before sunrise." He turned back to Henry and kicked him with a muddy boot. "Get up, Livingston, and meet your fate."

"Alex, no!" Eliza said, and he thrilled to hear his name spoken by her so intimately. "He didn't know what he was doing . . ."

Eliza didn't believe her own words, but she was desperate to defuse the situation, lest more violence ensue.

"That scoundrel knew exactly what he was doing. And he must be made to pay for it."

"She's right," Stephen said. "You cannot challenge him when he is in this condition. It is not honorable. If you did shoot him, you would be tried for murder."

"But I want to kill him!" Alex yelled. "I want to see him bleed to death before my eyes."

"As do I," Stephen said, looking at Alex with great sympathy. "But you will have to wait till he is himself again. Anything else is beneath your dignity."

"I care not a whit for my dignity," Alex said, but he knew Stephen was right.

"It doesn't matter," Eliza said. "I could never marry him now."

"You think he will release you from your engagement? You do not know these Livingstons as I do," said Alex. "If Henry released you, he would be admitting wrongdoing. And his father would never let him do that. William Livingston would rather have a dead son than a son with a cloud hanging over his head."

"But what if he doesn't die?" Eliza said. "What if *you* died? He is a soldier, too. He can shoot, too. What if he kills you? I can bear him getting away with this attack, but your death—that I couldn't bear. Please, Alex."

Alex looked down at her, and suddenly, she was in his arms. He didn't know if she had moved or he did. It was all he ever wanted, all he ever dreamed. She was not yet married. She was—*she could still be*—his.

He turned to Stephen. "Throw Livingston out on his face. If he tries to get back in, stab him."

WHEN THEY WERE alone, Alex finally spoke the words he had kept inside for so long. "Oh my dearest, it has been torture. I cannot bear the thought of you marrying him! I should have spoken sooner, but I was afraid I was not worthy of you."

"My darling," she said. "Do not despair, I will break it off myself." She laid her head against his chest. "I'll run away. You'll find me, and we'll elope. We'll flee to the west and live beyond the frontier. In a cabin or beneath the open stars. I don't care. Just as long as I'm with you."

He tilted her chin up and looked her in the eyes. He had wanted to do this since he saw her in her simple gown in Albany at her mother's ball. He had dreamed of this moment, and at long last, he bent down and their lips touched.

It was just a moment, but Alex felt all the fatigue and dampness leave his body.

He kissed her with all his heart and soul, and she melted under his embrace, kissing him back, so eagerly and so tenderly he thought he would die right there.

"I will be with you, Eliza," he said in a husky voice. "Whatever happens, I will always be with you."

32

Best of Aunts and Best of Women

The Cochran Residence

Morristown, New Jersey

April 1780

The following week passed in a blur of tension.

Eliza was able to put off the wedding by claiming illness. It helped that Aunt Gertrude was the most well-known nurse in the Continental army, and her uncle, even though he was away, was personal physician to the commander in chief. No one seemed to suspect her claim, and in fact she was so shaken, she couldn't get out of bed the next day or for days after that. She trembled anytime she heard a loud noise.

"It is unconscionable!" Aunt Gertrude said when she heard the whole story, a bit embarrassed too many glasses of wine had seduced her to sleep through the entire encounter. They gathered in the parlor a day and a half after the incident to discuss what to do next. "In all my life I have never heard of a gentleman behaving so outrageously. And no word from him still—no apology, no withdrawal of his engagement. Nothing!"

"He is no gentleman," Stephen declared. "I have a good mind to call him out myself."

"Absolutely not!" Peggy shrieked, causing Eliza to jump. "This assault is terrible enough, but to lose you on top of it!"

"Nor could I," Eliza said. "You have acquitted yourself with immeasurable dignity, Mr. Van Rensselaer, but Colonel Livingston has been a soldier these past four years and is bound to come off better in a duel. But even worse, if you were to duel, then the causes of the conflict would receive a public airing, and I simply couldn't bear that."

"This talk of duels is nonsense," Aunt Gertrude said now. "Boys posturing and preening. This is a simple matter. I shall write Colonel Livingston and demand that he rescind his proposal for your hand. He will have no choice but to withdraw. Honor compels it."

But apparently Henry did have a choice—or he had no honor—because less than an hour after Aunt Gertrude had sent a servant to deliver her letter to the Livingstons' rented house, a note came back in Susannah Livingston's own hand.

Dear Mrs. Cochran,

It is my understanding that some regrettable actions took place night before last when both my son and your niece celebrated perhaps a bit too much on the eve of their nuptials. It is one of the little-discussed casualties of war that the absence of our husbands and fathers lends a certain lawlessness to our households, and in this atmosphere our young people are not as well chaperoned as they would normally be. Henry tells me that when he mistakenly entered your husband's house yestereve—one white house looking rather like another when one is in a strange town—he was greeted by your niece in rather revealing attire, which he in his impaired condition interpreted as an invitation to behavior unseemly for a lady to commit to words. It would seem, then, that the fault for the altercation lies with both parties, and the most prudent thing for us to do in the absence of either paterfamilias is to put the incident behind us, and proceed with the union as planned. I gather that Miss Schuyler has been taken ill, but as soon as she is well enough to stand it is my fervent wish that the marriage take place, and we allow our young people to get on with the important business.

Yours very sincerely,
Mrs. (Governor) William Livingston

"Of all the—" Peggy was rendered speechless by the note, which Aunt Gertrude read out loud to her and Eliza. "Does she dare to insinuate that my sister is somehow to blame for being attacked?"

"She does not insinuate it, Sister," Eliza said wearily. "She says it straight out. Henry is her son, after all. I suppose it makes sense—"

"Stop," Aunt Gertrude interrupted her. "Never ever, ever make excuses for a scoundrel. The fault is entirely his, and anyone—even a mother—who defends it is equally to blame. 'Mrs. (Governor) William Livingston.' What pretentious poppycock!"

Eliza was first shocked, and then, for the first time since the attack, amused. She had always known Aunt Gertrude to be an unconventional, independent woman, but she never guessed that she carried quite this level of bile in her. She felt exceedingly grateful that she was under this remarkable woman's protection.

"Let us write Mama and Papa, then," Eliza decided. "It will take at least a week before we hear back from them, but we can say my condition has taken a turn for the worse. It is a lie, but a white lie, and I shall do penance for it later."

The letter to the Schuylers was duly sent, along with a second, surreptitious note that Eliza slipped to the footman when he went to post the first. The second note was to Alex, but to her dismay, Loewes brought it back with him upon his return.

"I am told that Colonel Hamilton has not been seen since the night of his return from Amboy," the footman said, tactfully not referring to the parties that had ended in such disaster. "General Washington is said to be furious. The spring campaigns are about to get underway, and Colonel Hamilton's absence is a great handicap to their organizational abilities."

"What?" Elisa said fearfully. "Has no one any idea where Colonel Hamilton has gone?"

"None, I'm afraid, but if you like, Miss Schuyler, I can continue to make inquiries."

"Please do," Eliza begged. "But do be discreet. I do not

want to compound an already scandalous situation by dragging him into it."

Loewes was gone much of the rest of that day and the next, and at least he was able to return with some positive news. Colonel Hamilton had been seen at the coach station in the wee hours of Wednesday morning, where he had requisitioned one of the mail horses. Last seen he was galloping north.

"North?" Eliza repeated. "But he knows no one in the north. Such friends as he has in North America—Colonel Laurens and General Lafayette and a few others—are all in the south."

"The clerk on duty said that Colonel Hamilton gave no hint as to his destination, but he did ask where he could change horses, and the clerk told him that the next stop on the Albany Post Road was at Boone-Towne."

Albany? Could it be...? Was Alex going to see...her parents?

But Loewes was still speaking.

"That said, Miss Schuyler, the clerk informed me that Colonel Hamilton never made an appearance at the Boone-Towne station, so it is entirely possible that he asked his question only to throw any pursuers off his trail."

Eliza didn't know what to think. Nor did she have much time to consider it, for the following day—a Monday—she had a rather unexpected visitor: Governor William Livingston himself.

The governor appeared in the late morning. He came on his own, on foot, and from the way he halloed at the people who passed him by on the street, you would have thought he was merely taking his morning constitutional, or even campaigning for reappointment.

But once the maid had shown him into the parlor, and Aunt Gertrude and Eliza had joined him, his countenance immediately turned sour.

"Mrs. Cochran," he said, addressing Aunt Gertrude, though his condemning gaze rested upon Eliza, "this siege has gone on almost as long as the British occupation of New York. It is time to surrender."

"Surrender, you say?" Aunt Gertrude repeated in an incredulous voice. "And is this how you would have your son commence his married life—with a bride he first attempted to defile, and then coerce into marriage? I wonder that you are not ashamed even to make such a request aloud."

"Mrs. Cochran," Governor Livingston said in a tight voice, "out of respect of your and your niece's femininity, I will not respond to such charges as I normally would. But I must insist that you do not slander my son's name even in such limited circles as these. He has his reputation to think about, after all. What occurred was regrettable, but it was a moment of youthful indiscretion, complicated by the pressures of war and the debilitation of alcohol. You cannot think this behavior representative of my son's character, let alone my family's."

"I cannot think anything else," Aunt Gertrude said, speaking on behalf of Eliza. "Such behavior cannot be seen as exceptional, but as the true measure of a man's character."

"This is my son you are speaking of, Mrs. Cochran," Governor Livingston said coldly. "I would ask that you consider your remarks."

Aunt Gertrude was unbowed. "And I would ask that you consider yours. You have raised a scoundrel, sir, and all of Morristown knows it. He moved seven injured men from their beds in the infirmary for the sake of throwing himself a party. To a house whose reputation I cannot bring myself to utter in the presence of my niece! It is a miracle none of them died."

"But none of them did die, and neither was Miss Schuyler harmed on the night in question. Let my son do the chivalrous thing and marry your niece, despite her own rather base attempts to slander his reputation."

Aunt Gertrude guffawed.

"I must say, Governor Livingston, I'm rather shocked you would invoke chivalry now, when it was so sorely lacking from your son's heart and actions several days ago. And as for reputation, the drunkard, rascal, and bounder whom you call a son is more than capable of staining his honor without the assistance of a couple of feeble ladies."

Governor Livingston's face turned beet red. "I have heard quite enough," he said, barely able to control his voice. "Miss Schuyler will present herself at my house on Thursday afternoon, exactly one week after the originally scheduled date, where she will marry my son in the presence of his family and of such of hers as are in Morristown, and that is my final dictate."

"Or what?" Eliza spoke up now. "You'll drag me there by my heels? I can only imagine how that will look."

Governor Livingston turned on her coldly. "Do you think I have no ammunition at my disposal, Miss Schuyler? Your family's financial troubles may not be generally known, but I can assure you that I know them and can destroy General Schuyler's reputation with but a few well-placed asides. Your elder sister has already caused a scandal by eloping with a British rascal who many believe to be a spy for King George, and your younger sister has all but been sold to the Van Rensselaer child so as to save your family's fortune. You yourself were known to have consorted with Colonel Alexander Hamilton until but directly before you announced your engagement to my son. Do you think that anyone will believe you did not throw over your paramour for the sake of our family's money? Your family may not have any money left to lose, but there are still many other things that can be taken from you."

Eliza was rendered speechless. She could only stare in shock at this, the most powerful man in the state of New Jersey, threatening to destroy her entire family for the sake of a petty grievance.

Aunt Gertrude also didn't say anything. However, she did stand up and go to a small escritoire on the far wall. She opened a drawer and pulled out a case, which it took Eliza a moment to recognize. It was her aunt's medical case—the same one in which she had once carried the supplies for the smallpox inoculation. She opened it now and pulled out a small vial—the same type of vial that had contained the inoculum.

She turned back to the governor and walked toward him slowly.

"Do you know what this is, Governor Livingston?"

"How should I know what that is?" Governor Livingston replied haughtily.

"Indeed, how should you? Despite your high station, you are in many ways a terribly ignorant man. This," Aunt Gertrude continued, holding up the vial with a flourish, "is a tincture of the great pox itself."

Governor Livingston gasped and drew back.

"Madam! You cannot be serious."

"Serious? Furious is more like it. That you could come into my house and speak to my niece with such effrontery. It is even more disgraceful than your son's action. No doubt we all now know where he gets it from. Well, I shall not have you in my house any longer. Either you leave this instant, or I uncap this vial and pour it all over you."

Governor Livingston stood up and stepped behind his chair.

"You wouldn't dare!"

"Wouldn't I? You have attempted to corner a mother hen, Governor. Yet there is no animal fiercer than a mother who fights to protect her young, and I think of Eliza as the daughter I never had."

"Madam, I implore you—"

"I am an old woman," Aunt Gertrude cut the governor off. "My hands have started to tremble of late, and in my agitated state who knows what might happen. I would suggest you leave before an accident occurs."

The governor hung fire for one more moment, then turned and ran out the door.

Aunt Gertrude turned to Eliza with a smile. Eliza drew back in horror at the vial, which sat carelessly in her aunt's hand.

"Aunt Gertrude! Do be careful!"

"Relax, dear, it's just smelling salts."

Eliza stared in disbelief for a moment, and then collapsed into the sofa in relief.

"Aunt Gertrude! You are a hero! Whatever else happens, I will always have this memory."

"I don't expect it will keep the governor at bay for long. I do wish we would hear back from General Schuyler. There is only so much a woman can do on her own."

Eliza nodded her head, but it wasn't her parents she was thinking of.

Where is Alex? she asked herself for the thousandth time. *How could he have left me now, when I need him most?*

As if he'd read her mind, Loewes entered the parlor. The footman had a concerned look on his face.

"Yes, Loewes, what is it?" Aunt Gertrude said in a commanding voice.

Loewes grimaced. "I just thought that Miss Schuyler might like to know that the horse Colonel Hamilton requisitioned from the mail coach was found yesterday."

"Found? What do you mean, found?"

"It wandered into the Boone-Towne station. It was still saddled but quite riderless. I'm afraid, Miss—I'm afraid there was quite a bit of blood on the saddle."

33

Ambush

The Post Road

Outside Boone-Towne, New Jersey

April 1780

After four years of army life, Alex had come to know a bit about men—the good, the bad, the heroic, the unspeakable. He had met Henry Livingston's type before. He knew that when Henry Livingston awoke in the morning, if he had any memory of what he'd done, he would find a way to blame it on Eliza or on alcohol. On anyone but himself. Which is to say, there was no way a man like Henry Livingston would do the honorable thing and release Eliza from her engagement. The Livingstons were a venerable clan, but perhaps too proud. They, too, would be more inclined to sweep the affair under the rug rather than admit wrongdoing. No, if anyone was going to put an end to this disastrous union it was going to be the Schuylers.

It was up to him to get to them in time.

Albany was some 140 miles from Morristown. If Alex rode

all night and through the following day, he could reach the Pastures by nightfall Thursday evening. He would need multiple horses, though, which meant commandeering them. The mail coach would have an ample supply, and as a colonel on General Washington's staff, Alex should be able to pull rank and commandeer one. No doubt he would be chastised for it when all was said and done, but this was the last chance to win Eliza. He would risk anything—even his career.

It took ten minutes of pounding before the station clerk opened the door, and another ten minutes before Alex was able to make it clear what he wanted and that he wouldn't take no for an answer. Ten minutes later he was mounted on a gray Arabian—the fastest horse in the stable, the clerk said.

A three-quarters moon lit the road, which the horse seemed to know quite well. Alex knew the road, too. It was the same route he had traversed almost every day for a week in February, when he was waiting for Eliza to show up. He settled into the saddle and let the horse have his head. He had been awake for nearly eighteen hours at this point, and already logged some thirty miles on horseback that day in the journey from Amboy and had been twice soaked through. He was exhausted, sore, and chilled, but alternating waves of anger and passion drove him on. An hour went by, then another. The moon sank low in the sky, and a hint of light appeared in the east. Not dawn, but its promise.

Alex didn't remember seeing the horses appear on the road ahead of him. Afterward he realized they must have come from the thick forest that shrouded the west side of the road and were crossing it to get under cover of the trees on the other side, but when he first saw them he had the impression that they had appeared out of thin air.

I must have fallen asleep, he thought.

The riders seemed as surprised by his presence as he was by theirs. They pulled up short, the horses' noses still pointing west but the riders' faces all turned south, to stare at him. Then he understood: Their faces were covered by kerchiefs.

Bandits!

He pulled his horse up short, but it was too late. The three riders had spurred their mounts toward him, and before he was able to turn around, they were on him. He had seen their muskets come unslung as they rode toward him and ducked down against his horse's neck just in time. He heard the crack of a gunshot and the whiz of a musket ball past his ear. A moment later he felt a searing pain in his shoulder and realized the ball must've grazed him as it flew by.

The shooter would not be able to reload on horseback, but there were still two others. Alex knew he was an easy mark as long he was mounted, and so threw himself off his horse on its lee side. The Arabian was agitated but stayed in place, even as Alex pulled his musket free. He stepped quickly from behind his horse, aimed at one of the two riders trying to get a bead on him with their muskets and fired. A shower of blood haloed the rider's masked face, and then he fell from the saddle.

As he fell, though, the man's greatcoat slipped open, and Alex saw a flash of crimson within.

Redcoats! They must be on a raiding mission from their

base on the island of Manhattan. It was incredibly daring of them to come this far. They must have been after some very big prize indeed.

The two remaining riders were on him now. Alex kept his horse between himself and his attackers, especially the one with the drawn gun; as they wheeled around the Arabian, Alex stabbed blindly with the bayonet mounted on his musket's muzzle. He missed the rider but felt his blade sink into the quivering muscle of the horse's croup. The animal was more frightened than hurt and reared back on his hind legs, sending its rider sprawling to the ground.

Alex didn't hesitate. He fell to one knee and drove the bayonet into the exposed red breast of the second raider. The rider had dropped his musket. Alex wasn't sure whether it was loaded or not, but he threw his own musket aside and grabbed it anyway. The remaining rider was wheeling around for a final charge, holding his musket in front of him like a lance, not planning to fire it.

Alex had the one loaded weapon remaining. He lifted it to his shoulder and took steady aim. The rider bore down on him in a clatter of thundering hooves. Alex waited until he was sure he couldn't miss, and then fired. The rider flew off the back of his horse as though his head had been caught in a wire. The riderless horse charged on, though, and Alex had to throw himself out of the way. He landed painfully on his wounded shoulder, which tore and throbbed all at the same time.

He forced himself to get up, his fingers scrambling for a weapon. But it was unnecessary. Three prone figures lay on the road, none of them moving. The Arabian had run off, but two of his attackers' horses remained. Though he was desperate to get on with his private mission, he knew he would be remiss in his duty if he did not at least search the three men who had attacked, since they were clearly spies of some sort. Two of them were devoid of anything other than common implements of war, but the third had a passel of folded papers in his hand, one of which was sealed with wax bearing the stamp of the Contintental army. There were perhaps a dozen officers in the entire army who commanded such an insignia. It wasn't his purview—and was probably above his station—but he couldn't stop himself from opening it. "*My dear Major André*," he read, followed by a list of American troop movements. But the signature at the end was the most shocking part of it all: "*Yours very sincerely, General Benedict Arnold.*"

Alex couldn't believe what he had found. Evidence of treason involving one of the most decorated American heroes. And with John André, no less, that handsome British officer who had nearly swept Eliza off her feet at the same party where Alex met her. He couldn't believe that he had stumbled across such a momentous discovery, and knew he needed to report it immediately. But other business called him north. Reasoning that André would not be able to act without this intelligence, Alex assumed he had a day or two before he was truly derelict in his duty. And who better to report treason to than another general?

Limping slowly and mouthing soothing words, he made

his way to the nearest one. Its nostrils flaring at the scent of blood, it was clearly an experienced warhorse, waiting cautiously while he approached it. Alex found he couldn't heave himself up with his right arm, and so had to pull awkwardly with his left, but eventually managed to get himself into the saddle, still warm from the heat of its last rider.

He took one last look at the three spies strewn across the road.

"No one will ever believe this," he said and, spurring his mount, jumped over the nearest corpse, and resumed his journey north.

THE NEXT THING he knew he was waking up in an exquisitely soft feather bed. His shoulder ached and his vision swam, but when he could focus again he saw the handsome trappings of a well-appointed bedroom, a boy's room, judging from the articles of clothing he saw here and there, and the musket and sword mounted on pegs in the wall.

"Are you awake?" a voice asked then.

Alex turned. Though he had never seen the boy before, who looked to be about eleven or twelve, he would know him anywhere. He had a Schuyler face: blue-gray eyes and high forehead and small, almost delicate mouth. This must be Philip Junior.

Alex nodded weakly.

"How—" His voice broke, and it was a moment before he could speak. "How came I to be here?"

Philip stared at him blank-faced for a long moment, then opened his mouth to call:

"Papa! The deserter is awake!"

34

Can't-Runaway Bride

Outside the Governor's Mansion

Morristown, New Jersey

April 1780

Tap-tap-tap.

The knock at the door was as soft as the scratch of a mouse behind plaster, but to Eliza it sounded like the blows of an axe against the trunk of a two-hundred-year-old oak. As long as the door to her bedroom remained closed, she was safe. She was Eliza Schuyler, with her whole life still in front of her. But once it opened she would be Eliza Livingston, counting down the days until it was over.

"Eliza . . . dear." Aunt Gertrude's voice was soft, but it rang in Eliza's ears. "It's time."

She looked at herself in the three standing mirrors Kitty had had Loewes drag into her room. Kitty had brought the dress, too, a crème moiré number with a double bustle saved from being too wan by an elaborate green motif on the overskirt, and an emerald underskirt in watered silk. It looked like the desert blooms she had read about, when a once-a-year rain falls and the sands erupt in shoots that will live and flower and die in a single day. The corset—her first in who knew how long—months, maybe even a year—gave her a waist almost as thin as Peggy's, and the décolletage was more than she had ever dared. She reached reflexively for a shawl, but Kitty slapped her hand away lightly. Lightly, but definitively.

"Not today," she said, dusting a little powder over Eliza's bosom. "Today you become a woman, and you display yourself with pride."

The wig was one of Kitty's, scaled down slightly, because Eliza could not hold still when it was piled too high, yet taller than any she had ever worn. The feathered hat perched atop it looked comically small to Eliza's eyes, but Kitty said it reminded her of the crest of some exotic jungle bird.

"A parrot?" Eliza whispered, thinking of Peggy's wig from the party last week.

"You're a cuckoo!" Kitty laughed, slapping Eliza lightly with the flat of the comb she was using to tease up the wig. Lightly, but not so lightly. "Now look!"

She turned Eliza to the mirrors, arranged so that she could see herself from three sides. Eliza looked like a painting of herself, a painting that the artist had done from memory. Instead of capturing her likeness, he had simply created an idea of womanhood—widened hips, tiny waist, full breasts, rouged lips—and animated it with traces of the girl who used to be Eliza Schuyler.

"I-I do not look like myself."

"Exactly!" Kitty gushed. "Isn't it grand?!"

Eliza found her childhood friend's eyes in the mirror.

"Tell me. Does it hurt?"

Kitty's brow furrowed, but then smiled it away. "You mean, the secrets of the marriage chamber? A thousand generations of women have survived it. I'm sure you'll be fine."

"No," Eliza said. She reached for her old friend's hand. "I meant does it hurt when you hide every last shred of your individuality and self-worth behind acres of silk and cups of powder and smiles that never, no matter how hard you try, reach your eyes?"

Kitty's smile grew rigid on her face, and did not, as Eliza had said, reach her eyes, which were cold and condemning.

"You are nervous," she said, pulling her hand away from Eliza's. "I will give you some time to yourself."

ELIZA SAT IN her bedroom listening to the rush of footsteps in the hall outside, the hushed voices of women getting themselves dressed for the wedding and maids making the house ready for the reception afterward. Three times she had heard a hand on the door, three times someone—Peggy first, then Stephen, then Aunt Gertrude—had told whoever was at the door to leave Eliza alone.

"She will come out when it's time," Aunt Gertrude had said.

And now it was time.

THE DOORKNOB TURNED; the door eased open.

"Eliza, darling? The carriage is waiting downstairs."

Gone was the woman who had waved a vial of smelling salts in Governor Livingston's face and called it the great pox. Part of the skill of being a good soldier, she had told Eliza last night, is knowing when a battle is lost. This was not a battle, Eliza had protested. It was the whole war. "Perhaps," Aunt Gertrude had admitted. "But there would still be other battles, other wars, and you must save your strength for them."

Aunt Gertrude held out a gloved hand to Eliza. She stood and let herself be led like a little girl into the hall, where the servants stood on either side, smiling at her as best they could. She nodded at them as Aunt Gertrude led her between their ranks and down the stairs, where Peggy and Stephen waited, their smiles even more forced. The door was open, sunlight streamed in like a shower of gold. At the end of the walk a red-trimmed four-wheeled carriage waited just the other side of the gate. Its top was thrown open so that everyone in town could see her as she was carried to her groom.

She let herself be led outside and helped into the carriage by a liveried footman she didn't recognize. One of the Livingstons', no doubt. Aunt Gertrude was installed beside her on the leather seat and the driver snapped his whip and the carriage sprang forward with a little skip. The Livingstons' house, where the ceremony would take place, was behind them, but the carriage set off gaily up Pine Street and then turned onto Dumon, heading toward the Green, where Eliza would be displayed for all the town to see.

"It's just like a wedding is about to happen," Eliza said, "when it's really an incarceration."

Aunt Gertrude put her hand on Eliza's knee.

IT SEEMED THAT spring, too, was in on the joke, for the day had dawned as glorious as any in the new season. The air was brisk, to be sure, but the breeze carried a hint of warmth rather than chill, and though the sunlight illuminated more than it heated, it still shone down through a sky dotted with birds: hawks, ducks, pigeons, jays, and finches, all circling or diving or darting through the buoyant air and singing their varied songs. The trees in the town green hung heavy with buds that seemed only seconds away from bursting into full leaf, while the pond at the park's center was ringed with golden daffodils, whose blossoms shone in the dark water like the reflection of a hundred little suns.

Sheep grazed on the verdant grass and chickens pecked at grain while sows rooted at the boggy end of the pond, their bellies full with litters about to be born. A half-dozen townsfolk were about, maids and grooms on their errands, and as many soldiers, who all stopped what they were doing to smile or wave or salute at the lucky girl who was about to marry into the most powerful family in the state.

"That elm tree there," Eliza said, pointing over the well-wishers, and past them. "The one with the strong horizontal limb, like a soldier's rifle held at his shoulder. That is the tree where convicts are hanged, is it not?"

"Eliza, please," Aunt Gertrude pleaded. "You are only making it worse."

THE TURN AROUND the green was completed, and the carriage headed back along South Street. The view was of white houses now, dainty and neat, with shutters thrown wide to let in the late-morning sunshine. A great furred calico cat, as big as a raccoon, with an orange patch over one green eye and a black one over the other, sat atop a fencepost and cleaned its paws lazily as she watched Eliza's carriage float by.

"Oh, I do so love a long-haired cat," Aunt Gertrude said, staring at the placid beast. "They are as twice as warm as a muff on a winter day. They can be a bit ratty, though, but that fine puss is as well groomed as a princess. Someone loves her!"

"Mama tried for years to keep cats at the Pastures," Eliza answered. "But the foxes killed them all. I don't think they were even eating them. I think they just killed them to spite Mama."

"You cannot blame Mrs. Schuyler for this, Eliza. You know she wants what's best for you."

"Does she? She offers me for sale to the highest bidder and then has not even the courtesy of showing up to see the final results of the auction."

"It is a three-day journey from Albany, under the best of circumstances and, with the wetness this spring, no doubt the route is even slower than ever. And I have heard reports of British raiders, too, making so bold as to attack even guarded mail coaches. Would you really want your mother to risk her life just to see you exchange a few words before a minister?"

"I think she ought to be here to see what she has wrought. Papa, too. It is the least they could do."

"Hush, now. We're here."

The carriage had pulled up before a large white house, which, if truth be told, looked like every other house in Morristown, and every other house in New Jersey, save that it was a little larger than most, with broader windows and a more ornate pediment over the door. Where once Eliza had delighted in the little touches that made each five-bay house a unique expression of its owner's taste, now she saw them as minute variations on a single repetitive theme, and that theme was, conform or be cast out.

And look at her! After all her talk of being her own woman, forging her own path, she was letting herself be led along like a sheep to be sheared and sheared again and again until, at last, it gives no wool and instead of having its hair cut, its throat is cut instead, and it winds up in a stewpot.

Aunt Gertrude alighted from the carriage with the footman's aid, and now held her hand up to Eliza.

"Come, dear."

"No."

"Eliza, please. It is the way things must be."

"No," Eliza repeated. "I will not hand myself over to my own doom."

"Then you hand your family over to their doom," Aunt

Gertrude said. "Are you so selfish that you would sacrifice your papa and mama and brothers and sisters so that you don't have to marry a man you don't love? Do you think a better man will take you, after word of the scandal gets out?"

"Are they so craven that they would sell their daughter? I tell you, I will not do it."

"Eliza!" another voice called then. "Eliza, wait!"

Eliza turned. She saw another carriage farther up the lane, wooden-sided and covered with mud, as if it had traveled some great distance. Its door opened, and a blue-jacketed figure was tumbling out of it so clumsily that the carriage rocked like a dinghy in the wake of a whaleship. The fellow stumbled to the ground and nearly fell, his three-cornered hat tumbling off his head and exposing a shock of russet-colored hair.

"It—it cannot be," Eliza breathed.

The ginger-haired figure looked up at her, and there were the blue eyes that melted her heart.

"Eliza, wait! I'm here!"

"Alex?" Eliza said, afraid to believe it. Still, she was standing up—no, scrambling up—and pushing aside her aunt's hand and the footman's and forcing her bustled hips through the narrow door of the carriage so quickly that she heard fabric tear. She pushed herself all the way through and hopped down onto the flagstone bricks of the Livingstons' front walk.

"Alex?" she said. "Is it really you?"

His face was flushed and he seemed somewhat thinner;

he handled his right arm gingerly, as though it pained him. His hands in hers were so hot that she could feel them through his gloves, and hers.

"It's me," he said. "I'm here. You don't have to marry him. You have to—that is—" He sank somewhat gingerly to one knee. "Elizabeth Schuyler, my darling Eliza, my one and only Betsey, will you marry me?"

When Alex knelt, a second pair of figures came into her view, emerging from the carriage that had carried him. Her parents. General and Mrs. Schuyler, looking on with grim but determined smiles on their faces.

Eliza found her mother's eyes. Her mother looked back steadily, then nodded.

Eliza looked down at Alex, who stared back at her adoringly, nervously, triumphantly. She opened her mouth to answer him, but no words came out.

35

Here Comes the Groom

The Cochran Residence

Morristown, New Jersey

April 1780

"But how did you . . . I mean, you just disappeared . . . and then your horse was found with blood . . . and I wrote and no one answered . . . and Governor Livingston was just so, so—"

"It's fine, Eliza, it's fine." Alex knelt on the carpet and stroked Eliza's hand where she lay on the sofa in Aunt Gertrude's parlor. "I'm here now. I'll explain everything. Or, well, your mother will, because I'm afraid I don't remember much."

"You don't remember?" Eliza asked, frowning. "I don't understand."

Catherine Schuyler's round face slipped into her daughter's viewpoint.

"Oh, Eliza, this poor boy was so delirious when he arrived at the Pastures that he had no idea where he was. In truth, I have no idea how he found us. It must have been God's will that he arrive."

"You rode all the way to Albany and back? In seven days?"

"Four days, really," Mrs. Schuyler answered. "Three of those days were spent abed—where he should still be, if you ask me."

"I am quite recovered, Mrs. Schuyler, all due to your good care."

"You do look rather peaked," Eliza said. "But please, tell me, what happened? Why did you run off? And how came you to be so ill that you were three days bedridden at my parents' house?"

Alex shrugged and moved from the carpet to a nearby chair, though never letting go of Eliza's hand.

"I knew that the only way you would break off the engagement to Colonel Livingston was with your parents' permission. And I knew that the only way they would grant that permission was if they were told, clearly, and without the tact that a feminine correspondent would undoubtedly put into a letter, exactly what kind of scoundrel he was. And so I requisitioned a horse from the mail coach and made my way there. It was a rainy day, as you recall, and I had already been some six hours on horseback during the journey from Amboy, and awake for some eighteen hours, so I was rather susceptible to the effects of damp and fatigue."

"And then you were ambushed by those British dragoons. As I said, it is a wonder you made it to us at all," interjected Mrs. Schuyler once more.

"Ambushed!" cried Eliza.

Even if Alex were at liberty to divulge the evidence of treason he had uncovered regarding General Arnold and Major André, he couldn't think of the words to describe it. He wasn't entirely convinced that he hadn't dreamed up the whole thing.

"Your father has handled it," he said gently. "Suffice to say that the culprits will be brought to justice, and history will remember them in infamy."

"Are you hurt?" Eliza said. "It seemed to me that you were favoring your arm earlier."

"Just a scratch," Alex said, releasing Eliza's hand just long enough to rub his wound gingerly, then taking it up again. The scab pulled when he lifted it, but the muscle beneath was uninjured. In a week or two, he would likely not even remember the cut. The attack itself was a blur, too, lost behind a wall of fatigue and fever.

"So that was your blood on your horse's saddle? But how came it to arrive at the coach station without you?"

"It was spooked by the gunshots and made its way home to the station on its own. I was able to catch one of my assailant's horses. I rode as far as the Sloat House coach station in Pothat and on up to Albany."

"And you slept not a wink during the entire journey!" Eliza asked incredulously.

"Not in a bed," Alex said. "Though there were times I'm sure I dozed on horseback."

"By the time he got to us," Mrs. Schuyler said here, "he

barely knew his own name, or why he had come. I tell you he was raving so badly that I thought the fever had gone to his brain and we would not have him back, but it seems to have been mostly the effects of three days without sleep and little food, a nagging wound, and a terrible chill."

"They tell me I slept for two days," Alex confessed sheepishly. "I must apologize for that, my dear Eliza."

"Oh, nonsense," Eliza said, stroking his hand. "I can't believe you risked your life for me!"

"I would risk it a thousand times more, to win your heart."

Mrs. Schuyler cleared her throat self-consciously. "While he slept, your aunt Cochran's note came, but I confess that your father and I could not distinguish between the jitters of a reluctant bride and the malfeasance of roué. Certainly we had heard nothing suggesting that Colonel Livingston's character was anything less than that of a gentleman, or we would have never consented to the marriage." Alex watched as Mrs. Schuyler fixed her daughter in the eye with almost desperate earnestness. "I do hope you believe that, Daughter."

"Henry was always a weak boy," Eliza said in a measured voice, not forgiving, but not condemning either, "but never a roué, as you say. I gather that his time in the army has not had the character-strengthening effect it has on so many of our soldiers. But you could not have known that. He has been stationed in Connecticut and coastal Massachusetts, far from Albany, let alone New Jersey or Philadelphia."

It was not exoneration, but Mrs. Schuyler seemed content with that.

"We thought to write you, but then Colonel Hamilton awakened and was able to give us a fuller accounting, and we were convinced that it was necessary that we travel here in person to stop the marriage. Colonel Hamilton insisted on accompanying us, but the doctor said he wasn't well enough. We managed to keep him in bed one more day, but then he said he would return without us, so your father commissioned a carriage and we came together. We had to hope that your aunt Cochran was able to delay the marriage until word came from us, or we arrived ourselves."

"Aunt Gertrude was remarkable," Eliza said. "I suspect Governor Livingston will never set foot in a house occupied by her ever again."

Alex looked over at Mrs. Cochran, twirling the small vial of smelling salts she had used to revive Eliza in the fingers of one hand. She caught his eye and winked.

Just then the front door clicked open, and a moment later General Schuyler stomped into the parlor.

"It is done," he said, removing his hat and coat, then handing it to a servant in the hall. He shut the door behind him and took a seat on a chair close to his wife.

"I have persuaded Governor and Colonel Livingston to release you from your engagement and to keep the entire matter strictly *en famille*. In exchange, Colonel Livingston will not be brought before a court-martial for callously and carelessly jeopardizing the lives of seven Continental soldiers in moving them from their infirmary so that he could throw a party, and of course, his most reprehensible and disgusting actions against a lady shall remain known only to the injured party and her family." He looked at his daughter with equal parts tenderness and anger. "Though I would prefer to shoot him myself, at least some manner of justice has been done."

"A scoundrel like that will seek out his own justice eventually," Alex said with disgust. "Although I, too, wish I could be the one to mete it out."

"It is behind us now," General Schuyler said, "and a much brighter future lies ahead. That is, if Eliza will still have you," he added with a wink at his daughter.

"What?" Eliza said.

"There was a question on the table," General Schuyler said, "that Colonel Hamilton put to you, before you so rudely fainted into his arms."

"Oh, I would not call it rude," Mrs. Schuyler admonished her husband. "I would call it charming."

"Well, charming or rude, she shouldn't leave the poor boy hanging!" General Schuyler managed a chuckle.

"The poor boy agrees!" Alex chimed in, looking at Eliza hopefully.

"Wh-what?" Eliza stuttered again. "I mean—" She looked nervously at her parents, but mostly her mother. "Can I? You seemed so against it before."

"There are families whose greatness lies in their past, and in their legacies," Mrs. Schuyler answered. "That is a quality much to be admired, for tradition is what binds us as a society. But there are some families, like some nations, whose greatness is a future development, and that quality, though harder to discern than the prestige of manor houses and coats of arms and titles of rank and office, is no less valuable, if, indeed, not more so."

General Schuyler put his arm around his wife and drew her near.

"What Mrs. Schuyler is saying," General Schuyler added, "is that it is the Schuylers who would be honored by a union with so brilliant and noble a personage as Colonel Hamilton."

"So I can marry him?" Eliza said, her eyes flitting between her parents and Alex. "I can say *yes*?"

"You had better," Mrs. Schuyler said, "or I shall never forgive you."

Eliza turned to Alex. Alex felt his body fall away from him. The only thing that kept him rooted to earth was his hand in Eliza's.

"Then, yes!" Eliza exclaimed. "Yes, yes, and yes, I will marry you! Yes! Yes! Yes!"

36

Poor Man's Wife

The Cochran Garden

Morristown, New Jersey

August 1780

For his entire lifetime Alex had been dragging his past behind him like a heavy chain. He was an open man with no secrets to hide, yet he had all the insecurities of an outsider. From his melancholy youth, he was ever needy to earn a foothold in respectable society. Whether by the zest in his pen or the zing of a bullet past his ear, he wanted to make a difference in the New World by his own merit.

It was true he had hitched his horse to General Washington's wagon with roaring success and was now on the verge of ascending into polite society by becoming one of the Schuyler family. And yet, as much as thriving as the right-hand man to General Washington and becoming the son-in-law to General Schuyler thrilled him, there were always the nagging doubts from the wounds of his childhood. Would people regard him as marrying into the Schuyler family only to access their wealth? How could Eliza Schuyler possibly believe he could provide for her as a husband?

He had written her reams and reams of letters, as well as a poem that she kept folded in a locket around her neck. Her letters were full of love and anticipation, matching his for enthusiasm and tenderness. He was the luckiest man in the world.

Their wedding was set for December, when there would be the winter lull in fighting, and he would be able to take a few weeks off for the ceremony and the honeymoon. But it was now August, and while he did not doubt her love for him, he wanted to make certain she knew what she was getting into.

Taking a few days' leave to be able to see his beloved, he returned to Morristown, his heart in his hands.

ELIZA DUG HER hands into the dark earth, happy to be out in the sunshine of Aunt Gertrude's vegetable garden on this hot summer day. Alex had returned from the battlefront unexpectedly that morning and just escorted her home from church. While checking the garden for any hint of greenery to add to Aunt Gertrude's luncheon table, she found small green squashes already gone to seed.

"Alex, is there anything more beautiful than dropping a seed in the earth and then waiting for it to become something perfectly useful? These tiny seeds will be cucumbers by next midsummer, sitting in the middle of Aunt Gertrude's table as finger sandwiches. How perfectly practical it must be to be a farmer's wife."

Alex circled the flagstone border that enclosed the garden

for the third time. It was not often that he could manage a visit, but it appeared there was a certain urgency to this one. He looked like a man who had something to get off his chest, and she'd unintentionally led him right to it with her innocent question.

"How practical must it be, you ask, to be a farmer's wife, Betsey?" Alex stopped in his circle and approached her straight on. "Rather the question, I should think, is, how practical must one be to be a farmer's wife? Or a poor man's wife? How practical must one be to forget about beautiful dresses and elegant dinners and a house full of servants to prepare it all at a moment's notice? How practical does a poor man's wife have to be to be content with a book by candlelight instead of a night at the opera? How practical to watch your hands grow rough with gardening and milking and churning and all the work that is to be done just to make it from one dawn to the next?"

Eliza looked at Alex. Ah, so that was his worry. He had said as much, in his lovely letters.

She saw the dread in his face and wanted to make it disappear. "But, my darling, I merely meant I love to garden. And I love to sew. I meant nothing more than that. What is it, dearest, what are you trying to tell me?"

"I fear, Betsey, that our love, deep as it is, is not enough to nurture a lifelong marriage. Marriage is in many ways a business partnership and I fear you are getting the rough end of the deal by marrying me."

Alex ran his hands through his hair and opened his

palms. "I confess I have not been as brilliant in managing my own monetary affairs as I have been in managing the affairs of state. Money and land never seemed to matter to me until now. But now there is you and our future children to consider. I must take care of you in the best way I know how. And I do not know that I am good enough."

Eliza put down her trowel and brushed off her hands. She'd left her bonnet inside, and her face had quickly pinked up under the sun. She opened her arms to him. "Come here, to me, Alex. I shall show you what I care about."

Alex found he couldn't look her in the eye. "Oh, my pretty damsel, when I think of the match you could have *made*—ah! And here you have chosen me, one who has so little to offer. If happiness were all that it took to make a thing such as marriage work, we would be set for life. But how can you be sure that ours will not turn into one of those tragic unions that unhappy couples share?"

Eliza laughed. "Perhaps you forget I was raised by a thrifty Dutch woman who managed an entire household while raising a large brood of children. Surely, there is something of practical value in all of that!"

"You make light of it today, but I entreat you. Consider me decades from now. Will you be as satisfied then as you are at this moment with being a poor man's wife?"

"Silly man. I know the man I am marrying is destined for great things, as the many remarkable things he has done thus far have brought him to such a high point already. Mark my words, Alex. You are a man whose future lies before him for all to marvel at one day. And you, Colonel Hamilton, are mine, and I am yours always."

He scooped her into his arms once again, his doubts quelled. "I shall never be worthy of you, my angel," he said. "I know I shall disappoint you in a thousand ways before our time on earth is through. But I hope that you will always see the good in me and know that this unworthy heart of mine will always be yours, no matter what obstacles or failures I bring to your life."

Eliza pulled away and looked him right in the eye. "I know you, Alex. I know you and I love you, and I shall always love you, come what may. I shall be yours, always."

37

Wedding March

The Schuyler Mansion, Also Known as the Pastures

Albany, New York

December 14, 1780

At long last, it was time for the wedding. Life being life, and war being war, the heady romance of the proposal endured a nine-months interregnum before it was consummated at the Pastures in Albany. For one thing, Eliza wanted to be married as far from the debacle of Morristown as possible—wanted only to remember Morristown as the place where she had fallen in love with Alex, and not where she had almost lost him, and herself. For another, it was the place where Alex had had his command of the 3rd New Jersey abruptly mooted when General Clinton of the British army stepped up his invasion of Charleston, which after a six weeks' siege, had fallen in mid-May.

It was altogether a disastrous turn of events, one that left General Washington scrambling to recover and unable to part with his most trusted aide. The Benedict Arnold affair proved even more tumultuous—General Arnold was one of the brightest stars in the Continental army, who had once served with General Schuyler. Thanks in part to Alex's discovery of his correspondence with Major André, the Continental army was able to foil Arnold's plan to hand the fort at West Point over to the British. General Arnold himself managed to escape but Major André had been caught and imprisoned. Though Eliza remembered him fondly as the dashing swain who had danced with her on the very night she met her future husband, Alex realized there had been something sneaky about him that night they bumped into him in Morristown at the bonfire.

Though General Arnold had initiated the plan and John André was merely the officer he managed to contact, everyone on both sides of the conflict thought Major André one of the most honorable men in either army. Yet the law was clear, and General Washington's position inflexible. Though Alex himself asked General Washington for clemency, on October 2, the dashing young officer was hanged for espionage behind enemy lines.

The death shook Eliza deeply, and it was some weeks before she felt ready to move forward with, as she said, "the rest of my life."

But at last there was a lull in Alex's duties, and by the end of November, he was able to escape north to the Pastures.

The wedding was on for December 14 at noon.

CATHERINE SCHUYLER STOOD in front of her looking glass, rocking her enormous belly. She was visibly pregnant for the twelfth time in her lifetime and decidedly cranky, but today at noon she would paint a smile on her face and play hostess at the Schuyler family's grand wedding feast for her second-eldest daughter, Eliza.

A second glance in the mirror did little to calm her nerves. "I look like a stout Dutch milkmaid," she groused. As the noontime wedding hour approached, there was nothing for it but to lift her chin high and wear a dazzling shawl. She chose a green-and-burgundy-velvet piece, patterned with feathers that spread across her shoulders and ended in gold threaded tassels that dropped below her hips.

Once a striking dark-haired beauty with a long elegant neck, she could hardly remember the pert figure she had been so careless with, but the vanity created by the overheated praise from her groom on their wedding night had stuck with her forever. But as the years passed in a lifetime spent raising her large brood, Mrs. Schuyler had developed a habit of rocking herself to generate a moment of peace. Now she caught occasional murmurs of being called the Rocking Horse by her children and routinely found her husband disappearing into his study each evening after dinner.

Nevertheless, for today—Eliza's special day—Catherine Schuyler would make every effort to be gracious.

It was to be a small family wedding in the Schuyler home, as was the Dutch custom of the day. Of course, there was nothing small about the Pastures or the extended Schuyler clan. And with the Schuylers, there were always songs to be sung and games to be played inside and out. The general recruited Mr. Vincent to ferry guests back and forth over the ice-packed Hudson in an open sleigh rigged out with the jangling bells of two liveried horses.

As the noonday sun glanced off the snow on that cold December 14, and the parlor began to fill up with first cousins, distant relatives and friends, a Bach sonata for flute and harpsichord signaled the wedding was about to get underway. The southeast parlor, being the grandest in the house, was chosen, wherein were gathered Angelica and John Church, and Peggy and Stephen Van Rensselaer, and Philip Junior and the younger Schuyler siblings, along with the requisite Schuyler, Van Cortlandt, and Van Rensselaer kin.

Anticipating the bride's entrance, all conversation came to an abrupt halt as guests took their places on either side of the great hall. The family sat in several tiers of chairs, exquisitely yet soberly dressed, except for Angelica, who could not resist a crimson gown.

Waiting in the vestibule for General Schuyler to walk their daughter into the room, Catherine Schuyler crossed her shawl over her large belly and began to rock herself. Not lost on her was the irony of the bride coming down the aisle on the arm of her father: the quaint concept that a woman is under the primary care of her father until she is given over to the keeping of another man. Well, her first daughter Angelica's ship had already sailed on that passage, so Mrs. Schuyler intended to relish every moment of this, her second daughter's most elaborate affair.

Although, in hindsight, as practical Eliza had reminded her mother after the wedding costs began to mount up, perhaps Angelica had done the financially strapped Schuylers a considerable favor.

BUT ENOUGH ABOUT her mother, for as much as this was Mrs. Schuyler's triumph, it was Eliza's day. And on this very special day Eliza remained true to herself to the last.

Entering the grand foyer to strains of Bach and heads tilting with oohs and ahhs, she represented the picture of modesty and grace in a simple dress of ivory, fitted but without a corset, with thick petticoats to give it shape but nothing so cumbersome or affected as a bustle or train. A thin silver diadem circled her hair, from which hung the palest veil, set with freshwater pearls. Aunt Gertrude's borrowed cameo provided the finishing touch.

Altogether, the first glimpse of his bride—which should have come as no surprise to Alex, standing there looking so lean and handsome himself—nearly brought him to his knees.

Of course, a young groom always tries to look his best, but Alex was particularly dashing in his blue-and-buff uniform with the gold epaulets and the green ribbon of an aide-de-camp. He had known all along exactly what he would wear—the same stiff number he'd chosen to sit for his portrait by Charles Willson Peale shortly after he joined General Washington's staff. The yellow buttons gleamed on his uniform, and breeches were as brilliantly white as the legs of a hawk. A single curled lock of his ginger hair had escaped the ribbon that held it back and fell rakishly beside his eyes.

But behind that confident façade, even on what should have been the happiest day of his life, there was a sadness he could not name. In contrast to his bride's enormous tribe, there was no one there to represent his own, despite his best entreaties. Yes, he had sent a written invitation to his estranged brother in St. Nevis to come meet his black-eyed beauty, and he had pressed hard for his father to come to America from the Grenadines, but neither of them had written him back. Indeed, no one from his remaining family would ever meet any of the Schuylers. For Alex to be enveloped into one of New York State's blue-ribbon families helped put to bed a lifetime of doubts and depression about his own dubious birthright.

Eliza fretted for her fiancé, but he seemed resolute. "You are the only family I need," he'd told her.

And now the moment had arrived.

The minister began the ceremony with the traditional question for Eliza's parents. "Do you, General and Mrs. Schuyler, give your blessing to these two, and promise them your continued love and support?"

"We do," said the Schuylers, "—with God's help." An amen chorus from their huge clan echoed their pledge.

Then the minister turned to Alex. There was no one beside him. "And who stands up for you, sir?"

There was an awkward silence as the guests looked around the room for the bridegroom's supporters. Finally, an unpretentious voice announced itself from the edge of the room.

"I do, sir." Stephen Van Rensselaer slipped through the guests and stepped up right behind Alex. Peggy's hand went to her throat, her eyes brimming with love for a man whose words always seemed to come at the perfectly timed moment. The familiar words of the Dutch Reformed marriage ceremony stumbled slowly out of Stephen's mouth. "I give my blessing and promise my continued love and support . . ."

"As do I!" Lieutenant Colonel James McHenry, Alex's fellow aide-de-camp, cut smartly through the guests to take up his post beside Stephen.

"And I, as well," said John Church, his voice booming from the other side of the hall.

The minister raised his eyebrows, patiently waiting for the coda to their pledge.

"—with God's help!" said the three in perfect unison.

"Well done," whispered Angelica to her very own new husband. Even she couldn't help but be moved.

The minister covered the bridal couple's clasped hands with his own and called for the exchange of the vows. In deference to his future in-laws, Alex had gone along with the conventional vows of the Schuylers' church. But when it came to writing his personal vows, the scrivener in him came to the fore.

Alex listened intently as Eliza recited the familiar vows: "I shall love you and give myself up for you, as Christ loved the church and gave himself up." The minister nodded for Alex to repeat the words.

He began true enough:

"I shall love you and give myself up for you, as Christ loved the church and gave himself up"—then Alex looked into Eliza's shining eyes and added a twist of his own—"and I shall serve you with tenderness and respect, and encourage you to develop the gifts that God has given you."

Eliza's eyes were so fastened on Alex that it was as if the words came directly from his mind to hers. The minister stood between the two of them with a perplexed look on his face. He drew in a deep breath and looked out over the affectionate expressions on the guests' faces. He must have decided the groom's choice of words would more than suffice.

"Therefore," the minister intoned, "what God has joined together, let no man tear asunder. By the authority invested in me under God and state, I now pronounce you, Alexander and Elizabeth, husband and wife." Eliza beamed at Alex, who exhaled heartily. "You may now kiss the bride, Alexander."

Eliza fairly flew into Alex's arms, and they kissed so sweetly and for so long that it drew cheers all around.

General Schuyler tossed his head back and roared

with the gusto of a contented man. He marched across the entrance hall, eager to congratulate the newlyweds with a hearty handshake for his son-in-law and a kiss on the cheek for his daughter.

"Eliza, my sweet girl, you have chosen well!"

The general rubbed his hands together and shouted to the musicians to play on. "Let's liven things up a bit around here!" They kicked off with a boisterous Old English wassailing song. "That's it, boys—now that's the spirit!"

Alex grabbed his beautiful bride for a reel that was more of a jog—and the house was suddenly full of life and laughter, music and food, children and dogs.

CATHERINE SCHUYLER STOOD in the middle of her crowded parlor rocking herself, surrounded by all the joys such a large happy family had brought her. Behind her in a swirl of activity, the servants were bringing out the largest quantity of foods in the best manner the Schuylers could afford.

Throughout the day and well into the evening, General Schuyler's valet, Rodger, presided over the busy kitchen staff, hard at work doling out clam chowder, stewed oysters, roasted pig, venison, potatoes, baked rye bread, Indian cornbread, and pumpkin casserole. Trays of nutmeats and candy dotted the parlor. Coffee and tankards of spiced hard cider were set up on fine linens in the library.

Even Aunt Gertrude's Morristown cook had been put to service to bake the wedding cake—a thick, rich, spiced fruitcake, made heavy with alcohol and nuts. A round table covered in a beautiful damask cloth was carried into the great hall for the ceremonial cutting of the cake.

As was the custom, the cook had baked a piece of nutmeg inside. Whoever received the slice with the nutmeg was supposed to be the next to marry.

Catherine Schuyler nearly fainted when it turned out to be Peggy.

38

Happiest They've Ever Been

Honeymoon Suite

Albany, New York

December 1780

The large, gabled mansion on the Hudson seemed eerily quiet after such a long, raucous day of celebration. The last of the guests had gone and the Pastures' kitchen had been returned to its everyday readiness. Dot banked the hearths high and headed off to sleep with a well-deserved hot toddy.

By midnight, every room in the house was dark except for the firelight coming from the secluded guest bedchamber at the top of the stairs. Covered from neck to knee in a ruffled white linen nightshirt, Alex stood beside the canopied four-poster bed, waiting impatiently for his bride to join him.

On the other side of the bath chamber door, Eliza passed the end of a fresh candle over the wall sconce's flame to soften the wax. Steadying her nerves as she waited for the slow dripping to begin, she pressed the pliant base of the warmed candle into the candelabrum and held it in place until the wax hardened.

She ran the candle's wick through the flame of the sconce and saw her reflection alight in the mirror above the washbasin. She liked how her white satin nightgown created a soft sheen against her skin. But something was still amiss. She reached behind her head to tug the pearl-handled barrette from her hair and let her thick dark curls fall loose around her shoulders—*Ah, that's it. I'm ready now.*

Eliza opened the door to the bedroom and went to meet her husband.

She stepped lightly toward the edge of the bed and kissed Alex full on the lips for the second time this night. Frank and tender all at once.

As gently and as slowly as he could, while feeling more impatient than he had ever been in his life, Alex took the candelabrum out of her hand and set it on the mantelpiece over the crackling fire.

Eliza stood in front of the hearth, luxuriating in the heat against her nightgown. The modest girl was not so modest anymore.

Cupping her chin gently in his hands, Alex bent forward to kiss her and inhaled her sweet scent. In an effort to slow himself down, he reached for her hand and took one step back for a good long look at his new bride—from head to toe. "Turn around, my angel," he managed to say. "Let me see you in the firelight."

Eliza pivoted in a dainty circle, excruciatingly slow. When she came back around, her dark eyes sparkled and a knowing smile played over her lips. She ran her fingertip down his freshly shaven cheek, playacting the role of a saucy little charmer. "Although I am inexperienced, Alex, I am not naïve. But, tell me true, do you love me?"

Bouncing on the balls of his feet like a besotted schoolboy, Alex crossed both hands over his heart. "More than any man has ever loved."

The dim light flickered across Eliza's shoulders, and Alex felt his blood rise tight under his skin. It was time for this soldier to rally. "Indeed, the truth is, Mrs. Hamilton—you take my breath away. What ever shall we do about it?"

Unbuttoning her white satin gown, Eliza let it drop to her feet.

ELIZABETH SCHUYLER HAMILTON stood next to her husband as he skimmed rocks across the Pastures' frozen duck pond. A nearby flock of geese rose from the riverbank and squawked at the two of them, switching directions in midair at the sound of Alex's sliding another rock across the ice.

She dug her gloved hands into her hips and turned her pretty face toward the afternoon sun. "They must think I'm going to bake them into a pie!" Alex laughed as the birds disappeared in noisy protest.

Eliza had never seen Alex quite so happy and relaxed. She shook her head and laughed at the incongruity of it all: *Imagine General Washington's famous aide-de-camp taking the time to stop and admire the birds!*

"One day, Alex, when you tire of being a soldier, we will spend all of our days just like this, watching birds and taking in the sun, surrounded by children of our own. You'd like that, wouldn't you, my love?"

"Eliza, you and the Pastures have already taken a perfectly fine soldier and turned him into a lovesick pup. And at this moment, on this very day, there's nothing and nowhere I would rather be."

A WEEK INTO their honeymoon, Alex had confided to his bride that this was his first few days off in five years. As General Washington's right-hand man, Alex was always at the general's beck and call, expected to be ready to write or ride at a moment's notice. Yet, here at the Pastures he was well away from his work-obsessed life. His days were tasked only with leisurely horseback rides and pulling his boots off by the fire, with Eliza reading at his side or challenging him to a shrewd game of backgammon. Surrounded by family for the first time in his life, he basked in the healthy glow of his wife and the entire Schuyler clan.

As Alex and Eliza spent the last few blissful days of their honeymoon traipsing through the snowy woods or adventuring out on that long-awaited open sleigh for a ride through the streets of Albany with loyal Hector out in front, their future stretched before them with all the hope and promise a new country had to offer.

And at last, the lonely young man who belonged to no one finally belonged to someone, forever, and the practical girl who would not settle for less than a love story for the ages found the lifelong romance she had yearned for all her life.

ACKNOWLEDGMENTS

This book would not be a reality if I hadn't taken my family to see *Hamilton* in New York City in June 2016. It was right after the Tonys and featured the original Broadway cast! (Except for the king, so to us Rory is the king, Jonathan who?) My ten-year-old daughter, Mattie, was so taken by the love story of Alex and Eliza that I was forced to do research to answer her questions and in doing so got caught up in their story as well. So I would like to thank Mattie, whose favorite character is Eliza ("*Hamilton* should be called *Eliza*, Mom; we wouldn't know his story if she didn't tell it"), for giving me the idea to write a book about their romance.

I would also like to thank my long-time editor, Jennifer Besser, for believing in this story from the first email. I heart you, Jen!!!! Thank you to everyone at Penguin for yet another awesome book together. Yay!

Many thanks to everyone at 3Arts including my agent, Richard Abate, and Rachel Kim, and everyone at Spilled Ink, especially my research assistants for making sure I didn't take *too* many liberties with history. (*Liberties*—get it? Thanks for the joke, Leigh Bardugo!)

Not very much is known about Alex and Eliza's romance, except that they fell hard and fast and were so in love that Eliza carried a poem he wrote for her in a necklace she wore until the day she died. Swoon. And so this is my fictional embellishment. I hope you enjoyed it.

Thanks to all my friends and family—you know who you are and I love you all.

And last but never least, thank you to my husband, Mike Johnston. I wrote a poem to him in our early courtship, too. (But he doesn't like to wear necklaces. Man jewelry—shudder.)

Turn the page

for a sneak peek of

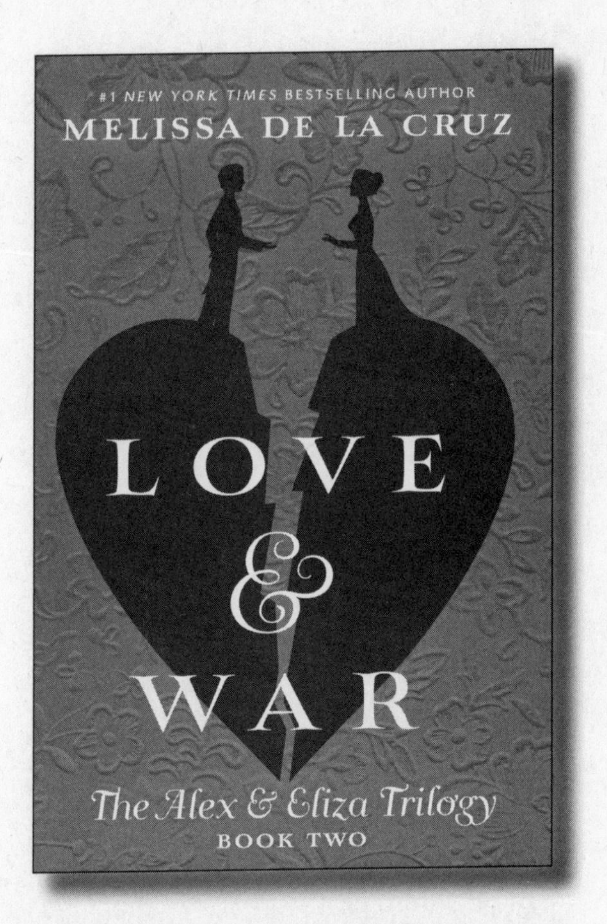

1

Spring Harvest!

The Schuyler Mansion

Albany, New York

April 1781

Forget Paris. The French could keep their croissants and the Champs-Élysées. Who cares about London? Rome? Athens? From what she'd heard, they were just a bunch of ruins. And what of Williamsburg, Virginia? Charleston, South Carolina? New York City? As far as she was concerned, they could all fall off the map.

In all the world, Elizabeth Schuyler Hamilton thought there was no place more beautiful than Albany at springtime. Of course, the Pastures was dear to her as her childhood home, and even more so as the site of her wedding to Alexander Hamilton just last winter. Time had done little to dampen their affection, and she was more in love with her husband than ever. Perhaps it was this love that led to Eliza's delight at anything and everything around her.

But rose-colored glasses or no, it was hard to claim there was anywhere more glorious than late April in her hometown. The air was warm and the sun was mellow. Bare trees had covered themselves in soft green foliage and the sharp, tangy smell of fireplace smoke gave way to the softer aromas of hyacinths and crocuses, lilac and dogwood. Swallows darted through the air, snapping up flies and gnats, and newborn calves, foals, and shoats frolicked about the fields and sties. The mighty Hudson River was wreathed in mist at daybreak and teemed with fishermen's boats in the afternoon. Their nets hauled in plentiful catches of shad, whose roe had a delicate, almost nutty taste that paired perfectly with a salad of tender mustard greens.

But best of all was the bounty of blueberries and strawberries. All over the estate, hundreds of bushes sagged beneath the weight of thousands upon thousands of red, burgundy, and purple fruit. Every morning for a week, Eliza and her sisters, Angelica, Peggy, and five-year-old Cornelia—joined sometimes by their youngest brother, eight-year-old Rensselaer, known affectionately as Ren—traded in their sumptuous silks and bustles for simple, sturdy muslin skirts that they'd tie up high, showing ankles and calves in a bit of a risqué manner, and joined the housemaids in the fields to pick bucket after bucket of plump, sweet, juicy berries. (Well, not Ren. Ren hadn't worn a skirt since his christening.)

By noon, their lips were as stained as their fingertips (after all, picking involved a fair bit of "sampling," as Eliza put it), and the three oldest sisters repaired to the kitchen to do their work. Some of the fruit was packed in ice in the cellar, and some more was baked into pies, but most was simmered in rich syrupy jellies whose tart sweetness would liven up many a winter meal, slathered on fresh bread or griddle cakes or dabbed on turkey or mutton. A portion of the fruit was pickled, making for a delicious snack, salty at first, before exploding in your mouth in a burst of sweetness.

But as tempting as all these rich cooked treats were, Eliza's favorite way to eat them was also the simplest: fresh and chilled. Each plump fruit tasted like a thimble-size dollop of liquid happiness. That early spring afternoon, standing in the dappled light by the stone counter, Eliza alternated between a basket of strawberries and a basket of blueberries, savoring them one at a time.

"I can't decide which is more perfect!" she exclaimed to her sisters, who were gathered around the long rustic table that ran down the center of the kitchen, sorting fruit.

"Blech." Peggy Schuyler pouted with lips that were nearly as fruit-stained as Eliza's. "If I ever see another strawberry or blueberry again, it will be too soon!" she said as she reached for yet another blueberry and popped it in her mouth.

"Peg's right," Angelica agreed. "Sometimes nature's bounty is too much. A week ago I couldn't wait for the fruit to ripen. Now all I want are peanuts! What I wouldn't give for freshly roasted nuts right now!" But before the words had escaped her lips, she was already rolling a red strawberry between her fingers, letting it disappear into her mouth as well.

"With this war, we can't have peanuts till September anyway," said Eliza.

"Stephen says the war may be over before fall," said Peggy, referring to her fiancé, Stephen Van Rensselaer III. "The American coastline is simply too long for even an army or navy as powerful as England's to cover, and with French forces now fully committed to the cause of our independence, King George's men will find themselves both outnumbered and outmaneuvered."

"It is hard to imagine this war being over," Eliza said. "I feel as though we have grown up with it. But I do hope he's right! Alex and I have been married for half a year already, but we have yet to establish a household."

Indeed, as much as Eliza loved the Pastures, she was impatient to move out of her parents' house and into one with her husband. After their wedding, they'd only had a few blessed weeks together before he had to rush back to General Washington's headquarters. These days, Alex was chafing at their present living arrangements just as much as she was, and both were eager for more time on their own.

Though she loved her husband dearly, and knew he loved her, they had spent more time apart than together during the course of their brief romance and even briefer marriage. The flame that burned between them was bright, but they had yet to live alone as husband and wife. In many ways Alex was still a stranger to her. Their lives were mediated by family and servants and soldiers, and as such, their private lives were not as private as they would have preferred.

At least he'd been home now for a spell, although he was scheduled to leave again in a few days. Missing him was the lot of a soldier's wife, and instead of weeping and worrying, Eliza endeavored to be brave. Still, it was difficult, even in the midst of so much beauty, not to feel bereft. When Alex was gone, she felt his absence as a physical ache. She chided herself for being so selfish. While she was his wife, he was a man of the world, of the state, and she owed it to her country to share, didn't she?

Her own parents had endured many long separations during their marriage. Even so, General and Mrs. Schuyler had at least had a few years to establish themselves and start their family before their first parting.

Since Alex was leaving soon to report back to duty, festivities had been planned for later that evening. She didn't want to surmise how long he'd be gone, but hoped when he returned they would finally be able to settle down on their own. "I am ready to live under my own roof," Eliza declared.

"Hear, hear," Angelica seconded. "I have been married a year longer than you, and my husband and I see less of each other than when we were courting. Tell me: Do you know yet where he plans to make his residence?"

Eliza shook her head. "It will probably be New York City, which is most conducive to a career in law. But if he is lured into politics, we may well end up in Philadelphia or perhaps someplace farther south, if all this talk of creating a capital in the midpoint of the country comes to pass."

"*Uuuuuugh.*" The sisters' conversation was interrupted by a low moan from a corner of the kitchen, where Cornelia was sprawled across a stack of burlap bags filled with rice. Her face from nose to chin to plump cheeks was painted dark purple from greedily consumed berries. "Too—much—fruit."

"I told you, Cornelia," Eliza said, laughing in sympathy. "You must pace yourself or you'll give yourself a bellyache."

"Too—late," Cornelia moaned, rubbing her aproned stomach with fingers that were as dark as her mouth. But even as she did, she sat up and was soon shuffling toward the buckets brimming with fruit.

"Wait till tea, dear, and you can have scones with fresh jam and cream," Eliza said, catching her sister and turning her around. "Please head inside now and have Dot give you a good scrub. We can't have you looking like a harlequin at the party tonight."

Eliza expected Cornelia to protest being handed over to their ladies' maid. Instead, a piercing scream filled the sweet-scented kitchen. "Party!" the little girl screeched gleefully, running toward the door. "Dot! Dot!" she could be heard yelling as she disappeared into the courtyard. "Eliza says you must give me a bath RIGHT NOW!"

Eliza stared fondly after her youngest sister, then returned to Angelica and Peggy. Just two and a half years separated all three older girls. Though quite distinct in appearance, they were nevertheless so close that they were often referred to collectively as "the Schuyler sisters," as if they were triplets.

"Speaking of husbands: Will Mr. Church will be joining us this evening as well?" she asked Angelica.

"Oh, Eliza, don't be so stuffy! We have been married for ages, you can call him John!"

"Ha!" Peggy laughed. "I heard her talking to her husband the other day. Do you know she still calls him Colonel Hamilton in public?!"

"Peggy!" Eliza exclaimed. "You ought not to eavesdrop."

"It's not eavesdropping when all three of us are in the same parlor," Peggy said with a smirk. "Tell me, sister dear. Do you *always* address your husband so formally? I hope there are times when your discourse is more . . . intimate!"

Eliza felt a deep blush color her throat and cheeks. She did call him Alex when they were alone, but in public, she followed her mother's model and addressed him by his proper title. Fortunately, the hot kitchen was filled with steam from pots of stew and consommé for the party, and she hoped her sisters wouldn't notice. Still, she found herself helplessly tongue-tied.

"Oh, Peggy," Angelica said. "Always the provocateur!"

"Me?" Peggy laughed. "I am but an unmarried maiden, whereas you two are worldly wedded women. How could *I* possibly provoke *you*?"

Angelica couldn't help but grin. "I suspect that our polite Eliza will continue to address him as Colonel Hamilton among company even when they have been married as long as Mama and Papa."

"Unless he gets promoted like Papa," Eliza said, finally finding her voice. "In which case, I'll call him *General*

Hamilton. And you never answered my question. Will *John* be joining us this evening?"

"I believe so. He accompanied your colonel and Papa when they went into town this morning to attend to some work of his own, and told me he expects to finish by early evening. And Stephen?" Angelica continued, turning to Peggy. "Will your young man be there as well?"

"He said he is bringing half the Rensselaer cousins with him," Peggy replied with a nod, though she didn't sound happy about it.

"Is Mother Rensselaer still refusing to allow him to propose?" Eliza asked.

"I'm afraid so." Peggy sighed. "She says he is too young, but I don't believe it. When we first began courting, she was eager for us to marry immediately, but after what happened with Papa, she grew noticeably less enthusiastic. It's almost as if she thinks I am after him for his money!"

It was true that the Schuyler fortune wasn't what it once was. Four years ago, General Schuyler had been unceremoniously replaced by Horatio Gates as commander of the northern army, at about the same time that the Schuylers' Saratoga country estate was burned to the ground by British forces, destroying the better part of the Schuylers' income. Between the loss of funds and the cost of rebuilding, it had been a lean couple of years. But the family coffers had begun to recover at last, especially after Angelica's and Eliza's marriages. John Barker Church, Angelica's husband, had a booming business in trade, and Alexander Hamilton, though far from rich, was well provided for by the Continental army, and everyone said he had a bright, indeed limitless, future ahead of him.

Alas, that did not seem enough for the snooty Rensselaers.

"She is being absurd!" Eliza scoffed now. "It is *Stephen* who chased *you*. Why, that boy has been in love with you since he was in short pants!"

"Oh, has he started wearing trousers at last?" Angelica quipped, to a swat from Peggy.

Eliza laughed, then patted her younger sister's hand. "The Rensselaers wouldn't dare forever object to joining their family with ours. We are already cousins on Mama's side, and for all their money and land, they haven't nearly the prestige we do." She sighed. "Well, it sounds like dinner will be a full house. I look forward to seeing all three of our lads in the same room. It's so rare these days."

"I know!" Angelica said. "And soon enough the war will be over and you will be moving to New York City or Philadelphia or, heaven forbid, Virginia. John has been talking about returning to England, and I'm sure Stephen will want to build Peggy a house on some plantation-size corner of his vast holdings. This may be the last time we're all together for who knows how long!"

"Well then, let's make it the best party ever!" Eliza said. She stood up and grabbed a pie from the cooling rack, placing it in a basket. "And now if you'll excuse me, I'm going to take Mama a snack. Peggy, please don't wear the crimson silk Stephen gave you," she joked. "I cannot bear to be eclipsed by your radiance yet again."

"Ha!" Angelica laughed. "Telling Peggy not to dress up is like telling a goldfinch not to shine. Face it, Eliza, you're going to have to cinch tonight."

"And put on a wig!" Peggy added with a laugh. "Dot was teasing mine up for an hour last night, and it is *at least* three feet high!"

Eliza groaned, dreading the pinch of a corset and the itchiness of a wig, then reached for one last berry.

Springtime! In Albany! Not even the thought of all the painstaking effort that would go into looking presentable could ruin her day.

Find out what happens next
in the final book of
the Alex & Eliza Trilogy!

Turn the page

for a sneak peek of

Melissa de la Cruz's new series!

Chapter One

Shadow

Something or someone is following me. I've been wandering the woods for quite a while, but now it feels as if something—or someone—is watching. I thought it was one of my aunts at first—it was odd they didn't chase after me this time. Maybe they didn't expect me to go very far. But it's not them.

I stop and pull my hood back to listen to the forest around me. There is only the wind whistling through the branches and the sound of my own breathing.

Whoever is following me is very good at hiding. But I am not afraid.

Slivers of light penetrate the dense foliage in spots, shining streaks onto the blanket of decaying leaves and mud under my boots. As I slice through thick vines and clamber over rotting logs, speckled thrushes take flight from the forest floor before disappearing overhead. I pause to listen to them sing to one another, chirping elegant messages back and forth, a beautiful song carrying warnings, no doubt, about the stranger stomping through their home.

Being out here helps me clear my head. I feel more peaceful

here among the wild creatures, closer to my true self. After this morning's argument at home, it's precisely what I need—some peace. Some space. Time to myself.

My aunts taught me that sometimes when the world is too much, when life starts to feel overwhelming, we must strip away what's unnecessary, seek out the quiet, and listen to the dirt and trees. "All the answers you seek are there, but only if you are willing to hear them," Aunt Moriah always says.

That's all I'm doing, I tell myself. Following their advice. Perhaps that's why they allowed me to run off into the woods. Except they're probably hoping I'll find *their* answers here, not my own. That I'll finally come to my senses.

Anger bubbles up inside me. All I have ever wanted is to follow in their footsteps and join the ranks of the Hearthstone Guild. It's the one thing I've wanted more than anything. We don't just sell honey in the market. They've practically been training me for the Guild all my life—how can they deny me? I kick the nearest tree as hard as I can, slamming the sole of my boot into its solid trunk. That doesn't make me feel much better, though, and I freeze, wondering if whatever or whoever is following me has heard.

I know it is a dangerous path, but what nobler task is there than to continue the Guild's quest? To recover the Deian Scrolls and exact revenge upon our enemies. They can't expect me to sit by and watch as others take on the challenge.

All the women I look up to—Ma, my aunt Moriah, and Moriah's wife, my aunt Mesha—belong to the Guild; they are trained combatants and wise women. They are devotees of Deia, the One Mother, source of everything in the world of Avantine, from the clouds overhead to the dirt underfoot. Deia worship was common once but not anymore, and those who keep to its beliefs have the Guild to thank for preserving the old ways. Otherwise that knowledge would have disappeared long ago when the Aphrasians confiscated it from the people. The other kingdoms no longer keep to the old ways, even as they conspire to learn our magic.

As wise women they know how to tap into the world around us, to harness the energy that people have long forgotten but other creatures have not. My mother and aunts taught me how to access the deepest levels of my instincts, the way that animals do, to sense danger and smell fear. To become deeply in tune with the universal language of nature that exists just below the surface of human perception, the parts we have been conditioned not to hear anymore.

While I call them my aunts, they are not truly related to me, even if Aunt Moriah and my mother grew up as close as sisters. I was fostered here because my mother's work at the palace is so important that it leaves little time for raising a child.

A gray squirrel runs across my path and halfway up a nearby tree. It stops and looks at me quizzically. "It's all right," I say. "I'm not going to hurt you." It waits until I start moving again and scampers the rest of the way up the trunk.

The last time I saw my mother, I told her of my plans to join the Guild. I thought she'd be proud of me. But she'd stiffened and paused before saying, "There are other ways to serve the crown."

Naturally, I'd have preferred her to be with me, every day, like other mothers, but I've never lacked for love or affection. My aunts had been there for every bedtime tale and scraped knee, and Ma served as a glamorous and heroic figure for a young woman to look up to. She would swoop into my life, almost always under the cover of darkness, cloaked and carrying gifts, like the lovely pair of brocade satin dance slippers I'll never forget. They were as ill-suited for rural life as a pair of shoes could possibly be, and I treasured them for it. "The best cobbler in Argonia's capital made these," she told me. I marveled at that, how far they'd traveled before landing on my feet.

Yes, I liked the presents well enough. But what made me even happier were the times she stayed long enough to tell me stories. She would sit on the edge of my bed, tuck my worn quilt snugly around me, and tell me tales of Avantine, of the old kingdom.

Our people are fighters, she'd say. *Always were.* I took that to mean I would be one too.

I think about these stories as I whack my way through the brush. Why would my mother tell me tales of heroism, adventure, bravery, and sacrifice, unless I was to train with the Guild as well? As a child, I was taught all the basics—survival and tracking skills, and then as I grew, I began combat training and archery.

I do know more of the old ways than most, and I'm grateful for that, but it isn't enough. I want to know as much as they do, or even more. I need to belong to the Guild.

Now I fear I never will have that chance.

"Ouch!" I flinch and pull my hand back from the leaves surrounding me. There's a thin sliver of blood seeping out of my skin. I was so lost in my thoughts that I accidentally cut my hand while hacking through shrubbery. The woods are unfamiliar here, wilder and denser. I've never gone out this far. The path ahead is so overgrown it's hard to believe there was ever anyone here before me, let alone a procession of messengers and traders and visitors traveling between Renovia and the other kingdoms of Avantine. But that was before. Any remnants of its prior purpose are disappearing quickly. Even my blade, crafted from Argonian steel—another present from Ma—struggles to sever some of the more stubborn branches that have reclaimed the road for the wilderness.

I try to quiet my mind and concentrate on my surroundings. Am I lost? Is something following me? "What do I do now?" I say out loud. Then I remember Aunt Mesha's advice: *Be willing to hear.*

I breathe, focus. Re-center. *Should I turn back?* The answer is so strong, it's practically a physical shove: *No. Continue.* I suppose I'll push through, then. Maybe I'll discover a forgotten treasure along this path.

Woodland creatures watch me, silently, from afar. They're perched in branches and nestled safely in burrows. Sometimes I catch a whiff of newborn fur, of milk; I smell the fear of anxious mothers protecting litters; I feel their heartbeats, their quickened breaths when I pass. I do my best to calm them by closing my eyes and sending them benevolent energy. *Just passing through. I'm no threat to you.*

After about an hour of bushwhacking, I realize that I don't know where I am anymore. The trees look different, older. I hear the trickling of water. Unlike before, there are signs that something, or rather someone, was here not long before me. Cracked sticks have been stepped on—by whom or what, I'm not sure—and branches are too neatly chopped to have been broken naturally. I want to investigate, see if I can feel how long ago they were cut. Maybe days; maybe weeks. Difficult to tell.

I stop to examine the trampled foliage just as I feel an abrupt change in the air.

There it is again. Whoever or whatever it is smells foul, rotten. I shudder. I keep going, hoping to shake it off my trail.

I walk deeper into the forest and pause under a canopy of trees. A breeze blows against a large form in the branches overhead. I sense the weight of its bulk, making the air above me feel heavier, oppressive. It pads quietly. A huge predator. Not human. It's been biding its time. But now it's tense, ready to strike.

The tree becomes very still. And everything around does the same. I glance to my right and see a spider hanging in the air, frozen, just like I am.

Leaves rustle, like the fanning pages of a book. Snarling heat of its body getting closer, closer, inch by inch. I can smell its hot breath. Feel its mass as it begins to bear down on me from above. Closer, closer, until at last it launches itself from its hiding place. I feel its energy, aimed straight at me. Intending to kill, to devour.

But I am ready.

Just as it attacks, I kick ferociously at its chest, sending it flying. It slams to the ground, knocked out cold. A flock of starlings erupts from their nest in the treetops, chirping furiously.

My would-be killer is a sleek black scimitar-toothed jaguar. The rest of the wildlife stills, shocked into silence, at my besting the king of the forest.

I roll back to standing, then hear something else, like shifting or scratching, in the distance. As careful as I've been, I've managed to cause a commotion and alert every creature in the forest of my presence.

I crouch behind a wide tree. After waiting a breath or two, I don't sense any other unusual movement nearby. Perhaps I was wrong about the noise. Or simply heard a falling branch or a startled animal running for cover.

There's no reason to remain where I am, and I'm not going back now, in case the jaguar wakes, so I get up and make my way forward again. It looks like there's a clearing ahead.

My stomach lurches. After everything—the argument and my big show of defiance—I am gripped with the unexpected desire to return home. I don't know if the cat's attack has rattled me—it shouldn't have; I've been in similar situations before—but a deep foreboding comes over me.

Yet just as strongly, I feel the need to keep going, beyond the edge of the forest, as if something is pulling me forward. I move faster, fumbling a bit over some debris.

Finally, I step through the soft leafy ground around a few ancient trees, their bark slick with moss, and push aside a branch filled with tiny light-green leaves.

When I emerge from the woods, I discover I was wrong. It's not just a clearing; I've stumbled upon the golden ruins of an old building. A fortress. The tight feeling in my chest intensifies. I should turn back. There's danger here. Or at least there *was* danger here—it appears to be long abandoned.

The building's intimidating skeletal remains soar toward the clouds, but it's marred by black soot; it's been scorched by a fire—or maybe more than one. Most of the windows are cracked or else missing completely. Rosebushes are overgrown with burly thistle weeds, and clumps of dead brown shrubbery dot the property. Vines climb up one side of the structure and crawl into the empty windows.

Above the frame of one of those windows, I spot a weathered crest, barely visible against the stone. I step closer. There are two initials overlapping each other in an intricate design: BA. In an instant I know exactly where I am.

Baer Abbey.

I inhale sharply. How did I walk so far? How long have I been gone?

This place is forbidden. Dangerous. Yet I was drawn here. Is this a sign, the message I was searching for? And if so, what is it trying to tell me?

Despite the danger, I've always wanted to see the abbey, home of the feared and powerful Aphrasians. I try picturing it as it was long ago, glistening in the blinding midday heat, humming with activity, the steady bustle of cloaked men and women going about their daily routines. I imagine one of them meditating underneath the massive oak to the west; another reading on the carved limestone bench in the now-decrepit gardens.

I walk around the exterior, looking for the place where King Esban charged into battle with his soldiers.

I hear something shift again. It's coming from inside the abbey walls. As if a heavy object is being pushed or dragged—opening a door? Hoisting something with a pulley? I approach the building and melt into its shadow, like the pet name my mother gave me.

But who could be here? A generation of looters has already stripped anything of value, though the lure of undiscovered treasure might still entice adventurous types. And drifters. Or maybe there's a hunter, or a hermit who's made his home close to this desolate place.

In the distance, the river water slaps against the rocky shore, and I can hear the rustling of leaves and the trilling of birds. All is as it should be, and yet. Something nags at me, like a faraway ringing in my ear. Someone or something is still following me, and it's not the jaguar. It smells of death and rot.

I move forward anyway, deciding to run the rest of the way along the wall to an entryway, its door long gone. I just want to peek inside—I may never have this chance again.

I slide around the corner of the wall and enter the abbey's interior. Most of the roof is demolished, so there's plenty of light, even this close to dusk. Tiny specks of dust float in the air. There's a veneer of grime on every surface, and wet mud in shaded spots. I step forward, leaving footprints behind me. I glance at the rest of the floor—no other prints. Nobody has been here recently, at least not since the last rain.

I move as lightly as possible. Then I hear something different. I stop, step backward. There it is again. I step forward—solid. Back—yes, an echo. Like a well. There's something hollow below. Storage? A crypt?

I should turn back. Nothing good can come from being here, and I know it. The abbey is Aphrasian territory, no matter how long ago they vacated. And yet. There's no reason to believe anyone is here, and who knows what I might find if I just dig a bit. Perhaps a treasure was hidden here. Maybe even the Deian Scrolls.

I step on a large square tile, made of heavy charcoal slate, which is stubbornly embedded in the ground. I clear the dirt around it as much as I can and get my fingertips under its lip. With effort, I heave the tile up enough to hoist it over to the side. Centipedes scurry away into the black hole below. I use the heel of my boot to shove the stone the rest of the way, revealing a wooden ladder underneath.

I press on it carefully, testing its strength, then make my way down. At the last rung I jump down and turn to find a long narrow passageway lined with empty sconces. It smells of mildew, dank and damp. I follow the tunnel, my footsteps echoing around me.

I hear water lapping gently against stone up ahead. Could there be an underground stream? The passage continues on, dark and quiet aside from the occasional drip of water from the ceiling.

At the end of the corridor a curved doorway opens into a large cavern. As I suspected, an underground river flows by. A small hole in the ceiling allows light in, revealing sharp stalactites that hang down everywhere, glittering with the river's reflection. The room is aglow in yellows and oranges and reds, and it feels like standing in the middle of fire. This space was definitely not made by human hands; instead, the tunnel, the abbey, was built up around it. There's a loading dock installed for small boats, though none are there anymore.

Then I see something that makes my heart catch. I gasp.

The Aphrasians have been missing for eighteen years and yet there's a fresh apple core tossed aside near the doorway.

That's when I hear men's voices approaching from the corridor behind me.

Chapter Two

Shadow

"Who's there?" a gruff voice calls out from within the tunnel. It echoes: *Who's there? Who's there? Who's there?*

Frantically, I search for somewhere to hide. *They heard me!* But the tunnel appears to be the sole way out and I can't go back the way I came. There's only the river below. The voices whisper to one another from inside the tunnel as I slide off the edge of the dock and into the water, trying not to make a splash. I hear clanging as the men run toward the stream, their boots shuffling on the ground as they turn around looking for whoever was there.

"Got away," one says. His voice is deep, gravelly. It's the same man who called out before.

"Could be you're hearin' things again," says the other. Higher-pitched, scratchy. Younger than the first, I think.

"Is that so? Then who moved the stone?" the first replies. "More like they jumped in the river."

The second scoffs. "Then they're dead for sure."

His words are prescient as the flow of the river drags me along, turns a corner, and slopes down, the current picking up speed. I try to retain control but the water swallows me. I struggle to push myself above the surface and gasp for air. *They were right, I won't make it.* The undertow is too strong.

I kick as hard as I can, barely keeping my head out of the river, which is splashing against my face and into my nose and mouth. I can't keep the water out and also let air in. *Don't panic*, I tell myself. *Never panic.*

I spot a heavy branch sticking out of the water. I reach for it and fail, falling back into the current. I should never have come here. I'm going to drown. *I'm going to die.*

Also: *My aunts are going to kill me.*

No, no! I absolutely refuse to give up! My arms and legs shove me on as if being controlled by an outside force. I manage to propel my body toward another floating branch and grab on to it.

Water washes over my head again. I keep my eyes closed and hang on to the branch with all my might. When my head emerges, I try to suck in air but immediately begin coughing. Wheezing. There's water in my lungs. My nose and throat are burning. The men at the abbey can probably hear me splashing now but I hardly care. I just want to make it out of here alive.

There's a light ahead. The mouth of the cave. I hear banging noises from behind me, where the men were at the shoreline. It sounds like some kind of battle, as if the men I'd heard back there were suddenly attacked. My breathing is returning to normal, though I still feel the sting in my nose and chest. If I hadn't come across the branch . . . or if my leg had caught on one under the surface . . .

I emerge with the river. I look around and see I'm on the other side of the abbey now. Right near the hill I saw in the distance earlier—the site of the great battle. I feel the oppressive weight of death all around me, even within the earth itself.

The branch runs up against some rocks near the shoreline, beneath an ancient weeping willow. My arms are weak. Shaking. I have to get out of the water. I can take refuge in the tree. Its full, low-hanging branches are spread out around its wide, trunk-like curtains. A good place to hang on, stay concealed.

Please just this one thing, I beg myself. *Get out of the water.* Gritting my teeth, I lift my upper body until I'm lying across the top of a stone. A horse whinnies from beyond the hill; a man shouts. Another man grunts again and again, as if he's punching someone. I rest a moment to catch my breath and listen to the brawl beyond the hill. The men are still struggling against some interloper, but it means they're not coming any nearer to me, so I swing my right leg up onto the rock and hoist myself out. The heavy boots I'm wearing definitely weren't helping me in the water.

The sounds of struggle subside abruptly, as if someone's won. Dripping wet, I crawl over to the willow and hide beneath its curtain of leaves. It's quiet now. They may have left—or killed one another. Either way, not my concern.

The sun is already setting; one of my aunts would definitely have started looking for me by now.

There hasn't been any other sound from beyond the hill for some time now. I don't like it here. Unlike the ruins, this place bears the stain of death. Violence. Its energy is an invisible fog. I place my palm against the willow's sturdy trunk to brace myself so I can stand.

A powerful shock surges straight through me.

Suddenly, I can see a soldier wearing the Renovian colors, bleeding out into the earth. Another soldier with a missing arm, leg snapped upward into a terrifying pose, is groaning. *I want to go home,* he cries. *I want to go.*

One man is almost fully submerged in the river, only his legs sticking out. And countless others are strewn about in the same condition, or worse. Everywhere. The dead. This is the Battle of Baer, playing out before my eyes. I can smell the stench in the air and hear the death groans, but it isn't real. I'm not there; this is just an illusion, a place memory. One so powerful that those with the sight can see it if they try. Even if they don't try. Aunt Moriah said sometimes such visions find the seeker, rather than the other way around.

I have been seeing visions since I was ten years old.

Then I look up. And there he is. King Esban.

I recognize him from his chiseled profile on Renovian coins. A striking figure, like the fabled shipbuilders of the north countries: tall, broad shouldered, bearded, golden hair flowing from under a dented silver helmet. Noble and brave, just as the stories say, but with kind eyes. They never mention that.

I feel the urge to go to him but I can't move. I know what's about to happen, and I want to call to him, to warn him. But when I try to yell, nothing comes out.

A man charges toward him, sword raised above his head. He's wearing a gray Aphrasian robe and their unmistakable black mask. The king is steady. Metal meets metal with a clang. They struggle, the rebel monk pushing the king back; the king shoves him off with equal force. The monk aims his right leg directly at the king's stomach, but Esban steps away so the kick lands off its mark, barely grazing his hip. He stretches his arm back and swings the sword at the rebel with all his might. The monk dodges the strike. The king is furiously red, chest heaving, teeth bared. He lunges at the monk again.

They go on like this. It seems that neither can win. The other soldiers haven't even noticed the skirmish on the mound yet. I try to scream, *Help him!* But I can't, because as real as it seems, I'm only watching. Witnessing the past.

I look back up.

The rebel is on the ground. The king walks over to him and lifts his sword. For a brief moment I hope King Esban will win this time. That the past can change. But the monk rolls and swipes the king's leg out from under him. He stumbles, falls. He's about to get up when it happens.

The monk drives his sword straight through King Esban's chest.

I yank my hand away from the willow. I start gagging, retching. I haven't eaten all day, so all I bring up is bile. Tears are streaming down my face. This is what my aunts meant when they told me to *be careful for what you wish*. For the answer might not be the one you seek. I wanted danger and adventure as a Guild apprentice, and alas, I seem to have found it.

I stand to leave. Based on where the sun hangs in the sky, I've a little time left until complete darkness. I'll dry off as I go, as long as I'm moving. Good thing it's still warm at night. I won't freeze to death, at least.

I walk away, just as something slams into me. I'm knocked straight onto my back, totally winded. For a frenzied second I expect to see the jaguar again—but no, there's a man standing over me.

Gray robes. The dreaded black mask of the Aphrasian order covering his face. The mask that's given children nightmares for centuries. The monk raises his sword.

This is no vision.

This is all too real.

This must be who was following me earlier. The smell is the same—of rot and death. I was right, there *was* a predator on my trail, one who is intent on killing me. I am too shocked to move.

I shut my eyes and cross my arms over my face, anticipating the blow.

But someone comes out of nowhere, swooping over me and knocking the assailant away, running a sword through his belly.

I open my eyes. A hooded man stands over my attacker, whom he has impaled to the ground.

As he leans over to inspect the dead man's pockets, I catch a glimpse of my savior.

I'd know that face anywhere. It's Caledon Holt.